Praise for The Caleb Trees:

"A warm, rich, exquisitely told story . . . This novel will join *The Deep End of the Ocean* on my bookshelf."
—Deborah Smith

"Dee Holmes tugs at readers' heartstrings with great insight and skill. *The Caleb Trees* is a book you won't soon forget."
—Barbara Bretton

Praise for RITA Award–winner Dee Holmes's previous novels

JONATHAN'S WIFE

"Fresh and wonderfully written." —*Publishers Weekly*

WHEN NICK RETURNS

"A truly gifted writer . . . a truly exceptional book. Ms. Holmes has a flair for creating realistic characters and great stories. Do not miss this one!" —*Rendezvous*

"Compelling and touching." —*Publishers Weekly*

"Profound description . . . well-written . . . a multilayered, classy novel." —*Painted Rock Reviews*

The Caleb Trees

DEE HOLMES

JOVE BOOKS, NEW YORK

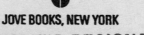

THE CALEB TREES

A Jove Book / published by arrangement
with the author

PRINTING HISTORY
Jove edition / September 2000

The Penguin Putnam Inc. World Wide Web site address is
http://www.penguinputnam.com

ISBN: 0-515-12904-6

A JOVE BOOK®
Jove Books are published by The Berkley Publishing Group,
a division of Penguin Putnam Inc.,
375 Hudson Street, New York, New York 10014.
JOVE and the "J" design
are trademarks belonging to Penguin Putnam Inc.

PRINTED IN THE UNITED STATES OF AMERICA

10 9 8 7 6 5 4 3 2 1

Chapter One

At six-thirty on that tranquil March morning, Meg DeWilde had no reason to believe it wouldn't be an ordinary day.

From the upstairs of their Rhode Island home came the blare of FM rock, running water, and the slam of a door.

"Caleb!" she called from the bottom of the stairs.

The music diminished and her sixteen-year-old son leaned over the second-floor railing. Shirtless and wearing holey sweats, he scowled down at her. "She's hogging the bathroom."

"Give her five more minutes. Don't forget to wear your white oxford shirt. The one you wear to church."

"Huh?"

"For the assembly this morning. Don't tell me you forgot."

"No one else is getting dressed up."

"Gregg is wearing a tie."

"No way."

"I talked to his mother last night."

"Shit."

"Caleb, cool it on the swearing," his father said as he passed him and started down the stairs. "You know your mother doesn't like it."

Jack DeWilde halted on the bottom step, impeccable in a gray suit, yellow shirt and a gray-and-slate-blue silk tie. "I have to get some papers I left in the study. You didn't throw anything on my desk away, did you?"

"Nope. Just watered the plants," Meg said.

"Good." He kissed her, then took the newspaper she'd brought in from the driveway.

"You smell good," she murmured.

"It's the aftershave your mother gave me for Christmas."

"Very hunky."

"Remind me to use it next time you're feeling sexy."

He glanced beyond her, his attention already on its way into the study.

Nevertheless, she touched his belt buckle. "I was feeling sexy last night but you were falling asleep by the time I came out of the bathroom."

His gaze returned. "I thought you had your period."

"That was last week."

He apologized, blaming his distraction on an overload of details at work. "Tonight, I'll make it up to you." He kissed her again before walking away.

Meg considered this most recent miscue. It was one of many in the past few months since Jack had expanded DeWilde Real Estate to include offices down in Newport. Meg had encouraged the growth just as she'd supported all his goals throughout their marriage. Jack, like any successful businessman, wanted to make the most of financial opportunities.

In the early years, she'd worked for him when he couldn't afford a full-time accountant. If she pitched in and helped again, it would relieve some of the pressure.

In the kitchen she set out cream for Jack's coffee, apple juice for Bethany and Pop-Tarts for Caleb, along with cold cereal and a pitcher of milk.

Sunshine poured through the double French doors that opened to a wraparound porch. Beyond lay a winter-weary backyard bordered by nests of bushes and carefully pruned trees, including three cherries. One was huge and old with obese branches. The other two had been saplings when they were given to Meg eleven years ago by a neighbor. She and Caleb brought them home in his red wagon, and he'd helped plant them. It wasn't long before they became *his* trees. He'd nailed some boards across limbs in the old one from where, for three summers, he'd perched and reported on the growth of the saplings. As the years passed, they became simply the Caleb trees.

Nostalgic memories. Treasured memories. Her memories.

"You're deep in thought," Jack said from behind her.

"Just thinking how lucky we are."

"Hmm." He poured himself a mug of coffee and pushed the raisin bread down in the toaster before opening the newspaper.

"I better check on the kids. Sounds awfully quiet," she said.

"Caleb's still in the bathroom. Shaving, I presume. Since last fall I think he's cut himself more looking for whiskers than shaving them off."

"He's growing up," Meg said. "I'm not sure I like it."

"You didn't like it those first weeks he was in kindergarten."

"I wasn't the only one. That first day you came home from work early to find out how he did."

He took his toast and buttered it. "Don't remember that." Bringing his plate to the table and sitting down, he added, "Bethany's on the phone."

"What else is new? I swear she sleeps with the thing." Meg glanced at the wooden wall clock. She broke off a corner of his toast, popped it in her mouth, then went to the stairway. "Hey, you two are going to miss the bus if you don't hurry."

"I can drop them off," Jack said when she returned. "I'm going in that direction." He opened the real estate section.

Meg heated her coffee mug in the microwave. "I wish

you would come with me to the assembly. How many times during the week do we get to see Caleb dressed in something other than jeans and tee's?"

"Is what he wears really relevant?"

"Yes." She tolerated the sloppy, oversized clothes that were currently popular, but special occasions like this one required dressing with a measure of care.

He shrugged. "Frankly I think you're overdoing the importance of this. He already knows he's getting the most-improved-in-chemistry certificate. The teachers would accomplish more if they focused on classroom work rather than organizing one of these feel-good sideshows. The kids know the score—to them it's just an excuse to skip a class."

"Aren't you being a bit harsh? Kids need praise and a public show of confidence encourages their self-esteem."

Jack looked at her. "Meg, the real working world doesn't give a rat's ass about encouragement and self-esteem. If those two things were the criteria for success, I'd be collecting a check for the permanently unemployed."

"You're different. You had a lot of responsibility that most kids never have." She touched his sleeve. "I still wish you were coming with me."

For a moment he seemed to waver, then, "I can't. I have an appointment in Newport and a meeting right after-wards." He paused, thoughtful. "If I could, I would."

"I know. Maybe I should come back to work for you." She hadn't planned to just fling out the suggestion in an unprepared burst, but now that she had she was glad she hadn't primed him. This way she'd have an honest from-his-gut response.

His attention was fully on her, and he wasn't smiling. "Don't be ridiculous, Meg. You have enough to do and I can afford to hire more help if that was the problem."

"Then what is the problem? You've already hired more people. Carl, Vicki, Dana, and that new manager for New-port."

"The problem is there's only one of me."

"And I know you better than anyone. We used to work well together and—"

"No."

"I just thought I could ease the workload on you."

"I said no." This time he said it more emphatically.

Then he reached for her hand and brought it to his mouth, kissing the palm and folding her fingers around the gesture. "I want you right here doing the things you love—gardening, staying involved with the kids and their school problems as well as their successes—like pushing Caleb to improve his grades. You get credit for that, too."

"His poor marks last fall were an abcrration."

"Just the same, if you hadn't pushed him, he'd be in some serious academic trouble. With those high SAT's contrasted by low grades, the message any college would get is here's a smart, capable kid who's lazy and not working to his potential."

"But he got his grades up."

"They could be higher," Jack said, never satisfied with good when better was within reach. "He knows it, we know it. With baseball season looming, Caleb's mind will be on improving his fastball."

"I suppose," she said, amazed at his ability to make her rethink her own plans.

Jack continued. "I want to know I can count on you to keep him focused like you did before. The last thing we need at this crucial point is both of us working long hours at DeWilde's."

She couldn't think of a valid argument to counter his logic. He'd always been a master at detailing his side of an issue and presenting it so flawlessly that any further discussion sounded redundant. "Of course I want the kids to do their best and live up to their potential."

For Meg, their children's happiness and safe progress into adulthood had been paramount. Bethany whirled along, managing to turn even the stickiest issue to her advantage—a trait she'd gleaned from her father. However, Meg had grown increasingly aware that their son didn't have the obsessive work-incentive that was Jack's hallmark.

"Do you think we're putting too much pressure on him?" she asked. "He has the job at Bushes, a couple of after-school jobs cleaning up yards, plus studying, playing baseball . . ."

"He had them all last year and had no problems."

She had no answer for that and concluded she was being too motherly.

He resumed reading his newspaper while Meg cradled her warmed mug.

Watching Jack so easily switch gears from a family topic to methodically analyzing the ads of competitive Rhode Island real estate companies was a lesson in focus. Deal with an issue and then move on—all facts and conclusions, not emotional waffling. It was a familiar pattern that had made him so successful.

Years ago, when interest rates were in double digits and no one was buying homes, Jack took a huge risk in a depressed business cycle. He bought a struggling independent realty company staffed by three demoralized agents. He infused an energy into the business, gave the agents bonuses and convinced them a bonanza of eager home buyers was only a sales agreement away. When borrowing became cheaper in the eighties, and the consumption of real estate went from picky to frenetic, sales at DeWilde Real Estate tripled. Though money and success resulted, Jack believed neither were tangible enough to indulge in laurel resting. He still personally screened every new agent, he worked longer hours than any of his employees and he constantly studied his competition.

Now he took a notebook and made some notes.

"Surely the competition isn't giving away any secrets in a newspaper ad," Meg commented.

"Businesses always give away secrets. The question is whether it's a deliberate revelation or an unintended one." He winked at her and slipped the notebook into his briefcase.

The disarming gesture unexpectedly pricked her. Not because he hadn't shown her the ad and what he had discovered, but that he assumed she wasn't interested.

Maybe she was. Maybe she wasn't. But she would have appreciated the opportunity to say so rather than be dismissed with a wink. She stared down at her hands. The missed lovemaking, shooting down her offer to help and now this. God, had she become too familiar in her role? Too easily appeased and too willing to just take what he said without thinking about where her own thoughts and feelings were on a given subject? Jack, in his wanting to protect and provide, had created a painless environment that Meg had slipped into as easily as she'd wandered through life before she ever met him.

For all of her thirty-nine years, Meg had few regrets. She had grown up in Cooper Falls, Rhode Island, the younger daughter of a middle-class family. Her father had volunteered for Vietnam along with some buddies who still believed in the war, but later he returned minus two of his friends and without his easy optimism and gung-ho enthusiasm. He went to work for the gas company while her mother maintained the household and kept her two daughters occupied with chores and volunteer activities. Clean, reverent lives that in her sister Kate's opinion were, "disgustingly boring."

For Meg, adversity and tragedy were experienced within the safe boundaries of books, television and her high school drama class. While her sister took on risks with relish—a lot like Jack—Meg preferred the safer paths until college, when she had been mortified by her small-town ignorance about sex and drinking and drugs. Presented openly by its proponents as sophisticated, hip and mind-expanding . . . Meg might have yielded beyond clumsy experimentation if not for falling in love with Jack DeWilde.

By contrast to her own uneventful life, Jack had been a survivor. The son of a gruff, embittered lobsterman and a cowering mother, his youth had been knotted with financial and emotional insecurities that carried ramifications even today. His colorful and contentious past made a powerful impression on Meg. Failure and struggle, family responsibilities and a dogged determination to succeed added to his mystique.

Though cool-headed and cynical, he was also charming and self-assured. She'd boasted to her family that Jack could handle anything, and knowing her father wanted his daughters married to "good" men, Meg knew Jack was the best. She still believed that.

Now at forty-two, his dark hair was gray-threaded at the temples, his face carried the forged lines of stubbornness and decisiveness. Yet he retained an engaging charisma that dominated a room and made him a man people liked to be around.

He peered at her over the top of his newspaper. His eyes crinkled at the corners. "Okay, babe, what's up?"

"I love you."

"I love you, too. Do I hear a lecture coming? Or another argument for coming to work at DeWilde's?"

She shook her head. "No argument or lecture. It's just that we miss you. We'd like to have you around more than you are." Meg didn't consider this a complaint, just a cogent observation.

He laid the paper down and took a deep breath, his expression open and understanding. "What can I say? I promise to do better, but real estate is hot right now, and with new offices to oversee, I'd be an irresponsible, careless business owner if I neglected them."

She sighed. "I guess I sound whiny, huh?"

"Nope," he said fondly, "you sound like a wife and mother." He went to the coffee carafe and refilled his mug.

A wife and mother. Yes, that's what she was and what she'd always been the most proud of, but perhaps she'd allowed her life to become too narrow and cramped. Caleb and Bethany were needing her less and less. Perhaps the time had come to open the way for interests beyond her home and her family and the volunteer work.

"By the way," Jack said, "the new owners of the Stratton house asked me if you gave advice on gardens. They saw the picture of our house at the office and when I told them my wife did the landscaping, they wanted to know if you did consulting. They're awash in catalogues and don't have a clue where to begin."

"You didn't volunteer me, did you?" she asked, thinking of her newly minted thought on exploring new avenues.

"Of course not. I said I'd tell you what they said and let you decide." He took out his wallet and handed her a slip of paper with their phone number.

She put it aside to deal with at another time.

Bethany and Caleb came into the kitchen. Bethany dropped her backpack by her chair. Sipping her glass of apple juice, she said, "I want raisin toast, not cereal."

"Help yourself."

Wearing the Red Sox jacket that Jack had bought him last year, Caleb headed for the door. Meg noted the white oxford shirt collar peeking out of the jacket.

"Caleb?"

"I'm not hungry."

Meg walked to him and touched his back. He was taller than she, and had been for the past two years. His build was wiry and lean with muscle in his arms and shoulders from workouts for baseball season, which began in a few weeks. Darkly handsome like his father, sensitive and emotional like she was; Caleb was a young man stretching with potential and intensity and a keen sense of right and wrong.

Now, she pressed her hand against his shoulder, and lifted the dark brown hair from the inside of his jacket. "Butterflies?"

He stiffened. "Huh?"

"Butterflies? You know, in your tummy? Nervousness over the assembly this morning?"

"Oh, yeah. I guess that's it."

On the pitcher's mound, Caleb could have been a poster boy for aggressive self-confidence, but in other situations he was often shy and reluctant. His reticence this morning didn't surprise her. The on-stage spotlight of the auditorium would not be a place of his choosing.

Jack put his dishes in the dishwasher. "Good job on getting those marks up, Caleb, but they need to be better for Brown or Harvard to take your application seriously."

Without turning around, Caleb's shoulders slumped indicating his father's words weren't new. "Dad, I've told you I want to pitch for the Red Sox."

Meg sighed. This had been a long-running, tense topic that never turned any positive corners. "Please? Can we not do this today?"

Jack ignored her. "I know what you told me and you know what I told you. You can play baseball in college."

"I don't even want to go to college. Coach Rivers said lots of guys do okay without going to some big deal college." Caleb turned around, his eyes hopeful. "I could take courses at night like you did."

"When I want your coach's advice," Jack said flatly, "I'll call him directly."

Caleb tightened his jaw, his voice barely audible. "Yes, sir."

Jack scowled and Meg shook her head at him, her eyes pleading.

Acknowledging her, Jack softened his voice, "Pitching

for the Red Sox is an ambitious and worthy dream, but it's not smart or realistic to blow off an educational opportunity and ignore the doors a degree can open for you."

"Oh, come on, Dad. That's a lot of crap. You opened doors all by yourself. You're rich and you got that way by working hard. I can do that, too."

"I didn't have a choice. You do."

"No, I don't. You won't let me have a choice." His voice rose. "You've already decided for me. You don't care what I want."

Meg had had enough. She started forward, but Jack stopped her. His eyes were fierce and unyielding. Caleb stared back at his father, the teenager's face flushed with anger. It was obvious to Meg that neither would give in. The silence continued. Bethany picked toast crumbs off her plate with her wet finger and Meg leaned back against the counter, her fingers curving around the edge. The furnace clamored on and somewhere outside a dog woofed.

Finally, Jack said, "A time-out would be best for this discussion." He put on his topcoat.

"What for? Nothing's gonna change," Caleb mumbled.

Bethany ate her toast, her gaze going back and forth between her father and her brother.

Jack glanced at his wristwatch, not reacting to his son's scowl or his complaint. "It will change when you understand that a dream isn't strong enough to stake your entire future on."

Meg thought she saw a flash of panic in her son's expression as if suddenly he knew he was going to lose this argument.

"Do you want a ride to school?" Jack asked.

"No! I want to play baseball!" Caleb slammed out of the house, letting the storm door bang and rattle. Jack lifted his briefcase, slipped some papers inside and closed it.

Meg unplugged the coffee, put away the cereal boxes, and unable to hold back her annoyance, she slammed the cupboard door. "Why do you insist on going round and round with him?"

"I don't want to go round and round. I'm his father and I'm right about this, and Meg . . . you know it." Then to add weight to his argument, he said, "And it would be enormously helpful if his coach allowed you and me to counsel our son rather than feeding his own ego by filling Caleb's head with unrealistic illusions."

"Sloane is enthusiastic about Caleb's pitching potential."

"He's interfering."

"But—"

"I don't want to argue with you, too, Meg."

They exchanged glances and Meg let the subject drop.

Bethany zipped up her jacket, pulling her long blond hair out so that it flowed down her back. She glanced from one to the other. "Uh, Mom? Is it okay if I go to the mall after school?"

Meg dumped the rest of the coffee and put the grounds down the disposal. "Just be home by five o'clock."

"How 'bout you, cupcake?" Jack said to Bethany. "Do you want a ride?"

"I'll take the bus." She lifted her backpack and slung it over her left shoulder. At the door, she looked at her father, her gray-blue eyes steady and fearless. "Caleb is the best pitcher we've ever had. Maybe you should talk to Mr. Rivers. He really is a cool guy." Then as if not wanting to alienate her dad too much, she crossed the kitchen and hugged him. He hugged back.

Over their daughter's head, Meg's eyes met Jack's. She saw his determination, his fierce refusal to allow his only son to lose precious years chasing what was very likely an unattainable goal. It was one thing to go easy on teenage rules as Jack was wont to do, but it was another thing to allow Caleb to miss an opportunity that Jack, himself, would have grabbed with both hands at Caleb's age.

"Gotta go," Bethany said.

"Sure you don't want a ride?"

She hesitated, shrugged, and finally said, "Okay. Can we pick up Erica? She thinks you're cool and she loves your car."

"Now there's an endorsement if I ever heard one." He gave Bethany the keys to his black Lexus. "You back it out of the garage. I'll be there in a minute."

The fourteen-year-old squealed in delight at this growing-up rite and went out the door.

Jack cupped Meg's chin. "Caleb and I will be fine. This will sort itself out. I don't want you to worry."

"You two don't seem close to a compromise."

"We have time." He kissed her, and when he started to pull away she pulled him back into her arms.

"Caleb is serious, Jack."

"So am I."

With that he walked out, leaving Meg wondering how the two stubborn, most important men in her life were going to resolve this one.

At Cooper Falls High School, Caleb yanked open his locker and flung his jacket and books inside. He slammed it shut, causing other students lingering nearby to move quickly away. Bracing his hands on either side of the door, he pressed his forehead against the cold metal. His insides hurt. He struggled to stop the tears that sprang too easily these days. Why did everything have to be so shitty?

For months his whole life had been jammed up with stuff and questions and pain and not one fucking answer. His dad kept hassling him about grades and going to some big deal college—Caleb had figured he'd get off his back when his grades got better. Why wasn't that good enough? Why did it always have to be more? Just because the old man lived life perfectly all the time . . . And he did. No screw-ups, no mistakes, no lies, no embarrassments. Never.

Caleb wanted to be like him, wanted to do things right, wanted to be so good that his parents would bust with pride. Instead, he felt squeezed and scared and more lost than the first time he'd cut through Sawyer's Woods and couldn't find the way out. Jessup had helped him then; this time he was on his own. He sniffled, feeling overwhelmed with problems, worry and terror.

He wanted to play baseball. That one desire would take work and sweat, guts and awesome determination just to get to a major league farm team. More work than getting into some geeky college. Anyone could do that. Then there was his girlfriend. She wouldn't see him, wouldn't talk to him and he didn't know how to fix it and that was tearing him apart. If only he was eighteen. Then he could do what he wanted. He wouldn't have to answer questions, or explain or beg or make excuses. He'd be free and on his own.

But eighteen was two years away, and meanwhile his whole life was a mess. He wiped his sleeve across his eyes, then banged his fist on the door. "Shit."

"Caleb?"

He spun around so fast, he got dizzy. "I didn't know anyone was there."

The kid was Donnie Paquin. He was a junior who'd moved to Cooper Falls before Christmas. Tall enough to play basketball, but he moved in such a clunky, weird way that Caleb overheard one of the coaches call him uncoordinated. He didn't make the team. Donnie, however, was a whiz in chemistry and Caleb took him up on his offer to help him with his homework. When a rumor spread that Donnie was a fag, the guys began to hassle him and ragged on Caleb about being his boyfriend. It wasn't long before a fight broke out and Caleb, seeing his grades going into the tank without Donnie's help, took his side.

The other kid got a bloody nose and Caleb wound up with a black eye before a teacher stopped it. Since then Donnie had looked up to Caleb with such goofy admiration it made Caleb nervous. He didn't need any more trouble.

"You looked pissed at someone," Donnie said, slouching against one of the lockers.

"I am. What do you want?" He wasn't in the mood to listen to Donnie's problems. Not today.

"I wanted to tell you that I did what you said."

Caleb gave him a blank look.

"You told me I should tell my parents I'm gay. Well, I told them and—" He hesitated, his hands diving deep into his pockets. "They sorta freaked at first. Then my mom cried and told me I needed to talk to the priest, and my dad—he said my mind was screwed and he wanted me to go to some shrink in Providence." Then he laughed self-consciously. "But they didn't kick me out or say I ruined the family. I showed them the pamphlet about gay teenagers like the one you have in your locker. They read it, Caleb. I mean they *really* sat down and read it. I'd figured if that pamphlet worked for you, it might work for me. And it did."

"Worked for me? I don't know what you're talking about."

"About you being gay."

Caleb straightened. He glanced around to make sure no one overheard him. "I'm not gay. I sorta thought I might be cuz so many of the girls made me want to puke . . . but, well, now I know I'm not. I mean, I did it big-time with a really cool girl."

"Oh." Disappointed, Donnie looked down at his shoes. "I thought, well, because you stuck up for me and you've been nice and friendly, uh, you know, letting me help you with chemistry . . ."

"You're smarter in chemistry than I am."

"You're smart. You'd just rather play baseball."

Caleb nodded. Then peering at Donnie, he said, "You

thought I was like you, huh? Man, I wish it were that simple."

"Being gay is simple?" Donnie laughed. "Boy, now I know for sure you aren't." He drew closer and Caleb backed up, banging his arm on the locker. Donnie said, "I'm not going to touch you."

"Then what?"

"You helped me, I want to help you."

"You can't. It's too much of a mess and blabbing about it would— I just can't talk about it. I gotta go."

"Maybe if you talked to the person who's making you crazy."

Caleb had taken a few steps away, and now he came back. Worried and cautious, he asked, "How do you know it's one person?"

"I don't. But if you could get that person on your side, or someone else—maybe a friend, you'd feel braver. I did when you took my side. You gave me the guts to tell my parents."

Donnie's words wound through his head like a stretch of clear road. He felt as if he'd stepped out of a strangling fog into the sunshine. One person on his side. That's what he needed. For baseball, Coach Rivers had told him he had to learn to do one thing better than anyone else. And he had. He and his well-honed and nearly perfected fastball could do miracles from the mound. This time he needed support, he needed just one person on his side.

Suddenly he felt light-headed and nearly giddy. He'd do it. He'd go and pour out his guts and just maybe, like with Donnie, everything would be all right.

"Hey, Donnie, thanks."

He grinned, a wide open smile. "Thanks for being my friend."

Caleb sauntered off to homeroom, feeling more confident than he had in months.

Life didn't suck anymore.

Chapter Two

Meg parked her sage green Ford Expedition in the front lot of Cooper Falls High School. She wasn't surprised at how few cars were there, recalling Jack's comment about a feel-good assembly. Other parents hadn't made it a priority either. Well, she had and she was looking forward to seeing Caleb get recognized for his hard work.

Inside, she joined students and teachers headed for the auditorium; she'd come early to get a seat near the front, but the crowd mirrored the parking lot. Sparse.

She chose an aisle seat about eight rows back from the stage. She took off her coat and was about to sit down when a male voice behind her said, "Mind if I join you?"

She turned around and smiled. "I was hoping to see you."

"Words for my heart." He grinned.

Meg let the comment pass. Sloane Rivers was Caleb's baseball coach as well as the high school's athletic director. He'd recently moved back to Cooper Falls after coaching at a prep school in western Massachusetts. His ex-wife and daughter lived here, and the director's position afforded him the opportunity to be closer to his daughter, Erica. She was Bethany's best friend.

Meg and Sloane had been childhood playmates. Their mothers had been best friends and had pushed them in matching strollers down County Street. Lorraine Hadley and Eve Rivers had chattered and planned how their two children would grow up and marry and make them devoted grandmothers. But Meg had never been seriously attracted to Sloane. A solid friendship, yes, but Sloane had been too much like her to generate any spark of passion.

Sloane and Jack were amicable, but more on the level of polite acquaintances than close friends.

"Jack's not coming?" Sloane asked. Wearing chinos, a blue oxford and a navy pullover, he looked very much like the approachable coach and ally that Caleb admired.

"No. He had appointments he couldn't break." She settled into her own seat, folded her coat and set it and her purse aside. The stage was set up with a podium, chairs for the faculty and risers for the students to step upon after receiving their certificates.

Sloane spoke to a couple who stopped to chat and they exchanged greetings with Meg. She listened to the conversation about the hopes of Cooper High in the upcoming baseball season, and after the couple walked away, she said to Sloane, "There's something I'd like to ask you."

"The answer is yes."

"No kidding around, okay? This is serious."

"Meggie, when it comes to you, I'm always serious."

Meg found his offhand comments flattering and fun and mostly meaningless. At the same time she wasn't oblivious to the fact that Jack was wary of Sloane for just that reason—his tendency to engage in facetious flirting. "This is about Caleb and this idea he has about pitching for the Red Sox."

Sloane tented his fingers, pressing the tips against his mouth. "The idea isn't totally implausible."

"That doesn't sound like a contract is in the mail."

"At this point, that *would* be implausible, but possibilities begin with dreams and hard work." He leaned forward, turning his head sideways to look at Meg. "Caleb is talented, he's young, he's obsessive about the game and with the right contacts there's no telling what might happen."

Meg was determined not to be swayed by biased enthusiasm for Caleb's talents. Jack certainly wouldn't be.

If he were here, Meg imagined him saying "exactly my point" to a comment such as "no telling what might happen." For Jack, a no-end-result plan was too vague, too slippery, too fraught with unimagined disasters. He had never been a dreamer nor an illusionist; he'd experienced too much sadness, too much tragedy, known too many faulty perceptions to trust anything as wispy and empty as dreams. He'd found his way by building on the only foundation he knew: himself.

Yet, this morning she'd understood Caleb's resentment. He wanted to pursue his dream of pitching professionally, and Meg had little doubt that he wanted his father's support in the same way he had Sloane's.

"How much have you said to Caleb?" Meg asked.

"I haven't sat him down and told him a major league career is in his future, if that's what you mean. That's way too iffy."

"Have you discouraged college?"

"Absolutely not."

Meg was silent for a moment.

"Is that what Caleb said?" Sloane asked.

Instead of answering, she said, "Would you do me a favor?"

"Anything."

"Don't encourage the baseball angle. At least not for right now. Caleb doesn't want to think about anything else. Jack and I believe that's shortsighted."

"Whatever you say."

For the next hour, Meg waited through a parade of students. She applauded and wished that Jack were here with her when Caleb's name was called. Bethany was sitting in the third row from the front and Meg grinned when her daughter clapped and shrieked for her brother.

Maybe this was just a feel-good assembly but that didn't

diminish her pride. Tears filled her eyes, and she applauded with such enthusiasm she got a cramp in her hand.

Caleb accepted the certificate from the principal, paused a moment to speak to his chemistry teacher, and then went and stood with the others.

After the assembly finished, Meg rose to her feet. She gathered her coat and purse. Sloane squeezed her arm. "Tell Caleb I'll congratulate him later. Say hello to Jack for me."

Meg nodded, glancing toward the stage where Caleb was surrounded by his friends, and getting a huge stranglehold squeeze from his sister.

Caleb grinned when he saw her.

"Oh, Caleb," Meg said, her voice breaking. "I'm so proud of you." She hugged him fiercely and he didn't resist despite all his friends standing around.

"It's not such a big deal, you know."

"Well, I think it's a *very* big deal," she countered.

Bethany yelped. "I think it's totally awesome."

"Yeah, it is kinda cool," he finally admitted, and Meg saw the pleasure of making his mother proud in his eyes. He gave her the certificate, which she promised to have framed. She gave him one last hug and watched him walk away with his friends.

Bethany tucked her arm into her mother's. "I like that he wasn't a jerk. You know, acting like some swelled-up toad doing high-fives and other gross things guys do."

"I know. He was humble and a little shy."

"Yeah. Like heroes are supposed to be."

Meg drew her daughter closer. "Exactly."

That good, settled, all-is-right-with-the-family feeling stayed with her as she drove home. Caleb had worked hard; he'd studied and applied himself and now he'd been publicly honored for his efforts. Her heart swelled with pride for who he was and his future potential.

When she turned onto Euclid Drive, she scowled when she saw the rusted Chevrolet. She'd called the police about the unsightly car on her way to the high school. That was an hour ago. Why was it still here?

The vehicle was parked near a fire hydrant—a clear violation, and now she noted some kind of fluid coming from under the engine and making a jagged path toward the curb.

Using her cell phone, she called the police again, and she was assured—again—that a patrol car would be sent to check it out.

It was nearly eleven o'clock when she walked into the house. She put the kettle on for tea, listened to a message from their accountant that their income taxes were ready and another one from her sister, Kate, saying she'd call her back. She was about to call Jack, when the phone rang.

"So how did it all go?" Jack asked when she answered.

"I was going to call you," she said, chuckling. "See, for all your huffing about this being a feel-good show, you want to know how it went."

"I confess."

"It went great, and I think Caleb was really proud of himself. He even let me hug him in public without wincing."

"Definite progress into male maturity," he said sagely.

"And I spoke with Sloane."

There was a strained silence. "And what insightful advice did he have this time?" he asked, the sarcasm thick.

Meg sighed, then decided not to mention Sloane had sat with her. It would only give Jack another reason to be annoyed. "I told him that I would prefer he cool it on his enthusiasm about Caleb's dream career in baseball. That you and I wanted him to focus on his grades. Sloane agreed."

"Good."

She waited a moment to see if he would say anything else on the matter, but he didn't.

"Jack, we should do something for Caleb. Reward him. Maybe give him some money toward that pickup truck he wants to buy."

"Good idea."

Feeling buoyant, she hung up, pleased by the way she'd handled Sloane and Jack. The two men both had Caleb's best interests in mind; Jack just needed to allow Sloane some slack.

She made her tea, adding milk and sugar before carrying it upstairs to drink while she changed clothes. The sun was bright and the temperature outside had climbed to forty-five degrees. She wanted to take advantage of the nice weather to rake out the winter debris that had accumulated around the bushes.

Outside, she pulled on gloves, took the rake and wheelbarrow from the garage and went to tackle the winter litter on the south side of the house. She worked steadily, losing track of time as she emptied load after load of leaves and twigs into a compost heap near the edge of the property. Surveying the raked ground, she stretched to ease the kinks jabbing in her back from a winter of limited exercise. But the kinks were worth it as she admired the results, noting lots of bright green growth in the rich soil that had been blanketed by layers of dead leaves. She returned the wheelbarrow and rake to the garage. Fifteen minutes later she stepped into a hot shower.

Afterwards, she dressed, blow-dried her hair and she'd just slipped on her shoes when her sister called again. Meg told Kate about the assembly, and that their mother had called from Florida the previous night to say she'd be home the end of April.

"So what's up with you?" Meg asked, and immediately wished she hadn't.

Kate railed on and on against Porter Delacourt, the man she was currently involved with. That was Kate. Always involved, but never committed.

"I caught them in bed, Meg, and I'll be damned if I'm going to be sophisticated about it."

"I don't blame you," Meg said, paying marginal attention. This was nothing new. Kate's love life blazed one moment and waned the next; it had never had the consistency and depth that Meg had found with Jack.

Yet, Meg listened while Kate ranted, whined, sputtered and cried for another twenty minutes. All Meg had to do was offer an occasional "I'm sorry" and a generous amount of "poor baby" commiseration. By the time she hung up, she knew more about Porter and the other woman than she wanted to. It was nearly two o'clock, and she still had groceries to get and library books to return.

She put on her jacket, grabbed the books, slung her purse strap over her shoulder and headed out the door.

She'd left her Expedition in the driveway, and now she placed the books in the backseat. She'd just put her purse on the passenger-side seat after getting out her car keys when a patrol car pulled into the drive.

Meg frowned. Still holding her keys, she nudged the door closed and walked toward the blue and white vehicle. The last time the police had been in the driveway was Halloween when an officer brought Bethany home after a brawl at a loud teenage party that a neighbor reported. Bethany hadn't been in trouble, but the boy she'd gone with had been drinking and she'd refused to get into his car. She'd asked the patrolman for a ride.

Now a tall, uniformed officer slid out from the driver's side.

"Can I help you with something?" she asked, her eyes flitting to the passenger side where another officer emerged. When neither spoke, she said, "If this is about filing a complaint about the rusted car, I don't want to do that. I just wanted it towed away. It was leaking some kind of fluid." She looked at one of the men and then the other. They both wore dark glasses; she noted their expressions carried that blank seriousness that revealed nothing, but at the same time projected a foreboding. She tightened up when their slow deliberate manner caused an alarm to clang deep within her.

"A tow truck took care of the vehicle, ma'am. I'm

Sergeant Lubella and this is Officer Kremer. Are you Mrs. DeWilde?"

"Yes. I can't believe that two officers came over here to tell me the car had been towed."

"Ma'am, we're not here about the car. Is Mr. DeWilde home?"

"At two in the afternoon? Of course not. He's working. What's this all about?" Meg's words rushed forward, not keeping time with the increased speed of her pulse, with the building apprehension.

"Any other family members home?"

Now a grinding panic. She swallowed, making herself speak evenly. "No. My son will be home from school shortly. No . . . wait a minute . . . I think he has baseball practice this afternoon. Or is that tomorrow . . . ?" Suddenly her mind scrambled and she couldn't remember. "I'm not sure. My daughter was going to the mall with her friends."

The tall officer drew closer. What was his name? She thought desperately, instinctively fearful now and unable to push away the dark whispers snaking and coiling about in her mind. Something was wrong. Terribly wrong.

"I'm afraid we have some bad news."

"Bad news?" she repeated as if she were hard-of-hearing. Some inner sense wanted to stall, to deny, whatever was coming. "Is it my husband's mother? His brother?" Hazel and Ford DeWilde had substance abuse problems that had been ongoing for years. Jack vacillated between worry and irritation to the point that if the phone rang late at night he immediately assumed one or the other had been hurt.

"No ma'am. It's your son."

"Caleb?" Her breath whooshed out in relief. Now she knew there'd been a mistake. She'd just seen Caleb a few hours ago. "Was there some ruckus at school? Why didn't they just call instead of sending the police and scaring me." She pressed a hand to her chest to calm and steady her thumping heart. But their expressions didn't change.

"Not at school. This happened in Sawyer's Woods."

Caleb often visited Louis Jessup at his cabin in Sawyer's Woods, but not during school hours. "No," she said, shaking her head. "That's impossible."

"Mrs. DeWilde, let's go inside."

But she stumbled back from his attempt to take her arm. "What happened to Caleb? I want to know."

Her gaze darted from one to the other. Clearly neither officer wanted to answer her.

Finally, the sergeant said, "There's no easy way to say this. Your son was found dead. Hanged. It appears to be suicide."

Chapter Three

Why were they telling her this? Why would they come here with such a wildly improbable scenario? Meg felt light-headed, dizzy, disoriented. Her entire body sagged as if life poured from her, scattering like a broken bag of marbles.

She stumbled. Her hands clenched and her knees went spongy. One officer caught her before she collapsed on the asphalt.

"Mrs. DeWilde?"

"There's been a mistake." Her voice sounded calm and normal. Well, of course she sounded okay. She *was* okay. Caleb was okay. He would come home just like always. Coming home and jumping off the bus wearing his white shirt and chinos and his Red Sox jacket. Hours ago he'd stood polished and proper on the stage, and she'd loved him for dressing the way she'd asked him. She could still feel his warm body from when she'd hugged him after the awards ceremony. He hadn't resisted, revealing for a few special seconds his soft, vulnerable side. Sure he was cool, sure anything important to adults was typically no big deal to him and his friends, but that was normal, that was the way of teenage boys. That was her son.

Any minute now he'd be crossing the cul-de-sac, sprinting across the driveway, slamming into the house, heading for the refrigerator, drinking milk from the jug . . .

Her eyes stung raw and scorched and she rubbed them with her coat sleeve. She had to move, to do something. Her car was still parked where she left it. She felt her keys bite into her hand, reassuring her she had things to do. She scowled, turning this way and that. What had she been about to do?

"Probably gonna pass out on us." The voice drifted above her.

Pass out? Her? Ridiculous. The only time she'd fainted was when she'd gone on that crazy starvation diet when she was in college. She couldn't faint. She had to drive.

"Let's get her into the house." A large hand gripped her arm, tugging her away from the car. What were they doing? She had errands—groceries, library books. She resisted the locked hold on her.

"Let go of me."

"Mrs. DeWilde. Come on. We want to help you. You need to go inside. Phone your husband."

"Jack?"

The other officer muttered, "Look, we can handle this for her. I met DeWilde last year. His business sponsored my kid's Little League team. We can do the notification. This is nasty stuff to deliver on the phone."

Meg stiffened, struggled, shoved at their hold on her when the full meaning of the past few moments swamped her. Her eyes widened, pupils dilated, body shaking. Her arms wrapped around her middle holding down some vile nausea that began to gather.

"We can't leave with her like this."

"We won't have to. Here comes someone."

The afternoon sun ducked behind the clouds and a cold northern breeze blew her hair against her cheeks. Three black crows landed beside an azalea bush. Meg stared at the creatures as if they were trespassing.

"Meg, what's going on?" The familiar female voice cut through her wooziness.

"Claire?"

Her neighbor's long, tent-sized brown cardigan flapped out and she tried to gather it close to her. *You always buy your sweaters too big, Claire.* Meg stared at the sweater, her mind latching on to irrelevancies. *And brown? You should wear blue. You have such pretty blue eyes.*

Claire took Meg by the shoulders. "What's happened? I was going out to feed my birds when I saw the police car." To the officers, she said, "I'm Claire Dozier. I live across the street."

"We appreciate you coming over. There's been an accident."

The air vibrated around them.

"Lord have mercy. Not her husband . . ."

"The boy. He was found dead. Hanged in Sawyer's Woods."

Claire dragged Meg even closer. "Caleb? But that's impossible. I saw him get on the bus this morning."

The officer sighed. "Ma'am, Mrs. DeWilde shouldn't be alone and we can't leave without making sure she's all right."

"You come here and tell her Caleb is—I can't even say it—of course she isn't going to be all right."

Both officers glanced at one another, exchanging some silent thought not answering her question. "Ma'am, we'll notify Mr. DeWilde."

Claire took charge of Meg as if she were a slow child. Protecting and pillowing her to the sweater that smelled of meatballs and fireplace ashes. "I'll take care of things here."

Meg heard them as if she were far away, yet the meaning of their words resonated louder and stronger and cutting with whole denial giving way for the enormous reality. Her son was dead. My God, her son was dead.

The officers climbed into their car, backed into a two

vehicle–wide turnaround and nosed the cruiser toward the street when the black Lexus pulled in and blocked their exit.

Jack scowled, his reason for coming home suddenly not important. What was going on? Cops? His wife being physically supported by Claire Dozier? He got out of the car, his concentration solely on Meg. The police car had stopped and parked, facing out. The engine stayed running as the two men stepped out, one walking to the front bumper. The driver closed his door and tugged his hat into place.

Claire saw him and turned Meg, saying something to her. She broke from Claire, running. Jack started toward her.

In those ensuing seconds every instinct for emotional survival that he'd honed years ago exploded open and splattered every nerve with terror. He caught her as she practically climbed into his clothes.

He gripped her, steadying her. "What? What?"

"It's Ca-Caleb . . . Dear God, Jack, C-Caleb is . . . is dead."

He pulled her back looking at puffy eyes, smudged makeup and lips pulled in as tight as a sealed envelope. Her spirit was vacant. His insides buckled and shifted down as if a hose had sucked out his guts. "That's ridiculous," but even as his instinctive denial died she was already shaking her head.

"How? When? Where?"

"He killed himself. Sawyer's Woods. He—" But she couldn't continue.

"Suicide? That's crazy. I don't believe it."

"The police told me . . ." She twisted restlessly. "They said it was true."

Jack stared at her, desperately trying to conjure up any bizarre reason for why the cops would say this, but he could barely think. His mind had thickened like a sluggish summer swamp.

She clutched him, her nails digging into his suit jacket.

Jack held tight unsure who was preventing who from collapsing. Claire stayed at a distance, her hands covering her mouth. Fuzzy slippers on her feet crouched like twin pink rabbits. One of the cops had stepped back near the garage where Meg's lilacs grew. He lit a cigarette and waited. The other officer leaned into the vehicle's open window, radio mike in hand, talking to someone.

It was all true. This was really happening. A siren whined in the distance and Jack recalled a siren he'd heard earlier. Oh, Christ.

Jack shrank from the "what-ifs" that lobbed through his thoughts. His gaze fastened on one of the cops. The man cocked his head indicating he wanted to speak with him.

Details about Caleb. Details they figured Meg couldn't handle. He didn't have to work his brain too hard to know he didn't want the details either. He wanted to get back in the car and drive far, far, far away. Big-time denial, pal, and nowhere to run. Meg's sobs had quieted into muffled hitches against his neck. Jack felt cloistered, airless, his own breathing heaving from so far down inside him he feared letting it out all at once.

He squeezed his eyes closed. He had to get a grip. For Meg, for Bethany . . . *Bethany!*

Jack pulled back. "Good God. Bethany. She doesn't know, does she?"

Meg looked blank, then the color drained from her cheeks.

She broke free, swinging toward the Expedition. Instantly, he hauled her back.

"Jack, she'll be hysterical. She needs us."

"I'll go get her." A band cinched tighter and tighter around his chest. "You go on in the house. Ask Claire to stay with you. I'll get the other stuff done."

"I don't know what to do. I don't feel anything. I'm all hollow. This is so unbelievable."

"Meg, sweetheart, if I could change this—make this untrue . . . make this easier . . ." Jack hugged her fiercely, cowered by his impoverished attempt to answer the unanswerable. He wanted it to go away. He wanted it to be some outrageous brutish joke. Meg grasped onto him like he was the buoy that would keep her from sinking.

And they stood, their bodies pressed so close, one heartbeat indistinguishable from the other. Holding and clinging and still.

Claire slowly came forward.

Jack drew back a bit, wiped the moisture from his eyes, keeping Meg tucked close.

Claire held her clasped hands up, fingers pressed against her mouth. "Oh, Jack, I'm so so sorry. How awful for your family. What could that boy have been thinking."

Jack stared at her. It wasn't a question, but a comment that implied he should have an explanation. Well, he didn't and it pissed him off that Claire Dozier would float a suggestion that he did. If he and Meg had been aware that suicide was in Caleb's thoughts, they sure as hell wouldn't have ignored it.

Jack clenched his jaw so tight that even his back teeth hurt. "If you would take Meg inside—"

"Surely to goodness, I can do that." Claire moved beside Meg. "I can stay as long as you need me, my dear."

Jack urged Meg to go.

"What are you going to do?" she asked, gulping.

"The police want to talk to me. Then I'll bring Bethany home."

"I'm going," she said flatly. The sudden resolve seemed to surprise and invigorate her. "I can't let you do this alone."

He debated arguing, then changed his mind. He wanted her with him. He needed her. And Bethany—God, he didn't even want to contemplate breaking this to his fourteen-year-old. Caleb was her hero.

Just this morning she'd taken her brother's side.

Just this morning Jack had rejected his son's nutty career dreams.

Just this morning he'd told Meg there was plenty of time; Caleb would come around. His son would see the wisdom of college over baseball. See the wisdom, for God's sake. And not just any wisdom, but *his* wisdom.

Now this. Suicide. The word, the act, the enormity of its implications simply wouldn't connect to anything he knew and loved about his son; suicide was a dive into an abyss he couldn't navigate. Jack pressed the heels of his hands into his eyes.

"I'll drive," Meg said, clearly realizing he was about to lose it.

"No, I'm—" he was going to say he was okay, but he wasn't. "I can drive. We'll go in my car."

"I'm so glad you came home," she said, latching on to him again as if he might scurry away.

She took a deep breath, straightened and walked to the Lexus. Jack watched her slip into the front seat, feeling inadequate and to his astonishment, angry.

Claire hadn't moved. She clutched her sweater to her flat chest, her eyes anxious and waiting. Well beyond sixty, she was known around town as a gossip and a snoop. Physically, she was a union of bones, her clothes large and colorless. Her helmet of brown hair resembled a whisk broom. She fed birds, mowed her own grass, kept a revolver in her pantry and never missed an opportunity to be a "helpful" neighbor. Odd, he realized, that this fragmented accumulation defined Claire. He couldn't recall ever noting any precise details beyond her overly solicitous manner whenever she visited Meg.

"Thanks for coming over," he said automatically.

"When I saw the police I knew something was wrong, but Caleb killing himself. Mercy. Such a young man. Such a terrible loss."

Her ruminations ambled around him like meaningless chatter. They made no impression because they changed nothing. Pleasing sentimentality that repeated the obvious.

In the arena of sudden death, Jack had potent knowledge

and disenchanted memories. He'd stood on a Newport dock, a skinny teenager in a Budweiser tee-shirt, grimy jeans and stolen sneakers and watched the cops haul his old man's body out of Narragansett Bay. Accidental drowning had been the official cause, but Jack hadn't been convinced. His father had been a fisherman; he knew the water. He'd survived a sinking boat in the rolling Atlantic during a fierce nor'easter. For him to drown in a few feet of lapping water beneath a rickety dock was as likely as a shark surfacing in the local YMCA pool. His old man had defied the sea's elements more times than he'd been drunk. Yet after peppering the cops with questions, nosing around the bars and quizzing the pub rats, Jack had no answers. He got sympathy, cheek pats, shoulder squeezes and advice to let it go. A drunk drowned. Accidents happen. Life moves on. End of that story. New story, kid, new direction.

Take care of your mother.

Take care of your brother.

Be the man of family. That's your responsibility,

There it was.

And here it is again.

Jack glanced at his watch. 2:35. Bethany told him that morning that she was doing some library work after school for about an hour before going to the mall. He had enough time to head her off at school.

"Do you still want me to wait until you get back?" Claire asked.

"Not necessary." He started toward the two cops when she took his arm and leaned close like she was his mother about to give advice.

In a low voice, she said, "Surely you must know that this will be all over town in the next few hours."

"Probably. What's your point?"

"I could do some phoning for you. Save you from that ordeal."

Jack could almost hear the excitement rumble beneath her words. She had firsthand knowledge. Spreading news when she was an inside source was more delicious than waiting on some gossipy speed-dialer.

She prattled on about how shocking and disturbing it would be for Cooper Falls. Very disturbing, yes terribly disturbing and, of course, tragic. Finally she took a breath, spittle at the corners of her mouth.

"Do whatever, Claire," he said flatly. "Spread the word. Answer the questions even when you don't have a clue about the circumstances. Gin up some frenzy of speculation."

She backed up, huffing. "Well, I've never—I came over here to help and this is what I get!" She wrapped her sweater tight, stomped past him across the drive to the side yard and then across the street to her house.

Jack loosened his tie, opened his jacket and shoved his hands into his trouser pockets as he approached the officers.

The taller one adjusted his sunglasses. "We're sorry, Mr. DeWilde."

"What happened?"

"This is what we know so far. Louis Jessup found him and cut him down thinking he could do CPR. That's what he told 9-1-1 when he called it in."

"Cut him down? He hanged himself?"

"Yes, sir. He used his shirt."

Jack lowered his head and closed his eyes at the enormity of what he was hearing. His shirt. The shirt Meg insisted he wear. That anger that introduced itself earlier flared like a suddenly lit blowtorch. His son was dead because of a goddamn white shirt that he hadn't wanted to wear.

Then a graphic visual of every tragedy he'd ever seen on television scrolled through his mind. The body bag, heavy and full and sling-shaped carried by rescuers to a waiting van, pushed inside, doors slammed and taken . . . taken to where? "Where is Caleb now?"

"In Providence. The ME will do an autopsy and give an official cause of death and then release the body. Louis Jessup was badly shaken."

Jack didn't give a damn about Jessup. He'd never liked Caleb's friendship with the old hermit, and for the man to be so closely associated with his son's death made Jack queasy.

"Sir, you'll need to make arrangements with a funeral home. They'll take things from there and notify you when the body is released."

The body . . . his dead son . . . God.

The wind blew cold and Jack shivered. "Anything else?"

"One other thing. There'll be an investigation. There always is when a death is unusual. A detective will want to talk to you about your son and—"

"Talk about what?" Jack's gaze jumped from one cop to the other. "Caleb isn't—" He cleared his throat. "Caleb wasn't ever in trouble with the police."

"It's just routine, sir. He'll be looking for anything that might have triggered your son to do this. He understands how difficult this is for you and your family."

"He does, does he?" Jack snapped, detesting the official patronizing. "Does he have a son who hanged himself?"

Their silence was their answer.

"Then don't give me any bullshit about understanding and difficulties." He turned and walked to his car.

Inside, he put on sunglasses, started the engine and backed out of the driveway. Claire stood on her front porch, looking frail and small and for a few seconds Jack wondered if he'd misjudged her. Then she turned abruptly and stalked into her house. Nope. He'd been right. He mentally tracked her steps to the closest telephone.

Meg slid her hand around his leg. "What did the police tell you?"

He covered her hand and squeezed. Tears burned and his eyes itched. "Nothing we need to talk about now. How are you doing?"

"Numb. Trying to get my mind around this."

"Too big for that. Don't even try. Think about Bethany.

The family will need to be called. I'll take care of making the funeral arrangements." Did he really sound so methodical and organized?

The police car behind them turned left at the light and Jack continued straight. Meg's fingers pushed into his leg and he welcomed the distraction.

"Call Carpenter Memorial," Meg said. "Floyd handled Kevin's funeral." Kevin had been a friend of Caleb's who'd died in a car accident more than a year ago. She leaned forward, her face damp, her hair tangled, her eyes hauntingly bright when she looked at him. "A funeral for Caleb. What are we doing? Just a few hours ago the biggest problem was whether he'd play baseball or go to college."

His throat thickened painfully. "Don't do this."

"Baseball or college, Jack! Innocent and irrelevant. Does it matter now? No, because now he isn't going to be doing either. We're going to bury our son." Silence draped and enveloped them through the next intersection. Jack wanted a cigarette and a drink and the second chance that he would never have. Meg slumped against the door, her tears bringing soft sobs. "I've always been able to deal with the stuff the kids did, but this, this is so impossible."

"Meg, no one is expecting you to be strong or to handle this," he said, the lame words more filler than meaningful. His responsibilities were already kicking in, preparing him for the coming days. At the same time he felt as if he were self-creating a bulwark against foes, friends and endless questions without answers. He'd been here before. He knew the drill.

She turned suddenly and looked at him. "You came home? But you didn't know. Why did you come home?"

"I wanted to talk to you about something. Not important now."

Jack flipped on his directional, slowed and turned into the high school parking lot. The buses were gone. A few student groups were scattered across the area. Jack noted the huddle of guys on the pitcher's mound, arms loose, heads down, feet shuffling. In that moment he knew word of Caleb's death had reached the school.

Meg was out of the car and headed inside with Jack following. She approached the principal's office when Arthur Squires came out and closed the door.

Jack had known the principal since 1990 when Squires and his wife, Eleanor, bought a house through DeWilde's. Meg and Arthur had worked together on a number of school projects. Distinguished, stern and in his late-fifties, Squires had a slightly pitted complexion and a small, brown mustache so carefully clipped it looked false. He wasn't known for warmth and coddling. Discipline not disruption was his motto. Today he looked stunned and confused.

He took Meg's hands and squeezed them gently. He only nodded to Jack, for which he was grateful. Shaking hands seemed obscene. "I just heard. Some boys saw the police and Rescue over at Sawyer's and naturally went to investigate. This is such a terrible shock, I don't know what to say." He paused, lowering his head as if words might be hidden in the red pattern on the gray linoleum floor. Finally, blinking and clearing his throat, he said, "Bethany knows. Just a few minutes ago. She's in my office with two of her friends. I just tried to call your house to let you know I would keep her here."

The twenty-step walk through two doors into Squires's office felt as if every step included lugging a cement weight.

Bethany was on her feet, tears streaming, running, crying. Screaming, she fell into Jack's arms, hysteria making her shake. Jack pulled Meg to them and held them both as Bethany cried, "No, no, it isn't true!"

Meg gathered her into her arms, saying nothing, her own tears sliding down her cheeks as she stroked Bethany's tangled hair. Erica Rivers covered her face with her hands. Another friend, Jenny something-or-other comforted Erica.

Jack plunged his hands into his pockets. The principal's eyes were grief-stricken and Jack had to look away.

"Jack, if there's anything Eleanor and I can do."

Bring him back. Make him alive again. "I wish there was."

"The school, of course, offers their support. Caleb was a fine young man." He glanced out the window as if ashamed of such an obvious cliché. Jack glanced too. There was simply nothing to say. The day had grayed, the clouds heavy and thick above a trio of more weeping girls, arms around one another trudging toward a waiting car. The phone rang and Squires answered, turning slightly, keeping his voice low. "Yes. Just a little while ago. We're all in shock. No, I don't know any of the details. You'll have to talk to Coach Rivers about what the team will do. We haven't had a chance to think about the school's response. I'm sure we'll have an answer by tomorrow."

Jack tuned it out, continuing to watch out the window, allowing his mind to shut down. Beside him Bethany's sobs had slowed and Meg was whispering as she led their daughter out into the corridor.

Squires touched his back, his voice catching. "Please call if there's anything you or your family needs."

What we need, no one can give us. Nevertheless he nodded in the affirmative, then followed his family, his head up, staring straight ahead and seeing nothing.

Never had he felt so powerless, never had he felt so useless and never so desperately aware that their lives had been forever changed.

Chapter Four

Every room Meg walked into had reminders of Caleb.
Framed baby pictures, a Little League collage and the most recent, a photo taken last year when Caleb pitched a no-hitter for the Cooper Falls Warriors. Atop a lamp shade sat a recent addition to his Major League cap collection. On the buffet in the dining room lay a forgotten history textbook with a broken binding and stuffed with wrinkled papers.

But here in the kitchen, tucked where Meg had returned it on Tuesday morning, was the box of blueberry Pop-Tarts. She drew her finger down the side of the box, touching the jagged rip. Caleb never had the patience to open the package according to directions. When she pointed it out, he would say, "Jeez, Mom, it's not a bomb, it's just a stupid box."

And she would answer, "You're too impatient."

"But I get what I want quicker." Then he would grin, bite down on the Pop-Tart and that would be the end of it.

The end of it. The end . . .

Meg sucked in her breath, the rawness of her throat now as familiar as her son's rejoinder. She should toss the box in the trash; nobody but Caleb liked Pop-Tarts. She stared at it as if physically removing and discarding it amounted to blasphemy. She couldn't. She wanted to keep it . . . yes, saving it gave her a tangible extremity of comfort. Comfort in a box of Pop-Tarts, for heaven's sake. She pressed her hands against her face, suddenly overwhelmed.

Finally she swiped the moisture from her cheeks. She closed the cupboard on the box and began clearing the table of breakfast dishes.

"Mom? I don't have anything to wear."

Bethany stood in the archway dressed in black leggings and a faded red sweatshirt that ended at her knees. Black polish announced her toenails. Her side-parted hair draped over her shoulder in a shower-wet hank and her expression was pinched into the same sad grimace she had been wearing since Tuesday afternoon.

Today was Friday.

Today was the funeral.

"You have lots of clothes. Wear whatever is comfortable." Meg dragged the sponge across the counter and spilled the crumbs into the sink. The past sixty-plus hours had ground by in a blur. She had no idea what she'd said to the throng of friends, neighbors and Caleb's school buddies who had come by. All she knew was that they had been bereft and devastated and struggling for words. Tears and silence became a mutual solace.

This particular day had loomed dark and heavy; she dreaded the funeral with its rituals and its form. The finality offended her and angered her; her son had left too many missing answers. She wasn't ready for a tidy beginning of tomorrow, for time to heal and strengthen as all the sympathy cards promised.

She picked up the latest batch that Jack had opened and placed them in a rattan basket to look at another time.

"Mom, you're not listening."

"What?" Meg looked at her daughter, momentarily forgetting she still stood in the archway.

"See?" Bethany's lower lip rolled out far enough for a pair of cardinals to perch.

"You have my attention."

She blew out an exasperated breath. "I don't have anything to wear to a funeral."

"Of course you don't. No one has clothes for a funeral. We do the best we can. Wear the blue dress."

"I don't want to." Stubborn. Meg guessed she was supposed to offer suggestions until one appealed.

She opened the dishwasher and began to stack dishes. "Then the plaid wool skirt and your dark gold sweater."

"I hate that skirt." She swung her hair back, the wetness making a smacking sound when it hit the wall. "It makes me look fat and the sweater has a gross spot right where my tit is. Everyone will look and laugh."

Meg paused, the upside-down mug in her hand dripping coffee drops. "Pardon me? Tit? Can we do without the slang?"

"Caleb said tit," she replied, belligerence in full boil. "I heard him and Gregg talking about tits and asses and if a girl wanted a guy to like her she better have big tits and a little ass." She cupped her hands over her breasts, rubbing her palms on her nipples. "Look. Nothing. Flat as old lady Dozier's." She spun around hiking up her sweatshirt to show what Meg thought was a nicely shaped bottom for a fourteen-year-old. Bethany grabbed a handful of one cheek and pumped it. "Isn't this disgusting fat? This is why I don't have a boyfriend. I have no tits and a big ass."

Meg stared at her, unsure what to make of such a strange conversation and too mentally exhausted to try and decipher it. Her daughter's success or lack of in the boyfriend department struck Meg as absurdly beside the point today. She put the mug into the dishwasher and closed it. "Then wear something else."

"You choose."

Meg frowned. "Bethany, why are you asking me when you don't like what I suggest?" She struggled to not be verbally sharp and impatient, but her insides churned. She wanted to slam her hand on the counter and shout: *I don't care what you wear. I don't care what anyone wears. I don't care about boyfriends and big tits and little asses. I don't want to be calm and logical and all-knowing. I want my son alive. I want—oh God.* Meg dropped her head, horrified at this calloused inner reaction to her own daughter.

Since the news, Bethany had cried or whined or argued nearly nonstop, and while Jack had been a paragon of patience, comfort and decision-making, Meg's grief had opened a score of angry reactions when she wasn't flailing in a numbing emptiness. She didn't know what to do, where to turn or how to find any surcease. She couldn't relieve her own pain, how in God's name was she supposed to handle her daughter's?

Deal with her as she is, give her what she wants, Jack had said. Her sadness isn't yours or mine. She wants to be close to us because she's the one left behind.

"All right, Bethany," she said, pulling deep on her inner resources and softening her voice. "Since you don't like my suggestions why don't you tell me what you'd like to wear." Meg was fully prepared to call Kate and tell her to go to Filene's and buy Bethany whatever she requested.

She perked up. "I was looking in your closet."

"Ahhh." *She wants to be close because she's the one left behind. Oh, Jack, how did you get to be so wise about your daughter?* Meg was dutifully thoughtful. "Not the crepe with the feathers."

She grinned, the first smile Meg had seen in days.

Bethany twisted her hands together. "I don't think it's, uh . . ."

"Appropriate?"

"Yeah." She paused, plucking at the front of her sweatshirt. "I was thinking . . . that, well . . . maybe . . ."

Meg waited; she loved this familiar jousting, and feeling to her own surprise, almost alive once again. "You were thinking what?"

Then in a burst she said, "I want to wear your black sweater and that long gray skirt."

It was what Meg had planned to wear and in fact the two pieces were hanging on her closet door. No doubt Bethany had seen them. She rarely asked to wear anything that belonged to Meg. More closeness? Perhaps. "The skirt will be too big, but wear the outfit if you like."

"You mean I can? I thought you'd say no."

"Nope. It's all yours. I'll find something else."

Instead of the smile she expected, Bethany looked trapped and then she erupted into tears, rushed to her mother and practically leapt into her arms, sobbing and holding on to her. "I can't stand it. I don't want to go to Caleb's funeral. I don't want to watch him put in the ground and covered with dirt."

Bethany had balked about going to the calling hours, too, but she'd gone, albeit avoiding the casket. Meg held her now and rubbed her back, welcoming the weight and life of her daughter. "Shh, I know. You wanted me to say no and then you'd have nothing to wear."

Meg felt the small nod. "Am I a terrible person for hating all of this?"

Meg hugged her even tighter. "Of course you're not. And you want to know something? I don't want to go either."

"Then why? Is there some law that we have to go and cry and listen to words that won't bring Caleb back?"

"No, sweetheart, there's no law. It's just what people do when someone dies. It's a ritual, a ceremony, a way of saying good-bye."

"Well, I think it's stupid," she said in a huff, swiping her fist across her eyes. "I don't want to say good-bye. Caleb didn't say good-bye to us. Why did he do this? Did he hate us?"

Meg took a tissue and mopped at her daughter's damp red eyes. "Of course he didn't hate us."

"Then why did he do it?"

The question Meg had been avoiding for days hit her like a cold punch. This was at the core of her own misery. *Why.*

"This has been made worse for us—" She hesitated, shuddering, cringing from the word. "Because it was suicide. If Caleb had been in a car accident like Kevin or had died from an illness, we would be sad and heartbroken, but we wouldn't be left with the mystery of what Caleb had been going through. We don't understand what was so terrible that he would take his own life." *My God, I sound like I'm delivering his eulogy.*

"It makes me feel stupid and ashamed." Bethany hung her head, her shoulders shuddering, her words carrying a raw pain. "I should have known what was wrong. He was my brother. I knew a lot of stuff cuz he told me things." At Meg's raised eyebrows, Bethany quickly said, "Oh just dumb stuff. Nothing bad. Well, nothing really bad," she amended.

Whether from not wanting to know at this precise moment or her own weariness, Meg asked no questions. "Let's have no more talk about you being stupid or ashamed. Okay?" At Bethany's silence, Meg cupped her chin and gave her a gentle shake. "Okay?"

"Uh huh."

"Now, I think you better go and get dressed. Where's your dad?"

"He's in the study. I heard him on the phone with Uncle Ford. He's coming over with Gram DeWilde. Mom, do I have to go?"

Meg turned her and headed her toward the stairs. "Go get ready. We have to leave in less than an hour."

Bethany grumbled and stomped off. Meg poured Jack another mug of coffee and carried it into the study.

The deep green and mahogany room faced the west. A trio of six-over-six windows alcoved a generous cushioned seat that invited her to sit, as she often did in the evening with a brandy and the sunset over her shoulder while Jack and she caught up on their respective days. The male mood of the space came from an oxblood leather couch, a duet of faux Tiffany lamps and a rolltop desk Meg had bought at a Tiverton barn sale; she'd cleaned it, but left the patina that gave it color and character. The piece was a surprise for Jack on his fortieth birthday.

Now dressed in his black suit pants, white shirt and somber tie, he sat hunched over a legal pad scribbling on a list he had started on Tuesday. He made notes and crossed off others. She was awed by his control and focus and seemingly endless ability to handle every detail, including Wednesday night's drive to Logan because her mother couldn't get a direct flight from Tampa into Green Airport.

Meg had been worried because a full twenty-four hours passed before she'd gotten in touch with her. Then when she'd called a condo neighbor and learned her mother had left the previous Sunday with some people that the neighbor didn't know, her concern increased. By late Wednesday afternoon when her mother finally answered the phone in a toothachingly sweet voice, Meg was so relieved, her fear burst into anger and poured like a cloudburst. She had demanded to know where she'd been and with whom; her mother, amid tears over Caleb, got testy and infuriatingly stubborn. Jack had taken the phone and within minutes had calmed her.

Later as they prepared for bed, Meg asked, "Did she tell you where she'd been?"

"No."

"You should have asked."

"No, I shouldn't have."

"Three days she's with God knows who and you don't think it's important to ask?"

He'd stared at her as if she were making no sense. "Meg, listen to yourself. Your mother doesn't have to account to you. It's none of your business. I'd think you'd be glad she's independent and has a life."

"I'm her daughter, for God's sake. I'm not supposed to care where she is or what she's doing?"

"Caring and wanting her to clear her activities with you aren't the same. If this hadn't happened with Caleb, you would have never known she wasn't home."

He'd been right, and her own sharpness had betrayed her real motives. She liked that her mother's activities had always been predictable—golf lessons on Tuesday, the hairdresser on Wednesday, bridge on Friday night. Meg liked that her own life was fulfilled and routine and she worked hard to avoid the stress of conflict and the ambush of surprise. Caleb's suicide had plunged her into an abyss that had collapsed her singular ability to figure out what to expect and then act accordingly. Her common sense and usual judgment had been halting or incapacitated.

For her mother to simply go on a trip without telling anyone had terrified Meg beyond the rational. What if something *had* happened to her? What if these friends were slick con artists or charming rogues looking to relieve her of her money?

When Lorraine had arrived, she'd immediately gathered her daughter into her arms much as she'd done when Meg's father had died five years ago. Meg abandoned her anger and allowed her mother to comfort and pet her, realizing how very much she'd longed for maternal soothing in the same way Bethany had searched for ways to cling and be close.

Jack simply looked relieved that another crisis, minor as it was, had been managed.

He'd handled the funeral arrangements, making sure she was included in the final decision of an open or closed casket for the calling hours—they opted for open. He'd agreed with Meg that Caleb would be buried in his baseball uniform. A church service at Trinity Methodist would precede the burial at Orchard Rest Cemetery.

He had fielded endless incoming calls, spoken with the cavalcade of neighbors who brought food and tears and generous hugs. Jack had held her through the past three nights when sadness replaced sleep.

Watching him now, she saw the exhaustion lining his face, and was it her imagination or had he lost weight?

Meg set the mug on the desk, then sank down on the window seat. "Sweetheart, you look beat."

"I am." Jack sat back, tossing the ballpoint onto his list, and glared at the phone as if daring it to ring. He lifted the mug to his mouth sipping, and squinting his eyes against the steam that rose from the liquid. "We're all set with the limo. Kate will pick up your mother and Ford is bringing Ma. Chuck and Mike want to do something so I asked them to organize the parking at the cemetery—they and their wives, plus Vicki Slocum, are coming here to follow us to the church."

Chuck Cabral, Mike Perry, and Vicki Slocum all worked at DeWilde's; Meg had spoken to them at the calling hours. Vicki had been particularly weepy and frazzled, looking younger than her twenty-eight years. Caleb had worked for Vicki since September. From Jack, Meg learned that the young woman frequently mentioned what a great kid he was—reliable, honest and best of all they'd become friends.

"Whatever you've arranged is fine," she said, worried by the strain and hoarseness she heard in his voice.

He put down the mug and extended his hand. "Come and hold me."

She moved immediately, climbing onto his lap and curling her arms around his neck. "Oh Jack . . ."

"Meg, I love you. My God, how I love you."

She gripped him even tighter, feeling the throb of emotion behind his words. Why, she wondered sadly, does it take something like this to bring out this lovely vulnerability in her husband. "I couldn't have gotten through any of this without you," she said.

"Without me? Jesus, I can't get through life without you."

Her eyes stung with tears of love. "Nor me without you." Not having Jack to anchor her was such an outlandish concept she couldn't fathom existing without him. His hands slid under her sweater and rubbed her back.

"When my old man drowned, Ma bought a quart of gin and locked herself in the bedroom. Ford had been running with a bad crowd, goofing off, stealing stuff, getting arrested on a weekly basis, and messing with pot and pills. Pop dying was all the excuse the kid needed to really fuck up his life." His voice was pensive rather than angry, reminding her of a recitation of facts after years had calcified the pain and disappointment.

"And it all fell on you to deal with," she said, very aware of how easily and willingly Jack had shouldered it all.

"I won't let this family collapse," he said adamantly, the pledge as solid as her beloved trio of Caleb trees. He stroked her hair, cupping his hand around her neck. "I just want these death details to be over. The past three days feel like ten years."

They sat quietly a few moments. "When are you going to talk to the police?" Meg asked.

His body stilled followed by silence, then, "Let me guess. Kate or Ford has been chattering."

"Closemouthed Ford?" She chuckled. "He would never tell me something you told him. If I ask him anything, I get, 'better talk to Jack.' It was Kate. She said the police wanted to ask questions about why Caleb killed himself."

"I'm not particularly concerned about the cops and their questions since we don't have any answers. I'm worried about you and Bethany and the three of us getting our lives sane once again."

"I want that, too." She heard the shallowness under her words. Even as she understood that sanity and routine would eventually return, their family and they, themselves, had been irrevocably changed.

"Good." He kissed her before she could say anything more.

"Hey, anyone here?" Ford called from the kitchen.

"In the study," Jack answered.

Meg slid off Jack's lap, holding on to his hand. "We should do it as soon as possible. Like tomorrow. Bethany is going off with Kate."

"What are you talking about?"

"Going to see the police."

Jack turned toward the door, signaling that the conversation was over. "I'll handle it."

"But I want to hear the questions. I might have some answers that would give us a reason, some insight into why—"

"No, Meg," he said turning and facing her. "I'll take care of the cops. We are not going to turn into some obsessive family living a mantra of grief, trying to find answers that don't exist."

Meg's eyes widened. "But that's silly. Of course there are answers. Caleb didn't do this because he was passing by Sawyer's Woods and spotted a convenient tree."

Her raw sarcasm startled her and Jack frowned. She resented the notion that this was some random act of her son's. After what they'd been through, the time for mincing words had passed.

"I'm not saying that."

"I know you're not and that's the point. He killed himself for a reason. Just because we don't know it yet doesn't mean it doesn't exist."

"Don't know it yet? What the hell does that mean? This isn't an unfolding drama. You're talking in circles."

"And you're confusing things. Of course, I'm vague, I don't know anything."

"Exactly."

Meg sighed. She had to take this one step at a time, and the first step was the police.

Ford hovered in the living room shadows, obviously not wanting to interrupt. Jack studied her, waiting for her to blink. When she didn't, he muttered, "We'll discuss this another time."

"No discussion, Jack. It's settled. I'm going with you."

Her words held authority and she guessed his neutral expression was deliberate. Humor her, she suspected.

Just days ago a similar disagreement regarding her working at DeWilde's ended with her deferring to him, which no doubt was what he'd assumed now. Well, this was different. Terribly, terribly different. *A determined purpose carries its own power,* she thought, recalling Jack's words to Ford last year when Jack finally persuaded his brother to check into rehab for his cocaine habit. Ford had been clean now for nearly six months and the relationship between the two brothers had never been better.

She considered repeating the wisdom to him now, but she'd made her point. Evidenced by his walking away and quizzing Ford about his mother. Hazel DeWilde might have been a disengaged mother, but just as sadly she was an expert on getting drunk.

Meg reached to turn out the desk light when her gaze fell on Jack's list. Most of the items had been crossed out, but she noted he'd written DET. SETH EIDSON. 10:00. SATURDAY. That he hadn't mentioned the appointment clearly indicated his intent to quickly and quietly keep it without alerting her. Then next week when she asked, he'd brush it aside assuring her it was all settled and nothing of importance had been learned. But if the police presented some insight, would Jack have told her? It was a question she couldn't answer with any assurance and that disturbed her. Yet, however protective Jack wanted to be, he was never careless. If his motive for not including her had been questionable, he would have never left the list here. He'd naturally assumed she wouldn't want to go.

A few days ago he would have been right, but the agitation stirring within her couldn't be contained by Jack's intentions no matter how altruistic.

She switched off the lamp and returned the coffee mug to the kitchen.

Outside Jack had put on his jacket and opened the garage door on the side that housed his Lexus. He hauled

out the trash cans for garbage pickup, and Ford followed
with a carton of recyclable glass. The two men walked
back to the shelter of the open garage. Ford's old red and
white Blazer was parked behind the Lexus and Meg could
make out the figure of Hazel on the passenger side, looking
through a hatbox-sized purse.

Ford and Jack lit cigarettes. To Meg they looked more
like the estate owner and the hired hand than brothers.
Physically Ford was bony and agile, while Jack was more
solidly built. Her husband was polished and self-confident
whereas Ford appeared cocky and smart-ass; attitudes,
Jack claimed, their old man had taught because Reilly
DeWilde hadn't survived by being a swell guy. Meg was
convinced Ford was basically shy and intimidated by his
brother's success and ease in social situations. Jack dismissed that; he insisted he was just like Ford, he'd just been
lucky, married Meg and mucked the crap out of his life.

The two boys had had their futures decided by the loud-
est authority—their father. Reilly, harsh and blustery,
hauled his two sons from their beds at daybreak on Jack's
thirteenth birthday (Ford had turned ten the week before)
sat them at the chrome-legged table with a red-and-yellow-
checked cloth and plastic cereal bowls. Hazel, telling Meg
a few years ago of this event, emphasized that she'd tried
to detour Reilly's heavy-handedness.

"Reilly didn't like no interfering," Hazel said, answering Meg's question before she asked it.

Hazel told of how he'd pounded the table, shouting,
"Life ain't no frigging cake and beer party and my boys are
gonna be fishermen. You hear me?" Ford nodded instantly,
eyes popped wide as a new recruit staring at the drill sergeant. Jack, stony-eyed, balked. Reilly glared and snorted
and threatened. Fishing was a DeWilde tradition and he
hadn't spent years keeping up the payments on the *Lucky
Louise* to have his snot-nosed kid flip him off like he was
some piss-ass with a leaky rowboat.

What Reilly hadn't understood was that Jack wasn't just

being ornery. He hated fishing, was terrified of deep water and flat-out rebelled by refusing to go near the docks, which so infuriated and embarrassed Reilly that he told Jack, "You're no goddamn son of mine," which had Jack firing back with, "I don't give a shit."

Meg had been appalled by the raw rancor, but Hazel took it all in stride. What could she do? Reilly expected obedience and no lip. Jack resented being told what to do. His deeply imbedded paternal bitterness shocked Meg; the kind of vicious exchange such as Jack and Reilly sparked in each other would have never happened between her and her own easygoing father. Ah, thought Meg, realizing the similarity of Jack's attitude toward Caleb. Their son had resented Jack for telling him what to do. She doubted Jack had ever thought through how much he mirrored the traits of his own father. Perhaps refinement had masked those nasty edges.

Yet Hazel defended "her men" as scrappers slinging out their emotions like a fresh catch dumped on the scale. Everyone saw and no one looked twice.

The breach never truly healed, although Jack avoided the docks and fishing boats with the same vigor a fugitive steers clear of roadblocks. But Ford reveled in the dangerous, backbreaking work, hanging around the piers and envying the fishermen in from weeks at sea, spending their hefty pay on straight whiskey and sturdy sex.

Then a few years later, Ford and Reilly faced a raging Atlantic storm that swamped and broke up the *Lucky Louise*. Ford, his father and one other man were the only survivors picked up by the Coast Guard. The toll of that tragic outcome was measured in decades. Reilly got hornswoggled out of his boat insurance by a smarmy, but clever boat dealer. He then settled himself in the Foolscap Bar when he wasn't standing on the dock staring into the narcotic swells of Narragansett Bay. Hazel's drinking increased and Ford, depressed from a back injury caused by the accident, went from pills for pain to pills all the time. And Jack tried to hold it all together.

Just like now. Meg sighed.

Kate's BMW turned into the drive. Hazel was walking toward the house with Jack and Ford. Meg quickly left the kitchen and headed up the stairs. She needed to move Bethany along and dress herself. They had to leave for the church in fifteen minutes.

"She refuses to go," Meg said a short while later as she reentered the kitchen wearing a black suit and pearls. She put her leather bag on the table. Seated beside her Florida-tanned mother was a winter-pale Hazel, showing a folder of snaps of Caleb that Meg knew were one of a dozen. Hazel actually put photos in albums and displayed them on a shelf.

Vicki Slocum sipped from a mug of coffee. Kate stood by the door with Ford. Both held cigarettes. The door was cracked open to let out the smoke.

Jack, leaning against the counter, straightened. Beside him were Chuck and Patti Cabral and Mike and Sue Perry. Coats had been shed and Chuck had just commented that the temperature was nearing sixty in the sun—a record-breaker for the first day of spring. Meg's words turned all eyes to her, for it was past time to leave.

"She sick?" Jack asked, walking forward.

"No. She doesn't want to see her brother buried," Meg said, thinking that avoiding this would have been her preference, too. "We discussed this earlier but I thought she would be okay."

"I'll take care of her." He glanced at his watch. "Why don't you all go on ahead. The limo just arrived. I'll bring Bethany in my car."

More than likely letting her drive, Meg thought, but said

nothing knowing that Jack took great pleasure in indulging his daughter. Today even more so. No one moved.

"Frankly, Meg, I can't blame her," Kate said, flicking the cigarette out the door. Always the thinner of the two women, she looked even more slender in a caramel-colored suit. Her caplet of brown curls had been corralled by twin ivory combs. Dark eyes that were usually provocative and ardent—vintage Kate—this morning were ringed with exhaustion. Fleetingly, Meg wondered if her sister's sleeplessness was over Caleb or a new crisis with her Boston boyfriend.

"I don't either," Meg said, listening for footsteps on the stairs. If anyone could convince Bethany, Jack could. She was her father's daughter, just as Caleb had been her son. Had been . . .

Her mother slid her chair back and stood. "Maybe it's best if we all go on as Jack suggested. If I know my granddaughter she'll be embarrassed if we're all here when she comes down."

Hazel rose and came around the table to take Meg's hand. In a low voice, she said, "Honey, Jackie will take care of everything. Just don't you worry."

"Hazel's right," Lorraine chimed in, causing Meg's eyebrows to lift at her mother's enthusiasm. The two women were cordial, but good friends was a stretch. "Jack is indeed a marvel." She then launched into an abridged version of her flight to Logan and Jack picking her up.

"That's my son." Hazel preened proudly as if she'd been a leader in innovative child-raising. She then explained how Jack had supported them when her beloved Reilly had gone to fish with the Big Fisherman in the sky. This sanitized version usually got more textured with each recitation. Ford rolled his eyes and leaned toward Kate, whispering. She covered her smile with her hand, their heads barely touching. No one interrupted, giving impetus to Hazel's colorful details.

Finally Vicki rose and carried her mug to the counter. At

the calling hours, Vicki seemed overwrought and uncomfortable. Now she was demure and flawlessly dressed in a willow green skirt and short, fitted jacket that showed off the slender hips of a woman who'd never had children. Her hair had been rolled into a hair-salon chignon, makeup deftly applied with full lips the color of wet cinnamon.

"And hasn't he been like a rock for you?" Hazel asked, causing Meg to glance from Vicki to her.

"Yes, he's been wonderful," Meg murmured.

"Well, that's what husbands are for. Reilly was that way. He showed Jackie how to be the strong one. My Jackie knows his place and family duty."

Meg squeezed her mother-in-law's hand and kissed her cheek, smelling a faint waft of gin mixed with breath mints and Charlie. Hazel had framed Jack into the role of all-around caretaker. What he did for his mother and brother was what he was expected to do for her and Bethany.

Jack returned. Alone.

"Where is she?"

He shook his head. "Short of dragging her there physically, she's not going."

"Terrific," Meg said, annoyed despite knowing she shouldn't be. "Now what?"

"We go without her." Jack flipped off the kitchen light and cupped Meg's elbow. "Let's go."

She pulled free. "I can't leave her here alone."

"Meg, she's fourteen not four," Jack said with that decisive tone that moments ago she'd praised. Now it made her angry. "She'll be fine."

"Fine? She'll be fine?" Her voice pitched higher and sharper. "That's what you said about Caleb. He'd be fine."

Her words rolled around the room like the small ball on a roulette wheel looking for a place to drop.

Jack stared at her without speaking.

Meg felt as if her heart had blown open revealing only an empty crater.

Kate, Lorraine and the two couples eased their way quietly out the door. That left only Vicki, Ford and Hazel. Meg set her bag down and unbuttoned her suit jacket.

Jack clasped her wrist. "No. You're not staying here. This is our son's funeral."

"And this is our daughter who is scared and sad and upset and God knows what else. I can't go off and leave her," Meg said, the implication being that Bethany might not be safe alone.

Jack drew close, his voice low. "Why don't you twist your goddamn blame in deeper?"

Meg's eyes filled with tears. "You think I don't blame myself? I do."

Jack exhaled then pulled her into an enfolding hug. Meg let the tension in her own body slip away. He murmured something and she whispered, "I'm sorry."

Slowly he released her, his arm, however, firmly around her shoulders.

"I have a solution," Vicki said.

Meg and Jack glanced at her.

"Let me stay here," the young woman said. "Seriously, you two need to be together. I'll be glad to keep Bethany company." She walked forward. "I was a teenager when my mother died and it was so hard. I'm sure Bethany is having a very bad time. Caleb had told me they were very close."

Hazel whispered, "What a lovely offer." Ford nodded. Jack looked at Vicki saying nothing. Meg looked at her, unsure of what to say.

Vicki placed her hand on Jack's arm. "Please let me. You need to be with your family."

Meg frowned. She was the one who intended to stay, not Jack. "This is very considerate of you, Vicki."

He hesitated, then nodded. "All right." Jack glanced at his watch. "Let's go. We're already late."

In the limo, Meg, seated next to Jack, leaned back in the leather seat. She tried to ignore the clutch of tension deep in her womb. She felt his weight beside her, inviting her to press close, to absorb his strength. She didn't move. She hadn't recognized this side of herself that had been emerging since last Tuesday. Forceful. Independent. Even cloudier was her lack of desire to question this change. The others chatted in low voices, Jack inserting an occasional word or two. Outside came the roar of a jet. He twined their fingers together.

She remained silent. Her heart hurt. They were burying their son and she had no idea why.

Chapter Five

Detective Seth Eidson and his wife, Mazie, attended the boy's funeral. They'd met the DeWildes a year ago at a local fund-raiser for sports equipment. While they didn't know them well, they'd come to the service out of respect and because Mazie remembered the rumpled-haired Caleb with the fearless blue eyes trying to sweet-con her into free ice cream when she worked the Little League concession stand. Yet even if the DeWilde boy had been a stranger before last Tuesday, Eidson would have been compelled.

When the medical examiner had found no drugs or alcohol, no marks or suspicious wounds, he'd listed the cause of death as asphyxiation caused by strangulation. Eidson wasn't surprised. From his own observation of the scene, of the victim and after questioning Jessup, suicide seemed probable.

Kids killing kids unsettled him, but kids killing themselves truly saddened him. He and Mazie were barren; something they discussed only when Mazie brought it up and then only when she'd had too much Zinfindel. Eidson admitted to occasional fatherly yearnings, and a promising sixteen-year-old from the Euclid Drive area of Cooper Falls hanging himself scraped at his brain like a pain he couldn't reach.

The service began at Trinity Methodist at 11:00 A.M. The 1880 church had been declared the oldest with continuing services in Cooper Falls thanks to a 1940's fire that gutted St. Luke's, the Catholic sanctuary that once owned and flaunted that honor. The gray stone Trinity zenith with recessed stained-glass windows commanded the corner lot of Haymaker and Ward, marked off by four sixty-foot-tall beech trees. The double-entrance oak doors were as weighty as Jericho's Walls. Cotes's Crane Service over in Westport had to be called in when the membership voted to take them down and refurbish them.

Those doors stood wide on Friday morning, organ music and airy reverence enfolded a who's who of Cooper Falls. The town council was there, as was the police chief and his second wife of three weeks. Business owners including Warner's Realty, DeWilde's competitor, attended or sent representatives. High school had been dismissed for the morning, and while lines of sobbing girls and somber boys filed into the church, earlier Seth had seen a bunch hanging at the water fountain at Lawton's Plaza when he'd gone to Dunkin' Donuts for coffee.

He'd made it his mission to do a twice-a-day check of "the tree." The Sawyer's Woods memorial began to take shape within moments of the yellow police tape being removed late Tuesday afternoon. Cellophane flutes of flowers, notes tied with ribbon fluttered on the branches and a massive white board had been nailed to the tree. The kids signed "To Caleb" with scribbled spiritual wisdom, nubs of nostalgic thoughts, tender directives and many, many, "We'll love you forevers" on torn notebook pages. Baseball gear appeared from an autographed Yastremski ball to enough gloves and bats to outfit a couple of teams. Stuffed animals that Eidson guessed once graced ruffly pink-quilted beds peeked from amongst the flowers. The tokens of sentiment covered enough space to park three cars although the tree itself was hidden from the road. The expanding memorial had changed a once trash-laden area into a rainbow shrine.

Now, he parked his blue Buick and he and Mazie joined the throng moving into the church. The doors closed for the service and forty minutes later they reopened to the exiting strains of "Amazing Grace."

As they returned to their car, Ford DeWilde stopped them and invited them back to the house after the burial. Eidson expressed his sympathy and Mazie hugged him. She knew Ford thanks to their mutual fastidiousness about eating fresh fish. She'd met him on the docks of Newport after watching him unload swordfish and getting a quick lesson in what "fresh fish" really means.

"Please tell Caleb's parents they are in our prayers," Mazie said, making clear that they didn't intend to intrude. Eidson nodded solemnly. He didn't care much for big social gatherings no matter what the occasion. Because he was a cop, he invariably got asked questions about a current case or worse had to politely listen to some cop-drama fan advise him on how to do his job. Since he would be meeting with Jack DeWilde for some routine questioning, Eidson knew his appearance at their house would be awkward.

He returned to the station, caught up on some reports that hadn't been filed, left around 4:00 and drove by "the tree." More flowers and more notes in addition to a stuffed baseball uniform someone had propped atop the autographed white board. Three girls at the edge of the piled remembrances sobbed in a tangle of arms and hair. He wondered if one of them was a grieving girlfriend.

Minutes later when he walked into the house Claire Dozier, garbed in a bulky sweater that could have warmed up a Sherman tank, was on her way out. A distant cousin of Mazie's, Eidson spoke to her and continued on into the kitchen to dig a beer out of the refrigerator.

A few moments later Mazie appeared looking spiffy,

giving him one of those quick dry kisses that Eidson found as dreary as a bird peck. He snagged her before she scooted away and kissed her wet and proper.

"Very nice. Are we doing the dirty deed later?"

"At your service, ma'am."

"And you do service well." She grinned.

He winked and she turned to the stove, where she lifted the lid on a pot of pea soup.

"Couldn't Claire have waited a few days before flitting over here with her funeral report?" Eidson had spotted her at the church swooping about like a sacrilege.

Mazie stirred and tasted, then added a shake of pepper. "She's lonely and gossip is her hobby. Besides in a few days she'll have all new stuff. Nothing more boring than gossip everyone else knows. Then it's just conversation."

He leaned against the counter, sipping his beer, watching his wife, marginally listening. Small, blonde and compact, she had generous breasts that she hated and Eidson treasured. High on her left thigh rode a starburst tattoo, first appreciated by Eidson on a Newport beach when she walked past him and his pals. They'd whistled and leered. Eidson had followed her. She was five years older than him and it took him a year to talk her into marriage. They were at twenty-five and counting. "Is the soup ready? I'm hungry."

"You don't want to hear what she said?"

He sat down at the table. "Summarize it."

She ladled soup into china bowls that had been her grandmother's and carried them to the table. A basket of crackers sat beside a green salad.

"I put in lots of ham the way you like it."

"Looks good." Eidson sniffed, the heavy aroma tickling his taste buds. He broke up a half dozen crackers, stirred them in and dipped his spoon. "So what did she say?"

"Why Seth Eidson, I do believe you're as nosy as you accuse Claire and me of being."

Seth peered at her. "Since this is gossip update twenty-two since the boy killed himself, I already know the main plot line. Jack DeWilde is a bastard."

Mazie poured wine into her glass. "She says he was rude and swore at her when all she was trying to do was help."

"Uh huh. Even without hearing DeWilde's side, I'm on it."

"You men all stick together."

"Hmmm."

She ate two spoons of soup and took a sip of wine. "Claire went back to the DeWildes' after the burial. By the way, she said Bethany wasn't at the church or at the cemetery."

Eidson waited.

"Claire said at least a hundred people were at the house, coming and going. Sloane Rivers—that's Caleb's coach—was there and Claire saw him hugging and whispering with Meg." She paused. "You did know that Sloane's mother and Lorraine Hadley were best friends eons ago and planned to have their kids marry each other?"

"Luckily for DeWilde their plans didn't work."

"Anyway, Hazel DeWilde had too much to drink and Ford drove her home, but then came back and drove away with Meg's sister. A caterer brought the food and Claire said there was lobster tails and huge cold shrimp like they do at weddings. I told Claire that they had decent food because Jack was probably sick of all those noodle casseroles. Lot of people from Jack's office were there and she overheard Lorraine talking on the telephone to someone named Ben." Silence fell in favor of more scoops of soup, some buttered crackers and forks full of salad.

Finally Eidson sat back, his appetite satisfied, folded his arms and watched her, not missing the coy waiting to pounce that she was doing. He decided a more delightful woman had never existed.

"Is that it?" he asked for he knew she expected it.

Mazie twirled her glass.

Eidson drained his beer, feigning disinterest. "Claire needs to get a grip. That isn't even decent gossip. It sounds like she just took down names."

Mazie set her glass down and leaned forward. "There's more."

"Ahh."

"Claire heard it from Erica Rivers. She's Bethany's best friend."

"Teenage gossip. Always a reliable source."

But instead of anymore dragging, Mazie folded her fingers around his wrist. "This is serious, Seth. It might help you tomorrow."

At exactly 10:00 Saturday morning, Eidson slid the folder into his top drawer, closed it and moved to answer the knock on his office door. Promptness impressed him and when Jack DeWilde stepped aside to allow his wife to enter first, Eidson raised his eyebrows. When he and DeWilde set up the appointment, he'd made it clear his wife wouldn't be coming. Too stressful. Eidson hadn't argued, despite a preference for speaking with both parents.

Meg DeWilde looked exhausted yet he sensed a resilience when her eyes frankly met his.

"Please come in and sit down. I'm sorry we're meeting again under such sad circumstances. Can I get either of you some coffee?"

Both declined. She slipped off her jacket, then sat very straight in the chair, handbag deep in her lap, her fingers wound through the strap the way Mazie's did when she was nervous. In black jeans and a white sweater, she appeared decisive and yet unsure where that would get her. Soft haircut, minimal face paste, and sparkly earrings that glittered like jewelry that came in those satin-lined boxes with raised gold lettering.

DeWilde took the other chair. He, too, looked weary,

withered and if escape had been doable, he would have done so. He clearly didn't want to be quizzed, folding his arms in a "don't fuck with my dead son's legacy" obstinacy.

Eidson perched on the edge of his desk, a position that made him appear less scary according to the seven-year-old daughter of the desk sergeant. "I appreciate you both coming so soon. I know this is difficult, but the department always looks into a death that shouldn't happen. I've read the autopsy report." He paused for the question, but wasn't surprised when the request for a copy didn't happen. He followed with what he knew they wanted. "There is nothing suspicious in the report."

They glanced at each other, mutual relief in their expressions.

"So let's get to the point of you being here. Tell me about Caleb."

She looked up, her eyes round with confusion. "I thought you wanted to ask us questions about . . . about his death."

"Let's start with his life."

She reached for her husband's hand, clutching it tightly. She opened her mouth, then closed it. "There's so much. I don't know where to begin."

"I don't know what you want to know," DeWilde said, tossing it back and impressing Eidson.

"I'd like to hear about how he'd perfected his incredible fastball," Eidson said.

DeWilde visibly relaxed, and she began a wordy explanation that covered everything from baseball, to Caleb's part-time jobs, to fishing trips with his uncle Ford the previous summer, to painting his grandmother's back porch and on and on. Eidson smiled, nodded and allowed them both to talk—they laughed a few times and in listening Eidson could have been convinced that on this very morning, Caleb was simply off doing Saturday chores, or Rollerblading down Euclid Drive. His character and accomplishments were a glowing froth of busy events; the boy wouldn't have had time to look up suicide in a dictionary.

"Girlfriends?" Eidson asked when they both finished.

She frowned and Eidson figured she was adding up a long list. A good-looking sixteen-year-old with Caleb's baseball star status surely amassed a covey of fluttering hearts.

Eidson waited expectantly.

She said, "Erica Rivers. She's at our house a lot because she's Bethany's best friend, and last fall she was pretty stuck on Caleb."

"And how did your son feel about her?"

She turned as if aware that she was doing most of the talking. "Jack?"

He straightened, then laughed uneasily. "Caleb never paid any attention to her. He really wasn't all that girl crazy. Baseball consumed his free time."

"In the winter, too?" Eidson's teenage winters were all about keeping Amy Kennedy warm in his Chevy with the broken heater.

DeWilde bristled. "Yeah. In the winter, too."

Uh oh. Eidson kept his face bland. No covey of fluttering hearts. Girlfriends were a touchy subject.

"He wasn't gay," Meg DeWilde said, answering a question Eidson hadn't asked. DeWilde's gaze tunneled into Eidson like he was chambering a round of ammunition.

"Did he tell you he wasn't?" he asked.

"He didn't tell us he was. Look, I know where you're going with this. Gay teenage boys have a high suicide rate and if that was his problem then you'd tell us that's probably why he died."

"Jack, I can't tell you anything. These questions and your answers are only threads looking for a knot. Even if Caleb had been gay doesn't rule out other reasons."

"He wasn't a homo. He wasn't."

Eidson surmised that either DeWilde was offended by the idea or terrified of it. He changed the subject.

"I saw Caleb helping Louis Jessup stack firewood one afternoon last month when I was out that way. Did he work for Jessup?"

She smiled. He scowled.

"Jessup and Caleb were friends," she said.

Eidson glanced at him. Clearly the subject of Jessup bothered him.

"Jack never liked Jessup," she said.

"Wrong. I didn't like him around Caleb."

"Could you elaborate a little?" Eidson asked.

"He's more than forty years older for starters. The guy's a hermit in a run-down shack that makes a homeless shelter look like an immaculate ranch with AC and an applianced kitchen. No one in town goes near the property and the council would be jig dancing if the place burned down. A few years back I approached him about buying and I sweetened the offer with a listing out near Beaver Pond that would have given him his privacy and a decent place to live. No dice." DeWilde took a breath, and Eidson jumped in.

"So how did he and Caleb become friends?"

"It was shortly after Kevin Frazier was killed," she said. Eidson recalled the fiery accident two years ago near the Connecticut border. The Frazier boy, fourteen, had been drunk and had stolen his mother's car. After jumping a guardrail, he'd slammed the car into the crumbling wall of an abandoned factory.

"Kevin was one Caleb's best friends. Our son was having a tough time and used to walk through Sawyer's Woods when he wanted to cry and he didn't want anyone to know. Once he got lost and Jessup found him. Jessup and my father were friends and served in Vietnam together. Caleb was intrigued by his back-to-basics lifestyle and that Jessup had been in Vietnam with my father. They'd been close friends and Caleb liked the idea of being pals with his grandfather's buddy."

"Did either of you know if Caleb smoked pot?"

The question caused his mother to turn abruptly and stare at Eidson.

"Caleb didn't do drugs," she said flatly.

Eidson looked at DeWilde.

"Do you know otherwise?" DeWilde asked.

"The autopsy showed no drugs or alcohol."

She sagged back.

DeWilde got to his feet, slipped his hands into his pockets and walked over to the window. Spits of rain hit the glass. "So why the question?"

"Jessup grows pot."

DeWilde turned and narrowed his eyes. "Last time I heard, grass is illegal."

"It was the last time I heard, too." Eidson rose and reached for his cold coffee, but drank anyway. "Tell me about last Tuesday."

By the time Meg finished, she'd mentioned the white shirt he hadn't wanted to wear, the breakfast he didn't want to eat, and the assembly that didn't seem to interest him.

"Was he usually that argumentative?"

She didn't answer immediately. Then, "He'd been juggling a lot of things—work and school and practice. I wondered sometimes if he was under too much pressure."

DeWilde sighed, sinking back down in the chair, his voice low. "Caleb and I argued."

"About what?" he asked, wondering if what Mazie told him would match.

"He wanted to play baseball for the Red Sox and I wanted him to be realistic and focus on going to college. It had been an ongoing disagreement—no, it wasn't just that. It was a battle and neither one of us wanted to give ground." He looked down at his hands and Eidson saw his throat working. "He accused me of running his life and slammed out of the house. That was the last time I saw him."

Eidson walked to the window and cranked it open. A biting wet breeze swiped at his cheeks. His eyes burned and he kept his back turned until the pain passed. He liked

DeWilde; he especially liked his honesty at a time when denial would have been easier. Eidson heard her sniffle and DeWilde shift around in his chair.

"Your son's suicide . . . it appears there was no single catastrophic event. It probably was the result of an accumulation of problems, disappointments, perhaps rejection . . ." He cleared his throat. "Some years ago in Maine a man lost his teenage son to suicide. His life, like your son's, seemed pretty normal. The only event that was out of kilter was his breakup hours before with a girlfriend. On reflection rejected love, while disappointing, didn't seem enough to push him over the edge, but combined with the trail of previous disappointments, the breakup appeared to be the rock that broke the scale. Not having a solid, defined answer isn't satisfying. Since Caleb gave no obvious clues, whatever particular circumstances caused him to kill himself would be speculation at best."

Eidson still stood near the window, hands deep in his pockets. Meg rose and her husband held her jacket while she slipped it on.

"Nothing is clear-cut to us, Detective Eidson. But there is a reason. There has to be."

Eidson said, "Speaking from my limited experience, this kind of thing can consume a family when the reason or motives *are* clear and known. For your family, the risk is even greater."

"Are you suggesting we just forget this, that we move on as if our son's suicide will fade away in time?" she asked stiffly.

"I'm suggesting that the living family must find a new road and go on." He and DeWilde exchanged looks and Eidson guessed this idea had already been floated.

His wife said, "I don't know how to process the mound of grief in some linear tidy fashion. To suggest that I'll ever process the fact that Caleb hanged himself for some secret or unknown reason . . . well, that's not possible."

After they left, Eidson stood at the window and watched

DeWilde open the passenger door of a black Lexus. The couple stood in the opening. Her hair blew and she tried to tame it. DeWilde stood close and then tugged her into his arms. At first she resisted, then wrapped around him as though saving this moment of solidarity would save their lives.

Chapter Six

By Wednesday, Jack would have welcomed a deaf and blind implant to escape the overload of visitors and the pissy remarks. The latest had been delivered by a foamy-haired female in a fur coat with bloodshot eyes and lumpy scrambled egg skin. Jack found her the previous night standing in the driveway between Ford's Blazer and the Perrys' Dodge Caravan with an IMPEACH CLINTON bumper sticker. Jack had no clue who she was or how she got there. Whatever curiosity he entertained evaporated when she wailed, "Didn't you know he was a mental case?"

His reply had been, "Ma'am, I'll call you a cab."

There'd been other comments from friends, that in a more spiritual mode he might have considered for their good intentions, but instead he groused to Meg that he was fed up with grief advice and analysis bouquets from people whose only intimacy with death had been aged relatives in nursing homes no one ever visited. Meg, on the other hand, had been demure and classy and patient with the assortment who tracked through as if history was being recorded and they wanted their names spelled correctly. Jack finally closed himself in their bedroom with a bottle of Dewar's and a better understanding of why his mother drank.

Thursday found him restless and claustrophobic. He

wanted to go back to work, or more truthfully he wanted to tunnel out of the strangling mystery of why, and thereby avoid the inevitable showdown with Meg for his disinterest.

Eidson's suggestion to move away and ahead paralleled his own to Meg the day of the funeral. And for the brief time it took to drive home from meeting with the detective, Jack had been fairly positive that she'd been satisfied and retired her questions. But then her sister breezed in wanting to know what the police knew and while Meg explained the unexplainable, Jack saw the fragile veneer of reason slip away. She and Kate talked and analyzed Caleb's days leading up to the suicide until Jack longed for the nostalgic past when motive analysis wasn't forked up and consumed like a plate of pasta. He resisted giving in to the grief as if it were a cobra in a dark room; the emotion worried him and scared him, for it had bitten and poisoned the family his father had left despite Jack's efforts to keep them safe and stable.

Since Kate's visit, Meg had not completed a conversation that didn't include some reference to what would cause Caleb to suicide. Then she'd look at him desperately for an answer. And God, he wished he could have given her a satisfying one. Instead, he'd felt the same inadequacy of cogent thought that plagued him when his old man drowned. Yet he listened and he listened and he listened some more, praying she'd stumble onto a rationale that would end the ruminating. The possible motives he'd heard puzzled over with whispered deliberations had all the silliness of leaping into a hundred-acre landfill of clamshells on the wild chance of finding a pearl.

Earlier this morning, he'd driven Bethany to school. Their daughter had been sullen and silent, spending too much time in her room and too little time on the phone. The latter worried Meg and Jack almost as much as the distinct smell of cigarette smoke when she'd come home the night before. Jack promised Meg, he'd talk to her. Privately, he viewed the issue as a minor flaunt at authority. Nevertheless, he went through the "smoking is bad" clichés while driving her to school and got an indifferent shrug in response.

Then as he passed two boys with ball gloves hanging from backpacks, she slid low in the seat, squeezing her eyes closed. Jack looked away, too.

Suddenly she popped into a straight-up position, and glared at him, tears choking her words. "Why did you fight with him? Why did you always have to make him do what you want? See what happened? See what you did? He was my hero and I wanted to be just like him and now . . . now he's dead. It's not fair and from now on, I'm doin' just what I want to do when I want to and you can't stop me."

The knot in Jack's stomach swelled to a basketball. For an instant he saw his old man standing over him—yelling, cursing, demanding "do it and do it my way." God, he'd treated Caleb the way his old man had treated him. Now his daughter was in full-throttle rebellion and he hadn't a clue how to handle it.

"Sweetheart, I know you're angry," he said lamely, unsure if her defiant outburst sprang from anger or shock or confusion and figured it was all three.

"Let me out," she snapped. "I don't want to talk to you. I hate you!"

He felt lost and inadequate and he wanted to refuse, but he stopped the car. Before she could get the door open, he tugged her close, hugging her stiff body and kissed her forehead. He said the only thing he could think of. "Mom and I love you very much."

For an instant she stayed, her breath bubbling against his neck. "You loved Caleb and look what that got him," she cried with more anguish than any kid should feel. Then she scrambled out and ran across the baseball field where just two weeks ago Jack had watched Caleb take batting practice.

Her words vibrated in his mind but he had no answers

even now as her shape grew smaller by distance. He'd waited to make sure she walked toward school. Moments later she was swaddled by a hundred outstretched arms rocking her in a personal healing service without music. Dramatic grief, close and sorrowful and oh so consuming.

Grimly, he returned home, figuring he'd botched things with Bethany and vowing to do something that didn't involve demands and arguments although he had no idea what. He left his car in the drive and rehearsed how to tell Meg he was bailing out for a few hours. A week's worth of backed-up office work appealed to him.

Halfway up the stairs to change clothes, he paused when he heard a car needing a muffler pull into the drive. No more, goddammit, no more. He leapt down the stairs and barreled for his study to hide like Caleb had whenever Bethany brought Erica home. Like that Saturday when Jack was struggling to finish the *New York Times* crossword puzzle before Sunday's new one.

Caleb had closed the door and crouched down beside the desk.

Breathing fast, his cowlick stood straight up, his cheeks stained like red lollipops.

"What's going on?" Jack asked.

"Erica wants my body." He'd winced as if Erica planned castration. "I mean she follows me and keeps trying to touch me."

Jack nodded in the solemn deliberation that he knew was expected.

Caleb wiped his sleeve across his nose. "She's a buffa-rilla." Translation: big as a buffalo and ugly as a gorilla.

"Definite reasons to avoid her, I'd say."

"Right. Did girls drive you crazy before you met Mom?"

"Yep. It's their chosen mission since Eve tempted Adam."

He thought about that. "Even Adam would be grossed out by Erica."

He'd marveled at his son, ripe with the promise of manhood, yet corded so tightly to the innocence of youth. Jack treasured these threads of candor.

"Give her a couple of years. I predict she'll be a knock-out."

"No way," he muttered, clearly not convinced that beauty would blossom from such an obvious weed.

Out the window, Jack saw Bethany and Erica walk across the yard toward the street. "Coast is clear."

Caleb peered through the glass to make sure, then grinned. "Thanks for letting me hide out." Then he strolled out of the room.

Jack had never told Meg of the short exchange; she had parameters of behavior she expected the kids to abide by, and she'd been particularly adamant on Caleb not being rude or unkind to Bethany's friends. That this girl was Rivers's daughter was coincidental, or so Jack convinced himself, for he had minimal fervor for disturbing Meg's rules. Just as he had zero appetite for mucking up his own memories by picking through his son's short life in search of negative dots to connect.

And he never had finished the crossword.

Now, he cracked his shin on the corner of the desk and cursed.

"Jack? Are you going to answer the door?" Meg called from the upstairs hall.

He remained silent, settling a pair of headphones over his ears, moving the switch to CD, settling back to the strains of Bolero and closing his eyes.

A few minutes later, her hand rested on his shoulder. He turned, feigned surprise and ringed his neck with the headset.

"Hi gorgeous."

She leaned against the doorjamb, arms crossed, eyebrows skidded together. Face flushed a pretty pink, her hair was tucked casually behind her ears and combined with shabby jeans and a faded sweatshirt, she looked like she had in college—young, daring and dazzling. His mental yardstick measured his chance of luring her upstairs for some morning sex.

"Why are you hiding in the study?" She wiggled the earphones. "Forget the ruse. I know you heard the doorbell." Eyes narrowed, frown wrinkling, mouth pursed like a ripe peach.

Jack sighed, sexual thoughts diminishing. "Because I couldn't get to the bedroom without passing you."

She scowled even harder. "Avoiding our friends isn't like you."

"Seeing them every day isn't like *them*. Look Meg, this is the longest-running funeral Cooper Falls has ever had. I'm appreciative of all their sympathy, but not even a man on bread and water for two years could eat one more noodle casserole."

"Why are you being so irritable?"

Because my son is dead and I'm weary of good intentioners telling me how sorry they are when they don't know jack-shit about our loss.

"I'm being truthful," he said aloud. "Surely you and I can handle truthful."

"Can you?"

He guessed where she was going with that and didn't answer. She swung around to exit, and he shot out of the chair and grabbed her.

"Come on, I don't want to fight with you."

"I don't want to fight with you either, but—"

He kissed her before she could add something that would recycle the tension between them. Her mouth was pliant and cool, and Jack coaxed her tongue to come out of hiding.

He repositioned her, lifting her against him, unwilling to hold back and letting her know. He was hard and he knew the moment she felt it. Instead of the resistance he half expected, she pressed even tighter.

"I shouldn't," she murmured.

"You should." Jack took eager advantage of her uncertainty. "We need each other."

She hesitated, and he waited for her to say that wanting sex was wrong because their son had just been buried.

"I have things to do," she dissembled.

"So do I, but for a half an hour we can do this together."

"You don't think—? I mean, what if someone comes and we're in bed? Your car is in the drive and they would know we're here."

He listened, astonished that this was the same woman who just a month ago had gone down on him in this very study with guests in the living room drinking cocktails.

"We'll lock the doors and they'll understand we don't want to be disturbed."

Before she could disagree, he sent her upstairs while he set the locks. A smile claimed his face as he took the steps two at a time.

In the bedroom, he closed the blinds to the morning sun. He rolled her beneath him, loving her giggle at his eagerness. They kissed and nuzzled and Jack worked her clothes off and his mostly so. When he cupped her mound, she raised her hips, and then as if she'd been poked by the grief police, she went limp before turning her head into the pillow. Jack breathed deeply, hearing her muffled sobs as his erection deflated.

He lay on his back, wanting to curse her while at the same time knowing he couldn't. He loved her—lovemaking or no lovemaking. He hooked his arm beneath her and pulled her into his arms, feeling like the sixteen-year-old who had comforted his kid brother after their old man died.

"I'm sorry, Jack. I thought I could."

"It's okay."

"It feels out of place, embarrassing, as if we'd had George Carlin jokes at the funeral."

The analogy measured too far out on the silliness scale, but the point had been made. Jack ventured neither agreement nor an argument, but instead kissed her forehead, then rose and opened the blinds. Two squirrels scampered about the backyard oblivious to a stalking calico.

"I'm going to take a shower and go to the office for a while," he said, aware that his earlier reluctance to leave her had evaporated with his erection. One of the squirrels raced up a tree trunk and back down again. "Will you be all right here?"

"Yes." And when he glanced back at her she had already dressed and begun straightening the bedcovers like a woman late for a suddenly remembered appointment.

Jack turned back to the cat and the squirrels. A beagle had wandered in, nosing the dormant ground. The squirrels headed up another tree and the calico backed up and crept behind a speckled boulder that in a few weeks would wear a skirt of daffodils.

Leave it to a trespassing mutt to snarl the strategy, huh guy? The dog nosed closer to the rock, and the cat flattened out. "Meg, come and see this." When he got no answer, he turned to an empty room. Bed made, the clothes he'd worn yesterday and tossed on top of the hamper were now inside and his bottle of Dewar's had been removed from the dresser. Suddenly he resented her goddamn efficiency.

When he turned back to the window, the dog had circled the rock, sniffing and squirting. The squirrels were up another tree and the calico had disappeared. Just like Meg.

Jack slipped his sport coat on and checked his pants to make sure he had his wallet and keys. He walked down the hall, the burgundy carpeting absorbing his steps. Caleb's bedroom door was open and Jack stopped to pull it closed. Then he saw her.

She was seated at the maple desk looking as prim and stiff as she had the day he'd helped her flip Caleb's mattress and she'd found the lurid magazines. Drawers sagged open as if a thief had been in a careless hurry. Her back was to him as she methodically examined notebook pages for significant implications. The room itself was orderly.

His son had never been a slob; he usually put his clothes away—unlike his father—and made good use of the wastebasket. From beneath the bed, however, poked a forgotten sweatshirt. Jack wished he hadn't seen it.

With no difficulty, he'd avoided the room since he'd taken Caleb's baseball uniform for his burial. His aversion gripped him anew.

Remaining in the doorway, he couldn't shake a disrespectfulness at going through these obituaries of his son's life. Meg apparently felt no such reservation.

"Is this one of the things you *had* to do?" he asked.

Startled, she twisted briskly toward him, confirming how concentrated she'd been on her task. She'd notched her hair behind her ears, glided her gaze to the next pile and stiffened her posture. "You know exactly what I'm doing. You don't like it and you refuse to understand, but you know." She swept a pile of loose papers into the trash. She was pissed at him, but then that was half the reason he wanted to leave; to give them both some breathing space.

When he didn't offer an immediate response, she returned to her sorting. Jack sighed. Bethany and now Meg. Back to back strikeouts.

"Since you're obviously going out, could you pick up some milk?"

From anger to asking him to buy milk. His mind boggled.

Since he had nothing to say that would make her happy, he was about to leave when she said, "I know I can't change what he did, but I need to find out what happened to him and why."

Jack rolled his lips together, adjusting his temper down to simmer. "How? It's not like he left a note, told his pals or had developed some sort of personality deterioration."

"All the more reason for me to do this."

Her cemented steadiness both impressed him and weighed him down. He longed for her to agree with him and follow his advice the way she'd always done, but he wasn't dealing with the Meg he knew before Caleb died. He could have handled her tossing off some accusatory remarks about his indifference. What he feared was the serious undertone of a crusade that had gravitas. She set aside a handful of baseball cards to give to Gregg.

Another approach, he decided. "Meg, I went through this classic need to know after my dad died. I should have been paying more attention to the wreck my family was headed for." *Which is what I'm trying to prevent with this family.* "In the end I learned nothing more than what I had the day he died. He'd fallen off a dock and drowned."

"And you're still blaming yourself for not saving him from himself. I'm not blaming myself or anyone else for Caleb because I don't know what happened. At least not yet."

"God almighty."

"Don't you understand? It's like here's our happy son with a full life and suddenly he hangs himself."

Jack heard her and his own ancient mistakes resurfaced. Those who ignore the past are doomed to repeat it. Is that what awaited them? More trouble spawned by a tragedy? Dammit, not if he could stop it. Jack scrubbed his hands down his face.

Meg stood, her expression relaxed, a peach-pretty mouth now that had him catching his breath at how much he loved her smile, how desperately he loved her. She came toward him, sliding her arms under his cashmere jacket and around his waist. She tipped her head back, licking her lips, her eyes totally on him. "I understand why you don't want me doing this. Really I do. You've had your share of problems with Ford and your mom and you're probably thinking, 'Holy shit, I don't need my wife screwed up, too.' "

"Exactly."

"But they had problems already, and your father had been depressed and unstable for over a year." He saw the softness, the understanding that was so classically Meg.

"Don't you see how losing his boat *and* his income triggered his drinking, his carelessness and more despair in your family? All the counseling in the world probably couldn't have diverted their lives from the road they chose. Caleb was different. He wasn't depressed or messed up. I can't and I won't just let this go."

Jack held her, his mind weary. This wasn't grief searching for closure, nor was she driven by some temporary need to find an answer; she'd thought this all out and unless he made her understand . . .

He slid his hands up and down her arms in a repetitive motion, then led her into the hall. "Meg, sweetheart, these are reasons that we'll never discover. Maybe there was some deep problem that only he knew about and couldn't deal with." He was backing into a potential trap here if indeed such a problem existed, but he was desperate. "Kids do stupid things, and when they aren't doing them, they're planning them." She was looking at him, clearly unsure but not closed off to the direction he was taking her. His hope revived. "You and I both know that how kids act when they are around their parents isn't the way they always act. Bethany is sweet and young, and wants to be treated like an adult, but she is still a kid needing guidance from us, a kid who does things she knows are wrong. Like with the smoking."

"You're not comparing Bethany smoking to suicide?"

"Of course not."

"Then what are you talking about?"

"That Caleb wasn't perfect."

She gave a short laugh. "Jack, please. I'm not naïve. I know he wasn't, but I knew Caleb."

"Did you?"

"Yes, I did," she said firmly, walking around him and back into the bedroom.

Just leave. Go to the office and forget it. But his inability to get her off this crusade kept him there as surely as if his shoes were glued to the floor.

"How the hell do you know?" Then without waiting for her response, he said, "Because he was sweet, charming and obedient around you? Because when we demanded he get his grades up, he studied harder and his marks improved? Because he wasn't coming home drunk or stoned or with the cops chasing him?" He'd moved while he talked and now, despite his aversion, he was squarely in the middle of Caleb's room. "Sometimes you treated him like he still believed in Santa Claus instead of a kid who—"

He hesitated—a big mistake for she stared at him with probing intensity. He picked up some pencils that were on the floor and examined them as if they were fingerprint clues. Now that he'd charged down this path, he realized the hazards.

"A kid who what?"

"Who was a lot older," he said lamely.

"No. That's not what you were going to say. Do you know something? Something you're not telling me?" Those brown eyes of hers showed tiny lights of green tenacity that meant she wouldn't give up. "Jack?"

He tossed the pencils onto the desk. Okay, face it. This is what she needs to hear. This will make her understand that knowing isn't always a pleasant experience. His stomach lurched and he swore his heart had come loose, but he rolled out the bad news. "During the February vacation, Caleb and Gregg and two other kids had too much beer and they trashed the cottage." The cottage was in Jamestown and mostly used by Meg and Kate for summer days on the shore. In recent years the kids only went down if they could take their friends.

"Our cottage?" She looked stunned. "Our Caleb? I don't believe it. Who told you this?"

"Someone driving by heard a lot of noise and called the cops. They went to check it out and when they found out one of the kids was Caleb, they called me."

"Why didn't you tell me?"

"You were in Boston with Kate. I knew you'd be upset

and since it was only a bit of rebellion that got out of hand, I took care of it. I was just glad it wasn't someone else's place or we could have been looking at a lawsuit."

Meg never blinked while he was talking and now she sat down on the edge of the bed. "My God."

Jack felt a guilty lift in his spirits. Finally. He sat down beside her ready to comfort her and explain that it really wasn't a big deal, even similar to discovering those magazines under his mattress. This was where he wanted to be, the protector, the husband ready to offer support and guide her out of this morass. "Honey—"

"What else have you been keeping from me?"

"What? Nothing."

"Gregg and the other boys. Did you talk to them? Did you find out whose idea this destruction was?"

"I talked to them, got an estimate of the damage and told them how much it would cost them to reimburse me. Relax, their fathers are making sure they pay the cost."

She stared up at him as if his brains had leaked. "I don't care about the money. I want to know why they did it."

"Isn't it obvious? They were drunk and rowdy and bored."

"That's not enough."

"It's all I've got."

"Why is it you men never ask any questions?"

He gave her a blank look.

"What did Caleb have to say?"

"That he was sorry."

"Well, of course he said that. I mean why."

"Christ, you should have been a prosecutor," he murmured, off stride from her persistence. "I didn't push the point." But he had asked why, and his son had started to cry. Jack had been so stunned by tears he hadn't seen from Caleb since his pre-teens that he'd put his arm around him in a father-to-son gesture and somehow that became the answer. A wordless remorse didn't require probing uncomfortable and tortured emotions and his son had apparently agreed. The moment had been significant, for Jack believed their mutual silence had spawned a trust that he'd never had with his own father.

"You should have demanded a reason." She began closing the drawers, busying herself in that way so common to Meg when she was trying to process something she didn't like or couldn't understand. Jack prayed that he was witnessing the return of her common sense. He knew her pattern. She'd be pissed, not talk to him for a few hours, but by the time he came home later, she'd have come around to his reasoning. She always did.

He touched her shoulder to turn her and take her into his arms.

She shoved him away and stepped back. "If you'd told me about this when it happened, what he did in Sawyer's Woods might have been prevented. You'll never convince me that Caleb willingly took part in trashing the cottage unless something was very wrong."

"Something was wrong—he was being a dumb kid. Why must you insist there was some deep unknown reason."

"Because he killed himself!"

Chapter Seven

So much for confessing, he thought as he parked his car in front of DeWilde Real Estate. Forty minutes had passed since she'd marched out of Caleb's room, down the stairs and into the kitchen where she silently ignored his attempts to explain his botched rationale.

Never should have told her about the cottage, he reflected as he pulled a manila envelope from beneath his seat, slammed the car door and pocketed his keys. He rounded the vehicle, waved when a delivery truck driver honked, then stopped when Seth Eidson pulled up to the curb and lowered his window.

"Jack, how is everything?"

"Fine," he lied.

"Your wife?"

"She's doing all right," he lied again.

Eidson paused. "Counseling can help or a support group." He paused again, but Jack didn't respond. "You had a chance to see the memorial at the tree?"

"No."

"It's causing traffic jams out that way." Jack couldn't be sure if this was an observation or a complaint. "It's given the kids a place to express their grief. You really ought to swing by."

"I'll do that." He walked on and entered DeWilde's.

The expansive reception room had blue walls, framed prints of some of the more elaborate homes DeWilde's had handled, wall sconce lighting and upholstered furnishings. Jack hated plastic and fake leather. Beyond were cubicles with paths that connected the maze into the waiting area. Jack's office was straight ahead, and to his right was the receptionist desk where Fredi—"only my mother calls me Frederica"—Monroe kept watch like a hall monitor. She was short and friendly and refused to turn forty; she sat with a phone idolizing one ear and a sugar donut in her hand. A Disney World mug of coffee sat beside the current copy of *People*. Divorced twice, with three teenage daughters, Jack had hired her one afternoon five years ago when she walked in looking for a job on the very day Jack had fired her predecessor for serial incompetence. Fredi was so competent, Jack had to literally order her to take her vacation every year. He had no doubt that if he dropped dead tomorrow she could have run DeWilde's without missing a beat.

When she saw him, she quickly ended the call, brushed the sugar from her hands and hurried over to hug him.

"We didn't know you were coming in," she said, her eyes darting around as if checking for dust and stray coffee mugs.

Jack smiled, liking her prim, normal response. "Is everybody here?"

"Everyone is working. Chuck and Vicki had appointments but should be back soon." Her eyes probed his face. "You sure you should be here? You don't look much better than you did at the funeral."

"I know. It's been rough."

Her eyes teared, her voice fierce. "Oh Jack, I just wish I could make things happy for you and Meg."

It was so like Fredi to want to solve every conflict. "If only, huh?" He patted her awkwardly, grateful when she nodded and stepped away. He headed toward his office.

"Would you mind getting me some coffee? Cream, no sugar."

"I remember. You haven't been out that long," she scolded, then sailed around the corner to the coffee cubicle.

His office was plush with real furniture, not the generics sold in office supply stores. The red tapestry carpet felt comfortably familiar as he closed the door and crossed to the kidney-shaped desk. Meg had suggested he personalize with family-posed photos, but Jack had opted for framed crayoned artwork of their house that Bethany had drawn in second grade, a picture of Meg in her flower garden wearing a floppy hat, and a blown-up photo of Caleb sliding into home plate amidst a flurry of limbs, cleats and dust.

Fredi brought his coffee, then left him alone. Jack slipped off his jacket, loosened his tie, rolled back his cuffs and sat down to sort through the mail on his desk. Into the wastebasket, he tossed the manila envelope that had been in his car. It contained information, snapshots and prices on used pickup trucks that Jack wanted to discuss with Meg as a surprise for Caleb. That envelope had been the reason he'd unexpectedly gone home.

He tossed some unopened junk mail, glared at the envelope as though it should have had the balls to disintegrate, then snatched it from the basket. Opening the clasp, he fed the pages into the paper shredder. What an ass he'd been on Tuesday morning. He should have told Caleb about buying him a truck instead of arguing with him about college.

He tried uselessly to concentrate, but those final tense words with his son were chiseled into his mind and as immortalized as the photo of his son's slide into home plate. Flinging the mail on the desk, he turned to open the window behind him. The late March chill smacked at him, the raw wind a harbinger of spring training sprints at the baseball field.

So much for the distraction of work. He didn't want to be preoccupied about Caleb and he was weary of feeling guilty for trying to open a passage for the rest of their lives.

The abrupt loss and the aftereffects had uncovered a deep resentment of his own role. Once again he'd been molded into a reluctant family anchor when truthfully his solidity was more porous than steely. He took no comfort that these hidebound perceptions were his alone.

He stared at pedestrians hurrying from warm cars to warm buildings. By July, they'd be rushing from cool cars to AC'd buildings. Life goes on, and by watching the familiar motion before him he collected some reassurance. In a few months, he'd be sitting here thinking back to this unbearable week and acknowledging that seasonal change had indeed bestowed adaptability.

This forward-looking approach made sense. He couldn't change what had happened and to argue and dig and obsess the way he feared Meg would do, promised only more heartache. Convincing his wife of that wasn't working, but enough dead ends and she'd see the elusiveness of her search.

He finished opening the mail, took a phone call from his brother and made plans to meet with him to discuss "something important."

"Sounds ominous," Jack said, hoping Ford wasn't boozing or snorting.

"I need some advice and I don't wanna fuck up."

"Well, you're talking to an expert on that subject," Jack said, his thoughts going in directions he wanted to forget about. They hung up with plans to get together confirmed.

He called Fredi and asked her to bring him another coffee and within a few minutes a knock came on the door.

"Come on in."

"Jack?" Vicki Slocum stood in the doorway, a mug in her hand. "I brought your coffee. Is it okay if I talk to you for a few minutes?"

He wanted to say no. "All right."

Her green pumps sank into the red carpet, looking like ornaments off a Christmas tree. She closed the door.

"Better leave it open. You know the policy."

She looked as if she might argue, but then opened it partway. Jack had initiated the office policy in 1993 to protect all employees from gossip or harassment accusations.

Dressed in a gray pinstripe suit and a light green blouse, her reddish-brown hair was neatly styled. She carried herself with a sensuality that she'd artfully enhanced with a refined sophistication.

He glanced away from her, keeping his demeanor professional and detached.

She set the mug down, the steam billowing up over her hand to touch the cuff of her jacket.

"I've missed you," she whispered. "It's not the same around here when you're away."

Jack showed no reaction, reaching for the coffee and taking a sip. He sat back holding the mug with both hands. "Thanks again for staying with Bethany. Meg and I appreciated it."

"I enjoyed doing it. We cried and talked about Caleb and how much she loved him. She told me some of the courageous things he'd done, like the summer he saved her from drowning."

Jack blinked, then scowled. Bethany almost drowned? When? He'd never heard about that. Why hadn't Meg told him? And in that moment he echoed Meg's earlier *why didn't you tell me?* regarding the cottage. Now he understood why Meg was so furious with him. She'd wanted details, and now he did, too. But no way was he going to ask Vicki Slocum what the hell had happened in his own family.

"Caleb and Bethany were very close," he said.

"It certainly sounded that way. She's very sweet and very sad."

"The entire family is sad." On this fact he had all the details he needed.

She pulled the client chair close to the desk and sat down, leaning forward. Lavender fingernails, a thin gold watch on her left wrist. She looked at him, a spirited joy in her eyes that made him uneasy.

Not today. He didn't want to discuss this.

Vicki cleared her throat. "I have a suggestion on how to get buying interest in the Griswald house. I think we should raise the price."

"I'm listening," he said, wondering if he'd misread that joy. God, he hoped so.

"I've shown it a number of times and when they hear the price the potential buyers get suspicious. Yesterday afternoon, a man asked me what the owners were hiding. It's a big house in an upscale neighborhood and I think customers are afraid we're trying to get it off our hands."

"We are. The furnace is ancient, insulation lousy and the electrical service needs to be brought up to code."

"The man I spoke with has a brother-in-law in the heating business in Providence and he said the furnace probably just needed a good cleaning. In other words, this guy is sure there is some hidden problem much more serious—he hinted at termites or an environmental problem with the ground water. Bottom line was that he'd said no thanks. It's the third serious buyer who changed his mind."

"And you think raising the price will cut suspicions that we're trying to dump a problem." Actually, he thought her idea a good one. Too cheap can fold a sale just as fast as too expensive. She'd worked in Boston real estate before moving here so he generally took her suggestions seriously.

"It's worth a try." Her eyes sparkled and she rose, coming around the desk to where he was seated. Jack felt trapped between the window and the desk. The tips of her fingers brushed his wrist.

"You'll have to call the owners," he said flatly, sliding his chair back and moving away from her.

She laughed. "I know they'll *really* complain about getting more money."

He didn't laugh, not wanting to extend this meeting

beyond business. "Let me know what they say. Now, I've got some work to do and you do, too." He picked up a folder that hadn't been filed and flipped through it, dismissing her with his silence.

Instead of the exit he wanted, she rested her hip against his desk and picked up the photo of Caleb, handling it with a reverence usually reserved for priceless artwork. "I know you need some time and I respect that. It was a terrible tragedy. Caleb was such a terrific kid. Meg must be having a very difficult time. She's fortunate to have you through all of this."

She replaced the picture, then looked at him with understanding eyes.

"Meg is incredible," Jack said, meaning every word and wishing he'd stayed home.

"So are you."

Jack sighed. "Vicki, I don't want to talk about this."

"About us, Jack." She came toward him.

"There is no us."

But she wasn't listening. "I understand that right now you can't—"

He shook his head, silencing her. He heard voices in the reception area and wanted to close the door, but realistically that would, at the very least, raise Fredi's eyebrows. She'd later lecture him, pointing out his carelessness due to his distraction and his coming back to work too soon. One glance at Vicki revealed she was on the edge of some teary clarification. Sending her away with this issue hanging would be a mistake.

He'd have to keep their own voices down and take his chances. This needed to be dealt with and ended.

"Vicki," he said taking her arm and leading her to the client chair. Once she sat down, he lowered his voice to a concerned resonance. "What happened shouldn't have and any impression I gave you that I wanted more than . . . more than what happened was my error and I apologize."

"What's wrong with you?" she asked in a raised whisper. "You're talking like we shared some silly kiss. You made love to me and I made love to you."

"I know what we did."

"Then why are you being so vague like you hardly remember?" She shuddered in dismay. "I wanted you and you wanted me. It was romantic and sexy and wonderful and I thought you felt the same way."

Romantic? Honest to Christ, romance had not once entered his mind. Romance went with Meg. This hadn't been wine and candlelight and long slow seduction. And what did she mean, *I thought you felt the same way?* About what? But he didn't ask. He didn't want to know. He didn't want to hurt her, he just wanted her to go away.

Jack's belly thudded like the homecoming of a dropped sledgehammer. "Look, I never should have allowed it to happen. It was a stupid and reckless mistake and I take full responsibility."

She withered as if he'd delivered the ultimate insult. Jack had never felt so ill-prepared. She was twenty-eight, and hardly some innocent he'd taken advantage of. How hard could this be to deal with? He was being honest and forthcoming, dousing any thoughts she might have about a relationship. He didn't want to be cold, but he definitely wanted to be clear. Yet he sensed he was flailing like a beached fish. Even more puzzling was a genuine empathy that urged him to take her into his arms and comfort her.

To make sure he didn't do that, he moved around his desk so that she was several feet away. She was emotional and headstrong and—oh, hell, face facts. Like it or not she thought there was something between them.

Not from his perspective, that's for damn sure. The sex had been stupidly self-indulgent, and the devastating guilt—which was certainly with him now—had been lost in a forest full of reasons from overwork, his mother leaving an AA meeting only to turn up drunk on their doorstep three hours later, to hassles with the kids, to Meg pressuring him to be home more . . . All minor stand-alone stresses that in the weeks before Caleb's death had piled up and overwhelmed him.

That morning after he'd spoken to Meg about money for a pickup, he'd gotten prices, pics and stats for a few trucks from a local Chevy dealer. Jack had felt optimistic about Caleb, knowing that helping him to choose a truck would buffer their other disagreements. He'd been feeling pretty mellow and cocky when Vicki paged him. When he'd called her he'd immediately caught her excitement. She'd gushed a torrent of words about the huge sale she'd closed—one that Jack had guided her through because the buyer had been a real pain. She'd been ecstatic and grateful and she wanted to celebrate by taking him out to dinner that night. Jack nixed that. He wanted to be home for dinner. Vicki's enthusiasm fizzled like a fireworks dud. She might have whined, but Jack only heard her disappointment. He'd recalled his own first big sale and it had indeed been a heady moment and needed to be shared. He suggested a bottle of champagne at the office later that afternoon; she liked that, but couldn't he stop by her house and have just one glass to celebrate with her?

Oh, he heard the alarm alert. He knew he should say no, but he could handle this. Mentally, he played out the celebration as he drove. They'd toast her future—she'd be grateful for his professional guidance, he'd be modestly flattered and that would be that. And it almost followed that course until she kissed him. He should have backed her off, he could have walked away . . . should have, could have, would have . . . But he didn't.

They'd ended up in a tangle of clothes on her living room couch. That it happened at all was disastrous. That it happened when it did was his nightmare.

Jack glanced down at her, wondering how a man as smart as he could have been so dumb. Vicki's shoulders sagged and she lowered her head, but not before he saw her tears.

Terrific. If she went out of here red-eyed and sniffling

Fredi would be asking questions. Jack slipped a hand beneath her elbow and drew her up and into his arms. He felt no desire, only sadness. "I'm sorry . . ."

She curled against him, rubbing her cheek into his shirt. "Please don't hate me for wanting to see you, to talk to you, to be with you."

"Vicki, listen to me. You and I and what we did isn't really the point."

She clamped her hand over his mouth. "I know what you're going to say and you're wrong."

He circled her wrist and drew her hand away. "The timing is too coincidental. And we both heard the siren."

She shook her head vehemently. "It could have been anything—some old person going to the hospital, a car wreck over on 103. It wasn't . . . It wasn't."

Ah denial, he was well acquainted with it. Here they were discussing it without mentioning it. Before she could say anything else, he pulled a tissue from a box on the desk and handed it to her. She dabbed her eyes while Jack shoved his hands into his trouser pockets and leaned back against his desk. Head down, legs extended, his mind was sluggish and exhausted. His own idiocy more scorching by the terror that Caleb was dying while he was banging a pretty employee.

At the door, she called his name.

He glanced up.

"I love you."

Then she was gone.

He stayed put for a long time until he convinced himself she was being overly dramatic. Of course, she thought she loved him—it justified the encounter. Given a few weeks she would love someone else. He just had to avoid any more of these one-on-one meetings.

He worked until nearly six, leaving without seeing

Vicki, drove almost home when he remembered the milk
and backtracked to the 7-Eleven. Maybe he could talk Meg
into going someplace for dinner. Bethany, too. Envision-
ing the three of them away from the house memories gave
him a boost of optimism.

Turning into his drive, he scowled at the parked Dodge
4 x 4 truck. Inside the house plenty of lights were on and
the faint sound of some rap group CD assured him Bethany
was home.

But when he opened the back door and stepped into the
kitchen, his earlier optimism plummeted.

Meg and Sloane Rivers were seated at the kitchen table,
a glass of wine and a bottle of beer between them. But
what riveted Jack was Rivers's hands holding Meg's.

"What's going on?" he asked, the milk jug dangling
from his clenched fist.

Rivers moved, but Meg didn't. She glanced at Jack as if
his demeanor was out of line and his question ignorant.

"Sloane and I were making plans on how to go about
this."

Jack set the jug on the counter with a deliberate thud. "I
can hardly wait to hear what *this* is."

Sloane pushed his chair back, stood and lifted his leather
jacket from another chair. He swung it around, hooked on
his thumb so that it hung over his shoulder like some cool
imitation of a motorcycle jock. Jack wanted to snatch the
jacket and bag his head with it.

To Meg, he said, "Let me know what you want me to
do. I'll talk to his friends at school. Maybe we can put
together a pattern." He looked at Jack who saw a tiny glim-
mer of victory behind the good old schoolboy chum
façade. "Good to see you again, Jack."

"A moment I've waited for all day."

"Jack!"

But he was out the door and Jack glowered at Meg.
"What the hell is going on?"

Meg rose, put the milk in the refrigerator, closed the

door and stood motionless with her back to him for just long enough to make his insides grip ominously.

Then she turned on him. "What's going on is that someone besides me wants to know why our son is dead. His father isn't interested, but his baseball coach is."

"That's bullshit. His baseball coach wants to get into my wife's panties. Period."

"You've never liked Sloane so your accusation isn't surprising, but I'm not going to argue such a ludicrous statement. Besides, I'm perfectly capable of handling Sloane. As for your behavior, is this possessiveness another attempt to keep me from finding out about Caleb? Because if it is, you should be ashamed of yourself."

Jack gaped at her, the outlandishness of her accusation made him wonder how much wine she'd had.

"I've made an appointment with Caleb's guidance counselor." She poured the half bottle of beer into the sink and picked up her glass and dumped that out, too. "Bethany wants pizza tonight. Do you want to go get it or do you want me to have it delivered?"

"Christ, what's happened to you?"

"I'm making my own decisions because I can't live with myself if I do what you want, which is nothing."

When he simply stared at her, she went to the phone and called for the delivery.

Jack went to the bar and poured himself two fingers of Dewers. But he didn't lift the glass to his mouth. His head ached and the exhaustion he'd been fighting all day suddenly overwhelmed him. He left the glass and started out of the kitchen.

"Where are you going?"

"To bed." And then because he felt put upon and hurt and ornery, he said, "Call the ever-helpful Sloane back to eat pizza. I'm sure you two would like to talk with me out of the way. Just watch it with the hand-holding, our daughter might object."

She marched up to him and slapped him. "Damn you."

Jack flinched but inside he felt only sadness and confusion. She stepped away as if suddenly comprehending that she'd never hit him before. Seconds became a minute became another minute. She looked lost and anxious. Jack wanted to draw her close and beg her to leave Caleb to rest. But he guessed that would only begin the argument anew. So instead, he walked out of the kitchen and up the stairs.

He let his fury at Rivers salt his thoughts. He could knock the shit out of him, a delicious possibility that harkened back to his raucous days on the docks in Newport. Or he could shut up and pretend today never happened.

Pride goaded him toward the former. Being a grown-up with an angry wife convinced him to embrace the latter.

For now.

Chapter Eight

"Hi. I sort of thought you might be here," Erica said, stepping carefully through the wealth of flowers to where Bethany sat beneath the tree. With her knees pulled up to her chin, her black-lined eyes and dark rum lips, she could have been a pouting rock groupie. She wore a blue jacket, navy cords and heavy buff-colored boots. "How come you didn't let me know at school? I would have walked over with you."

She shrugged, drawing deep on the cigarette. "I'm meeting someone."

"Who?"

"Stick around. You'll see."

She'd come here to hang out, but she was worried about Bethany, too. "Did you see the flowers I brought this morning?" She indicated a huge bundle of spring blossoms. The message to Caleb that she'd finally settled upon mirrored her heart. *I miss you so much.* "Dad said it was kinda a lot of money but since I wanted to spend it for Caleb I didn't care." Erica's gaze swept over the crowd of memorial tokens. Some had died, more had wilted, many were bruised. Her bouquet was the freshest and occupying the spot of the autographed baseball; it was gone—stolen or retrieved by the second-thoughts owner.

Bethany seemed to not notice, studying instead the cigarette tip as if it was a mystical light. "Caleb doesn't know any of this stuff is here."

"Oh yes he does," Erica said passionately. She arranged herself beside Bethany who scooted sideways to make room. "I think he can see us and that he's sad that he made so many of us cry."

"That's stupid. He knew how wild everyone was when Kevin died. He should have known I'd be freakin' out and depressed and he didn't give a shit."

"That's not true!" Erica believed this vehemently because she'd loved Caleb, and with the same zeal she knew Bethany was her very best friend despite her nastiness in the past few days.

"Then why did he kill himself?" She smashed out the cigarette, flinging it aside. "You got the answer to that? No, you don't. Nobody does, I mean he didn't even leave a note or a letter or anything. Mom is totally crazy trying to find a reason and Dad wants to like forget it ever happened. Why didn't my brother come and talk to me? Why?"

"Maybe he was afraid."

Bethany got to her feet, fumbling in her backpack and pulled out a package of Marlboros. Her hands shook and she dropped the pack on the ground, the butts spilling among the flutes of flowers. She scrambled for them, putting them back, then lighting one.

"Bethy?"

"Don't call me that," she snapped. "It's a baby name and I hate it. If he was scared of anything, it was that I'd blab to you."

Erica gulped, crushed that her best pal was treating her so mean. She wasn't some fair-weather friend, but she also wasn't going to get stormed on when Bethany was the one being a dork. She folded her arms and took her on. "I don't believe you. You're just pissed that Caleb didn't come to you. You don't know what was so horrible in his life. That's the real truth, isn't it?"

Bethany took a threatening step, getting in Erica's face. "Shut up!" she hissed. The air between them vibrated, a sweep of wind crackling the flutes. Erica rolled a bit on her heels, but she didn't blink. Bethany backed away, looking down at her boots. "I can't talk about him anymore. Just please, please shut up."

"I'm sorry," Erica said, truly meaning it. "But something isn't right with you. The way you're acting, the smoking, the way you're talking."

But Bethany was already tracking away from the tree, moving toward the path that led to the road. Cars passed by, slowing, gawking at the memorial that had grown to a shrine. Within hours of his death, kids had gathered to cry, remember, question and share at this place less than a mile from the high school. Erica came the first time with Bethany. They had sobbed and held one another, and privately Erica was angry that Caleb had done this. Bethany was angry, too; just more honest about expressing it.

The red truck with big wheels and black swooshes on the fenders stopped on the road's shoulder. Music boomed, making the ground rumble. The window slid down and the driver hooked his arm over the opening, hand slapping the shiny door, keeping time to the blasting drums and electric guitars. "Hey, baby, what's happenin'?"

Erica grabbed Bethany's arm, concern hiking into pure fear. "Oh my God, that's Brandt Foley," she said as if he were a prison escapee instead of a senior and a football player. He had a wild rep and a new girlfriend every week and he'd been expelled last January for ten days for coming to school drunk with a knife and threatening to kill all the fags. "What are you doing? Caleb hated him. He warned you to stay away from him. He'd be flippin' out if he saw this."

"He doesn't care. If he did he'd be here. I can do what I want. I'm not stupid, you know."

"Wait."

"Let go of me."

But Erica couldn't, not before saying, "Please don't go with him, you'll get in trouble."

Whether it was Erica's words, her sudden glaze of tears or the ties of friendship, Bethany hugged her hard and fast. "Don't worry. And if you're really my friend you won't go blabbin' to my parents."

And with that she climbed up into the truck and Erica shuddered as she watched the vehicle roar away.

Meg opened the back door, holding it while Sloane eased through with a cardboard box marked DEL MONTE SLICED PEACHES on the side.

"Just one box?"

"This is it."

He placed the box on the kitchen table.

Meg hung back, easing the door closed. Oh how she wanted his locker contents to give her a direction or some clue that his room had not.

"Jack here?" Sloane asked. "Figured he might want to go through this with you."

She stared at the box, keeping her distance. "What?" She tried to ignore a sudden squeamishness that she was snooping. "Oh, no, Jack's back to work. It's just as well. Lately all we seem to do is argue."

"He sure wasn't happy to see me the other night." Sloane opened the flaps, but didn't take anything out.

There was something sacred about a locker's contents, like a private journal or a locked briefcase. Her own locker in high school had hidden a dog-eared copy of sexual fantasies that she and her girlfriends had read with jaw-dropping awe, cherry-red blushes and utter fascination. She recalled her absolute panic when she heard the rumor of a drug sweep. She'd gotten the book out just in time.

Surely Caleb had his secrets, too. Everyone had private compartments that were out of bounds. She'd believed in that, but she'd apparently embraced maternal blindness, too. The proof of her lack of attention, or worse, a sense she'd been clueless, had been clarified and escalated since Jack told her the cottage story. Sending the box, unexplored, to the basement would surely please him. What she was doing was about finding answers; she was confident that once she had them, Jack would not only be pleased but would understand how wrong he'd been in trying to thwart her.

"So did he say anything after I left?" Sloane asked.

"He thinks you want to get me into bed."

"He's right."

So Jack *was* right, she mused. "I can handle myself. I told him that and I'm telling you that," she said finding this guy-on-guy rivalry more irritating than serious.

She began taking things from the back of the box. Textbooks, a dirty pair of sweat socks, a Valentine from Erica and rolled into a corner was the Red Sox jacket Jack had given him. Meg experienced a visceral pain in the vicinity of her heart as she lifted the garment and touched the back where she'd touched Caleb that last morning. She squeezed the fabric at the left shoulder as if to capture some essence of him and make it her own.

"I'll be right back," she said haltingly, hurrying from the kitchen with the jacket.

She went into the bathroom and closed the door. She sat on the commode lid and pushed her face into the jacket and wept with a sorrow that was a closer companion these days than her husband. She could literally smell Caleb, that unique scent that was him. She drew it, absorbing it, committing it to memory. She never wanted to lose it, never wanted to forget it . . . never, never.

She opened the bathroom door and heard Sloane on the phone. She clutched the jacket close to her, sprinting upstairs to Caleb's room where she put it in the bottom drawer of his dresser with the sweatshirt from beneath the bed and the holey sweatpants he'd worn that last morning. These were clothes she hadn't washed, couldn't wash. These were her last connectors to her son.

Minutes later, she returned to the kitchen. Sloane had finished his phone call. Looking at her closely, he asked, "You okay?"

"I'll be better when this is done." She took out a bunch of crumpled papers and set them aside. Sloane straddled a chair, a beer bottle swinging from one hand.

"You know what I've been really thinking about?" Sloane asked, watching her. "I think about you being married to him and how he doesn't deserve you. Then I realize that the longer he acts like an idiot the sooner you'll realize he is one."

Meg lifted a spiral-bound notebook and began flipping through the pages. Some papers flitted out onto the table and the floor. "Give it a rest, Sloane. Helping me find out what troubled Caleb doesn't mean I'm going to listen to you trash Jack."

He sighed. "Always loyal, aren't you? And the bastard isn't clued in enough to appreciate you."

She opened her mouth and closed it again. He'd flirted and teased with her for years and she'd known he was half-serious, but surely he didn't expect her to respond like some mealymouthed victim, whining that yes, indeed she was loyal and Jack was unappreciative and out-of-touch. His attempts to make Jack look bad irritated her enough to question Sloane's motives.

And what did he really want? For her to engage in some provocative game? Do phone sex? Have an affair? Leave Jack for him? In eagerly accepting his offer of assistance, she hadn't ever intended to send some coded signal of interest.

"Scare you?" he asked, picking up on her long silence.

"Of course not."

He chuckled, sipping from the bottle. "That's because

you know I wouldn't hurt you and I only want the best for you. Jack better watch out. If he acts too much like a jerk, you're gonna come running to me."

"Pretty sure of yourself, aren't you?"

"Just an old friend who's been waiting a helluva long time."

Meg felt a twinge of unease at his directness. He was stepping beyond some passive flirting. "You're an old friend of Kate's, too," she said on a lighter note. "She's the one with a jerky boyfriend. Why don't you ask her out?"

"She's all sop-eyed over Ford. Besides she's a little too hard-assed for me. Too much like my ex."

Meg blinked and stared. "Ford? Our Ford? You're mistaken."

"Nope. They left here together after the funeral. Then I saw them at the Blue Shark over on County Road. This morning when I was driving to school, I saw her car at his place."

"That doesn't mean they're involved."

He raised both eyebrows, lifting the beer to his mouth. "You think she was just stopping for coffee? Not even you would be that naïve. I saw the car at about six-fifteen."

"Kate and Ford in a relationship," she murmured, trying to wrap her mind around the possibility. There were no two people as opposite unless it was her mother and Hazel DeWilde, but then they had astounded Meg at the funeral with their newly born closeness. She sat down, the notebook forgotten on the table. Caleb's death had brought some startling and odd ramifications. "She never said a word. She always tells me everything."

"She probably figured you have other things on your mind."

"I wonder if Jack knows." Pensive for a moment, she said, "Now that I think about it, I did see them with their heads together at the funeral. They've never paid much attention to one another before."

"Hey, he's a bad boy, she's a bad girl. Like meets like."

"You're crazy. Kate would hoot with laughter if she heard you say she was like Ford. He's a fisherman. She doesn't even like seafood."

"It's probably a safe guess that his job or her food choices aren't what has her at his place at six-fifteen in the morning." He shrugged and pulled the box closer. "Found anything in there that looks like it might mean something?"

She started to shake her head when she caught sight of the pamphlet on the floor. She picked it up and stared while an icy jam of realization froze her breathing.

"Meggie? What is it?"

"I don't believe it."

Sloane reached over and took the pamphlet. Two students were ovaled on the front, both smiling as if they were on their way to an amusement park. At the top it read: GAY TEENAGERS—WHAT YOU NEED TO KNOW. "This is no big deal. These printed PSA's cover all the hot teenage issues. Drugs, smoking, drinking, safe sex—they're placed in public service racks in the school library. The kids are always taking them although how much reading and heeding is anyone's guess." She turned away. "What, honey?"

"Caleb wasn't gay."

"Okay."

"Okay?" She faced him. "That's all you can say?"

"I don't know if he was gay."

"You saw him at school every day. You coached him, did you ever see any signs that . . . ?" Her mind snatched at moments past with her son, probing for any word or gesture. "I certainly didn't. Did it ever look to you like he wanted to be with boys? Oh God, Jack will be furious."

"Now hold on a minute." He rose, set the bottle in the sink, then pushed the box aside, tucking the flyer back in the spiral. "You're getting way ahead of yourself."

He reached for her arm, but she backed away. "Don't you understand? If Caleb was gay that could be why he killed himself. Seth Eidson, the detective we spoke with, raised that possibility but Jack didn't want to hear it. Caleb would have been scared and ashamed, afraid his friends would make fun of him, terrified to tell us, knowing his father would be angry and I would be disappointed and his grandmothers—Sloane, they would never understand."

He was quiet, hands in his pants' pockets, head down, studying his Reeboks.

"Say something."

"I don't know what to say. Look, why don't we talk to Bethany. Kids are usually savvy about what's going on. If there was anything—"

"Bethany would get hysterical," she said flatly, realizing she knew her daughter a lot better than she had her son. She went back to the box, pawing through the rest of the contents and finding nothing else related to the pamphlet. "Why would he have it if it wasn't significant?"

"Curiosity is my guess. Cooper Falls isn't on the cutting-edge of tolerance and easily available information, you know. Gay adults aren't all that visible, but we know there are some. Just as there are probably some gay kids."

"Probably? Don't you know?" she snapped, weary of his vagueness. "You're at school every day." She watched him walk around the table, unease dogging him. "Sloane, the time for protecting me from shock or disillusion passed well over a week ago."

"I don't want you jumping to any—"

She smacked her hand on the table. "Dammit, stop with that stupid disclaimer!" Jack had tried that with the cottage story, and he had offended her with his "I know best" presumption. "He killed himself. What could possibly be worse than that? What is so unmanageable about just stating the truth?"

"I don't know what the truth is. And what I do know doesn't prove anything."

"Let me be the judge of that."

He sighed. "There was one boy that Caleb was pals with who was gay." Sloane told of the fight at school last winter when Caleb defended his friend. Her son not only got a black eye from the kid he fought, but now she learned he'd endured the wrath of others who called Caleb a fag-lover.

Meg remembered the black eye. He'd come home from school late and she'd just returned from the mall where she and Hazel had been to a January white sale. Caleb had been in the downstairs bathroom, examining his eye in the mirror with all the pride of a winning boxer. He'd told her a bunch of guys had been pushing a new kid around and he'd evened the odds. The other guy had a bloody nose *and* a black eye. This declaration brought a triumphant grin. Meg had folded her arms, amused by his proud swagger. That evening she'd been treated to a more embellished recitation when Jack heard the story. In neither accounting had Caleb mentioned that the boy he defended had been gay. Leaving that detail out plus finding the pamphlet now opened new questions.

"What was his name?" she asked, reaching for a pencil to add it to a list of Caleb's friends she'd begun talking to in the past few days.

"Who? The gay kid or the puncher?"

"Caleb's friend."

"Donnie Paquin."

Meg scowled, the name catching at some thread in her mind. Yes! Donnie was the boy who was helping Caleb with chemistry. But as soon as his name made the connection, she wondered why Caleb never mentioned that Donnie was gay? Had he thought she and Jack wouldn't approve? Or was there more between Caleb and Donnie than a fight and chemistry tutoring?

On Sunday afternoon, Jack was stretched out on the couch in the den watching a Boston Celtics basketball game. Erica had come over and she and Bethany were closeted in Bethany's bedroom, coming out only when Meg knocked on the door and said there was a special delivery downstairs.

Five minutes later the teenagers tramped into the kitchen. Erica smiled shyly and Bethany, wearing black and purple, pouted her plum lips. Her recent "maturity" appeared to Jack more like a cosmetic-overdosed witch looking for a house to haunt. He mostly ignored the awful transformation, awaiting some signal from Meg. She seemed happy to ignore Bethany's mutation, causing Jack to conclude this was a "stage" and would go away. He'd become so accustomed to her ongoing snippy attitude that he wondered if he'd ever again have back his once sunny and lovely daughter.

The two girls took the warm pepperoni and mushroom pizza Jack had ordered for them. Meg added two cans of cold Pepsi. He heard music and giggling chatter, convincing him that Meg's urging Bethany to invite Erica for an overnight proved his wife's deft handling of the current family tenseness.

"The pizza made an impression," Meg said, handing him a bottle of beer just as the phone rang.

"Sure wish her makeup mysteries could be solved by a call to Domino's." Jack peered around her so as not to miss the final minutes of the game. The Celts were down by four.

Meg answered. "Yes, this is Meg." She paused. "Why hello, Vicki, how nice to hear from you."

Jack went still, game forgotten, beer souring in its path down his throat.

"Actually, he's collapsed on the couch watching the Celtics." Pause. "Bethany is still having some difficulties, but we're sure she'll be fine." Pause. One. Two. Three. Four. Jack counted his own pulse beats and the endless vacuum of silence. What was Vicki saying?

And why the hell was she calling? What did she want? His thoughts bounced around like a poker player searching for a strategy to bluff a loser hand into a winner.

"Yes, she enjoyed spending time with you, too." Meg glanced over at Jack who instantly shifted his gaze to the television. "How sweet of you to say such things about Caleb." She listened, leaning against the side of the desk.

She straightened some papers on the desk, arranged the pencils in the holder, replaced the caps on two pens while Jack waited like a trapped rat for Meg to swing around and drill him with fury and accusations. His chest muscles seized into a major cramp and he knew he had to get out of the room.

"Oh my God. I had no idea," she said turning and looking at Jack.

Jack rolled to his feet, but when he walked past her, she grabbed his arm, indicating he should stay. He pulled away and headed for the bathroom instead of out to his car where he wanted to drive around and decide whether to strangle Vicki before or after he faced Meg.

Inside the bathroom, he closed the door and cranked open the window. An enthusiastic April breeze cooled his face and boosted a lone kite that sailed from an invisible tether. Watching it brought Caleb to mind along with Jack's morass of guilt. He peered in the mirror, half expecting to see a confession in bloody letters where his face used to be. Instead, the pulse in his jaw pounded and he was sweating. He gripped the sink and lowered his head.

Breathing deeply, he shoveled through the chaos of his own overreaction. Get a grip. She's not going to call here and say to Meg: *Just thought I'd tell you that Jack and I were fucking when Caleb died.* Of course not. She might be young and emotional, but she's not whacked out. He frowned. Or was she? He vaguely recalled her saying champagne made her giggly and talky when Jack had soon learned it made her hyper-horny. He shuddered. Christ, his son was dying and he was wrapped up in illicit gratification. It was a disgusting picture and the memory sickened him. He turned on the water, splashing cold water on his face as panic gave way to annoyance.

What the hell was she calling about? No, a better question was *why* in God's name was she calling at all? She was his employee, not some friend of the family. He dried his face, swabbed it with a yellow towel and tossed down three aspirin in anticipation of a headache.

He opened the door, expecting Meg to be waiting, arms crossed, eyes flashing. She wasn't there. He walked far enough into the dining room to see that she wasn't on the phone in the study any longer. He found her in the kitchen wearing her coat and looking for her car keys.

He spotted them where they peeked from under a tower of tied-up, unread gardening magazines that any other spring would have been dog-eared instead of shuffled from mailbox to the house and now bundled for the waiting room at the medical clinic. Briefly he wondered if she'd kept the phone number of that couple wanting help with their yard design. Probably she hadn't.

"Looking for these?" he asked holding up her keys.

She glanced at him. "Yes. Where did you disappear to?"

"Had to pee."

She caught the keys he tossed to her. "Vicki wanted to know if you would come to her house and get some things that Caleb had left there."

Jack blinked, relief jackknifing through his gut followed by irritation that he'd so totally misread her phone call. "She needs me to come to her house? I haven't got time to do that." Nor did he want to face another scene with her. Feeling much more invigorated, he said, "Whatever tools she's got she can bring to the office."

"The snow thrower?"

"Shit." His relief collapsed, replaced with a bone-deep wariness of Vicki's motives. She could have told him this yesterday at work. Then he could have arranged to have it picked up by someone. But she didn't do that because she wanted him to come and get it, and what better way to accomplish that then to go through Meg.

"What's wrong with you?" Meg asked, scowling.

"I don't want to go over there."

"Why not?"

Jack opened the fridge and took out a jug of cranberry juice. He splashed some into a glass and drank it down. "Because she's an employee and I don't think it's a good idea."

Meg grinned. "Oh, for heaven's sake, that's silly. She was Caleb's employer, not some dirty girl in fishnet hosiery. I swear Jack, sometimes you can be as prim as my mother."

Prim? *Goddammit, Meg, don't be so trusting.* But what to do. He'd call his brother. The two of them could get it, or he could just ask Ford to go by himself. He was reaching for the phone when she cried out. He swung around.

"Oh no." Her hand clasped her mouth, her eyes distraught. "Is it because the things are Caleb's? You're remembering how you surprised him with the snow thrower last winter, aren't you? Oh Jack, how could I have been so dim-witted about this? But honestly, I didn't even think when Vicki asked. She was concerned that you would be looking for it and she'd forgotten until today when she was cleaning out the garage." She crossed the kitchen and hugged him. "I'm sorry, honey."

"It's okay," he said latching on to her ready-made reason and feeling stinkier than the bottom end of a sewer pipe. He pressed her tight against him, soaking up her softness and her understanding and wished his motives had been the grieving ones she so believed he possessed.

"Well, never mind," she said reaching up and kissing him. Her mouth came full and warm and he coveted a dozen more kisses. "I'll stop by after I check Mom's house." Lorraine had returned to Florida and Meg was picking up mail and feeding a couple of stray cats that her mother had adopted. "Vicki and I can wrestle the snow thrower into the Expedition."

Jack grimaced. He could navigate a client through a real estate deal with more sticky clauses than a porcupine had quills, but steering his own life away from a thirty-minute sex blunder staggered his usual deftness.

"You're not going to lift a snow thrower. I'll take care of it," he said wearily, his anticipated headache arriving with all the subtlety of a sledgehammer. "You take my car."

"Honey, are you sure?"

Hell, no, he wasn't sure. He'd rather crawl into a barrel of scorpions. He took his own keys from his pocket and gave them to her, taking hers in return. "I'll be home before you are."

She had the door back open when she turned to him. "Oh and tell Vicki thanks for commenting on what a devoted son she knew Caleb must have been. While she was saying all those sweet things I remembered that Caleb had a crush on her. Isn't that terrific?"

Jack raised his eyebrows, unsure how he was expected to answer. His son's crush on Vicki after the boy went to work for her had caused more than a few smiles between Meg and Jack for the months that his infatuation raged. Caleb, of course, denied it, but his boundless enthusiasm about helping her clean out her late aunt's house and his goofy grin whenever Vicki came near him were classically obvious. "Why is remembering that terrific?"

"It proves Caleb wasn't gay."

"What?" Had he missed something? Or was this some new angle that Meg was measuring? Jack had reframed from caustic comments since good old Sloane had sat in their kitchen and taken up his mantle of helpmate to her mission. "I don't want to hear this."

"Oh, but you do." Then as if she were that kite he'd watched earlier, her words sailed in a bounce of energy and joy. "After I found the pamphlet I was feeling so down because if he was gay I never figured it out and that made me feel dumb and out of touch with my own son. But I'm still going to talk to Donnie. Oh, you don't know about Donnie. He's gay and he and Caleb were friends. Sloane told me all about it—the fight, I mean."

"What would life be without good old Sloane," he grumbled, while she gestured and her words gained steam.

She ricocheted into retelling him the story behind Caleb's black eye of a few months ago. Given the dizzying maze of the conversation, it was easier to stay mute then confuse himself more by asking questions.

She continued. "It was that fight where he defended Donnie. For two days I've been trying to figure out a way to tell you that your son might have killed himself because of his shame over being homosexual. But now I'm not worried about upsetting you because he wasn't—gay, I mean. How could he be when he had a crush on Vicki? But then I never really believed he was, not deep in my heart, yet I feel like I've leapt over a huge hurdle and now I can focus on finding the real reason."

With his mind in gridlock, all Jack could manage was, "Wonderful."

Chapter Nine

Jack backed the Expedition into Vicki's drive, got out and raised the hatch. The backseat was folded down and he'd laid an old bedspread in the back to protect the vehicle's light green carpeting.

The garage door was closed but the side one was open. Jack peered inside, flipping on the light switch. Vicki's four-year-old blue Camry was parked inside and the snow thrower had been stored in an accessible corner so it could be rolled in and out without moving the car. Jack had cautioned Caleb about making sure he didn't scratch anyone's vehicle when he was maneuvering the blower.

He guided the machine out of the corner and through the door. He lifted it, winced at the weight, but managed to wrestle it up into the back of the Expedition. He went back to the garage to get the other things.

Into a box with Caleb's name on the side, Vicki had put a ripped sweatshirt, work gloves, a pair of hedge clippers, a couple of comic books, a jar of nails and an envelope of photos. Jack looked through the pictures taken last summer when they'd gone to San Francisco for vacation. Behind him he heard the back door open.

He shoved the photos into the box and set it beside the blower then closed the hatch.

"Jack?"

"Yeah. I think I've got everything." The afternoon had darkened into a murky twilight; rain clouds bulged. Wind snapped at his jacket and he zipped it.

"I have something else."

In her hands she held a sweater and before he could ask, she turned and went into the house.

Now what? He didn't want to go inside, but at the same time, if he blew her off and drove away she'd probably assume he was leery of being alone with her. He was, but letting her know that would be dumb as dirt. He was the older adult here, the one with confidence, the one adept at disconnecting from problematic situations. And he'd done that at the office—today would simply reinforce it.

He opened the door and stepped into a mudroom that smelled of aged wood, vacancy and wet rubber. Against one wall was a brown bench for sitting to put on and remove boots, and on another wall stretched a line of coat hooks. A plaid scarf and umbrella hung on two and on a third a lone yellow jacket with ski lift tags hanging from the zipper. Jack had no idea that she skied.

There was also a bag of groceries with a loaf of bread sticking out of the top. He picked up the bag and carried it into the kitchen, setting it on the counter next to the sink.

The room was clean and too neat, making him think of his mother's kitchen; she never cooked, merely opened cans and unscrewed bottles. Vicki had take-out menus beneath magnets on the refrigerator door.

Meg's kitchen jumped with old-fashioned chaos and family clutter and the lingering smells of some meal. *When did eating become a twenty-four-hour event?* she would ask with sarcastic humor. Magazines and mail always filled one particular area of the counter beneath the telephone. There was the fat jar of wine corks Meg was collecting for some craft project, the twisted phone cord that Bethany tied around herself while she talked, smeared on lipstick and combed her hair in front of a framed mirror

Meg had hung on the side of a wall cabinet. Caleb's glove and hat and Walkman had once been part of the clutter, too. Even Meg's galloping conversations that he often inhaled into his consciousness without overtly listening—all were part of the DeWilde kitchen.

Looking around at this sterility, he wondered if Vicki knew how to prepare a meal, if she read anything beyond *People* and the real estate trades—he'd seen those in her living room—or if neighbors ever dropped in and who her friends were. He realized he knew more about how Vicki liked her sex then he did about her as a person.

She sat in the tiny breakfast nook with high-backed benches set permanently in place and built tight to the rectangular table. The seats would barely accommodate shriveled old ladies drinking tea. Jack liked chairs and stretching room. The nook mirrored his mood—claustrophobic.

On the table was a gray and red shetland sweater that Vicki brushed with her hands over and over again. She hunched forward, turning her head so that he saw the tears slip down her cheeks. "I remember him wearing this. It was one of his favorite sweaters and just looking at it, touching it, reminds me how much I liked him, how special he was . . ." She gulped. "And how lousy it is that's he dead."

Jack's throat convulsed over a raw lump. Maybe he should have let Meg do this—this wrenching expectation of comfort and solace was out of his league.

"Do you remember him wearing this sweater?" she asked.

"Uh, sure." It was a lie and his ease in saying it sprang not from deception but the embarrassing recognition of his habitual detachment. Like not knowing Caleb had saved his sister from drowning. He'd been a disconnected father. He'd never paid much attention to the details of raising his kids; Meg had done that stuff. Jack went for the big picture, the turning points, the life changing events. Then Caleb's death became the *only* event.

"He was such a good kid," she said.

"Yes, he was." Jack wanted to grab the sweater and leave. "Vicki, look, I'm sorry you had to deal with all of his things. I've already loaded the stuff from the garage."

Instead of coming forward and giving the garment to him, she pressed her face into the wool and then slowly refolded it, straightening the sleeves like it was going into a gift box. "Do you know how many things he did for me? He'd carry the groceries in and put them on the counter just like you did. He cleaned out my car one afternoon and washed and waxed it. He brought me chocolate-covered cherries on my birthday. I didn't know he knew when my birthday was."

"I mentioned it one night at supper. I'd noticed it on your resumé because it was the same day as my brother's."

She stared at him, her eyes swimming with tears and angst. God, he had to get out of here.

"How sweet of Caleb to remember."

"Hardly a miracle. He had a crush on you," Jack said flatly, gruffly, wishing she'd ease up on the drama.

"Did you ever have a crush on an older girl?"

"Probably. Listen, if there's nothing else—"

But it wasn't going to be that easy.

She slipped out of the seat, holding the sweater like a delicate rare object she'd never relinquish. "He would have grown up like you, Jack. He was so very much your son."

"I like to think so. I was very proud of him, although I don't think he knew and I regret that."

"He wanted to please you. He would tell me how hard you worked and how smart you were and that you deserved the money you had because you always earned it, no one gave it to you."

Jack gaped at her, having no idea that Caleb had bragged about him. Talking hard work and financial security usually got a "not again" look which Jack ignored in the way Meg waved off Caleb's protests that eating oatmeal would turn his hair to paste.

His own old man rarely missed a morning without bellowing a "You know who gives the orders and it ain't you punk kids," diatribe that rattled Ford and infuriated Jack. The parallel father-to-son pattern jarred him by its obviousness. Jack couldn't recall if he'd ever praised his old man, and yet Caleb had praised him. "It seems he was even more remarkable than I'd realized."

"He told me you taught him that he could have anything he wanted if he worked hard enough."

"Yes."

"And what happens when you work hard and fail?"

"You get up and start again."

"I wonder what he failed at. What was so awful that he couldn't get back up again?"

"I don't know," he said, her musings spurring his thoughts on his parental ignorance. Guilt now for ignorance it was too late to repair.

"Have you ever failed? I mean in a big way?"

"Too many times."

She nodded. "Me, too." She kneaded her fingers into the yarn. "I never knew my father and I spent a lot of time a few years ago trying to find him. I never did. When I sold real estate in Boston, I did very well until Madison died. Did I ever tell you about him? He was wonderful and generous and I adored him."

The woman was amazing—she'd bounced from Caleb to him and now to herself with the ease of a three-handed juggler. "This Madison was a boyfriend?"

"Yes. We were going to get married. He died of a sudden heart attack while I was here last autumn. I didn't find out until I returned to Boston."

Odd, he thought, that she wasn't notified, but he didn't ask. This was Vicki and that meant emotional mystery and tangles—God knows what the other side of the story involved. His gut wanted no involvement while he fervently hoped she'd find someone—anyone—else to confide in.

He wondered, however, if the Madison shock accounted for her being so traumatized by Caleb's suicide. Twinges of understanding compelled him to say, "I'm sorry, Vicki. I really am."

She grasped his arm and squeezed her thanks before putting the sweater on the table. She took a cigarette from a pack on the counter, handing Jack the matches. He lit it for her, shaking his head when she offered him a drag. Inhaling and exhaling, she pushed the yellow daisy print café curtains aside and looked out the window where rain had begun in earnest.

"It was a very difficult time and I couldn't work," she said so softly Jack stepped closer to hear her. "I took a lot of personal days—I really needed an extended time off but eventually I realized I couldn't stay in my apartment that held all those pieces of my life with Madison. Even living in Boston became painful. I had to get away from all that sadness."

"I assume that's why you changed your mind about selling this house and returned to live here."

"Partly." She turned and waited a few seconds, as if expecting Jack to ask. When he didn't she added, "You made that job offer when I'd been here earlier and, well, my aunt Rose always hoped that I would keep the house. Since I had nowhere else to go, coming here and beginning a new life with a new job and new friends seemed ideal."

Jack leaned against the counter, setting his mind to work on how to change the subject and get out of here with the sparest amount of further conversation.

Watching her, he gauged the terrain. She'd moved away from Boston because of sad memories and poor job prospects. Now she lived and worked here, and once again she was wallowing in sad memories. She was a good employee with tremendous potential, and although not seeing her every day would be his choice, implementing a transfer to the Newport office would be dicey, especially given the number of clients she had here. But there was a temporary solution.

He paused in thought, then said softly, "Now there is sadness for you here."

"You do understand."

"I certainly do." Pause. "I was thinking." He stretched the spacious silence a bit longer, then in an unhurried tone asked, "Would you like to take some time off? You know, kick back and relax away from here? Maybe take a cruise? Or go down to the Islands for a vacation?" He handily remembered the yellow jacket. "Perhaps even some late spring skiing at Killington."

"I didn't know you liked to ski," she said brightly, as if discovering something they had in common. "I love it and I'm really very good. I bet you're an expert."

"Not quite." He'd last skied in the late eighties when a broken leg short-circuited a family weekend in New Hampshire. The injury also played havoc with his work mobility, bringing him to the conclusion that injury-related sports weren't worth his time or the induced stress.

"Madison didn't ski much. He used to take me a lot, but he liked the lodge better than the slopes."

Jack kept his expression impassive, but he'd bet that it was Vicki who took Madison. No single guy that Jack knew would spend a weekend with skiers if he didn't ski— even for a hot number like Vicki.

She put out the cigarette, her smile big and her eyes sparkling. "Oh, Jack, getting away would be fabulous. Leave here, relax and soak up the sun—oh, yes."

She drew close to him and he was disturbed by how vulnerable she seemed without her usual makeup, without her "upscale real estate" sophistication clothes. In sweats and an oversized sweater, she looked terrifyingly younger than her twenty-eight years.

"Tell you what," he said, wanting to nail this down before she got off-track again. "I have a friend over at

Ocean Travel, Bud Aldrich. I'll call him and he'll put together a vacation package with lots of comps."

She tried to hug him, but he deflected her, his thoughts turning to his own situation.

And while she was getting solaced by some muscled beach dude under the Caribbean moon, he'd take care of things here. This meeting that he'd dreaded had actually worked out okay. By the time she returned from all that sun and fun, their encounter would be a stale footnote in her sexual history. He'd disinfect his own conscience and rid himself of this lie that was choking him. No more bullshit—just get it done.

He'd sit Meg down, confess his tryst with Vicki, express his shame and guilt about where he was when Caleb was dying. And if she wouldn't forgive him?

That possibility chilled him, for then there'd be no turning back and he would be left with only the ashes of his marriage. He pushed the odious thought away. He'd make sure she forgave him. God, she *had* to.

"I think you'll have a great time," he said.

Vicki's eyes widened anxiously. "You want me to go alone?"

"The Islands are full of interesting people, and a lot of them are your age. Great looking guys—"

"No. I want to go with you."

"I can't go away with you."

"Why not? You go away on business. It would be very simple. Just think, Jack, we could relax and get to know one another and make love. Remember how good it was? And we were together only one time. I know you haven't forgotten. I can see it in your eyes." She shivered. "Just think what it would be like for days and nights and having each other whenever we want. It will be delicious." And as if experiencing some exotic taste sensation, she licked her lips.

Jack felt nothing. Not arousal or anticipation or even a far-flung provocative fantasy. Five days of raw sun, steamy sex and potent rum drinks should have at least conjured up some curious interest, but she might as well have been suggesting they watch paint dry.

She reached for his hand. "It would be so perfect."

"Perfect is a non-starter." He didn't bother to hide his annoyance with her persistence. "I won't repeat the obvious reasons."

She grinned. "Oh, Jack, obvious reasons are only dressed-up excuses. You want to come with me." She pouted, eyes slanting with mischief at her double entendre while she fiddled with the zipper tab on his jacket.

Jack recalled Meg calling him prim and saying Vicki was no dirty girl in fishnet hosiery. Suddenly it made him furious that his wife was so damn sure of him. Get real here. *It's not that she's oblivious to other women looking at you, it's that Meg trusts you.*

Then he thought of good old Sloane. Sloane and Meg. If she was off visiting Sloane on a rainy Sunday afternoon, Jack wouldn't be checking mail and feeding a couple of stray cats. And while he was fairly confident of Meg's faithfulness, Jack figured Rivers probably stayed awake nights planning ways to seduce her. He rezipped his jacket.

"What are you doing?" she asked, genuinely puzzled.

"I'm going home."

"You want me. I know you do."

He stepped around her and headed toward the mudroom. He glanced back. She didn't look angry about his disinterest as much as confused and disappointed. He didn't know what to say, but he sure didn't want to restart any conversations, so he muttered, "Enjoy the vacation," and quickly walked out the door.

Chapter Ten

Meg leaned forward, her eyes bright with interest. "This is just the kind of help I've been looking for."

Donnie Paquin gulped. Obviously uncomfortable, he slid farther away from her on the mall bench. His Coke sat between them next to a bundle of books and an expensive leather jacket. "It is?"

"Absolutely."

Earlier at the high school, her expectations of getting her questions answered came from Sloane. He had assured her that her son's friends would cooperate. The girls had either burst into tears or spoke of Caleb in such sainted tones that Meg judged the comments to be more post-tragedy revisionism then actuality. Then she faced the boys. After speaking with Gregg, despite giving him some of Caleb's baseball cards—Jack called that bribery—Gregg assured her that the cottage incident had been just some horseplay that got messy. Caleb was an okay guy and if he'd been in trouble, he'd kept it to himself. The other three boys had little to add except that one handed her a picture taken after the awards assembly. The photo unnerved her and she put it in her handbag, unable to look at it. Besides she didn't want a picture that would only sadden her, she wanted answers. She was about to find Sloane and vent her irritation for pushing her hopes so high.

Then she saw Gregg rib one of the guys, and they all looked down the hall toward a tall boy carrying a lot of books. The guys guffawed and one made a limp-wristed gesture. The blatant sexual mocking wasn't lost on Meg or on the boy she'd planned on talking to next.

She introduced herself and instead of the shyness she expected, Donnie Paquin froze like a cornered puppy. Meg convinced herself the panic came from what he knew about Caleb.

She pleaded for him to at least listen to her questions, and whether he'd decided that she'd haunt him until he did or he genuinely felt sorry for her, he agreed to talk to her at the mall by the center fountain. He had a job interview at a computer store and he'd meet her afterwards.

Meg arrived first and bought Cokes, not at all sure he'd show. But Donnie came across the mall, glancing around like he didn't want to be seen. He was gangly, as thin as a sapling and distressingly clumsy. He tripped three times between the fountain and the bench.

Meg had removed her coat, crossed her legs and took a notebook from her handbag. Her notes contained her own nagging questions, such as what had changed her son's upbeat attitude after she last saw him at the awards ceremony, plus her own reasoning about his motive. She refused to accept that he'd suddenly become so distressed that he'd randomly chosen suicide—there had to be more. Into her colony of scribblings, she'd added the cottage trashing, the discovery of the gay pamphlet and the lovely things that Vicki had said.

Donnie had just finished telling her how he'd urged Caleb to find a good friend and tell him what was bugging him.

"So it was something serious. Did he say what it was?"

"No." Donnie still fidgeted.

Meg made herself slow down. She was so anxious for answers that she was perilously close to scaring him off. She put away her notebook, leaned back to assure by her body language that she wasn't really pushy. She sipped her Coke, thinking how best to get Donnie to relax. Donnie ducked his head when a trio of boys slouched past them.

Meg said, "You know, I've talked to a lot of his friends and honestly, if I hadn't known better, I'd wonder if they even knew Caleb."

"Everybody knew Caleb. He was cool and popular."

"I know he was, Donnie. I wasn't being critical, and I understand the natural reticence of teenagers not wanting to squeal on a friend. Actually, I don't think they knew very much. They were more intent on telling me about the memorial at the tree and that they were circulating a petition to get his number retired."

He barely nodded.

"Have you signed the petition?"

"No." He glanced down, dragging his wrist across his upper lip.

"Well, I'm sure there's lots of time."

"Sure."

Meg's heart broke for him. He hadn't been asked; she was sure of it. He was gay and the guys doing the petition—all sport jocks—didn't like him and they didn't want his signature. The mocking she'd witnessed wasn't limited to Gregg and the others, it had been vigorously widespread.

"Cruelty isn't limited to getting beaten up, is it?" When he jerked and shuddered, she guessed he was remembering the fight. "You really miss Caleb, don't you?"

"He was my friend. I've never had one like him. He showed me how to be brave and not to let jerks—" He watched that same trio join another foursome. "Jerks like them say who I am."

He was my friend. A profound statement that illustrated how unfair she'd been when she'd suspiciously pondered what Caleb had done for Donnie in exchange for chemistry tutoring. She'd reacted to his homosexuality and not to Donnie, the teenager. What truly disturbed her was that she knew better. Her son, she now realized, had never stooped to such imbecilic thinking.

"You make me very proud to have been his mother." Beats of silence rippled between them.

"I need to get going," Donnie said, getting up to throw his half-finished drink away.

"No, wait. You said he was going to talk to a friend. And that you had this discussion before the awards ceremony. What I need from you is this friend's name."

He glanced away, pulling on his leather jacket. Meg feared that if he got away she'd never convince him to talk with her again. She couldn't let him go. Not yet.

"Donnie please. I know you believe you're honoring Caleb by keeping silent, but this has been very difficult for our family because we don't know why he killed himself. You've helped me tremendously by revealing that Caleb was upset enough about something to seek help from a friend."

"I don't know who upset him or what it was all about. I just know that he was pissed and angry about something. He said it was too messy to talk about right then. Then he walked away. I figured he was gonna go talk to him."

"Him?" Meg latched onto the pronoun. "Was it someone at school? Another friend? A teacher?" She eliminated Sloane. He'd already told her he hadn't spoken to Caleb that morning. "Someone outside of school?"

He shrugged, his discomfort level obviously rising higher with every question.

"Donnie, look, I feel like I'm playing twenty questions."

"I don't know anything!" Donnie whipped around, baggy pants flapping around his legs. He stumbled and righted himself. His fingers nervously worked at the snaps on his jacket. "I wanted him to tell me. I wanted to help him with what was buggin' him because he helped me. But he wouldn't tell me. Instead he takes off and the next thing I hear he's hangin' from some friggin' tree." Meg shuddered at the visual, but he offered no apology.

He turned his back on her, started to walk away, paused then hurled around, coming close, spewing words, spittle and anger. "I know what you really wanted to ask me. Not all this crap about friendship. You wanted to know if he was a fag. If I was his boyfriend." He lowered his voice. "If we had sex. If I was the reason he killed himself. Isn't that true? Isn't it?"

Meg sat speechless, her eyes huge, her body so tight it felt like a bundle of Chinese knots. Unfortunately her tenuous silence confirmed his accusation.

"Donnie, listen to me—" He shook his head. "Wait a minute. Let me finish."

"I know what you're gonna say. You're sorry? You didn't mean it? Just forget it. I've heard it all before and it doesn't mean shit." He turned away. Meg, wanting to clear up his misperception about her—and it was, it really was—grabbed his arm. His books fell and scattered across the floor. "Look what you did. You're crazy."

He stooped down, frantic to gather them and escape.

Tears sprang into her eyes. Frustrated tears. She wanted to hug him to her heart while at the same time shake him into making him listen. She had jumped to the wrong conclusion early on, but she'd changed her mind and she'd done that days before this meeting. She hadn't judged him, and in fact she honestly admired him, and here he was treating her like some homophobic nitwit.

She kneeled to help, putting papers into one of the textbooks.

"You're not being fair," she said soothing him like she used to do with Caleb after they'd clashed. "Caleb is dead and I don't know why. Naturally, I'm going to look closely at any motive that would have led him—"

"It wasn't me!" he shouted.

A few shoppers had stopped and other bench-sitters leaned forward to hear what was going on.

"Donnie, take it easy. I'm not accusing you of anything."

But it was too late. Panic and terror filled his eyes. "Leave me alone. Leave me alone!" He clutched his books, backing away, turning and stumbling once, then disappeared into the crowd of shoppers.

Meg sat back down on the bench, her legs shaky all the way to her ankles. Slowly she slipped on her coat and gathered her handbag. She glanced up at the huge mall clock. Somehow, in less than a half an hour, she'd botched a few simple questions and frightened a young man into fleeing as if she were a demon.

Meg drove home, pondering. For all the fear she'd generated in Donnie, she'd learned that Caleb intended to talk to someone. Had he done so and who was it? Or if he hadn't, what changed his mind? Think. Reason it out. He was sixteen and desperate; he wasn't negotiating some master plan. Since he'd died in Sawyer's Woods, had Jessup been the friend? He'd found Caleb. It was certainly possible Jessup might have been worried because of what Caleb told him, or because he'd expected the teenager and he never arrived. It occurred to her, too, that while Jessup had attended the funeral, he hadn't come to the house the way he had after her father died. Perhaps he was deliberately avoiding her. Yes, she was sure that he knew something and that called for a visit.

Her spirits lifted despite a drizzling rain. She was getting closer, she could feel it.

If he'd been prone to blame anything for the direction of his thoughts, he would have blamed it on the rain.

Making love on a rainy afternoon.

Before this horror of losing Caleb, Jack could have come home and surprised Meg. Then without a word exchanged, their clothes would have been flung off and he would have been inside of her within moments of walking into the house.

And so a half an hour ago when he glanced out his office window and saw the raindrops, his body reacted with an explosion of sexual interest that not only stunned him but reassured him that just maybe their lives might return to normal.

Midafternoon sex had not been planned, and in fact, it was damn inconvenient since he had a logjam of appointments that a distressed Fredi had waved at him when he pulled on his suit jacket and told her he'd be back later.

At home, he wandered through the empty house, nerves itchy and anxious. Where was she? And would she? He didn't want just compliance, he wanted her eager and breathless.

He tried her cell phone but she must have been out of the car. He nixed calling around—he sure didn't want a caravan of cars arriving with friends worried about Meg.

No, he'd wait.

Fifteen minutes passed.

He tried the cell again.

This time she answered.

"Where are you?" he asked.

"I'm on my way home," she said. "What's the matter?"

"Other than being horny as hell for you? Nothing."

He heard her breath catch. "Oh Jack. . . ."

"Hurry, Meg," he whispered.

Then a brief silence and a sigh that made his heart beat faster until she said, "Yes . . . oh, yes . . ."

Moments later from the study, he heard her truck, then the back door closed and he listened to her steps across the kitchen. He moved silently to the doorway, his body roaring like a jackhammer.

She halted, sliding her purse off her shoulder followed by her coat, looking him up and down before moving forward. The rain splattered against the window. He leaned against the doorjamb watching her, wanting her and pounding with the need. He straightened, and then made his way to the couch. His body hurt and he worked the belt of his trousers loose before her hands halted his.

He closed his eyes, sucking in his breath when her hands slid into his underwear and he felt the coolness of her fingers.

Her mouth was at his shoulder, her hands dragging off his shirt. He brought her around to face him, his eyes devouring, his body skittering with the intensity of a teenager in the throes of losing his virginity.

Clothes slipped away and the rain poured down. The afternoon gray shaded to stormy black. Their sounds rose heavy and ragged and once when she cried out, he kissed her so deeply he thought he'd never breathe again.

She was under him, the couch pressing around them like a cloak. He entered her with buttery ease and her legs came up around his hips and locked him into her as if to keep any intrusion at a distance.

She arched, and he squeezed his eyes closed, trying to hold back, while knowing he might have well tried to stop the rain. She came with a dizzying, high-flying rush and sent his own control speeding into infinity.

They lay spent and satisfied and he mustered the energy to tell her he was scared to death she wouldn't come home.

She looked at him and grinned. "Even if you hadn't called, when I saw your car, plus the rain I would have known. . . ."

"Thank God." He kissed her soundly. "I sure wasn't going to listen to any nutty excuses."

"Hmmm, so I gathered from that X-rated phone call."

"You loved it."

She punched his arm. "Such a stud."

"There you go." He smiled his best raffish grin and she melted like she always did.

Suddenly she tried to wiggle free. "Bethany—oh my God, Jack, she could come home any minute and—"

"She's already been home. I headed her off, gave her forty bucks and sent her to the mall."

"Bribery so you could have your way with me. I'm so flattered." She gave him a broad smile then a kiss quickly followed. She slipped her arms around him once again. "It was good, Jack."

"Good, hell. It was fantastic and we need to do it more often."

"Maybe you should come home in the afternoon even when it isn't raining."

"Works for me."

He looked down at her—all disheveled, cheeks stained red and warm, mouth swollen and eyes full of love and desire for him. Satisfaction filled him. If only he could seal these exceptional moments, or even better, shut out all the questions that had no answers.

Then as if the intrusion of reality couldn't be held back, the telephone rang, reminding Jack he had appointments at the office that he'd promised to return for.

That night, while they were getting ready for bed, she told Jack about the plan she'd formulated after her talk with Donnie.

"Louis Jessup? No, you're not, Meg. You're not going over to that hermit's dump."

"Then come with me," she said deflecting his bluntness. She slipped into bed, plumping the pillows, arranging the covers and snuggling beneath them. The lamplight glowed on his night table.

"And do what?" Jack asked, tossing his shed clothes over a chair.

"Help me ask some questions. He might know something. He did find Caleb."

"The police already talked to him. If he knew anything Eidson would have told us." Jack went into the bathroom.

She listened while he brushed his teeth, peed, flushed the toilet and returned. He opened the window that overlooked the side yard. A cool wind fluttered the curtains.

"But he and Caleb were friends," Meg continued. "Eidson would only have asked about what Jessup knew that was directly related to the suicide."

Wearing only dark blue boxers, he stood by the side of the bed, hands low on his hips, giving her his full attention. "This is insanity, and you know it. Caleb is gone. You have a daughter and a husband who are here and we need you. Instead, you're running around with Rivers—"

"I am not running around."

"Let me finish. You're spending time with him, you're jumping to way-out conclusions about Caleb being a homo and you're chasing down some poor kid who probably doesn't know squat-shit about what happened. And now you want to trot over to chat with some messed-up loner Caleb should have stayed away from." He climbed into bed and shut off the light. "The answer is still no."

Meg sighed. "Why are you being so negative? I know you're hurting from losing Caleb—I just don't understand why you're not at least on my side. It's almost as if you're afraid of what I might learn. Is that it?"

"No, that is not it," he snapped. Lack of light made his voice harsh and hollow. "I love you. I want you back as my wife yes, the delightful one of this afternoon, but also the one who is Bethany's mother. I don't want you off on some senseless crusade that consumes you. That woman over on South Reardon whose daughter went down on Pam Am 103—she's still holding vigils, writing letters, lobbying Congress, still looking for answers. In the meantime, her life and her family have been on hold for more than ten years. Okay, you're not that obsessed, but you're not letting this go. You're not gardening, you're not popping in to see me at the office and talking me into a runaway lunch with you. When was the last time you and Bethany went shopping? Your mother called me at work because every time she calls here she gets the machine. You've changed, Meg, and this mission of yours is the reason."

Meg, of course, had a perfectly logical explanation for all of those things—if he were more cooperative and supportive, she'd probably have had her answers quicker, but instead she had to do it alone. That comment, however, only brought a long silence from him followed by, "So now it's my fault?"

"Well, you certainly haven't been helpful." Then before he could counter, she added, "Tell you what, you come with me to see Jessup and if he doesn't know anything, you can say I told you so and I won't argue."

"I can say I told you so right now and save us both a trip."

"Please." She slid down and put her arm around him, sliding her hand into his shorts. To her satisfaction, he responded. "Hmmm, this feels good. As good as this afternoon."

"Using sex is pretty obvious."

"Whatever works, and you guys never complain."

"Was this the approach to convince Rivers?" he muttered.

"He was easy," she said, loving his flare of jealousy. "All I had to do was ask. You're always tougher to charm." She kissed his neck and drew her fingernail lightly across his scrotum. "We can make this a memorable moment, but if you say no, I'll have to try and sleep while I'm all frustrated and hot."

"Can't have that." He turned onto his back. "And what do I get out of this after I make you come?"

"I'll let you take me to see Jessup."

"My lifelong fantasy." He grumbled in disgust, but took her kiss and deepened it. She purred like she knew he liked, and rubbed her body against his.

"I want you," she whispered.

"I can tell," he returned with a bit of sass, then said, "I'll go if you agree that if you don't learn anything, you'll quit this mission of yours."

"You'll come with me? Oh Jack . . ." She flung herself across him, kissing him, gripping him.

"Promise me, Meg."

"Yes, yes, yes. Oh, I love you, love you."

And for the next forty-five minutes she showed him how much.

"What did he do to you?"

"Made me feel like a monster."

"That doesn't sound like Donnie," Bethany said. "He's so wimpy."

Meg was stirring pancake batter on Saturday morning. It was after nine with a weather prediction of a warm April day. She planned to take advantage of the sunshine and garden for a few hours. Later in the afternoon, she and Jack had plans to visit Jessup. To her, his agreement was a major concession and proof to Meg that once she got Jack involved in finding answers, his emotional miserliness would disappear. With unexpected irony, the debacle with Donnie had actually been a plus in that it focused her on Jessup and in turn pulled Jack in, too.

To Bethany, she said, "So you heard about our mall meeting? From Donnie?"

"Nah, the kids were talking about it. Some guys saw him with you. Donnie wasn't in school yesterday. He got into a fight."

"Not again. Was he hurt?" And this time there was no Caleb to side with him.

Bethany looked at her like she'd stumbled over the dumbest question of the week. "That's what happens in a fight. You need to get a clue, Mom."

"Well, excuse me for my extensive ignorance," she said,

spooning a bit of test batter onto the skillet. It sizzled, she scraped it off and poured four circles. "Let's try this. How well do you know him?"

She shrugged. "I see him in the hall and he goes to the basketball games. He tries to stay out of trouble. But it always seems to find him. Maybe he was scared you were going to raise a stink about him being with Caleb. He's pals with a couple of chemistry nerds." She grinned. "Maybe he's more than a pal."

"He and Caleb were friends, too. I don't think you'd make a double-meaning dig about the two of them."

"Caleb was my brother," she said hotly, which didn't really address the issue. Meg let it go. "Anyway, it's what you think when a guy is gay. You see him with another guy and you think—well, you know—they must be doing it. I mean why else would anyone want to hang around a fag?"

"That's a bit rough."

"It's what I think."

Since when? she wondered. "Friendship isn't reason enough to hang out?"

She shrugged.

"My roommate in college was a lesbian and she was a good friend. I trusted her as much as I trusted Kate." Meg flipped the pancakes, waited a few seconds and then slid them onto a plate and put them on the table. "She called from Paris when she heard from Kate about Caleb. She sent that huge arrangement of yellow and white roses for the funeral."

Bethany stared at her, mouth agape. The pancakes steamed. Meg placed butter and the pitcher of warm syrup beside Bethany's place. "Better eat while they're hot."

"You mean that friend that came a couple of summers ago for two weeks?"

"Riva Winchester. Yes."

"I didn't know she was—uh, well, that way."

"Hmmm, well, now you do."

"Wow. I really thought she was cool. She had all that

funky jewelry and that wicked tiger tattoo." She forked pancakes onto her plate, skimmed them with butter and syrup, cut a stacked triangle and ate.

"Donnie being friends with Caleb shouldn't be any more startling than my friendship with Riva." Meg thought her flow of logic quite reasoned, and waited for Bethany's equally reasoned answer.

She swallowed a second forkful before asking, "So, were you two lovers?"

Meg dropped the spatula. "Of course not."

"She never hit on you?"

"That's enough, young lady. I told you about Riva to illustrate a point about Donnie and Caleb."

She washed it down with her orange juice. "Then she did—move on you, I mean. Hey, no big deal," she said expansively. "It's not any different than a guy hitting on a girl he wants. The girl says cool or get a life. With two girls, I just think it's kind of weird, but well, it's not my thing. Bet Donnie found out quick it wasn't Caleb's either." She thought for a few seconds, then as if reaching a major conclusion, said, "I can buy that doin' it with Riva wasn't your thing if you say so."

Somewhere in her lexicon of responses to teenagers, she must have something that would apply here, but she drew a total blank. The daughter who just a month ago had been embarrassed by the explicitness of a sex education class was now pontificating an opinion on gay sex. And Jack thought Meg had changed in the past few weeks. It would appear a lot of things were changing.

Finally, Meg said, "Thank you for that vote of trust." She picked up the newspaper and put the sections back in order to give her hands something to do besides shake. Bethany pushed her plate away just as Meg sat down with her mug of coffee and the lifestyle section.

"Mom?"

Meg glanced up.

"I didn't mean to sound like a jerk. Donnie isn't so bad.

I kinda didn't think of him and Caleb being friends like I am with Erica. Donnie is sorta an outsider and most of us just left him that way."

"Except Caleb."

She sniffled and reached for a tissue. With her voice breaking, she said, "My brother was pretty cool, wasn't he?"

"None of us appreciated him as much as we should have."

"I wish . . ." she carefully dabbed at her black-outlined eyes, and Meg drew her close.

"I wish he was here, too, sweetheart."

And for a few minutes, Bethany leaned into her mother while Meg gathered close this more familiar daughter. Jack should see this, she thought. Shopping might appear to be mother-daughter closeness, but these moments of honesty held more value.

Bethany put her dishes in the dishwasher and Meg began to read an article on spring planting when the back door opened.

Kate breezed in wearing a cranberry suede coat and knee high leather boots and slung herself into one of the chairs. "Hey, beauties, what's new?"

Meg lifted her eyebrows at the sight. Perfectly made-up, perfectly tousled hair, perfectly toned body. A manhunt special if she ever saw one. No wonder Ford was intrigued. Bethany got her a mug and poured coffee. Kate took off her coat, revealing a black knit jumpsuit accented with a gold necklace as wide as a ruler.

"Aren't you kind of dressed up for a Saturday morning?"

"I have a date later."

"Ah."

Bethany stared in flattering awe. "You're so cool looking."

"Why thank you, chickie. You look gorgeous. How old are you now? Sixteen? Seventeen?"

Bethany straightened, drawing herself up as if to reach

one of those wondrous ages. "Almost. I'll be fifteen in December."

"Meg, remember when you were fifteen? You were crazy about that guy with the blue Trans Am? He used to zoom by the house every Sunday afternoon and you made sure you were home so you could wave to him."

"The Trans Am was black and waving to a guy in a car doesn't mean I was crazy about him." She rattled the newspaper to a new page and said to Bethany, "Your auntie loves to rewrite my past into some dreadful soap opera."

"The many secrets of sister Meg," Kate said dramatically, sounding like a television voice-over.

"Oh please."

"So what was his name?" Bethany asked, obviously intrigued by another peek into her mother's past. "Did you go out with him?"

Before Meg could answer, Kate added, "His name was Charlie and he unloaded boxes and crates over at Klein's Hardware. We knew that because his car was always parked by the side door and we saw it from the bus when we went to school. Sometimes we saw him, too. God, could he fill out a pair of Levi's."

"I never noticed," Meg said, wondering if it would do any good to kick Kate under the table.

"The truth was that she was too scared to go out with him. He was a hunky eighteen."

"The real truth is that Dad would have killed me."

"Were you scared? I mean about going out with him?"

"Certainly not. He wasn't my type and unlike Kate, getting in trouble was not my raison d'être."

Kate laughed. "Translated that means she couldn't have gotten away with it."

"Oh." Bethany sagged back in disappointment. "Gee, Mom, you never did anything. Didn't you get bored? Didn't you want to try stuff or do things that were exciting?"

"I did do things that were exciting. I just didn't think of rebellion and bad behavior as cool."

"But don't you ever wonder what could have happened with Charlie?"

Meg knew exactly what would have happened, which is why she only waved from her front yard. "I didn't really think about it," she said, daring Kate to argue with her. "Until Kate mentioned him, I'd forgotten him."

Kate's eyebrows slid up, but she didn't argue. "Your mom never gave your grandparents any grief or worry, which I know they appreciated because I was such a disaster."

Bethany shook her head. "No. You turned out great. You're rich and beautiful and guys think you're sexy." Bethany's adoration of her aunt's sophistication needed no translation. Meg felt very uncool.

"What better endorsement could an auntie want from her favorite niece?" Kate asked, grinning.

"She's your only niece."

"That's why she's my favorite." She looked Bethany over carefully. "I wish my hair had all those natural blond highlights. And your smooth skin. Is this fair or what? Thank God for Estée Lauder or I'd be as dried out as a bag of beans."

Meg rolled her eyes. Her sister's need for compliments and supportive accolades had reached the gag point.

On cue, Bethany said, "You'll always be pretty even when you're old."

Kate wrapped an arm around Bethany and tugged her close, whispering, "So when are we going shopping again? Summer is coming and you're going need some new shorts and a new bathing suit. I was thinking we'd go to Boston, poke around Newbury Street, pig out on Italian in the North End and hang out."

"Cool. I can go anytime."

"There's a small problem called school," Meg interjected, feeling like the cog in the fun wheel.

"She can miss a day."

"Uh, no, she can't."

"Ah, come on, Mom. One day is no big deal."

"Sorry."

Kate squeezed her hand. "We'll work it out."

"Spoilsport," she muttered to her mother before tossing her hair back and stomping out of the kitchen. She returned moments later wearing her jacket and a mouth coated with an inch of dark plum lipstick. A horn honked and Meg glanced out the window. A red truck crouched in the drive, its engine rumbling. She scowled, trying to recall if she'd seen it before. Nope. She hadn't. Bethany was at the back door when Meg asked, "Who is that?"

"It's not a date, Mom. A bunch of us are going to the baseball game and then over to the mall."

"That 'bunch' looks like one guy from here."

"He's picking the others up."

"He could come and knock on the door."

A heavy, dramatic sigh followed that comment. "Now you sound like Daddy. Geez, Mom, it's a ball game not an all night sleep-over."

Kate peered into the cream pitcher. "Is this cream?" At Meg's nod, she poured. "Your mom's afraid some boy is going to sweep you away before she's ready for you to go."

"You're a big help," Meg grumbled.

Kate wrinkled her nose. "Bethany keeps telling me how pretty I am. I have to make sure I stay on her good side."

"Oh Aunt Kate, I'm always on your side."

"There you are. And I haven't slipped her a twenty yet."

Meg rolled her eyes, feeling swamped and overruled.

The horn double-honked and Bethany hauled the door open. "I gotta go."

"When are you coming home?"

"Later. There's a party tonight and I have to get dressed."

"What party?" Meg was beginning to feel like the most uninformed mother in Cooper Falls. "You didn't mention any party."

"He's gonna leave without me. Ask Dad, he knows about it." And with that she was out the door. Meg watched as she ran to the truck and climbed in. The vehicle squealed out of the drive, leaving Meg feeling helpless and dumb for allowing her to go so easily. Kate sipped her coffee and glanced through the celebrity snippets in the newspaper.

"Want some pancakes?" Meg asked, thinking she'd rather stomp her feet, kick the wall and scream than fry batter for her "oh so pretty" problem-free sister.

"Thought you'd never ask." Kate pushed the paper aside. "Not that it's my business, but aren't you being a bit clutchy with her?"

"You're right," she said tightly. "It's not your business." Meg counted to three and decided the hell with it. "For all your defense of her, did you notice how she deftly deflected telling me the boy's name, a definite time she was coming home and used her father to skip explaining this sudden party? I'd bet my wedding ring Jack knows zippo about it."

Kate blinked, her mouth opening and then promptly closing.

"Furthermore, I'm well acquainted with the bob and wiggle routine. She's been either a suffering stranger or a pouty pain the past few weeks. Mostly I've ignored the rebellion, but it worries me. And a guy in a fancy red truck honking a horn like she was some easy piece of ass doesn't fill me with ease and confidence." She vigorously stirred the batter as if she were busting up cement, then clunked the griddle onto the burner. "And it ticks me off that every time I ask a question I'm paranoid, old-fashioned or out of touch with reality."

"Jesus, guess I struck a nerve."

She poured batter and grabbed up the spatula like she was going to hit a writhing snake. "I'm not supposed to ask questions *about* Caleb, and I'm not supposed to ask *any* questions of my daughter." The empty pancake pitcher landed in the sink with a thud, followed by utensils and a yank on the coffee plug. She swung around to Kate. "And you're not helping by talking to her like she was a grown-up when she's mostly a foxy kid with a flippy attitude."

Kate held up her hands. "Okay, okay. I'll treat her like she's a mush skull."

"She *is* a mush skull, like every other fourteen-year-old. She wants to be older, thinks she's smarter and is convinced she's got life by the tail. I'm supposed to be understanding and patient and sensitive—well, hell, you know what? Screw sensitive." She bore down on the pancakes. Flip. Splat. Sizzle. Then she slid the three onto the spatula and plopped them on a plate. "And dammit, I hate dancing around and wringing my hands and trying not to disturb her self-esteem when I want to shake some sense into her like Mom did to you and me. And for godsakes, I don't want to lose her to some horny goof in a red truck."

Kate stared at her, a grin working its way to a full smile. "Hey, I'm with you. God help her from horny goofs."

"Amen." She handed Kate her plate of pancakes.

"Thanks. For what it's worth—I know, you don't want my opinion, but I'm going to give it anyway." She buttered, poured syrup and cut into the stack. "Here's the way I see it. Bethany's okay as in teenage normal—if there is such an animal. Beyond the cosmetic counter look and the discipline-challenged agenda of wanting to be and act older, nothing she did seemed too weird."

"Maybe not, but this isn't the Bethany of a month ago. It's unsettling to watch and scary to think about. Caleb being the oldest allowed her to be the baby even after she wasn't. She was defended and protected by her brother and able to watch what he did to get some idea what she would be able to do. Now, it seems as if she's drifting like the forgotten member of some washed-up rock band. She's lost and trying desperately to pretend she isn't." Meg pushed her hands through her hair. "So I'm worried and trying not to act worried or God forbid, come off like some 'clutchy' mother—to use your word. In addition, I'm frustrated by not finding anything out about Caleb."

"Jack still keeping his distance?"

She nodded. "I know he's dealing with this in his own way, and I respect that, but I'd like to discuss things and he just doesn't want to hear it. He is going with me to see Jessup, but with all the enthusiasm of an appointment for a root canal." She refilled her mug, and Kate's, then sat down. "I'm tired of getting nowhere, so I'm going to try a new direction. I'm going to call Vicki Slocum this morning and invite her to lunch."

"The babe with the DKNY wardrobe?" Kate poured more syrup. "Why?"

"She knew Caleb, she likes to talk about him and I like to hear things about him. In that arena, she may reveal some pieces of his life that I haven't considered or that she didn't see as important."

"More than likely she was too busy trying to catch Jack's eye to pay any attention to what Caleb was doing."

"You noticed that, too, huh?" Meg commented, thinking of Vicki's soft, worshipful looks at Jack the day of the funeral.

"At her age she hasn't learned the fine art of subtlety. I thought it was kind of a cute hero worship. But just the same, I wouldn't trust her. These breathless adoring types like the pert-breasted airhead who's keeping Porter's shorts in a tent look innocent, but mostly they want men who can afford to buy them airline tickets and jewelry. Your Vicki might be sizing up Jack as the wallet in her life."

"Jack isn't that stupid."

"All men are stupid some of the time."

"Just the same, he doesn't like being alone with her. He's probably already got her figured out." She told Kate about his reluctance to get the snow thrower.

"Hey, he's a smart guy. What can I say? Where is he, by the way?"

"Meeting his brother for chourico and eggs over at Jingle's."

"So that's where he went."

"Uh huh. That's where *Ford* went, too."

Kate stared at her. "You know?"

"I do. Sloane told me."

"Shit. I wanted to tell you."

"You can tell me how serious you are about him."

She pushed her partially eaten breakfast aside, leaned back and took a cigarette from her purse. "Yes," she said wearily, "I suppose I could do that."

Chapter Eleven

For the nighttime crowd, Jingles had a reputation for being low-down, bluesy and raw, but on Saturday mornings, the first-floor eatery welcomed the swarm of Cooper Falls enthusiasts looking for a hearty breakfast before weekend chores or an outdoor sporting event. Stale crushed Marlboros had been swept out the door and the beer and sweat of Friday night had been overwhelmed by bacon, hot sausage and the best coffee in Rhode Island.

Seth Eidson was eating waffles and talking with two uniformed officers waiting for take-out. Sixty-seven-year-old Samuel Norbert, the DeWildes' attorney, sat with his granddaughter at a table by a window that framed the Strand, the only movie theater in town. The minister who had spoken at Caleb's funeral straddled a stool at the counter. Wearing an open-necked shirt and a plaid sweater, he ate eggs and home fries while he read the *Boston Herald*. Three waitresses worked the tables and booths while Jingles and his wife, Belle, did the cooking.

A short, chunky waitress with braided blond hair coiled into a slightly frazzled figure-eight and a smile lurking around her eyes, wove in and out of the crowded tables to set her tray down beside booth number four where two men sat drinking from thick white mugs.

She placed the plate of scrambled eggs, fried potatoes and chourico in front of the lighter-haired man. Then she added another plate with the same order in front of the dark-haired man. She added a platter of stacked and buttered toast, barrel-shaped glasses of orange juice and topped off their coffee mugs.

"Can I get you anything else."

"We're all set." Jack glanced up from the sports section of the *Providence Journal.* "Thanks— Ma?" He blinked and blinked again when he saw the crisp apron and the name tag saying Hazel. "You're working here? Since when? Why didn't I know? Ford? You knew about this?"

"She wanted to surprise you."

"It worked. When did all this happen?"

"About a week ago." Pride oozed from her. Jack couldn't believe over a week had passed since he'd spoken with her. He'd planned to call on Tuesday, but a hellish week of mixed-up sales agreements, a mortgage loan that fell through at the last minute, tedious calls and conversation with Bud Aldrich at Ocean State Travel, plus a minor break-in and vandalism at the Newport office, had tied his mind in knots. He'd forgotten all about phoning her.

"Belle asked me if I would fill in last week." Belle belonged to AA and she had met Hazel during one of her attempts at sobriety. Jack noted now that her eyes had lost the waxy vacancy that he could spot in an instant when she'd been drinking. Nor did her hands fidget.

"I did good, Jackie," she said softly, looking at him with a steady gaze that in the past had promised she'd stay away from the bottle, but now asked only for another chance. "I didn't mess up any orders and I got some good tips. Belle says I can stay on and that Jingles likes that I don't whine about my feet hurting."

Jack slid from the booth and hugged her as hard as he had as a kid when he still believed in spoken promises and unspoken hope. "I'm glad, Ma, real glad."

"I want you to be proud of me, Jackie," she mumbled

against his shirt, her voice halting. "I want to do good. After Caleb, I started thinking you and Ford don't need no more bad endings."

"I'm for that." Jack kissed her cheek, gripped by a flood of warmth for this woman who'd always wanted her family to be like Ozzie and Harriet. In the early years she'd had fringes of success when Reilly hauled in the big catches and per-pound prices brought hearty profits for the crew of the *Lucky Louise*. Then the market turned sour, the government made that worse when it imposed restrictions within the three-mile limit, forcing the fishermen to take their boats out farther for the same catch. Profits got eaten by expenses and Reilly never caught up enough to recover when his boat sank in the Atlantic nor'easter. Jack's own rebellion, his mother working when Reilly wasn't and wouldn't, Ford doing coke, the old man's boozing, her drinking . . .

Jack had struggled to support them, doing the oldest son's duty amidst a seething anger at his careless and self-indulgent father who he blamed for most of the problems.

Now here, serving a three-dollar breakfast just weeks after her grandson's suicide, his mother had her life as orderly and neat as a freshly set Harriet Nelson table. He was too used to the good times backing into disasters to be too optimistic, but this change looked more storm free than most.

Ford smiled as if the Harriet Nelson-and-two-boys scene worked despite the absence of Ozzie. Hazel fumbled for a tissue in her pocket.

"You two best eat before Jingles's food gets cold."

"Good idea," Jack said, feeling awkward.

Hazel went away to take another order. Jack forked his eggs, then dunked a toast corner into his coffee. Ford, too, ate silently.

After their plates were half emptied, Ford wiped his mouth, sipped his coffee and said, "You really were surprised, weren't you?"

"I still am. She hasn't worked since the early seventies."

"She doesn't have this booth, but she and Patsy switched after she took the order. Ma wanted you to see that she really was steady enough to carry a tray of hot food."

Jack watched his mother work a couple of the tables, reap a few laughs and from a third table, she pocketed what appeared to Jack to be a hefty tip.

Shaking his head in continual amazement, Jack returned to his breakfast. "Caleb's death seems to have rattled some old habits."

"Ma took it hard."

"So did I," Jack said grimly. He pushed his plate aside. "How about you? Haven't seen you much. You okay?"

"I haven't shot up if that was your question."

"Good. You clean and Ma sober, Christ, this is a joyous day." He leaned across the table and gave his brother's cheek a pat. "I'm serious, kid. You all right?"

"I got something I need to talk to you about."

"The thing you didn't want to mess up?"　　　　·

"Yeah."

"Go."

"I'm thinking about going up to Boston."

"Okay."

"I know I could work off one of the boats down in Galilee, and Sharkie offered me a place on his trawler, but I'm kinda tired of fishing and I'd like to do something else."

"Like what?"

"Boat building." Ford and Jack had worked together rebuilding an old lobster boat for Reilly to replace the *Lucky Louise*. After his death, Jack sold it and used the cash to buy his mother a car.

Jack thought for a moment. "Sounds promising, but why Boston? There's a boat-building industry right here in Rhode Island."

"There's another reason."

"There always is."

Ford took out a pack of cigarettes and offered one to Jack. They both lit up, leaned back while Hazel hurried over and cleared the dishes. After she refilled their mugs, she stood back and looked at her two sons like she couldn't quite believe they were hers.

Ford smirked. "You suppose she's gonna expect us to tip her?"

"You mean she isn't waiting on us for free because we're her sons?"

"Don't think so."

"Bummer. So much for being blood-related."

Hazel looked from one to the other, her smile bigger than Jack had seen in years. "You boys stop your teasing. You're gonna make me cry." She turned to leave, and Jack saw a flash of the strong-willed mother of his childhood whose stony-eyed looks could curdle milk. Once she'd marched him to the corner grocery and ordered him to confess and make restitution for the girlie magazines he and some pals stole when old Henry wasn't looking. The other guys caught the CRS disease. Jack bellowed about the unfairness, but his mother had been as rigid as the starch in her dresses. Now, she squinted at Ford and Jack laying down the law they'd better not break. "I still want a big tip."

Jack teased, "We might drop a couple of dimes."

"Just you make sure there are bills holding them up."

Jack shook his head, still awed by this abrupt and positive direction. She made her way to another table to do refills. "What a difference a boy's death can make."

"Proves what the preacher said at the funeral about the ripples of a life going on and on forever."

"The sterling influences of a worthy man," Jack murmured, feeling the deep tug of grief and awe that his son had brought about bigger changes in death than most men did in life.

Ford turned his mug around and around, stalling and starting and stalling again.

"You're on," Jack said, changing the subject. "Whatever it is, it can't be that hard to tell me."

"I don't know how you'll take it."

"I don't either until you spill it."

"This is so weird for me and I want it all to work."

"Ford, wanting it to work is the second half of the anxiety. Let's have the first half."

He leaned back, blew out a breath and tapped his table knife against his mug. "I want to go to Boston because I want to be with Kate." He glanced quickly at Jack for reaction, but got none. He went on. "We've been seeing each other steady since the funeral, and well, I think I'm serious about her. Since she works there, I'd like to be closer so we could see each other more often." He exchanged the knife for a spoon, hunching forward as if protecting himself in case Jack grabbed him by the shirt.

Jack lifted his mug, took a careful swallow of the hot brew and eased it down beside the folded newspaper. A burst of laughter came from the counter area where Jingles was telling one of his famous blond jokes. Jack turned his attention back to Ford. "You're involved with Meg's sister. I presume this is sex and not a reassessment of your portfolio."

"You mean I shouldn't have asked whether to sell my ten thousand shares of Microsoft or the fifty thousand shares of General Motors? Don't be a smart-ass, okay? And it's a lot more than sex."

"A lot more of what?"

"Like we get along good, she likes beer and we both like to dance. Neither of us wants kids. That's a big agreement, isn't it?" He gestured vaguely. "We're still gettin' to know each other. Jesus, it's only been a few weeks. It's a good reason why I should go to Boston. I mean, how do you get to know someone when she's clear up there and I'm clear down here?"

"Sounds like you've already decided. So what are you asking of me?"

"What you think."

Jack brushed his thumb around the handle of his mug, pressing his lips together in thoughtful contemplation. Finally in a friendly tone, he said, "I want to say this in a way so that there's no misunderstanding. Meg tells me I'm behind the curve on the softer, more sensitive strides that men have been making in conversation tactics in recent years. I want to give this my best shot. Ah, I think I have the right words." He looked at Ford. "Are you out of your fucking mind?"

Ford's beginning grin collapsed, and his mouth turned down. "I never should have told you. I should have just done it."

"You've already *done* it, the trick now is quitting."

"She's not a bad habit, and why the hell are you rakin' me out? You never did when there were other women."

"The other women weren't Kate. Not even close. Get real here. Kate isn't some dock floozy who's looking to ease you through some drug haze while she's cuddling with your cock on a cold night." His hard-ass analysis took the familiar track of past talks with Ford. Here's the truth, pal, you don't have to like it, but it's in your face and you gotta deal with it.

Ford looked as if he was measuring the outcome of punching his brother in the mouth. "Don't you think I know that? Cut me some friggin' slack, will ya? That's why she's different, why I'm different with her. Why I feel different."

"No slack, kid. That you feel different is only touchy, fuzzy cloud cover between your fantasies of life and reality." Jack leaned forward. "Look, I don't want to see your heart diced and fried, okay? I like Kate, personally. She's easy to talk to. She's fun at a party, she generous and mostly loyal. She could make most men forget they swore off hot chicks when they hit thirty, but she's not a woman an out-of-work fisherman can afford to keep in designer water, never mind getting serious about. I mean can you imagine her in here?" Jack's gaze swept the restaurant. "To Kate, these kind of places should be closed with 'condemned by the health department' signs on their doors. You, like the guys Jingles is over there ribbing, would vote to make the joint a national shrine. You see that difference, I know you do, and that's just for starters."

Ford's eyes flashed. He got to his feet, body tight, mouth grimly set.

"Come on, kid, sit down. You think I like pissing you off?" Jack crushed out his barely smoked cigarette. "Look, I'm being straight with you. Don't make this complicated. Sleep with her when she's here, but don't follow her to Boston."

Ford stared off into the distance, then flattened both hands on the table and slowly sat back down. In a bitter tone, he said, "You've got a helluva lot of nerve, you know that? You've got your life all neat and stacked like a new poker deck. I'm the one with lousy cards and I find one person I want, ask you for nothing more than 'fine with me and good luck' and what do I get? You exploding like I'd OD'd on smack."

"You asked my opinion not my blessing," Jack said, unmoved. "You know they never come with good tasting guarantees." He'd been over this "new life with a new woman" map before; each one, his brother later admitted, had cuddled up for a meal ticket or a weekend boyfriend. Jack would have been cheerfully calm if this new love had been a dock floozy. Ford had written the book in that arena, and within a few weeks, the freshness would have soured and he'd have forgotten why he ever got involved. But Kate?

Jack shuddered. His sister-in-law was high-strung, ditzy and probably looking to rejuvenate her ego after the wandering Porter Delacourt. What better pick-me-up than a carnal digression with a nice younger guy like Ford. That Kate was serious about his brother as in lifetime and forever didn't pass the sanity test. And in the end, Ford would be crapped on and Jack would be the one to haul the pieces of his brother out of another depression or drug binge.

After the long silence, Ford finally said, "I shouldn't have told you."

"You thought you'd keep it a secret? You know better. This is Cooper Falls, home of Claire the phoning wizard. A third of the town already knows."

"And doesn't give a damn."

"True. But I do, because I love you. You knew telling me wasn't mushroom time where I kept you in the dark and fed you shit. I know it tastes like it, but you'll chew it and digest it and in a few months . . ." Jack grinned a little, showing his confidence in his brother's eventual agreement. "Then there's this. You knew I wasn't going to blow this off with a sappy congratulations followed by how do you think the Red Sox will do this year?"

"Lousy, and I don't wanna make any side bets." Then like a drowning man not ready to sink for the final time, he said, "This can work with Kate."

"It can't and it won't, Ford." Jack looked at him, his eyes softening. "More than anything, I want you to be happy, but a longtime happy with a woman who can do more than make you hard."

"It ain't a bad place to start."

"It's not enough . . . it's not nearly enough."

Ford and Jack held each other's gaze for more than ten seconds. Ford slid once again from the booth. He said he was going to the men's room and walked away, leaving Jack pondering the ramifications of telling the truth. It rarely got a thank-you, mostly riled up the defenses and didn't even allow for a later "I told you so" without Jack feeling like it was his fault his brother screwed up.

Truth, he concluded was a helluva burden. And what he'd just waded through was a puddle compared to the deep dark well he faced in confessing to Meg about Vicki. The huge difference was that with Ford, Jack knew he was right on the substance. About Vicki, he had only messy, embarrassing excuses.

As of a few days ago, Vicki was booked for her week-long vacation in the Islands. He'd made sure Bud had included lots of extras plus got her into a villa where the under-thirty crowd partied. She'd told Jack how she was shopping for clothes, doing the tanning salon routine and not once had any gestures, intimate or flirtatious, passed between them.

He prayed she was already resigned to the pointlessness of wanting him. A Caribbean trip and his total disinterest in a relationship with her had apparently worked. Now if he could just find some courage under his own guilty betrayal of Meg . . .

Ford returned after a few minutes, added more to the tip Jack had left and caught up with his brother at the counter talking to Seth Eidson.

"Seth, how're you doing?" The two men shook hands.

Eidson said, "Mazie sure appreciated those lobsters you brought to her." He winked. "I did too—great eating. I made a pig of myself."

"Anytime. Jack, I gotta split. Next time it's on me."

"You got it."

Ford ambled out.

"Good guy, your brother. Last week, Mazie had driven to Newport to get some fresh fish and ran into Ford near one of the docks. He remembered she'd once told him how much she loved lobster. Ford appeared at the door the following day with two three-pounders. Wouldn't let her pay him, just said he wanted her to have them."

Jack nodded. "That's my brother."

"He's really got his life straightened out. You gotta be proud of him."

"I am." And Jack resolved right that minute to call Ford and tell him so. His brother had guts and potential and kindness. Jack had never had a lot of time for kindness; mostly he left that up to Meg who like Ford walked with it spontaneously.

"So how are things with you and your family?" Eidson asked.

"Meg is still determined to find out why it happened."

"Mothers are stubborn."

The two men walked out of the restaurant, with Jack fishing his keys out and heading for his Lexus. Eidson didn't move on.

Jack looked at him. "You're like a persistent dog who doesn't know what he wants to hunt."

Eidson dug his hands deeper in his slashed jacket pockets. "I think about you, Jack. About you and your son and your family."

"Probably because unexplained teenage suicides are a rarity. Thank God."

"More than that. I liked what I knew about Caleb. Mazie and I can't have kids so I sorta like to hang out at the ball field, or cruise through the malls to see what kind of action the kids are into."

"Had you ever met Caleb?"

"Not personally. Watched him pitch a few times, though. Saw him give some pointers to a freshman whose slider wouldn't slide. He didn't have a fat head or a sarcastic mouth. Guess what I'm saying is what you and your wife are thinking. Why would he do such a thing?" He held up his hand when Jack started to protest that he didn't want to discuss it. "I know what you're going to say, but Caleb wasn't the reason I wanted to talk to you anyway."

Jack folded his arms and leaned against the Lexus, his eyes squinting against the late morning sun. Meg would be gardening and tonight he'd take great pleasure in rubbing the kinks out of her wintered muscles. He needed to buy some Ben-gay and maybe some of that Mudslide mixture she liked. The coming evening held a bundle of anticipation.

". . . a little while ago."

"I'm sorry, what did you say?"

"I saw your daughter a little while ago."

"Oh?"

"She was with Brandt Foley."

"Sorry, the name doesn't sound familiar."

"You've never met him?"

Jack shook his head. "Bethany has a lot of friends. I don't know all of them."

"This one has had some trouble."

Jack straightened, his meandering mind immediately focused. "What kind of trouble?" Eidson related the incident at school when Foley was drunk and was threatening to kill all the fags.

"Your son got into a fight with Foley a few months back when he went after one of Caleb's friends."

"Donnie Paquin."

"I think that was his name. Foley hasn't been in any trouble since then, but when I saw him with your daughter—well, to be honest, Jack, I like you and Meg and figured you've had enough pain to last a lifetime. I'm guessing your daughter is a nice young woman. I wouldn't want to see her messed up."

Jack's heart plummeted at the thought. "Where did you see her?"

"Over at the ball game."

Jack unlocked his car, but before sliding in, he asked, "Do you usually take this kind of interest when you don't have to?"

"Sometimes. I know this. No family deserves to be plunged into this kind of unexplained tragedy."

Jack extended his hand. "Thanks a lot."

"Sure. And if you ever want to talk, my door is always open."

Jack started the engine and drove away, glancing in the

rearview mirror. Eidson stood there, hands jammed in his pockets, watching him. Jack looked again before he took a left turn, but Eidson was gone.

Now why would Seth think Jack wanted to talk? About what?

Maybe he was a frustrated shrink and figured him for a head case. Nah. Eidson was too canny, too aware of what he was doing and why. Jack didn't doubt his sincerity, and for sure he appreciated the heads-up on Bethany, but the only one Jack needed to bare his soul to was Meg. And he would. Soon.

Chapter Twelve

He'd been wonderin' when she'd show up.

Louis Jessup watched through the window as Ray Hadley's youngest climbed out of the green SUV. Wearing a suede jacket over a brown sweater and jeans that hugged witch boots, she picked her way around his mud-caked pickup and through the chopped wood he'd been carefully stacking after he found the nest of baby rabbits.

He rubbed his hands down the sides of his overalls, his eyes darting around the crowded cabin, paying little regard to the pile of pine boards destined for some future project. He built furniture sporadically and sold it reluctantly. Dealing with strangers gave him hives. He peered behind a sagging cardboard box of rags looking for the two raccoons who had been eating lunch. When he didn't see them, he quickly moved the stack of *National Geographic*s from the guest chair. The Windsor had been crafted by his brother, Billy, and Jessup made sure it stayed polished and clean in his honor.

The door squeaked when he opened it before she'd climbed the cement block steps. He'd seen her from a distance at the funeral; he hadn't ventured close enough to whisper his pain for her and the boy. He didn't fit with the grieving folk and when DeWilde spotted him, Jessup felt

the thunder rumble in his bones. The two men rarely
spoke, never mind tryin' to exchange mutual sadness. The
boy's friendship with him would have brought on ran-
corous sniping or cold, tense silence.

Jessup figured DeWilde was wishin' he'd been a better
father, and Jessup sure wouldn't have taken too many
breaths before agreeing.

The daughter that Ray had doted on looked at him now
and her mouth began to tremble, scaring him. He'd cried
when he found the boy, eyes swimming so thick that he
could hardly see to cut him down. After the funeral, he'd
rolled a few scores of Kona gold, opened a new quart of
rum and fuzzed himself into a mellow three-day haze.

"Now, Meggie . . ."

"Oh, Jessup." And she was in his arms crying, and shaking and sobbing so hard he had to concentrate on staying
upright. He eased his arms around her and patted like she
was delicate porcelain. She was having none of his unease;
she burrowed in as she had when he'd come when her
father died. Jessup could save baby bunnies and pull a
buddy out of danger from a buried land mine, but sobbing
women left him all confused and awkward.

She pulled away, taking a tissue from her pocket, dabbing at her eyes. "I'm sorry. I've been doing really well,
but seeing you and knowing how much Caleb loved to
come here—it just all came back."

"He was like you. Too soft and too caring for a kid." He
closed the door and waved in the direction of the Windsor,
then put a dented teakettle onto the old hot plate. She took
off her jacket and sat down, not quite relaxing, fiddling
with the tissue. The woodstove crackled, its heat warming
the chill of the spring afternoon. "I figured he'd toughen
like Ray," Jessup said. "Fucky world for a kid to grow up
in if he isn't tough. You want tea or coffee?"

"Tea. His father is tough and so is his sister. Caleb was
more like me."

"You're tougher than the lot of them."

She smiled. "You sound like Dad."

"Nope. Nobody could sound like Ray." He took tea bags from a round brass bowl that he and Ray had stolen from the hardware store and used for target practice when they were kids. "Nobody could be like Ray either." He paused. " 'Cept maybe the boy when he wasn't lost and searchin' like that day a couple winters ago that I found him."

"I remember. He told me about it," Meg said.

"Did he now," Jessup murmured, knowing the boy shrank the story to satisfy his mother so he wouldn't have to say Jessup found him blubberin' like a girl. He had shown the boy the trail out of Sawyer's Woods, but instead of seeing a kid who got lost, he saw a lost kid; Ray Hadley's grandson battling to grow up without Ray's wisdom.

Jessup took that struggle upon himself to honor Ray, if the boy was willing. At first he'd been like a lonesome and grateful puppy, eager and shivering. He'd lapped up the stories of loyalty and friendship and keeping promises and not being a sellout. Jessup told of honor and trustworthiness that had taken him and Ray through high school, jobs with a local utility, Ray's marriage to Lorraine and the birth of two daughters. They stuck together through Jessup's stillborn son and his divorce and they'd had easy times like when they played Saturday night poker in the back of George Mendonca's garage. Their forged friendship took them to Vietnam along with Billy, Mendonca, Calvin Wells, a shoe salesman, and Tukie Slidger, the son of Jingles and Belle.

Jessup told Caleb of the war, of the terror, the sacrilege, of a jumbo of wanton deaths; of soldiers lost but alive, buddies alive but lost. Then finally, Ray and Jessup returned. Their poker pals, including his kid brother, Billy, came home in flag-draped coffins.

"Dad thought so much of you, Lou."

"Yeah." Jessup honked into a handkerchief, shoving it back into his pocket. *Ray, wish I could've saved your grandson.*

He set out a white mug and a chip-free cup and saucer. Clearing his throat, he said, "So you came for what?"

"Not details about the hanging. About Caleb."

"Hard to separate the two now."

He heard her breath catch and figured she'd married the two despite not wanting to.

"I don't know what happened or why."

Jessup shrugged. "What's to know? You expectin' some sign or a surprise witness comin' out to tell all like in the movies?" His bluntness neither endeared nor infuriated.

The flash in her eyes revealed exasperation. "I just want some pieces that make sense. I need to know, Lou! I—oh, God, why is this so hard for everyone to understand? I can't just accept this wasn't preventable. I'm his mother, I should have known he was sad or depressed or despondent. I saw him angry and stubborn but never in a million possibilities did I think he would kill himself." She paused, studying her lap. "I haven't told Jack, but I spoke with a suicide-prevention counselor."

Jessup remained bland; he'd had a belly full of such useless canned chatter after the war. Nothin' but talky advice-presenting broads who flung around buzzwords like they were fallen leaves from an October tree.

"She said my guilt and questions were common because suicide is usually sudden and mysterious and there are always unresolved issues. She said Caleb probably had problems that should have been handled by counseling— maybe a psychiatrist. I didn't care too much for that. She made it sound like we should have known something was wrong and we were neglectful because we didn't."

"The boy didn't need no shrink."

"She asked me about any signs such as previous suicide attempts, drug or alcohol abuse and conduct disorder. It all sounded professional and sterile like one of those lists in magazines. Read the list, attach a troublesome behavior and there's the answer."

Jessup folded his hands, pleased she wasn't convinced.

"She asked if there was a family history of suicidal behavior, if either Jack or I had a history of depression or substance abuse, if Caleb's life was stressed because of personal difficulties or overly harsh discipline. *Overly harsh discipline!* Like what? I asked her. Those smacks on his bottom when he was four? She looked aghast, and the more she talked, the more I began to wonder if our family was dysfunctional. If you're a good family the secrets are buried under the guilt; if you're a messed-up family, well, then the secrets are known and you're still guilty. I did tell her of Jack's father's depression and Hazel's drinking."

"Every family has someone who drinks, and if I heard right, Reilly DeWilde had good reason to be depressed. He lost his manhood and his pride when the boat sank."

"And Jack has worked since then trying to keep his family from falling apart. Maybe we were so concerned about them that we lost sight of Caleb. Then there was the trashing of the cottage. That, the counselor said, could be conduct disorder."

"In my day they called it delinquency and mischief, and you got punished and that was the end of it. It wasn't somethin' that dogged your life like losin' a leg in the war."

Meg propped her elbows on the chair's forearms. "You know, you're right. Jack dealt with Caleb, and he was satisfied it was an aberration and not a pattern of vandalism. If Caleb were alive, it would be a forgotten issue."

Jessup waited to see if she wanted to say anything more. When she simply looked at him, he said, "Okay, here's the way I see it. The boy got into something and couldn't get out. Trouble? Maybe. Pain for sure, but something he couldn't talk about or make go away by coming to you or me or his old man." He rose and poured more hot water into his mug. "Guy I knew in 'Nam, he came home with one good leg and one sawed-off stump. Wanted no part of a false leg—that stump was his proof he was in the war. Got real good movin' around. Even did a funny dance, smackin' that leg as he rocked. Pretty good attitude, too, 'cept sometimes when he got drunk. Then a year later he went to prison for murder. Swore he didn't do it, but wouldn't say why he had the knife and how the guy's blood got in the trunk of his car. For sure he was hidin' somethin' or protectin' someone. Anyway, when he figured out he wasn't ever gonna be free, he hanged himself in his cell. Lots of guys in prison die using their clothes as weapons. That's what came to me when I found Caleb. This boy died like they do in prison."

Jessup settled back in the brown tattered La-Z-Boy rocker, careful of his full hot mug. He liked tea in the afternoon; it gave him peaceful thoughts of when Caleb came to visit. Watching him craft the boat, gluing the wooden pieces, inspecting his work with a critical eye and bringing it to Jessup for the final okay.

He waited for her to talk, but instead she held her cup suspended between the saucer and her mouth. Her cheeks were bleached dry like petrified wood. "What are you telling me? That Caleb did something horrible and that's why he killed himself?" The tea spilled and she set the cup in the saucer. Jessup handed her a clean rag from the box. She dabbed at the spot on her jeans. "That's just not possible. Caleb wasn't capable of doing anything horrible. He was a good boy."

"I didn't say he wasn't good. He had troubles."

She sat silent, her fingers pressing on the damp spot of denim. Jessup waited, rocking and sipping.

"Tell me," she whispered.

"The boy was in some kind of prison. Either in his mind or by his own design. He didn't plan to kill himself when he got out of bed that morning or he would have made preparations. He wasn't impulsive—he planned and then acted. Something he didn't expect blew up inside of him and this was his way out."

"Way out of what? He had a good home, parents that loved him, a sister who believed he was a hero. He worked, loved baseball and had a lot of friends. What could possi-

bly—I want a reason, Lou, something I can understand."
She told him her thoughts on Caleb being gay.

Jessup shook his head. "Caleb and me, we talked about
what made him horny and it wasn't boys."

"Now you sound like Jack."

"Lord help me," he muttered under his breath.

"He's having a hard time," she said, shifting the subject
so suddenly that he guessed new worry about DeWilde
threatened to swamp old worry about Caleb. "I'm trying to
understand but sometimes—" She lifted the cup, then put it
in the saucer without sipping. "Oh Lou, I need him with
me, not throwing up walls between us. He had a terrible
relationship with his father and I think he's afraid to learn
what happened with Caleb for fear it was his fault."

Jessup remained silent, then said softly, "And you want
to know what happened in case it was your fault. And then
what? After these answers are found. If it was DeWilde's,
you gonna forgive? If it was yours, will you then believe
you couldn't have stopped it? Or will you beat yourself
more because you should have?"

"I don't know. I guess it depends on what the answer is."

"An answer you'll never know for sure if it's the right
one. In the end you won't never be satisfied. Only Caleb
has the truth—"

"He didn't leave a note, he didn't say anything to his
friends, to you . . ."

He shrugged. "Maybe to him the truth was cruel, maybe
the truth hurt him so bad he couldn't find a way to make it
okay. Like my friend who hanged himself in prison. We
don't know if he was a murderer. And if he wasn't, why he
wouldn't say who was."

Dispirited, she sank back in the chair, crossing her legs
and turned toward the window where a pair of jays snarled
over a favorite maple branch.

Jessup offered more. "The boy felt things in a heavy
way, felt them whip his guts. Like he was pretty freaked
when his pal Kevin got killed. Punched me with questions.

Wanted to know why God let him die, and why all the things that Kevin tried to fix—getting his dad to move back home and give up his girlfriend so his mother would quit crying all the time . . . Your boy wanted to know why all of those got fixed after Kevin died."

"What did you tell him?"

"That dying changes trying to doing, effort to action."

She looked thoughtful. "His death has changed our family."

"Yep. Never gonna be the same again." He watched her and if he could have performed miracles for Ray's daughter, well, he would have done a full basket.

"Caleb was going to talk to someone the day he died. I was hoping it might have been you."

"Nope, wasn't me."

"You found him . . ."

"I took him down, tried to make him breathe . . . I tried everything I knew to try."

"I know you did." She reached for that tissue again, pushing it into eyes. Taking a breath and then another one, "When you last saw him—"

"Two days before. He came to tell me he wasn't going to any big deal college no matter what his old man said. We talked about baseball and his chances for the majors and I told him he should get educated, too. Sure couldn't hurt. Seemed reasonable to me, but he was having none of it—accused me of siding with his dad. He said his girlfriend would understand."

Meg's eyes widened and he noted she tried valiantly to hide her surprise. "Did he mention her name?"

"Nope."

"You never asked?"

"Figured he'd tell me if he wanted me to know."

"Weren't you curious?"

"About a sixteen-year-old with a girl? That would be like being curious about why the sun comes up. It's just the way things are."

"Had he ever mentioned a girlfriend before?"

"Can't say if I remember."

She sagged like a rag doll missing her stuffing. "I feel as if I'm spinning in circles. Nothing but vague answers." She bent down to lift her purse from the floor, staring to her right and then slowly straightening. "Lou?"

"Yep."

"Did I just see two raccoons crawl under your bed?"

"Really?" He leaned forward, relieved the critters were okay. "Glad you spotted them. They're suppose to sleep over here behind the box."

She reached for her jacket, keeping a close eye on his bed. "Are they friendly?"

"Now, Meggie, would I be letting dangerous things come in here?"

"Probably."

He grinned. "Want to pet them?"

"I don't think so."

He grinned even wider, whistling lightly and the furry, black-ringed eyed animals scurried toward him. Shy, they tucked themselves close to the cardboard box. He reached down and drew his large hand down the back of the one closest to him. Meg didn't move. Then, like her son, she was too saturated with curiosity to stay away. She took a step and knelt down.

"Put your hand out palm up." She did so and Jessup put a piece of bread in it. The raccoon waddled forward, then reached out a long-clawed paw and lifted the bread as if her hand was a delicate feather. The procedure was repeated with the other one. "Found them when they were babies last October. They miss Caleb. He brought them those trick-or-treat Snickers bars."

"He loved Snickers," she murmured.

He rose to his feet when she stood. "I have something for you." He went to a cupboard and took out a brown paper bag. "Caleb made this."

Meg looked in the bag, her eyes wide and then moist.

She took out the wooden boat. It was the size of a large tissue box and not quite finished, but on the side in hand-painted blue letters were the words *Lucky Louise*.

"It was to honor the grandfather he never knew."

Meg's sob broke his heart. "Oh, Lou, this was my Caleb. This was the son I knew."

"You need to rest in that—the other stuff just makes pain."

She touched the wood at the starboard, she fingered the wheelhouse, she pressed her fingers on the name. "Sometimes I think I miss him more than I loved him. I just keep thinking of all the what ifs, the if onlys and the whys. Then a part of me is afraid to know—it's all such a jumbled mess in my mind." She slipped the boat back into the bag. "Can I have this?"

He nodded and a few minutes later he watched her back her SUV out of his yard. The taillights disappeared down the rutted road. Then he closed the door and looked at the two raccoons.

"It's good I didn't tell her about the journal. The boat made her happy. She needs to be happy again."

"I didn't know you'd be here."

"Hey cupcake, I wondered when you were coming over to say hello."

Bethany grinned, puffing from her dash across the ball field, eyes sparkling like the spring day despite the garish makeup. Her smile refreshed him with memory-making moments of how proud he'd always been of her and Caleb. "Quite a game. Cooper Falls really pulled out a win with that ninth-inning homer."

"Stinko pitching. Not if Caleb had been on the mound," she said as if he might have just been absent for the day. "I mean, no way would he have let Windmere get all those guys on base."

"Like the beginning of last season when he'd had the game won in the seventh," Jack said. He'd pitched a no-hitter and struck out the last six batters.

"Yeah, like that," she murmured, taking that perfectly played game as the marker of her brother's talent with a baseball.

He dropped an arm around his daughter and she leaned into him, closing in on his heart, which she'd immediately captured since her squalling arrival one fiercely cold December morning.

Jack had driven here after the talk with Seth, spotted the red truck and then Bethany with the Foley kid. Since the truck was blocked by two cars, the two of them weren't going anywhere. That reassured Jack. Nevertheless, watching them holding hands, and Foley's thigh too close to hers, touched off an overriding instinct to rescue Bethany that staggered him. Not in the rational, sensible approach of talking to get a fix on the guy, or even calmly striding over and telling the moron to get lost.

Nothing so civilized. Jack wanted to grab him by the balls and turn his swaggering possessiveness into a road map of cold sweat. Not complicated or elaborate—just a move that would absolutely establish *his* rules of how life worked when it came to his beloved daughter.

A ferocious thinking process that resurrected his ancient battles to save his perishing family. This primal need went beyond mere fatherly protection into the arena of desperate survival. The intervening years of comfort, money, success and Meg's deft ability to soften his edges felt as ineffective as the babblings of a drunk.

But he hadn't moved. Restraint limits later consequences, he'd decided, a concept he should have applied with Vicki.

He'd bought a cup of coffee and stood by the fence. Some other fathers were there and they made small talk without any mention of Caleb, proving that chance meetings went as awkwardly as the planned ones. Caleb's death was the elephant in their midst that everyone knew existed, but wouldn't discuss—including him.

Within moments, he'd been caught up in the game. He'd come to them all last season—the most memorable being the final one against Fairmont Academy when Caleb gave up a single, then pitched a wobbly curve ball that the batter had clubbed over the right fielder all the way to King Avenue. Jack had winced, closing his eyes, hoping the hit might blow foul.

It hadn't.

"Ah, shit," one fan howled. "No way. No damn way."

"How could DeWilde have thrown such a piss-assed pitch? He's suppose to hose them down, not send them a gift."

"We got last bats. Lighten up. We're gonna win."

"And win big. We're the hottest team in the state."

A Cooper Falls victory had been declared days before; the actual game would just be a wipe-up operation for the record books. Bets had been made with the odds on a Fairmont win so long, the local bookies were asking twice to make sure a Fairmont wager wasn't a mistake. "Fairmont Farts" had been written with sidewalk chalk and spray paint all over town. The victory streamers in blue and white were waiting to be flown, celebration parties planned in a dozen places, and even a parade had been arranged for the following Saturday.

If winning could be declared by enthusiasm, cash and enough chourico and pepper sandwiches to sink the *Titanic,* then Caleb's team was the winner. But, of course, winning was declared by the most runs on the scoreboard. Cooper Falls lost by two.

The town wailed, the fans groused, the players whined, but his son had been filled with guilt, second-guessing and—more troubling to Jack—Caleb had a distraught sense of having let down the team, of disappointing the town and blowing all his chances for a big league career.

Second-guessing such as he should have thrown a fastball instead, or he could have walked him because the next guy never hit beyond second base, and if only he'd thought a few seconds longer before hurling that pitch. It all culminated with his refusal to be in the team picture.

Jack abided Meg's "poor baby—we understand your pain" approach until he wanted to retch. Losing built better character than winning, he'd told her, waving aside her empathy and taking Caleb to the cottage for a man-to-man chat. Once there, he shoved in videos of other games his son had pitched and lost and made him watch each one twice. Being a hero on a winning team is a no-brainer. A hero on a losing team takes guts. Jack didn't know a lot about heroes, but he was an expert on guts.

A good pitcher takes his lumps, shoulders his share of the blame and then closes that chapter and starts practicing for another game. Too many days dragging in the cellar of self-indulgent pity would make him a worse pitcher the next season. Caleb had absorbed it all, saying little, but he'd been in the team picture that Jack had subsequently placed on his desk in the study.

But this, he noted now, was the next season, and being the father of the worst pitcher would have been preferrable to being the father of a dead son. Yet, remembering and appreciating wasn't a bad thing. All thanks to Seth Eidson.

He considered him an unusually discerning cop and wondered if the detective had Caleb in mind as well as Bethany's new boyfriend.

He'd gotten to the field in time for the last two innings, realizing he had to keep reminding himself that Caleb wasn't on the mound. From this distance, he could easily put Caleb into the pitcher's place. His son crouching forward, hat pulled low, eyes focused on his catcher, right hand behind his back massaging the ball. Then the slight nod, the straightening, the position, the windup and a fastball that made enemy batters dizzy with its perfection.

Jack had stood right here through two seasons, nodded to Caleb as he took the mound and by his presence assured his son he was proud of him in the not-so-great games just as he was when he pitched a winner.

"I miss him so much, Daddy," Bethany said with a hitch in her voice. She didn't call him Daddy very often, mostly when she wanted something, but here with the April wind slicing down the third-base line, he felt his heart reach out, wanting to give her an answer that no longer existed, the answer that would never be.

"I know you do. I do, too."

"Do you think Mom will find out what happened? Mr. Rivers said it's really important that she knows."

Jack hadn't heard of any visits lately by Rivers, but realistically Meg wouldn't say much to him. He'd made his ill-feelings known. Maybe the two of them were meeting elsewhere. Like here at the school or for coffee at the Creamery. "When did he tell you that?"

"One day this week. He's been a really good friend and Erica says he'd done a lot of asking around school trying to find out if anyone knows anything. He's really trying to help."

Help, my ass. He braced himself for the next question—shouldn't you be doing that with Mom? Bethany drew herself up and set her expression as if she'd practiced. "I'm like you, Daddy. I don't need to know because it won't bring Caleb back."

The relief he wanted to feel didn't come. Was she just saying that to make his disinterest okay? Besides what he felt wasn't disinterest as much as resignation. Caleb's suicide could never be changed—motives, reasons, answers were speculative at best. However, in a basic way, he and Bethany really did agree.

"You and I always did think alike, didn't we?"

"Is Mom gonna be okay? I mean after she finds out?"

"Sure she is. Your mother is a most remarkable woman—strong and resilient and smart, and she likes all the pieces to fit. When they don't she asks questions to make sure that they do."

She sighed with appropriate drama. "Yeah, I know."

"Uh oh. Sounds like you got quizzed."

"Just about Brandt. Oh, Daddy, she's acting like I'm going out with a convict," she wailed. "I mean, do I look that dumb?"

Jack chuckled. "A little heavy on the eye goop, but definitely not dumb."

She rambled right past his comment. "She thinks he should come in and be introduced just to bring me here to a ball game. It's all so juvenile."

"But a parental necessity," he said easily. "We get the gene when you're born."

She pointed to the kid slouched against the fender of his red truck, arms crossed, legs spread. "That's him."

"Hard to miss."

"He's cool."

"I bet." And horny as a horse watching a mare prance in the barn.

"Wanna meet him?"

"You didn't want your mother to meet him, but you want me to. What am I missing?"

"You're cool. Mom makes a big deal about everything."

Saying clearly to Jack what Meg had been telling him for years. He was too easy on Bethany.

"He's going into the gym," she said when he straightened and walked away from the vehicle. "Come on, we're gonna be late."

Bethany was tugging him toward the open double doors where the players and a herd of other kids were making their way inside.

"What's going on?"

"Oh, you weren't here when the game started. It's a special request by the team. They have a petition with a zillion names to retire Caleb's number. Mr. Rivers has to say it's okay."

From what Jack could tell, he, Rivers and about five other men were the only adults. He allowed himself to be pulled inside and introduced to Brandt Foley. The kid had to be six-two and possessed enough jock hormones to make Jack's grip on his daughter permanent. Later he intended to call Eidson and thank him for the heads-up.

Bethany giggled, leaning into Jack. "Isn't he the coolest, most gorgeous thing in the world?"

"Dangerous was more the word I had in mind," Jack muttered.

Bethany's eyes widened with interest. "Really?"

"That wasn't an endorsement."

"I can take care of myself."

"No, you can't."

"Now you sound like Mom." Then she squeezed his arm, "But I love you anyway."

Sloane Rivers hit a bat on the floor to get everyone's attention. "I'm told there's to be a request made to me." Chuckles and giggles spread throughout the crowd indicating no one had been surprised. "The team captain informed me that Bethany DeWilde is going to do the deed." He winked at Bethany and stepped back indicating the moment was hers.

"Come up with me," she whispered.

Jack blinked. "Me? No, this is your show."

"Please I want you to. I need you with me and it would make Caleb happy."

He thought immediately of that last argument when everything Jack had said and suggested had made him unhappy. Was there irony here or what? Short of making a scene he had little choice but to make his way to the front of the gym with Bethany holding his hand like he was a lost child.

Then she let go and took a few more steps toward the assembled team. The pitcher handed her a sheaf of papers that she looked through as if verifying the authenticity of the signatures. Then with a poise and sophistication that made Jack wish Meg could see this, she cleared her throat and turned to Rivers. "On behalf of the Cooper Falls students, these signatures represent a desire to have Caleb's number nine permanently retired to honor his name, his memory and his contribution to Cooper Falls High School sports."

Rivers took the pages, looking suitably impressed and at least to Jack, it seemed obvious the coach was overdoing his smarmy moment. So why all the fanfare? Was the ceremony for the kids or to center the attention on him? Jack's cynicism and mistrust of Rivers ran thick. All this public hoopla was to make points with Meg. In no time, this would get back to her and make Rivers look like coach of the year and the president of Caleb's fan club.

Rivers said, "Consider it done. Caleb made us all proud—proud to be a teammate, proud to be his coach and proud to be in his family." The place erupted in applause, whistles and shouts of "Yesss!"

Bethany turned to him and fell into his arms weeping, but smiling, too. Jack held her, his own throat raw, his insides a snarl of pain too similar to what he'd felt when Meg told him Caleb was dead. This moment proved to him that Caleb had ceased being just a good memory, but a memorable icon. Bigger in death than in life. And there, Jack realized, lay another tragedy.

Chapter Thirteen

On Tuesday, Meg deliberately arrived at the restaurant early, and slipped into the ladies' room to check her makeup and hair. She'd worn a red suit and a navy blouse and had a fresh manicure.

Checking herself in the huge mirror, she was relieved she didn't have to go through this every day to go to work. Kate did; and of course so did the young woman she was meeting for lunch.

Then again, she doubted Vicki Slocum ever looked ordinary. She'd never seen her when she didn't look sensational. Which raised the question of why Meg cared a fig. This wasn't competition, this was a lunch about Caleb. Yet that morning, after Jack had left for work, she'd stared at her reflection in the mirror on the side of the kitchen cabinet. Pretty, but hardly dazzling, greeted her. That analysis was followed by an inspection of her hands. No perfectly buffed and polished ovals at the end of delicate fingers. Working hands, Hazel had called them when Jack had introduced her, and her future mother-in-law had smiled with approval.

Well, today she'd wanted model's hands to match the stylish sophistication she intended to create out of her closet. A frantic phone call got her a last-minute appointment for the manicure. But first she'd showered and dressed—a bundle of indecision—until she'd settled on the red wool suit she'd bought on sale after Christmas. She hadn't worn it since the Mother-Son Valentine's buffet lunch at the high school.

"Mom, you look great," Caleb had said when he'd sat down with her. Then he leaned closer. "I like red on women."

She almost laughed, until she realized he was serious. Laughter would have been a catastrophe. "You do? I didn't know you paid a lot of attention to how women dress."

He sat back and grinned, causing her to understand immediately why Erica Rivers was nuts about him. Her son, the hunk. It made her feel a bit foolish that she'd just fully comprehended that her son stood on the cusp of becoming a man.

"Not most. Only the gorgeous ones like you."

Meg felt flattered along with a heavy dose of pride. "I don't know what to say. Thank you."

"Dad thinks you're gorgeous, too, in case he hasn't told you lately. I mean, I didn't just figure it out."

It had been a lovely moment—her red suit moment. A special moment with Caleb.

Oh God, don't cry now. She touched a tissue to the edges of her eyes and drew in a deep breath. Here she was pressed, manicured and looking, well, sensational. She smiled at her reflection—she really should dress up more often. She took one last look and exited.

The dining room had white tablecloths, blue vases of tulips on each table, and a massive green plant that anchored the room.

"I have a reservation for two at one-thirty," she said to the Barbie-shaped hostess. "The name is DeWilde."

She looked at her list. "Yes, right this way."

Meg took the booth seat, ordered a glass of chardonnay and no sooner had she taken the first icy sip, than Vicki appeared and was shown to the table.

Wearing a white dress trimmed in blue, Meg noticed the suntan immediately. The honey color enhanced her already lovely skin.

"Am I late?" Vicki asked as she slid into the opposite seat. "What a morning. I have a million things to clear up before I go away. Plus, I have new clients."

And obviously not the cooperative kind from her impatient look, Meg deduced. "Difficult?"

She sighed. "You said it. I did a walk-through of the house to see if the price they wanted reflected what they were selling. Sellers think profit rather than how to attract buyers." She rolled her eyes indicating to Meg that the seller must be asking champagne prices for six-pack real estate. She opened her purse, taking out a pack of cigarettes.

"This is the no-smoking section," Meg said before she struck the match.

She blinked. "Oh. Do you mind if we move?"

Meg did, but since the purpose of this lunch was to learn all she could about Caleb, she didn't want Vicki jittery and wanting to leave before Meg got all her questions asked.

They moved with their menus and Vicki ordered a diet Coke since she had to return to work. Once she had lit her cigarette, she resumed her story about the new clients.

"Anyway, apart from the clutter, the house had a lot of interior cosmetic flaws. I suggested they hire a professional stager. Jack has used them with great success. Once the stager has pointed out the problem areas and the potential spike in profit for the seller, Jack usually gets eager compliance. The goal is to get top dollar, right? I mean, it's not an insult, just good business. When I wanted to show my aunt Rose's house, I removed a lot of things she cherished because they were too personal."

"I've heard that buyers want to be able to visualize their own things in a home and not be distracted by the sellers'."

"Exactly. But this couple took my suggestion of stagers as an insult." She sighed. "I knew Jack would want me to press them, and I was very diplomatic. But the house—well, it needs interior painting, the wallpaper is very sixty-ish, and many of the furnishings screech thrift shop." She sighed again, sipped and tapped her cigarette on the ashtray.

Meg asked the expected question, though she really didn't care. "And what do the stagers do?"

"Basically, their job is to accentuate the house's value and keep the prospective buyer's focus on space and their own imagination of possibilities, rather than call attention to furnishings and personal items of the seller. The stager will want to rent some less obtrusive furnishings, and definitely want to install carpeting, especially in the family room." She lowered her voice as if about to reveal bloodstains from an old murder. "They have shag. Shag! I mean, my God, I didn't think there was any of that stuff left on the planet."

Meg decided not to mention the burgundy shag in her finished room in the basement. Jack had suggested changing it numerous times, but it was durable, never showed dirt or stains and for the basement it worked just fine. "So what decision did the seller make?"

"They want to talk to Jack," she said, clearly offended that her suggestions weren't immediately adopted. "Of course, he'll agree with me. He always does. Recently I suggested a house's price be boosted rather than lowered. He told me to try it, and within two weeks, it had sold."

"I'm sure he's glad he hired you."

"He's certainly told me a number of times. He's a wonderful boss. You're very lucky to be married to him. I bet he's the ideal husband."

Sometimes. "He is."

They ordered lunch and when the server had gone, Meg asked, "You said earlier you were going away. A vacation?"

"To the Islands. Jack urged me to take some time off, and I couldn't go down there looking like a pale fish." She brushed her hand lightly over her honeyed cheek. "I'm leaving in a few days."

"Well, I hope you have a wonderful time," Meg murmured, thinking that Jack was the one who needed a vacation.

"Actually, I'd wanted a friend to go with me, but it didn't work out."

"I'm sorry."

"I am, too."

Meg wondered if it was a man, but she honestly didn't care. She was more fascinated by a side of Vicki she'd not encountered before. Always the young woman had been soft-spoken, deferential and concerned. But the Vicki across the table appeared to be trying to prove something—a newly dawned self-assurance in her job, perhaps?

Then, as though turning on a dime, she said, "But we're here to talk about Caleb, not me. I'm still having a hard time believing it happened. This must be a nightmare for you."

"For our whole family."

"He was a great kid. Honest, a hard worker, always wanting to help. Curious and interested in so many things. He always had good things to say about you and Jack."

Meg had heard this before, and while she appreciated the flattering words, the good things her son did weren't what caused his suicide. "Vicki, did you know that Caleb had a crush on you?"

Vicki concentrated on putting out her cigarette. Their lunch arrived—a chicken club sandwich for Meg and a Caesar salad for Vicki. She sipped her Coke, while the waitress put fresh ground pepper on her salad and brought Meg vinegar for her fries.

"Did he tell you that?" she asked, forking some greens.

"Actually, Jack and I guessed. It wasn't surprising. You're quite lovely and Caleb commented once or twice that the two of you had a lot of fun when you were cleaning out your aunt's house. You liked the same music and he said you were interested in his baseball aspirations."

"I told him to follow his heart."

Meg winced. Idealism had a tantalizing fantasy element, but Jack would have scoffed. Meg, too, believed that only the young truly embraced such a capricious philosophy. If she'd followed such an impulse at sixteen, she'd have pursued being a ballerina. Never mind that her dance lessons at Miss Vachon's had been unremarkable; she couldn't perform and maintain the "line" of elegance required in a ballerina's performance, and she had neither the stamina nor the waif-like body. Heart-following required a whimsical desire—then came the hard work. "Is that what you did when you moved here? Followed your heart?"

She gave Meg a starry-eyed look. "I always follow my heart."

Meg paused between bites. She didn't quite believe that selling real estate made the top-ten list of anyone's dream career. What else did Vicki fantasize about? She'd have been more likely to find a young woman's dream fulfillment in Boston. "You told us the day of the funeral that you'd lost your mother when you were sixteen. Does the rest of your family live in Boston?"

She shook her head, appearing suddenly sad and hopeless. "My father walked out on my mother and me when I was just a baby. My aunt Rose was his older sister. After my mother died, I lived with her for a while and we used to talk—or I should say, I talked and asked questions about him."

"That must have been hard not knowing anything about your father," Meg said, reminded once more how much she'd taken her own family for granted.

"I thought he was romantic and tragic because he drifted around and let life carry him along." She smiled and picked through her salad. "Aunt Rose called him a deadbeat drifter who leapt tall buildings only in his mind. Of course, I was sure that once he met me, we'd be the happy father and daughter. I finally convinced Aunt Rose to tell me where he lived. It was in California, and I went out to see him."

Vicki paused, her head down, her hair falling forward. Meg wanted to take her hand and squeeze it, for she'd guessed this story didn't have a happy ending. "Did you find him?"

"Yes and no. He'd promised Aunt Rose when she called to tell him I was coming that he would meet with me, but he didn't. He disappeared the day I arrived. His landlady told me he'd packed his old duffel and caught a bus. She didn't know where to."

"Oh Vicki, I'm sorry. That must have felt like the worst kind of rejection."

"I didn't understand why he hated me so."

"Maybe he just didn't know what to do with a daughter and he was afraid to try."

She studied Meg, her eyes seeming to search for some answer. "Or he knew what he did was wrong and couldn't face the consequences."

"Perhaps. You never tried to find him again?"

"No." She paused. "And he's never contacted me." She brightened. "I know his rejection of me was his fault and not mine. I still believe in following my heart to get whatever I want."

"Well, it's certainly a better outlook than getting bogged down in what might have been."

"I'm so glad you agree with me. And I bet that when you married Jack, you followed your heart."

Meg laughed. "Yes, I guess I did. Nevertheless, often reality conflicts with what my heart wants. Like now, my heart wants to know why Caleb killed himself, but reality isn't being very cooperative."

"Did you think that because Caleb worked for me that I would know something?"

"Perhaps. I thought he might have told you if he was troubled or depressed or having a problem he didn't know how to deal with."

She shook her head. "I hadn't seen a lot of him in the

few weeks before. I would leave him a list of chores that he would do, and then I'd leave him his money on Fridays." She fiddled with her napkin and then lit another cigarette. Sitting back and exhaling, she said, "Jack kept me so busy that Caleb and I always missed each other."

"What about anytime before those recent weeks? During the late winter for example? Did he ever indicate he was worried or frightened?"

"No."

Meg sank under a weight of discouragement. Perhaps Jack was right. Perhaps there were no answers. But dammit, she wasn't ready to believe that.

"I did want to return this." She handed Meg a Filene's bag. "I intended to give it to Jack when he came for the snow thrower, but, well, we got to talking—you know how it is—and he left without it."

Meg puzzled over the multitude of references to Jack, not with jealousy but with curiosity. Vicki was obviously in awe of her husband, a response she'd observed numerously through the years. Charisma and success with the added bonus of good looks attracted attention and admirers—especially women. This wasn't news, but Vicki's insinuation into their lives not just as an employee of Jack's, but with Caleb, too, then her staying with Bethany the day of the funeral caused her some skepticism about intent that would not have occurred to her if Caleb were alive. Bethany had chattered later about Vicki, and how they discussed the latest in clothes, the rap groups and how many times both had seen *Titanic*. Vicki had done follow-up phone calls to her and to Bethany. Was it lack of family? One parent dead, the other as good as dead. A desire to be included and involved with a real family who cherished and loved one another?

Lunch today had given her little insight into Caleb, but it had revealed more about Vicki—lack of family connections plus she'd abandoned a successful career in Boston for Cooper Falls. While a pretty town, it was hardly cosmopolitan. Then again, her aunt had a home here and if nothing else that gave Vicki an anchor of sorts. Perhaps Vicki was, as Meg sensed, simply a lonely young woman seeking friendship and the closeness found in a small town.

That seemed a bit simplistic, and yet . . . Of course, Meg thought suddenly. She'd call Kate and ask her to find out what she could. Besides, days had passed since Kate called all excited because Ford had moved to the city to be with her. Meg wanted to find out how they were doing.

"Is anything wrong?" Vicki asked.

"No, just thinking of some things I need to do this afternoon." Meg pushed her plate aside, finished her wine and then opened the bag. She took out the red and gray shetland sweater she'd seen Caleb wear numerous times. Her eyes smarted and she pressed her lips together to stop them from trembling.

Finally, she said, "My mother gave this to him last Christmas. He'd seen it in the Gap and she'd gotten the last one in his size. I can still see the smile on his face when he opened it."

"I can only imagine," she said abruptly, causing Meg to frown. Perhaps the Christmas reference. Not everyone loved the holidays, and since she lacked family connections the celebration would be doubly difficult. Meg was growing more convinced that Vicki simply envied what Meg had—a wonderful marriage and family.

Meg said, "It did strike me as unusual when Jack brought the other items home. Caleb wasn't one to leave his things at friends' houses."

"He knew I'd take good care of them."

"I'm sure you did. I wasn't insinuating otherwise."

"It wasn't my fault he forgot things. I reminded him." And in that instant her defensiveness brought Bethany to Meg's mind. This was the kind of response her daughter would make. Then as if Vicki had realized how immature she'd sounded, she added, "He used to tease and say that if he never left anything behind then he'd never have an excuse to come back."

But Meg's mind had latched on to her own earlier comment. That it was unusual that Caleb had left things at Vicki's, or anywhere for that matter. *Unusual.* Out of the natural order of his life. Why hadn't she concluded this when Jack brought the other things home? Instead of thinking about the motives and what they meant, she'd gone through each piece as if it was holy and then put them all in the drawer in his room. One conclusion could be that Caleb acted differently with Vicki because of his crush on her. More clumsy, more forgetful, more anxious to see her. And as she'd said, if he left things behind, he always had an excuse to come back.

Then as if the young woman had crawled into her thoughts, she asked, "You're not angry about that crush, are you?"

"Actually, I was thinking how a crush on a pretty, sophisticated woman could easily cause a young man to abandon his usual habits."

"I was very flattered, but since he had a girlfriend, I didn't take it very seriously." At Meg's stare, she added, "You did know he liked Erica Rivers, didn't you?"

"Yes, of course." She made herself smile as if none of this was news, while at the same time wondering why Vicki, and Jessup—Erica had to be the girl Jessup didn't ask about—why they knew but his family didn't? How odd.

By the time she'd paid the check, wished Vicki a pleasant vacation and climbed into her car, she realized she had some reasons to chew on. An unusual behavior by Caleb could indicate he was troubled by something and therefore forgetful. But keeping Erica a secret? Why? Unless he was sheepish about admitting he now liked a girl that a few years ago he was hiding from and using "gross" to describe whenever her name came up.

When had all that changed?

• • •

Later that afternoon, Meg was walking through the green-house at Bushes Galore trying to decide between the numerous flats of pansies—mixed colors or all the same variety. Although early to plant, the best selection was available now and the plants would be happy in the garage windows. She intended to use pansies as a ground cover around the Caleb trees as she'd done last year when Caleb helped her plant. It was more work than the traditional pachysandra, but the colors were exquisite. And this year she wanted bright, life-affirming colors.

"Mrs. DeWilde?"

Meg glanced at the slender woman with a birthmark stain that nearly covered her left cheek. She wore her dark hair long so that it fell forward. Meg judged her to be around Vicki's age. "The manager pointed you out to me. I'm Hannah Ellsworth," she said offering her hand. "My husband and I bought the Stratton house. Jack was so wonderful in helping us finalize the details. In his office, I saw a photo of your house—"

"Of course, Jack mentioned that you were looking for some landscaping advice."

"I'd been asking the manager about what you planted at your house and when he saw you come in he suggested I talk to you directly."

"Jack gave me your phone number. I intended to call you."

"Oh, no, please, I don't want you to think I was faulting you. Oh, God, I'm not doing this right." To Meg's astonishment, Hannah's hands began to shake, and she held her package more tightly to stop them. Meg waited, having no idea what she should say. The woman continued, "I'm sorry. I'm making a mess of this. I should have called you. I've thought about you so much in the past few weeks."

Meg guessed what was coming, unsure if she wanted to spare herself or the uncomfortable woman.

"I heard what happened to your son," she said so softly, Meg had to lean closer to hear her. "I'm so very sorry. Gary and I lost our daughter, Lily, to SIDS last September. She was two months old. We have so little that's tangible—her cradle, a blanket my mother made, some pictures and our memories. It's like we loved her for a lifetime in those few precious weeks."

Meg's eyes welled up. "Oh, Hannah, how tragic and sad—"

"But so unspeakable for you, too. When I heard about Caleb, my heart ached for you—to have a child for so many years and share his laughter, dry his tears, to watch his potential develop and then to lose him. I can't even begin to imagine what a horror this must have been for your family."

Meg took her hand. "How very kind of you to be so forthcoming," was all Meg could manage around the huge lump in her throat. Hannah's words were some of the most precious she had received since Caleb died. No clichés or ritual musings, no search for words, no attempts to understand. Two mothers who had lost children . . . a bond born from excruciating losses.

Customers wended their way around them. Meg stood between the flats of pansies and Hannah carried a handful of flower seed packets.

Meg straightened, an inner push coming alive inside of her. Whether because they shared a mutual grief, or for a genuine liking of Hannah, she wanted to do this. This was definitely heart-following, instinctive, and necessary. "I'd like to help you with your yard, Hannah."

Hannah blinked and then grinned. "Why, thank you. I have neither a green thumb nor any clue as to what needs to go where."

"I'll stop by tomorrow morning about ten if that's okay."

"Wonderful."

Meg lifted up the flat of mixed colors, then said to Hannah, "When I come, I'd love to see some pictures of Lily."

The young woman raised her hand to cover her mouth, tears clouding her eyes, her voice breaking, "No one ever asks to see pictures. No one ever wants to talk about her. It's as if she never existed."

Meg squeezed her hand, saying with a touch what she couldn't express without crying. "I'll see you tomorrow."

She paid for four flats and six bags of cedar mulch with her credit card, noting that the boy who waited on her had been at the funeral and yet gave no indication he knew her.

He carried her purchases to the car, setting them into the back, all the while making no mention of Caleb. To make his silence more condemning, the job he now had had once been her son's. Meg would have taken a small reference such as "We sure miss Caleb around here" and treasured it. She knew kids were often tongue-snarled, but saying absolutely nothing infuriated her.

She rearranged the flats so they were level. Her heart thumped as heavy as the six bags of mulch. Hannah was right, and she saw it was clearly true when it came to Caleb. With some, it's as if he'd never existed.

Her tears came as she moved the bags to brace the flats. Not delicate, quiet drops on her cheeks, but a deep wrenching despair. She didn't bother to wipe them away, uncaring if anyone saw. She shoved the last bag of mulch into place, slung her purse over her shoulder and slammed the hatch closed. Maybe she should scream. She had a right to scream, to be depressed, to be frustrated and angry. Life wasn't going on for her, it was sinking underneath her right here in a shopping center parking lot.

"Meg?"

She jumped as if prodded by a hot poker. But when she turned and saw who it was, she threw her arms around him. He would understand, he would hold her, care for her, want to make her better, tell her how important her son was, that he should never, never be forgotten. "Oh, I'm so glad you're here," she wailed, grabbing fistfuls of his leather jacket.

Sloane drew her close, brushing his hand down her hair, his whisper gentle in her ear. "Ah, God, Meggie . . . Is it Caleb?"

She gulped. "It's always Caleb, but no one else gives a damn." She knew she was verging on hysteria, paranoia or both, but she continued anyway. "That kid in there has Caleb's job, he knew Caleb at school and he never said one word to me."

Bless his soul, he didn't look at her like she was crazy. He only nodded in understanding. "It's hard for the kids. Sympathetic language is strange for them—the boys more than the girls."

"I didn't want some trumped-up condolence sentence. I just wanted him to say he misses Caleb. How hard is that?"

"Sometimes harder because then you cry."

And when she pulled back and looked at him, she saw the moistness in his eyes. "Oh, Sloane. I'm sorry."

"I miss him, Meggie. I miss his ability and his spunk and smile and loyalty. I miss him like hell."

Meg clung even harder, that heart pain easing into a comforting ache that at least someone understood, that one of her best friends was there to hold her when she needed holding.

His arms remained around her, unmindful of passersby, moving only when someone honked that they wanted to get into the parking place they were blocking.

"Come on, I'll buy you a drink."

She almost refused. "I need to get home."

"Home can wait."

"What are you doing here, anyway?"

"Looking for you. Bethany said you were out buying pansies."

"I did get that done."

"And?"

"I'll tell you over that drink."

Chapter Fourteen

Never in his life had Jack paced, and he wasn't about to start now. But he'd looked at the kitchen clock at least ten times in the past six minutes.

Where the hell was Meg?

It was getting dark; there was no note, no voice mail message and the worry he'd told himself twenty times was juvenile had begun to thicken.

Bethany sashshayed in from the other room after a whispered phone conversation with Erica. He'd been half listening when he wasn't looking out the back door.

A leopard print shirt showed under her unzipped jacket, the bottom edge of which barely met the hem of her black skirt. Another inch longer and she'd look like she wasn't wearing a skirt.

"Where are you going?" he snapped, alarmed by her too adult clothes and irritated, not only that she was so calm but that she could leave when her mother was missing.

"Date." She murmured the word through a pursed purple mouth she was examining in the mirror. Didn't anyone wear plain red lipstick anymore?

"It's a school night, and you're too young to date." Then dispensing with that topic, he moved to the one that had him so jumpy. "Tell me again what your mother said when she called."

Bethany rolled her eyes, then leaned closer to study herself. "She said she was going to Bushes to get some flats of pansies and that she'd be home later."

"What time did she call?"

"Around three."

"It's close to seven."

Bethany shrugged, clearly more concerned about her makeup. "She got tied up. You know how Mom is in the garden shop. I can't believe you're this wired about it. It's not like she's some kid."

"Speaking of kids, you still qualify. You're not going out."

"What!" The sultry, full lip look she'd been practicing vanished into one of horror. "You can't do that to me!"

"You have school tomorrow, I don't trust Brett or Bunt or whatever his name is and your skirt is too short."

"His name is Brandt. Brandt!" she shouted. "You're treating me like a baby. It's not fair and it's insulting. I'm almost fifteen."

Jack didn't want to hear it. At another time he might agree he was being ornery, but right now he didn't give a goddamn. He was scared and angry and allowing his daughter to go riding off with that horny jock when he didn't know where Meg was just wasn't going to happen. Worrying about one of them had him crazy enough. "You're not going out. End of discussion."

"What's wrong with you? You're acting crazy. I'll be the joke of the week at school." She stomped over to the door.

"Bethany, I'm warning you."

"I'm going and you can't stop me." She yanked open the door, raced down the steps and ran up the driveway where she halted beneath the streetlight. Her long legs were too naked in the short skirt, her hair blowing about in the brisk breeze. She huddled there like some curbside pickup.

He stared after her, stunned by her absolute disobedience and his own powerlessness with a purple-mouthed fourteen-year-old. *She's like you, Jack. She has your charm and your resistance to authority.*

Meg's assessment of their daughter had been made when Bethany was three and had used her mother's red nail polish to color the white flowers on the living room wallpaper of their apartment. Jack regarded the painting as an artistic improvement over the bland white on beige paper. Of course he immediately became Bethany's hero, a status he'd held and enjoyed with only minor exceptions until Caleb's death threw their lives into daily chaos. Skirmishes now with Bethany were becoming far too frequent, not unlike arguments with Meg.

The real issue was where to lay the blame for the skirmishes. On his wariness, his guilt or his inability to embrace Meg's cause.

He stood in the doorway watching her, the chilly night descending around him like flotsam. He jammed his hands deep in his pockets. Shadows in the yard swayed and crouched like the trawls of his boyhood wreckage. Too many bottomless nights when he'd waited for his old man to come home, nights he'd hidden under the house so no one would see him cry, nights when his parents fought and screamed and he and Ford considered it progress if only one of them was drunk. Fear. A net of fear then and now still.

His head throbbed, exhaustion dragging at him. His options curled through his mind in a kind of freefall. He could march up the drive, literally pick up Bethany and bring her back. He could wait, get in his own car and follow them, or he could call Seth and tell him to have the truck stopped and deliver his daughter home like a delinquent. Or he could do nothing.

Nothing was what he'd always done. Avoid the hassle. Be the easygoing father, the good cop to Meg's bad cop.

She made the rules and she enforced them. Jack only had to back her up. Except tonight she wasn't here.

The red truck stopped and Bethany climbed into the cab seat. With the dome light still on, she leaned toward the boy and he kissed her, then she slammed the door. That was for his own benefit—in-your-face rebelliousness.

He expended the breath he'd been holding. Had he really hoped she would tell the jerk she couldn't go? Had he waited, cemented in place, expecting that she would run back because he was her father and that made his slingshot approach to discipline easier? He slumped against the door frame feeling old and defeated. Goddammit, this was all Meg's fault. If she'd been home then she would have dealt with Bethany. Given the opportunity, he'd clumsily blown it.

He opened a bottle of Dewar's and poured some into a glass, then returned to the back door to watch for Meg.

"I'll follow you home," Sloane said, taking her arm as they left Michael's Pub.

"I'm fine."

"Uh huh. Three glasses of wine along with nachos and cheese wasn't much to eat. Humor me, I'd feel better."

"You think I'm drunk," she asked, sucking in the chilly air to clear her head. Truthfully she was more sleepy than tipsy.

"Just a little too relaxed. On second thought, maybe I should drive."

"You're very sweet, you know that?"

"I love you. Being sweet isn't hard," he said so nonchalantly, it could have been the twentieth time instead of the first.

She didn't argue and in fact she was delighted that he cherished her, pleased that in the past couple of hours he'd made clear she was all he'd thought about since Caleb died. It was a heady concept to know that Sloane was entirely focused on her. He would do anything for her; all she needed to do was ask.

They'd talked about Caleb, she'd told him about the *Lucky Louise* model and her decision about helping Hannah Ellsworth, plus she'd griped about the boy in Bushes. Just having someone listen and agree with her without arguing reinforced her will and determination not to give up on Caleb.

Mostly, however, they'd talked about the good times they'd had growing up together. Nostalgia and memories—how she loved them. Those innocent years viewed through the prism of pleasant company seemed so ideal and perfect that by the time Meg was sipping her third glass of wine, she wondered aloud why she and Sloane had never followed their mothers' desires and married.

A major mistake, he'd said, leaning forward to whisper that he should have swept her up and taken her away to live happily ever after.

But she *was* living happily ever after, she reminded him. Just not with him. The wine made her blunt and she didn't quite notice the hurt look in his eyes.

They reminisced. She'd gone to college and met Jack, while Sloane got involved with Rebecca Laurent, a columnist who wrote about the gossip and soirees of the summer people in Newport. When Meg and Sloane met again, she was wildly in love with Jack. Rebecca and Sloane were living together.

They'd wished each other well, married their respective lovers and launched into their own futures. Kids arrived. First Caleb and then two years later, Bethany. Rebecca gave birth to Erica a few months later. Then when the girls were around nine, Sloane discovered Rebecca was having an affair with one of the rich men she wrote about. The marriage ended and while Rebecca and Erica remained in Cooper Falls, Sloane had moved away for a few years.

"Why did you *really* move back here?" Meg asked after they left the pub and were making their way between cars in the parking lot. He'd returned three years ago to take the coaching job at the high school, but Meg knew he'd had offers from bigger schools with a better salary and a more generous benefits package.

He had his arm around her, and she welcomed the cozy support of his body. "Hmmm, let me see," he mused as if contemplating something deep and wondrous. "I wanted to be closer to my daughter. Besides, this was my hometown and returning had advantages beyond material. There was you, of course. Erica hated going back and forth between here and Massachusetts. I felt it was important she have stability in her teen years, plus she liked going to school with Bethany and Caleb."

"Did you know that she was Caleb's girlfriend?" she asked, wondering why she hadn't hours ago, while at the same time realizing her chatter even now was as bouncy as a new tennis ball.

"Uh, I don't think so." Amusement laced his voice and for an instant he sounded like Jack.

"Well, I know so. I heard it from two people."

"Then by God it must be true." He grinned and turned her so that the parking lot lights fell on her face. She liked winning disagreements this easily. In fact, she liked Sloane and the lovely tension of standing this close with him absorbing her as if she were the most important person in his world. His eyes adored her, making her feel young and so necessary. "Is it true that if a guy kisses his favorite girl under a streetlight on a starry April night that all his dreams will come true?"

"Hmm, dreams. Like following your heart. So nice," she said, her body floating weightless, her mind swirling anew with chardonnay and the naughty possibility that she was going to be kissed by a man other than Jack. "Maybe we shouldn't."

"And pass up this momentous moment? Not a chance."

His mouth eased over hers, gently and then more consuming. He drew her into him and her arms climbed around his neck. Intimacy rushed through her; kissing him, feeling his tongue brush inside her mouth. Not deep and probing, more of a careful waltz that was at once romantic and endearing. Some distant wisdom urged her to pull away but the less cautious side pushed her closer. She'd never done this before and she wanted to make sure she experienced it all. Being naughty, her fuzzy logic reasoned, wasn't any fun if you couldn't remember the details to mull over later.

She tasted him, taking her time to slide her arms down and away. She licked her lips, the sweet kiss singed with just enough fire to make it shameless.

He tipped his head to the side. "You surprise me."

"What a lovely compliment," she said, feeling very sure of herself. A sudden burst of worldliness made her thoughts loose and buoyant. "I'm weary of being predictable."

"I figured you'd stiffen up and shove me away."

"Are you disappointed?"

"God, no. I think I'm floating on a golden opportunity. When am I going to see you again?"

She laughed. "Are you asking me for a date?" At his raised eyebrow, she said, "That would be a bit awkward since I have a husband who would definitely be opposed."

"Don't joke with me, Meg. I'm serious. I want to see you again."

How could he be so sure of what he wanted? Or was it just easier for men? Meg had little doubt that more kissing would lead to touching and then sex—not exactly the logical progression for a woman married happily forever after to another man, despite the airy worldliness she'd just found. A small kiss was only a little improper—sex was messy and complicated, never mind that Jack would probably kill him. God, she *must* be tipsy if she was this blasé about sex and murder.

She sidestepped his seriousness with a light laugh and a

squeeze of his hand. "I think a relationship between us is not a topic for a starry night after too much wine."

"All right, I'll hold it for a cloudy night when we're both cold sober."

She unlocked the door to the Expedition and climbed inside. She took his hand and squeezed it. "Thank you, Sloane. Thanks for listening and reassuring me I'm not nuts to be pursuing this."

"I'm at your disposal anytime. Anyplace." He winked. "I'll follow you home."

Twenty minutes later when she pulled into the drive, she expected him to turn around and go on home. Lights blazed in the house and a confrontation between Jack and Sloane—she definitely wanted to avoid that. Then he stopped behind her, waiting.

In her headlights, she saw Jack open the back door. The tension the wine had eased barreled back. *Sloane, go home. Please. Please.*

She opened the garage, drove in and cut the engine. She sat momentarily, hands gripping the wheel while she organized her thoughts from a momentous and disturbing day. Tomorrow promised more. She wanted to call Kate about Vicki, go to Hannah's and, now inspired by Hannah's talk of pictures and her own nostalgic trip with Sloane, she intended to get out all the pictures of Caleb and start a memory book. His growing-up years had been happy and she wanted to rekindle the joy her son had given his family.

Meg gathered the Filene's bag and her purse, deciding the flats could wait until tomorrow to be unloaded.

By the time she stepped out of the garage, Sloane's car was indeed gone. Thank God. She walked toward the back door that Jack was holding for her.

"Hi," she said, feeling ridiculously guilty and hating

herself for her unworldly reaction. How many nights had Jack come home late with nary a word beyond "Sorry, I'm late." She seriously doubted he ever felt guilty. Ever.

"Good evening, Mrs. DeWilde."

Uh oh. Never positive when he pulled that Rhett Butler formality. She could smell Scotch and took note of the open bottle.

"Did you and Rivers have a nice time?"

"We had a couple of drinks. No big deal."

"You doing anything with Rivers is a major deal. Every time. All the time. Did it occur to you that I might be worried about you?"

The man had mastered the neutral-toned voice. No rise, no inflection, no hint of emotion. It taunted her now to make him react. She took a few seconds, considering her answer. "You mean call and let you know where I was and then explain why I wasn't here when you thought I would be?"

His gaze followed her as she moved deeper into the kitchen. "It would make for an intriguing start."

She set down her purse. Hard. The Filene's bag got plunked in a chair. Maybe she should *start* by saying Sloane kissed her. That would rattle his damnable control. "Let's consider us even."

She shrugged out of her coat and slung it over the chair where the bag was. She picked through the scattered mail on the counter. A postcard from her mother saying she'd had a great time in Miami; she and Ben, a widower in her golfing foursome, had gotten tickets to the Masters in Augusta and had extended their stay a few days. Meg mulled that over, almost smiling at the thought of her prim mother traveling alone with a man. This was the same woman who once advised her that sleeping with Jack before she married him would ruin her. She fully intended to tease her about the "trip" the next time they spoke. There were bills, too, and she needed to get these

paid, plus those she had on Jack's desk. A few cards—
late-arriving condolences and a gardening magazine.

She set that aside to look through later, adding a mental
reminder to find the pictures of Caleb climbing the biggest
of the Caleb trees. And she needed to buy a scrapbook.
Bethany had done some scrapbooking with school photos . . . Yes, the two of them could work on the memory
book of Caleb.

At the sink, she got a glass of water, and when she
turned back to him, Jack still stood between the Scotch
bottle on the bar and the back door. Except now, the empty
glass had been set down and his hands were fisted in his
pockets. His eyes had the flinty seriousness that Meg
hadn't seen in a long time. It didn't frighten her, but made
clear this wouldn't be a happy gathering around the hearth
night. Well, dammit, she didn't care.

Still, his voice stayed low and even. "Let's consider you
owe me an explanation as to why you're out drinking with
Rivers."

"We're friends. We grew up together. He's been very
supportive and . . ." She drank some more water and
wished it was wine. Standing here, explaining her
actions—that with the exception of the kiss were perfectly
innocent—infuriated her. She faced him, eyes defiant and
cool—yes, worldly cool. "I had a really tough day. Or is
that not good enough?"

For a moment she thought she caught some amusement
in his eyes, but then it was gone. "How much did you have
to drink?"

"I am not drunk!"

"He followed you home, unless I'm being too naïve of
his sterling motives." She didn't miss the sarcasm. "Perhaps he'd hoped I was out and then he could come in and
finish whatever bedroom scenario he's been fantasizing
about doing with you since he was twelve."

Meg giggled, and she shouldn't have. Vestiges of the

wine, she supposed, but the idea of Sloane coming in for some quick sex, like she would even allow such stupidity, was just too ludicrous for seriousness.

"I'm not amused, Meg."

"Well, you should be because this is a silly discussion. Why would I want anyone else when I have you? No one does sex better than you. In fact, the last party we were at, it was you with the bevy of women hanging on your every word—and I'm sure at least five of them were trying to seduce you."

"Just three."

"Three more than were interested in Sloane. He could barely get the attention of the female bartender."

"I'll give him some pointers on the condition that he stay away from my wife." Then as if Sloane were a dead issue, he poured himself more Dewers, took a swallow and asked her, "You said let's consider us even. About what?"

"Wait a minute. I don't like that, Jack. You assume I'm some passive or worse, a willing female who would simply cave in to sex with him because it's what he might want."

"Not might. Does. I didn't mean it as a slam at you, but you always assume he's still the boy next door that you can trust. I'm telling you he's not and you can't."

"Your conclusion, not mine. Why shouldn't I trust Sloane? Because you don't? Do you believe I'd have sex with him while I'm married to you?"

"Meg, married people have affairs."

"We're not talking generally. We're talking about me. And this married person doesn't," she said, despite her earlier passing thought about "something" with Sloane. Passing thoughts don't count. "Do you think I would?"

His eyebrows crinkled in that way they did when she'd asked what he considered a no-brainer question. "No. You have too much honor and loyalty."

She swallowed, the shared kiss with Sloane suddenly sour rather than worldly.

"But Rivers covets you. I've seen it in his eyes when he

looks at you. I know the seduction game, Meg. Signals aren't always obvious until it's too late. Take your sister. She's done a number on Ford—not just sex but his ability to think straight. He thinks he's in love with her."

Meg guessed he was a little drunk. Not slurry or sloppy, but not purely sober; Jack never veered off to a topic that could change a subject until he had all his questions answered. But since he had . . . Meg picked up on the issue of Kate and Ford.

"I know you feel the need to protect your brother from my wild-eyed sister, but frankly I don't think it's your business. Or mine. And what if he is in love with her? Kate is crazy about him—she told me so. I think it would be lovely if they found happiness together."

"A reverse Cinderella story. How touching."

"You prefer those dock babes he usually takes up with?"

"I don't want the kid to get his clock cleaned. We've had enough of that in this family."

"The kid?" She lifted both eyebrows. "Please. He's in his late thirties. At what point are you going to quit living his life so you can shield him from making a mistake? You've done entirely too much of that with your family and what has it gotten you?"

And how has it helped this *family?* she thought. How did it help Caleb? But she kept those questions to herself. The ramifications were too new and troubling.

"Not much beyond a belly full of headaches," he conceded to her surprise. "So your advice is I should abandon all of them?"

"Of course not, but don't prejudge before anyone is in trouble. Ford and Kate will figure out soon enough if this will work. I think it was good that he moved up to Boston. He'll see her in the arena she works and socializes in."

"Her arena—ah, yes, the one of health clubs, upscale boomer bars and Porter the Back Bay bachelor," he said in disgust. "Ford is worth six of Porter Delacourt."

"You undervalue your brother. He's worth ten of

Porter. I don't want to see Ford hurt either and I told Kate that. Soon enough, they'll realize whether this is a fling or serious."

"Soon enough," he murmured. "I just hope soon enough isn't too late." He set the glass down and didn't refill it; instead he opened a box of crackers and took some cheddar spread from the refrigerator. "You still haven't told me what we're even about."

Meg put a cold chicken and noodle casserole into the microwave. While she prepared the greens for a salad, she debated whether to keep on Kate and Ford or just get to the core. The same core that had laid deep within her, silent and simmering for days. "We're even in that you made a promise to me and you broke it."

He looked at her, cheese mounded high on his third cracker. "What promise?" he asked, perplexed.

"Not only did you break it, but you've never even given me a reason or an explanation, never mind an apology. It's as if you dismissed it because it wasn't worth your time."

He put the cracker down, uneaten. "Meg, I don't know what you're talking about."

Suddenly the buildup of disappointment and anger couldn't be held back. "It was about our son, Jack. About Caleb. About finding out things from Jessup. You promised me you'd go with me last Saturday and you never came home, never called, never did anything. It was like your promise to me was meaningless, not worth your time, like you truly don't care at all what made him kill himself. I've waited for days for an explanation and even now, while I'm telling you this, you have the nerve to sit there looking dumb and blank."

Then the tears came, and she turned her back and folded her arms against the rolling pain in her chest.

His total and complete silence dominated the room.

Finally, the emotion she'd coveted from him for days filled his voice. "Meg, I forgot. Honest to Christ, I did."

She hadn't expected this. And it made her feel worse

than a broken promise. "You forgot? Forgot? This was about our son! How could you just forget?"

"I did. I swear it." He shoved his chair back and came toward her. "I had breakfast with Ford, and then Seth Eidson suggested I might want to check on Bethany. She was at the ball game with Brandt." He scowled. "Yeah, Brandt. That's his name. I talked with her, watched the end of the ball game and then there was the ceremony where Caleb's number was retired." He touched her shoulders, turning her and looking deep into her eyes. In a softer voice, he said, "I wish you'd been there to see Bethany. She presented the signatures, and you would have been so proud of her poise in front of all the kids. Afterwards, I called Seth to thank him and we met for a beer. I forgot all about going to Jessup's with you."

He made her dizzy when he made things so clear and logical. How did he always make it seem that she was the one being unreasonable?

"You talked with Seth?" Meg had liked him—his low-key approach that gave her a sense he truly had been upset by Caleb's death in a more personal way than he needed to be. A flowering hope opened within her. Perhaps Jack had forgotten, or he'd broken his promise because he didn't want to go, but if he was meeting with the police . . .

Maybe she'd misjudged, and Jack had been doing his own investigating. He really cared, he just wanted to wait until he knew something before he told her. "When did you get to be friends?"

"I'm not sure. He's like one of those people who always seems to be there when I turn around. I see him a lot. We've talked a bit. He's concerned about us because of what happened and—I don't know, he's just an easygoing guy. I like him. He's easy to talk to. He's not pushy, he's not looking for anything, he's just around." He shoved his hand through his hair. "I know it sounds corny, but he's become a good friend."

"It's not corny. He sounds like a great guy."

But again, if she'd expected a sheaf of details about Caleb, she'd expected too much. But this was Jack. He never dealt in possibilities or fanciful hopes. If he learned something definite, then he'd say something and not before.

He slipped his arms around her. "I'm sorry, Meg. I really did forget. It sounds like a weasly excuse, but it's the truth."

She sighed, sorry now that she'd let this simmer for so many days. "I believe you." She took his hand. "Come on. I want to show you something Jessup gave me."

In his study, she opened a cupboard in the bookcases. "Close your eyes."

He did so and when he opened them, the model of the *Lucky Louise* sat on his desk. For a few poignant moments, he simply stared as if it were an apparition. He reached out and touched the wood, the hull, the stern, the painted words. He had his back to her, and when she tried to turn him, he brushed her away, clearing his throat. "How did he know what it looked like?"

Meg drew a photo from the bag. It was of Jack and Ford and their father taken months before the boat sank. "He must have gotten this from your mother."

"It's amazingly accurate. I can almost smell the salt and fish guts," he said softly, his full concentration on the model. "Caleb made this . . ." Awe magnified his words. "I had no idea he knew how to work with wood."

"Jessup advised him, but Caleb did the work. The boat was to honor his grandfather—a tribute to his hard work." She touched Jack's back, sliding her hand down and around his waist. "It's yours. Caleb made it for you."

Chapter Fifteen

"Oh, shit."

"What's he doing here?"

"Whatever it is, he's going to see Squires." Bethany backed up by a row of lockers so she couldn't be seen from the principal's office. She shivered, despite a heavy sweater. The truth was that she'd been in a freakin' panic since her date last night with Brandt. She kept thinking about Caleb and how wild he'd be if he knew. And her folks—Jeez, they'd totally lose it. But then she thought of Brandt and how crazy she was about him, and she shook off the crummy details. Besides, she hadn't done anything *really* wrong, she rationalized. She hadn't had *real* sex with him. Everyone did what she'd done.

She had to get it together. This wasn't life and death. This wasn't even—

Erica jerked her sleeve. "Answer me. How would your dad have known? I mean it's not like the cops brought you home or anything."

"I don't know, but he's here, isn't he? He was pissed when I ran out last night. He was already asleep when I came in and Mom was on the phone with Aunt Kate. I kissed her good night and went to bed. He was gone this morning and Mom didn't say anything. But Dad, well, he has a way of finding out stuff. Like when he showed up at the ball game. How did he know I was there with Brandt? When I left the house he'd already gone to meet my uncle." Her eyes darted around, looking for her boyfriend. He was supposed to meet her before her first class and he'd never showed. That made her scared and angry at the same time. After what she'd done, he should be kissing her feet.

"You're gonna get caught doing all this sneaking around," Erica said, shifting her armful of books while she watched Squires's door.

Bethany leaned back against a locker, a smile spreading across her face. "Oh, wait a sec. Maybe he doesn't know and Squires is just gonna give him my name."

"I don't see how that's a happy thought."

"You get gloomy over anything I do or say."

"You mean stupid and risky."

"Yeah, yeah, yeah." When another student stopped to open her locker, Bethany lowered her voice to a whisper. "What can Squires say that proves anything? I mean, like the cops didn't take me to the station and call my parents. There's no proof Brandt and I were even there. Someone ratted out a lot of names and Squires probably called all the parents. But hey, I can just tell Dad that Squires got confused."

"But wouldn't he have all the parents come in at once? He could just tell what he knows—kinda like one of his 'heads-up' pronouncements. That way he wouldn't look like he was accusing when he doesn't know for sure?"

"Whose side are you on anyway?" Bethany snapped. "Besides, why is he sticking his nose in my business or in anyone else's? It wasn't like it happened at school or anything."

Erica stared at her aghast. "I can't believe you're talking like this. Since you didn't do anything wrong, why don't you just say you were at the party and left after a few minutes?"

"Hello? Get a clue, will ya. My parents would ground

me forever if they found out Brandt took me to a party where there were drugs."

Erica almost dropped her books. "He knew about the drugs before you went?" Her voice carried and a few heads turned.

"Shut up, will ya?"

But Erica seized on this new turn, her words tight with hindsight rebuke. "You wouldn't be in this mess if you'd listened to me and hadn't started going out with him. Now some kids get busted for drugs and you're gonna get in big trouble. Brandt was a jerk for taking you to that party, but he's a jerk all the time. No news there. No wonder Caleb had good reasons to hate him."

"That was because of Donnie. Not drugs." She fluffed her hair and gave Erica her most practiced pose in sophistication. "Besides, it wasn't Brandt's fault. I wanted to go," she said defensively. "It was a private senior party and Brandt wanted to see a couple of his friends. You know how hard it is for a freshman like me to get into a senior party? I mean, this was major and I wasn't going to miss out. Besides, we stayed only for a few minutes. The cops came after we left."

"The only lucky thing about this."

"Yeah," she said, but not with any enthusiasm. What she didn't tell Erica was that when she saw all the drugs she had to practically drag Brandt away.

At first, she'd tried to act cool, but the way some of the kids were spacing out sent off too many alarms in her head. In a dark corner of the living room, she'd found Brandt sucking on a pint of vodka and leaning over that slut Dara Lane. Bethany wanted to claw her eyes out for her pouty mouth, big boobs, and the way her fingers played over his zipper. Then she wanted to smack Brandt for the lusty-eyed stare he was layin' on Dara. Bethany had already witnessed one guy gettin' a bj. No way was she gonna look the other way so Brandt could get one from Dara.

He'd flipped out when she pulled him away, and for a

few frightening moments he balked, shoving her away as if he didn't know her, as if she were nuts. She'd screamed at him that she was going home, then marched out the door, fully intending to do just that—never mind that it was dark, rainy and four miles to her house. He caught up with her just as she exited the driveway and headed down Route 8.

He begged her to get into the truck, and for a few moments she felt righteous and powerful. He looked so pained and she truly believed he was going to say he was sorry, but then once she was in the vehicle, he took off, gravel skidding, tires squealing.

Throwing her ugly glances, he cursed and yelled worse than her dad ever had. He called her a baby who always dumped shit in the sugar. This is the thanks he got for makin' her his main girlfriend. Main girlfriend? Like Dara was one? And Karla, his ex, too? Bethany had seem them laughing together plenty of times. Were they still getting it on? But she had no chance to ask because he just kept yelling about what a baby she was.

All the kids did drugs. All the kids drank. All the kids did mouth sex. And she didn't buy all that bullshit that bj's were like real sex, did she? Bj's were the same as a kiss good night. Girls begged to do them. Why was she actin' like she didn't know the score? Was she the only weirdo in the school?

Hurt by his cruelty, she'd curled against the door, wishing she'd done as her dad had told her and stayed home. This wasn't the way acting older and sexy was supposed to turn out. For all her belief that Brandt wanted her as much as she wanted him, the events of the night and him making her feel like a snot-nosed kid devastated her.

Later, she hated herself for it, but the tenseness and the very real terror that he was going to take her home and say "see you later," had her burrowing against him and saying she was sorry. She just knew if she didn't he'd break up with her and she loved him and she would absolutely die if he dumped her. Then she'd cried.

He didn't say anything, just kept driving as if he were waiting for her to beg some more. She told him she loved him, that she'd do anything for him. Again she said she was sorry—she kissed him and kissed him, wanting to make things the way they were before the party. Then he told her how to make him like her again. And she'd been so grateful . . . so relieved there was a way to keep him . . .

"Are you sure you're okay?" Erica asked. "You look kinda white."

"Oh, God, I think I'm gonna be sick."

Bethany started to hurry away when Erica halted her. "Wait, look, there's your dad."

Bethany swung around, her stomach churning. She pressed her arm against her middle, nauseated by her own shame, dizzied by the scene now before her. Her father stood in the open doorway talking with Squires, and Bethany had the most urgent need to run down the hall and throw her arms around him and say she loved him and that she would never do anything to hurt him, that she was sorry she ran out last night. This was her father and he always understood, always forgave her, always made her feel cherished and loved and wanted.

Then he turned so that she could see his face and she saw the anger. Not wild, reckless anger like she'd seen in Brandt, but a deep fury of untested proportions.

In that moment, she knew she'd never convince him to believe her. He'd already made up his mind and she was in major trouble.

Seth Eidson glanced up when DeWilde walked into his office. He slammed the door and Eidson winced.

"I assume it didn't go well."

"Christ, I wanted to wring his fucking neck."

"That does explain a lot," Eidson said, gesturing to the chair. "Sit down."

He dropped into the chair like a marionette whose strings had just been cut. Eidson opened a bottom drawer, took out a bottle of whiskey, poured some into a foam cup and slid it across his desk. "I keep it for just such luckless occasions."

DeWilde tossed it down and shook his head when Eidson offered a refill.

"Okay, so tell me what happened."

"I told him I wanted to set up and fund a baseball scholarship in Caleb's name. Fifty grand cash with a scholarship of five given every commencement to a graduating senior beginning this June. With the remaining balance invested, it will eventually pay for itself."

Eidson gave a low whistle. "Impressive."

"I'm not interested in impressing anyone. I'm doing it to honor my son." He rose to his feet, his fury not yet abated. Eidson was glad to see it. He worried that he hadn't seen enough raw anger. A beloved son hanging himself was cause for some very raw anger.

Now DeWilde flung his hands in the air, then dropped them into his lap, curling them into twin fists. "They got some memorial that stops traffic where he hanged himself, and that's okay. Rivers retires Caleb's number and comes off the hero of the year, and that's okay. I wondered why that ceremony didn't get more attention. No one but the kids seemed to know anything about it. I asked Squires and he gave me some bullshit about it not being school policy to glorify self-inflicted death. The quiet ceremony with only the kids was okayed, but anything that drew more attention—anything like the local newspaper doing an interview or taking a couple of photos? No. Oh no, we can't allow that."

"I think I know where this is going," Eidson said quietly, not getting even a pause from DeWilde.

"Then I presented the scholarship idea. Squires stammers and stalls and plucks at his sleeve and in the end tells me it would be a problem. A problem! Free money to help a kid go to college and that's a problem? I was speechless and furious."

"Furious, yes. Speechless, I doubt." Eidson got to his feet while DeWilde slouched even lower in the chair, his expression bleak. Seth poured coffee, pondering this momentary setback.

When Jack had called him at home earlier that morning and explained his idea, Eidson had agreed that a monetary memorial that honored Caleb and the game he loved sounded inspired. He'd heard a father's enthusiasm and his own heart had done a bit of an emotional lurch. However, he'd warned him that it might not be as simple as telling Squires and getting the okay. He would need the school board's approval, but DeWilde had paid scant attention. Not surprising since he was accustomed to finessing expectation into reality. Squires's rebuff had honestly dumbfounded him.

Eidson pressed a mug of coffee into his friend's hand and then he perched on the edge of his desk. Even as he anticipated the answer, he asked, "Why did he say no?"

"Suicide isn't politically correct." He stood and crossed to the window, then turned and leaned against the sill, lifting the coffee and sipping. "He reaffirmed the school policy of not glorifying self-inflicted death and turning the person into a hero."

"Squires fears copycats. A couple of school districts upstate had this problem and set up similar rules. Kids glamorize things, and the scholarship would give Caleb a permanency most would envy. Like winning some award, but with more clout and prestige that would be noted every graduation when the scholarship is given. That enviable legacy has magic to a mixed-up kid who feels underappreciated. And if a kid has tried or considered suicide, the lasting tribute could make him think he'll be more popular, more glorious in death than in life. Just like Caleb."

"Glorious in death? God, that's sick. So my son's memory and place in Cooper Falls high school history is buried just like we did his body. Erase him on the chance that some other kid might think suicide is heroic. Well, I'm not going to let it happen. Caleb didn't kill himself to be glorified. I'm going to call the head of the school board and ask for a meeting to discuss this unwritten policy. If they refuse, I'm going to raise hell."

Eidson waited and when DeWilde didn't elaborate, he asked, "Then you've learned something?"

"What? Learned something about what?"

"You said Caleb didn't die to be glorified. Have you and your wife learned something new?"

"No. Not about his death, but about the kind of kid he was." Jack told him about the model of the *Lucky Louise* and his realization that his son had honored not only the grandfather he'd never known, but had done so with the one thing—re-creating the boat—that had meant so much to Reilly DeWilde.

Eidson listened, aware that this insight about Caleb had aroused in DeWilde a deep certainty that he had never allowed himself to acknowledge. Even amidst entrenched and hardened resistance toward his own father, DeWilde held respect for a man who, until the loss of his boat, had lived the life he loved without apology.

"If Caleb had lived, he and I would have fought about the baseball verses college issue until the real casualty would have been my relationship with him. I never considered pro ball as a serious career he would love; I saw it as some wistful dream that played better in the movies than in real life. When I saw the boat model, it was like looking at my own badly handled past. My old man wanted me to fish and I hated it. I ended up hating him for all the grief he caused me . . . the family . . ." He paused. Eidson didn't speak and the silence lengthened. "You know what kept me awake last night?"

"What?"

"That I benefited from Caleb dying. Isn't that a helluva thought? If he had lived, he would have grown to hate me because I would have squashed his ambition."

"A profound conclusion, Jack, but leave some room for the possibility that he would have respected you for insisting on college."

DeWilde gave him a stony look. "No wiggle room, pal."

Eidson shrugged. "Hey, I'm just calling it as I see it."

"And I'm telling you how it would have been. I'm just like my old man. Never listened, just demanded and expected obedience. I did it in that last argument with Caleb. I did it to Bethany last night. Then with Squires—"

"Bethany adores you and a simple apology will redeem you, whatever happened. But with the head of the school board, you could try a more subtle approach than wringing his fucking neck."

Jack sat back down, stretched his legs out and leveled a meditative look at Eidson, further convincing Eidson that his instincts about Jack DeWilde had been correct from the very beginning. Wisdom came hard and with a price, but it always came.

DeWilde asked, "You think that would make things worse, do you?"

"Marginally."

Meg had gathered pictures from the den, from the bottom drawer of her dresser and she added his chemistry certificate of excellence. Now she was in Caleb's room sorting through a Reebok box of baseball snapshots. It was late afternoon, and after meeting with Hannah and making some garden suggestions, she'd given the young woman a list to take to Bushes. They'd looked at Lily's baby pictures, and Meg wept with her for this tiny life that arrived and then died so swiftly. Hannah spoke of having another child, wanting but fearing. Meg offered no advice. Beyond trusting instincts, or as Vicki would have said—following their hearts—advice was schlock. For surely they wanted Lily in her cradle, sleeping and breathing and growing. They wanted what couldn't be just as Meg and Jack and Bethany did.

After leaving, she'd stopped at a local specialty shop and bought a scrapbook, rubber stamps, ink pads of colors, designer papers she thought Caleb would have liked, plus ribbon and a calligraphy pen.

All of it was spread out on the dining room table when Bethany came in from school. She'd seemed out of sorts, causing Meg to assume it was the month anniversary that had upset her. When she probed, Bethany burst into tears, flinging herself into her mother's arms. Meg held her and they'd both cried.

Bethany was intrigued by the scrapbooking idea and Meg quickly pushed a pile of photos toward her, leaving her to sort while she went in search for more.

Now Meg emptied the memory drawer. His baseball jacket, the clothes he'd worn that she hadn't washed and the sweater that Vicki had given her. She put the items on the bed, and lifted out the pictures she'd been looking for.

Downstairs, Bethany grinned when her mother came in with more snapshots. "This is a really cool idea."

"I thought so. I just wish I'd dated all these after they were developed. Like that one there at the cottage. Caleb looks about ten." He stood in wet trunks, goggles around his neck and enormous fins on his feet. His creature picture, she recalled. "I remember. 1993. Your father bought the boat and then sold it a few weeks later."

"He never has liked boats, has he?"

"Because he spent so much time on fishing boats when

he was young. He thought a pleasure boat would be different, but it wasn't."

"I saw the one Caleb made. It's cool."

"Very cool." Meg arranged a fan of Christmas photos, trying to decide which ones she liked best. "By the way, I talked to Erica a little while ago."

Bethany's eyes widened. "You did? About me?"

"About her being Caleb's girlfriend." Was that relief she saw in her daughter's face? "Nothing to add."

She shrugged. "If she said Caleb was her boyfriend, she's telling you what she wished, not what was true."

"So she liked him and he didn't like her? Or if he did the relationship was so new that nobody knew about it."

"Where did you get the idea? From Erica?"

She told of Jessup talking about a girlfriend and Vicki naming Erica. "I'm trying to pin down who Caleb wanted to talk to before he died. No one seems to have any idea."

"It wasn't Erica, Mom. Caleb wouldn't talk to her about anything because she's had a crush on him forever. He never did anything to make her think she had a chance with him. What did she tell you?"

"That she was sure he liked her as much as she liked him." Meg poured herself and Bethany a glass of Coke. "I took that to mean she liked him, but he didn't return the affection." She sighed. "It's just one more dead end. There's been so many that this one barely caused me to blink."

They worked silently, sorting pictures and trying out different arrangements for the scrapbook.

"Mom?"

"Hmmm." She picked out three Christmas ones she liked, set them aside and then pondered the one where he was opening the package from his mother with the sweater Vicki had returned.

"Is Dad upstairs?"

"Yes, he was making a phone call."

She cleared her throat and Meg glanced up. "Is he mad at me?"

"For disobeying and running out last night? Probably. And he should be."

She looked penitent and pale. "I'm sorry."

"Honey, you owe the apology and the explanation to your father. If you'd done it to me, I would have grounded you for a week. What he has in mind, I have no idea. Why don't you go find him and ask him."

She slid the chair across the carpet and got to her feet, hands rubbing down the sides of her leggings. "Yeah."

"Bethany, are you okay?" Her daughter had always been so self-sufficient, always on top of problems that Meg tended to regard minor mood swings as passing teenage angst and gave them minimal attention. But the last month had been horrendous and, no doubt, Bethany needed some special attention—just for her. "You'd tell me if anything was wrong, wouldn't you?"

"Sure."

Seeing a despair in her eyes, Meg didn't want to push, but at the same time she didn't want to be dismissive. "I had a thought today." Truthfully it just occurred to her. "Why don't we plan that shopping trip to Boston that Kate mentioned? We could get you some clothes for summer and then pig out on all that great North End Italian food."

She almost smiled. "That sounds great."

"Good. I'll set it up," Meg said, convinced Bethany was as cool to the idea as she would be to spending an evening at a Neil Diamond concert. "I'm expecting to hear from Kate in the next few days on another matter, so I'll ask her when we can get together."

She nodded, then left the room in search of her father.

Meg wanted to believe that her disobedience the previous night accounted for her low mood. Probably. And that was good if bad behavior bothered her, proving her conscience was in good working order.

She returned to her picture sorting, glancing up when she heard the knock. Rising, she went to open the back door.

Jack had been on his way downstairs when the sweater on Caleb's bed brought him to a halt. He stared as if it were some apparition sent to haunt him, which it probably was—by Vicki, of course. Had she decided to return his coolness by going to Meg? Using the sweater as her entree and then telling Meg of the tryst? Wouldn't that be a coup for Vicki, he thought, too aware of the sinkhole forming in his belly. On the eve of her trip to the Islands, she confesses to Meg and then safely flies away so that she's out of the firestorm.

Brilliant and underestimated suddenly seemed more appropriate descriptions for his employee than young and in love.

Wait a sec, pal, you're getting way ahead of yourself. He'd kissed Meg when he came home; she'd returned it with spit and tongue and a whispered promise of what she wanted to do to him. If their daughter hadn't been ten minutes from coming home, he would have done his best Rhett Butler sweep and taken her up the stairs right then. But instead he simply enjoyed the appetizer and the happiness in her eyes. Joy like he'd seen that rainy afternoon they'd made love. He didn't even mind that her beaming smile was about a scrapbook she'd described in minute detail. The photo spread and all the accessories that she showed him were hardly the reaction of a woman who had just learned she had a cheating husband. Nor was that kiss. Or the promise.

"Daddy?"

He swung around, his heart barreling around in his chest. His face burned as though he'd been caught with dirty pictures. Grateful that he hadn't switched on the light in Caleb's room and have her asking questions, he murmured, "I didn't hear you."

Bethany stood just a few feet away in the late afternoon light. Her hands were clenched, her posture itchy like she had sand on her skin. "Last night—uh, I wanted to talk to you about it."

"All right."

She seemed to study him, obviously gauging how deep the shit she'd have to plow through to earn his forgiveness or at least avoid major "get to your room" time. If not for the sweater and his desperate need to find out how Meg got it . . . but he couldn't let this go. He'd blown it the night before—no excuse today.

He left the sweater on the bed and walked toward her. "I owe you an apology for coming down so hard last night. I did treat you like a baby," Jack said, cupping her chin and lifting, never tiring of noting how pretty she was. Her eyes were sad and troubled and he would have drawn her into his arms if her body hadn't jerked back.

"*You're* sorry?" She swallowed as if comprehension alluded her.

Catching her off-guard delighted him. It rarely happened. "I am. However, going out of here like that is not acceptable behavior, young lady. Understand?"

She lowered her head. "Yes."

He started past her, when she grabbed his sleeve. "That's it?"

"You expected a lecture, privileges revoked and a steady diet of brussels sprouts?"

Her shudder showed her lasting hatred of brussels sprouts. "I fucked up. You're not going to do anything?"

Jack raised his eyebrows, about to chastise her for bad language then realizing how stupid that would be. What a great message. In your room for a week for saying fuck, but you get a pass for major disobedience. "No. I'm not going to do anything."

Instead of the relief he expected to see, instead of

"thanks, Dad, you're the best," instead of a hug and a kiss, she burst into tears and ran to her room, slamming the door.

Jack stared at the closed door, confusion churning through him. Females. Vicki claiming she loved him, Meg pissed one minute, forgiving the next, his daughter hysterical because he didn't punish her. Emotions and melodrama and unpredictability. So much for Seth's easy redemption.

He lifted the sweater from the bed, glancing at the other items and then seeing the open drawer. Again, confusion gripped him. Why had she put the baseball jacket in the drawer? Then he picked through the other items. A book report, sweats that hadn't been laundered, his baseball cap—all things Caleb had touched or worn in the days before he died. Fraught with memories, he realized, because they were worn by Caleb. He pressed his nose into the jacket, the sweater, the sweats and found his fading scent.

Meg's connections. Like the box of Pop-Tarts in the kitchen cupboard, like her buying pansies for under the Caleb trees because she'd done it last year and Caleb had helped her plant them one Saturday afternoon.

Harmless and okay, he guessed, feeling adrift in emotional overload. He left the other items, closed the door and although he wanted to ignore the sweater, he couldn't. This was a present connection, his connection and he wanted it broken.

Chapter Sixteen

When he paused in the kitchen doorway and saw her, the sweater weighed in his hand like a live grenade; throwing it at her lunged through his thoughts. *You're beyond insane, pal.*

Jack had covered his ass enough in business and in life to know that an easy charm plus a firm but nonthreatening approach dismantled a situation quicker than a defensive posture peppered with a barrage of accusations.

"I thought you were taking off early today to finish your trip's last minute details," he said easily. "No problems, I hope."

Wearing a yellow suit that showed off her salon tan, her smile at seeing him had to be a hundred-and-fifty-watt. "I had some work that needed to be finished."

Yeah, I bet. "Dedication. That's what I like." He casually placed the sweater over the back of one of the chairs. When he once again glanced at her, she was gazing at him as if being in his life would make her dreams come true.

She'd told him she'd wait for him and that she loved him; Jack had given neither any credence. Love and commitment based on a onetime sexual incident was the stuff of diaries and B-movie love formulas and beach blanket declarations that were no more realistic than a sand castle withstanding the incoming tide.

But here in her crisp suit of sophistication, she reminded him of when she came to DeWilde's last fall about handling the sale of her aunt's house. Jack had been impressed by her decisiveness and her maturity and, yeah, he hadn't missed her understated sexiness. He wasn't naïve. He knew that dynamic was as much a part of her ability to sell real estate as her professionalism and her command of detail. Whatever worked. Something usually did for she got the sale 89 percent of the time. Clearly, she had concluded she could get what she wanted in her personal life, too.

By ignoring her, by keeping a safe distance, by giving her zero reason to hope, he'd assumed—and fervently hoped—her feelings would lose their moorings and drift away. They obviously hadn't. Considering her logic, she could believe that he would eventually realize he did love her, divorce Meg and marry her. That thinking scared him and it saddened him.

However insignificant he'd viewed his intimacy with her, she'd taken it very seriously. Instead of gaining ground with time, he suddenly felt as entangled as he'd been that day in the office.

"I just finished showing the Cardinal Drive house and since it was just a couple of blocks, I didn't think you'd mind if I dropped the keys here. It would save me some time and a trip back to the office." She came around the table and pressed the keys into his hand. A brush of a touch, but enough to feel her chilled fingers.

Jack put the keys in his pocket and squeezed her arm in what he hoped she would interpret as good-bye. "Have a nice trip," he said, turning to the side so she wouldn't notice the rapid fire thump in his chest. His mouth felt dry and his thoughts, a feast of old-time survival tricks, presented innovative, but illegal ways to get her out of his life, none of which were subtle or realistic. This is why men murder their mistresses.

His told-you-so conscience suggested that if he'd given Meg the truth weeks ago, *she* wouldn't have let Vicki into the house. Then again, he might not be here either.

That dismal possibility had snuck out of his closet of probabilities when she'd told him she'd never cheat on him. Jack adroitly pointed out that good old Sloane had no such scruples. However, if the question had been posed to him, Meg wouldn't be swayed by his word parsing, nor was she likely to succumb to his charm and memorized excuses. Not now. He could imagine her disgust: "And *you* accused Sloane? You hypocrite!"

He winced painfully just pondering the various outcomes—all of which had disaster carved into them.

He moved close to Meg, but resisted overdoing it by putting his arm around her. Vicki stood on the other side of the table where Meg had been piling the pictures she didn't want to use. "I'm going to get all these labeled and then ask your mom to put them in albums for me."

"Good idea. What's for supper?"

"Supper? Oh, I hadn't thought about it. I see you found the sweater."

"Yes." Stay cool. Don't ask. Let her tell you.

"You're not upset, are you?"

"By the sweater? Should I be?"

"Maybe, and about Caleb's other things." Suddenly she looked sheepish. "Keeping his clothes in a drawer—it seems silly sometimes, but there's something about having them, his scent in the folds, touching them, knowing they're nearby . . ."

"They give you connections to him."

"Yes! You do understand."

"I understand." And he did. He understood because he'd had exactly the same reaction to the model of the *Lucky Louise*. He'd examined the boat with the minutest of detail, reveling in the pleasure of knowing his son had worked the wood. He'd constructed the pieces and where he'd found his son's marks he'd rejoiced. Imperfections made it Caleb's.

"You don't think I'm being morbid or paranoid or obsessive?"

"I think you're being his mother and you miss him and want to feel close to him."

The relief in her eyes made him feel like a horse's ass. She'd so obviously expected either an argument or a diminishing of her memories. Had he really acted so callously these past weeks? Dwelling in these sad places seemed so pointless to him for he couldn't fathom a way out. Maybe that's where he got messed up as a kid—he'd tried to make the bad stuff disappear by pretending it didn't exist. Meg not only acknowledged the bad stuff, she never flinched from its most tangible reminders. Her patience and faith in her family comforted him with its steadiness, and he was reassured by her strength. She was an incredible woman.

She hugged him now, her fingers digging in, holding on as if understanding his struggle had taken some momentous turn. Vicki watched the entire exchange saying nothing and yet, not for a moment did Jack believe her mind floated with rosy goodwill.

"I should go," Vicki finally said and not a moment too soon for Jack.

"Hey, have a great vacation." *And if you call and say you want to stay another week, I'll tell you to enjoy yourself.*

"I just wish I wasn't going alone," she said, shouldering her purse and turning her mouth down at the corners. Jack stiffened. Now what? Was she going to say she'd invited him? "It seems I do everything alone these days."

"I'm sure you'll meet lots of people," Meg offered and Jack said nothing.

"It's just that going with a friend or a boyfriend is much more fun." She fiddled with the bottom button of her suit jacket, while Jack's blood turned to ice. He glared at her, his eyes chips of fury. *Don't do this. Turn around, walk to the door and say good-bye.*

Meg had begun pulling food out of the refrigerator, and to Jack's everlasting relief, Vicki read the message and opened the back door.

Meg, a pan of lasagna in her hands, looked at Jack with her good host expression. Oh God, he knew what was coming. *Don't do it, Meg. Please, baby, don't.*

"Well, I should go. Thanks so much, Meg, for the other day. I hope we can do it again when I get back."

Jack blinked. The other day? Was that how Meg got the sweater? And what else did Vicki give her? But before he could frame a reason to walk Vicki out to her car and find out, Meg said, "Listen, since you probably don't want to bother with cooking when you have all the last minute things, why don't you stay for supper? We have plenty if you don't mind pot luck. And you can tell me what happened with the stagers."

Jack felt his heart drop like a hammer. No way was he enduring a meal with Vicki. He had to get her out of here.

Meg lifted Caleb's sweater and pressed it into his hands. "Take this back upstairs, and tell Bethany we'll eat in about twenty minutes." She frowned. "Are you okay?"

"Uh, yeah, look why don't you go tell Bethany. She's not real happy with me at the moment."

"Then you did punish her. I agree she needed to be, but today . . ." She sighed. "She had a bad time of it down here."

Jack's mind scrambled. He glanced at the wall calendar. One month. Jesus. "Obviously the reason she was so upset," he said so smoothly he winced inwardly. How could he have forgotten? "I told her I was sorry for coming down so hard on her. She reacted as if I'd threatened to lock her in her room until she was eighteen."

"Some days it's tempting," Meg murmured. "But I'm glad you didn't do it today." She took the sweater, glanced at Vicki. "Thanks for returning this." She then reached up and brushed her mouth across his cheek. Sweet, sweet

Meg. His Meg. "Set the table and get things started. I'll be right back."

No sooner did Jack hear her on the stairs, he looked directly at Vicki. "What the hell do you think you're doing?"

Startled, she took a step back. "Nothing, I was just dropping the keys off to you."

"You don't have time to take the keys to the office but you have time to stay and eat?"

"I didn't come to stay—you're acting like I did."

"Call me cynical and wary. How did Meg get the sweater?"

"We had lunch yesterday and—"

"You had lunch? You and my wife? Are you nuts?" He shuddered at his imaginings of what they talked about. He was damn sure Vicki hadn't called her to discuss house stagers.

She folded her arms and glared at him. "For your information Meg invited me for lunch. Someone in your family cares very much why Caleb killed himself."

Jack felt the sucker punch. "And I suppose you had the answer all wrapped up for her."

"No, but I sure have wrapped up where her husband was when it was going on."

Jack closed his eyes, the word bitch coming to mind, but he lacked the energy or will to even say it. The truth sucked, and hearing it here in his own kitchen turned his stomach sour. For about the hundredth time, he asked himself why he hadn't thought of the ramifications of betrayal. *Ego, pal. Plain garden-variety male ego. You underestimated her and overestimated yourself.*

She walked to the back door. "Give Meg my apologies for not staying. I'm sure you'll find a suitable explanation. By the way, if I wanted to let Meg know about us, I would have told her weeks ago. I'm in love with you, but right now I don't like you very much."

She closed the door behind her.

• • •

It was a phone call Meg never expected.

"Hello?" Her breath was reedy from rushing in from the yard. There'd been a number of hang-ups on the voice mail so she'd shut it off while she was home. The day had been sunny and warm, fueling her need to get some of the pansies planted to add color beneath the Caleb trees.

"I got something to tell you." No greeting, no small talk.

"Jessup?"

"You wanna come here. I'm home." And he hung up.

She didn't question his abruptness. He'd never liked phones, refused to talk to an answering machine and she guessed he'd gone to the 7-Eleven pay phone. She glanced at her watch. Bethany would be in from school, and she'd wanted to be here, but she was very sure what Jessup had to tell her was about Caleb.

She washed her hands, pulled off her sweatshirt and threw on her jacket. She left Bethany a note, grabbed her shoulder bag and fifteen minutes later, she'd parked in Jessup's yard.

He stood in the open doorway, his face grim, his shoulders slumped. The two raccoons flanked him like curious sentries.

Meg crossed the muddy yard. "What is it?"

Again no small talk, no social amenities. "I didn't think you needed to know. I wanted no piece of adding pain to what you have. Last night I was thinkin' I had no right not to tell you if I really believed you were strong. I do, Meggie. I do. But Ray, well, he always tried to protect you and when he died I wanted to honor him and do as he did. I don't know if this is the right thing." He wiped his sleeve across his eyes, shielding his face. "Don't know if it's a good thing."

Confused and dizzy from his ramblings, she whispered,

"You're scaring me. What thing? Protect me from what thing?"

"I don't know. I don't even know where it is or if it still is. He might've thrown it away. Maybe he never even put things in it. Maybe it's only good things."

Meg wanted to scream. "Jessup, what are you talking about?"

He stared at her as if she were slow. "The journal. Caleb's journal."

Meg clamped her hand over her mouth to contain the frantic flurry of excitement. Jessup watched her with grave concern as if she might faint or run shrieking in hysteria.

"Caleb kept a journal?" she finally managed to whisper as if saying it aloud would frighten away the angels that convinced Jessup to call her. A journal and its potential for answers was so mammoth, her mind just blanked out. "My God."

He simply stood silent, as was Jessup's habit. Meg's legs felt like kindling that had snapped in too many places. She gripped the 4×4 post where morning glories would twine in a couple of months.

"Where is it, Jessup? Where did he keep it?"

"Only saw him with it one or two times. After Kevin died he had lots of trouble understandin'. I showed him the book I kept in 'Nam, told him how it helped to write things down."

How it helped to write things down. In times of war, times of sadness, times of trouble and pain. Oh, Caleb, sweetheart . . . Meg tried to breathe deeply and found her lungs were empty. "Where do you *think* he kept it?" she asked again.

He glanced down, hands shoved deep into brown overalls.

"Don't know."

You don't know? You called me. I'm here with my hopes raised to the heavens and you don't know? How can you not know? Her mind ached as much as her heart. "But you must know. My God, how many places are there?"

He shrugged.

"Do you think he hid it?"

The shrug again.

"Jessup, help me, please. Some suggestions. Tell me what you're thinking because I know you're thinking something." She paused, her motive shameless, but she didn't care. "Dad would want you to help me with this. You know he would—"

"It's not here," he said abruptly. "I tore the place apart. Even looked under the house. It ain't anywhere around here."

"Okay, that's a start. Knowing where it isn't eliminates places. I know it's not in his room for I've already been through all his things."

"Maybe at that house he trashed," he offered.

She thought about that. Possible. For sure it was worth a look. She walked close to him and hugged him. "Thank you. You don't know what this means to me."

"Hope it don't hurt you more'n you already been hurt."

"Nothing could hurt as much as losing him."

But she didn't find it.

Meg drove down to the cottage two days in a row and turned the place upside down. When she wanted to go the third day, Jack objected.

Jessup's journal revelation had jerked Meg from the stable emotional arena of memory drawers and scrapbooks and dumped her right back into an obsessing new turmoil. Well, Jack had just about enough of Jessup and his interference.

"We're going out to an expensive lunch, you're going to have a mudslide and we're going to try and remember when our lives included runaway lunches and simply a time for us."

She looked stricken, then clutched his hands. "Jack, listen to me. The journal is so important."

"We're more important. Being together is more important."

"It could tell us why."

"It could not exist. Get your jacket. I made reservations for one o'clock."

"Not exist?" Her eyes were as big as the purple pansies she'd planted. "Are you crazy? Jessup told me he saw Caleb with it."

"Jessup told the cops he wasn't growing grass anymore. Seth knows differently. So much for his truth-telling." He took her arm and walked her out the back door.

"Why are you so insistent we do this today?"

"Because the reservations are for today."

He had the passenger door of the Lexus open. "I guess I should be flattered that you prefer my company to Murph the mortgage lender."

"Murph is out of town. Thank God."

She giggled for she knew he hated having lunch with the ubiquitous Murph. She slid into the seat and he leaned in and kissed her. "I like hearing you laugh and watching you smile."

She touched his hair where he knew the gray was spreading faster than the speed of light. "I have missed doing lunch with you."

"I've missed you."

"Oh Jack, I know I've been distracted—"

He touched his finger to her mouth. She kissed it and nodded. Thoughts transferred without words, he decided, were one of the pearls of a long marriage.

At the crowded restaurant, they were shown to a table for two with a glass top over a blue tablecloth. A small vase of daffodils displayed the early bounty of spring. A waiter filled their water glasses, took their drink order and left them with menus. They both nodded and smiled to some people they recognized at a nearby table.

When her mudslide arrived along with his Dewar's, he lifted his glass. "A toast." She lifted hers. "To many more lunches, many more years."

"Yes," she whispered, tears springing in her eyes. "Many more years to love each other. For I do love you very much."

Her words stirred his heart and left him choked for a response. If only he deserved her words, deserved her . . . In that moment he knew that what he'd done with Vicki was so odious, so wrong, so selfish that he'd not only defiled a marriage vow of faithfulness, he'd deeply dishonored Meg.

Christ almighty. Vicki would be back on Monday and he was running flat-out of time. No doubt, she would still be pissed and pissed-off women were volatile and unpredictable. His own tornado of guilt had spun to the point that he expected trouble before it happened. His behavior and thought processes were way over into the paranoid. Fredi had told him that morning of a female tourist drowning in St. Thomas during some party.

"Poor thing, but thank God, it wasn't our Vicki," she'd said somberly. For a dead, cold moment, Jack wished it was. His own survival and escape from adversity were finely tuned instincts that Jack hadn't seriously needed in years. He'd not forgotten how brutally those instincts bleached his emotions into hollow shells. Empty to the point that Vicki drowning had nothing to do with sorrow or shock, but only that if true he'd be spared ever having to tell Meg what a bastard she'd married.

Yet realistically, his betrayal remained a fact whether Meg knew or not. And that was the crux of the issue. Not whether he had the balls to confess or if he had the skills to create an excuse whereby Meg would forgive him, but that his silence to protect himself was another lie.

Meg was staring at him, her eyes puzzled. "Is anything wrong?"

Here's your opportunity. Tell her what's wrong. Not with her, but with you. Tell her you love her, tell her you betrayed her, tell her how sorry you are . . .

"Jack? Is it something at work?"

"No, not at work." He gripped his glass, not looking at her. "Meg . . ."

The birthday celebration at a nearby table got noisier and someone spotted Jack, wove his way to their table and urged them to join the party for a birthday toast. Meg agreed when she saw the birthday gal was the former principal at the high school the years that Meg attended.

"Come with me to wish her well, Jack. She was so kind about Caleb, calling and offering to help. My goodness, she must be near seventy-five."

"At least," he murmured, rising and taking her elbow as they made their way toward the crowd.

Just as well, he told himself. A busy restaurant was a lousy place to bleed.

She wasn't drunk, but by the time Jack dropped her off at the house, she was feeling giggly and relaxed. Vaguely she wondered why he hadn't told her what was bothering him, but after they'd returned to their table and lunch arrived, he seemed to be his old self. He'd taken a phone call from Fredi and another one from Murph who wanted to meet for lunch the following week. Jack rolled his eyes, but agreed.

He'd assured her he didn't have to rush, then proved it by lingering over coffee and dessert. She suspected he had work waiting for him—when didn't he? Yet, he'd made her his priority for a few hours, and she'd loved him all the more for the sweet gesture.

There was a note from Bethany that she'd gone with

Brandt to the mall. She checked her voice mail. There was a call from Hannah and one from Bushes. She returned Hannah's, answering her question about how far from the house to put the rhododendrons. Then she returned the call to Danny, the manager, at Bushes.

"Meg, I got two requests from customers for gardening advice."

"Since you sell plants that makes sense."

"Very funny. But it's not me they want advice from."

"Don't tell me. It couldn't be that—" she was going to say idiot. "Not that boy who replaced Caleb."

"No one could replace Caleb, and that's a fact."

"Yes." Meg's mind floated trying to follow Danny's point. "Maybe we should start this conversation over."

"No need. The customers want advice from you."

"Me?"

"One woman overheard Hannah talking about you, and I guess she told a neighbor. Anyway, you know me, always looking for innovative ways to increase business. Here's the deal. Would you do a workshop here for beginning gardeners? Not like school, but in the greenhouse where they can get their hands dirty. I figure twice a week to see how it goes. I'll do some advertising, but word of mouth will probably do the job. I'll put you on the payroll as a part-timer. Maybe you could even come in a couple of mornings and help out. What do you say?"

"I'm speechless."

"Just say yes."

She should clear this with Jack, but then decided that was silly. She wouldn't clear a volunteer job at the local women's shelter. Plus Jack would no doubt be happy she'd found something to occupy her mind besides the missing journal. A couple of hours twice a week would be fun. And giving gardening tips and advice to women as enthusiastic as Hannah could hardly be classified as work.

"Okay, Danny, I'll give it a try."

After she hung up, she walked through the house, down

to the basement and up to the bedrooms. She walked slowly, letting her mind roam into where a teenage boy would hide something. Meg had always allowed the kids their privacy and their adolescent secrets, believing that as long as they did nothing to betray her trust, she had no reason to snoop. Therefore it puzzled her that Caleb would not have just put the journal in a bottom desk drawer or on the top shelf of his closet or even under the mattress. She wouldn't allow herself to think he threw it away. It had to be in the house somewhere.

She began in the basement, going through the cupboards in Jack's work area, plus a cabinet of old toys and even checking between the cushions of the stored porch furniture that would need washing before use this summer.

After an hour, she came back upstairs picking a stray cobweb from her hair and got a bottle of cold water from the refrigerator. So much for the basement. She glanced around while uncapping the bottle and drinking.

Well, there was nothing left to do but tear the house apart. That's what Jessup had done at his place.

She began in the den. Pulling books from the shelves, searching under furniture, even digging into the couch and removing all the cushions. Besides crumbs, some loose change and the earring she'd been missing since last Thanksgiving, she found nothing. She did break a fingernail, then banged her ankle on the edge of the desk when she reached to get the telephone.

"Oh, Kate. Hi."

"You sound overjoyed to hear from me," she said with some pique.

"Try frustrated," Meg muttered, hauling open the middle drawer of the desk.

"My news ought to take care of that. It's about our sweet—and I use the word loosely—little Vicki."

"Don't you want to know about what?" She dug through the top drawer, looking for a nail file.

Kate sighed. "Jesus, I've been bustin' my butt to get

this stuff and you want to tell me why you're frustrated. Let's see. Bethany is wearing black lipstick, only two million of the three million daffodils in your yard came up, Jack can't get it up. Wait, wait, I have it. Mom ran off and eloped with Ben, the hairless golfer who has all his own teeth."

"Are you finished? This is serious." She found the file and went to work on the ragged nail.

"So tell me. What?"

"Caleb kept a journal."

Silence rolled across the connection.

"Like in a diary?" When Meg didn't add anything, she said, "So, don't keep me in suspense. What does it say?"

"That's why I'm frustrated. I don't know. I can't find it." She recounted the visit with Jessup and her fruitless searches.

"Did Jessup get it wrong? Maybe he just thought—"

"No. I was there. I talked with him. There is a journal." She dropped the file in the drawer, then closed it. She sat down, glancing at the mess around her and turned the chair so she couldn't see it. "So tell me about Vicki. I really am curious."

"I called a client who sells real estate and asked him if he could find out where Vicki had worked. He did and I called them asking for her. I ended up speaking with a secretary who had been a pal of hers. We met for a lunch and she expressed concern that Vicki was going to get hurt like she had with Madison Rhinelander."

"A boyfriend?"

"A much older boyfriend. Like in his late fifties. The secretary, a nervous number named Stephanie who chewed the ice in her ginger ale and blinked a lot, told me the graying Madison was rich so I called Porter. First time I've spoken with him since I hung up on him after his satin-sheeted afternoon with that redhead."

"I bet he was surprised."

"He thought I wanted him back, the prick. But that's another story. I asked if he knew Rhinelander. He did—they belonged to the same country club. Porter told me the old guy croaked last year. Sudden heart attack. He also had a very young mistress."

"Vicki?" Meg sat up straight.

"Bingo. The guy was married with three kids, sat on about ten corporate boards plus owns pricey Back Bay real estate. So with this hot new piece of information I went back to Stephanie. I pretended to be understanding of Vicki fucking a married guy—you know the drill? True love that's willing to wait until he sheds his tiresome wife. That sort of nonsense. Stephanie, bless her quivery little heart, decided I was a loyal friend of Vicki's."

Meg shifted uncomfortably. "This sounds pretty seedy and devious."

"Well, hell, of course it's devious. When you want to find out something from someone who doesn't want to tell you, you get devious."

Meg sighed. "Okay, what did Stephanie tell you?"

"Vicki loved Madison and confided to Stephanie that he'd promised to divorce his tiresome wife after the youngest kid was cozily enrolled in Harvard." Kate chuckled. "I resisted humming a few bars of 'My Heart Will Go On,' by the way. Here's the point. Rhinelander died last October while Miss Vicki was in Cooper Falls putting her auntie Rose's house up for sale. She didn't hear until she returned to Boston. According to Stephanie, she took it bad. She got depressed, couldn't work, lost a couple of big sales. Guess they asked for her resignation and she gave it. Of course, with Rhinelander gone, she also lost those all-expense-paid trips to Newbury Street jewelry stores. She moved into her aunt's house and went to work for Jack."

"How sad for her," Meg said. "She told me a boyfriend had died and I wondered why she hadn't been notified. Why didn't Stephanie call her?"

"She was visiting family in New Jersey. Don't get me sidetracked. Remember I said that Stephanie was worried that the same thing would happen to Vicki again like what happened with Madison?"

"Somebody she loves will die?"

"Oh for God's sake, what do I have to do? Spell it out like you're demented? The man she's in love with now is married to someone else."

Meg hesitated, drinking a long swallow from the bottle of water. She didn't want to hear this and she wanted to counter what she knew was ridiculous. Kate loved drama, and at times like this Meg wanted to just hang up. "I presume I'm supposed to conclude she's in love with Jack."

"Very good, Meg. A gold star on your paper. Stephanie said a man named Jack owned the real estate firm where she worked. That pretty much eliminates the other guys in town named Jack."

Meg said nothing.

Nor did Kate.

After a minute passed, Meg asked, "I'm not jumping to the conclusion you're dangling, Kate. Women falling for Jack isn't new. As I recall at one time you were nuts about him. Vicki is young, a bit starry-eyed and drawn to him. We talked about this before. She'd been through a bad time, she was new in town and Jack sent her Caleb, gave her the names of a couple of reliable contractors, plus he gave her a job. She's obviously grateful and mistaken that for love."

"No, you're mixing up the time line. The 'bad' time came after her *first* trip. When she made her second trip, she already had Caleb working for her and she knew Jack because of listing the house. She came back because of Jack, and not for the job he offered."

"Oh, please. Where else would she go but back to the place where she'd made some friends and had at least a semblance of family roots with her aunt's house? She lost her mother when she was a teenager, her father abandoned both of them and then later rejected her when she found him. She sounds more like a lost young woman. I just can't buy that what you've told me is some grand plan on her part."

"You believe Jack doesn't know anything about how she feels?"

The double-edged question caused her to hesitate.

Truthfully, she wasn't sure what she believed. From her own encounters with Vicki, there was no question of her loyalty and devotion to Jack. It certainly wasn't too big a stretch to conclude she might love him. But Jack's knowledge of her infatuation . . . ? That was another angle and if he did know . . . then what? To know and ignore? Wise and prudent. To know and enjoy? A guy thing that was probably harmless, but with obvious risks. To know and encourage? That would be a whole new direction and the bridge to an affair—

She made herself stop. She would not dwell on this. She would not allow herself to think things that she had no basis for.

"Meg?"

"I think we should change the subject."

"You need to tell Jack what I've told you and ask him if he knows she's in love with him. If he does, letting her continue to work so closely with him is reckless and even cruel to Vicki . . . unless . . . he's enjoying all that nubile attention. He is over forty and he's not blind or stupid."

Meg was seething. She resented Kate for slotting her husband into some midlife scenario that instantly raised doubts she hadn't had before this conversation. Doubts that two months ago she would have dismissed with a laugh, but then she would also have dismissed any idea that her son might commit suicide two months ago.

Just what she needed—more unanswered questions. She'd had enough with the mystery surrounding Caleb. This one would just have to wait.

"As I said a moment ago. Let's change the subject or I'm going to hang up. How are things going with Ford?"

"Did you have to ask that?"

"Uh oh."

Kate's breath caught, her voice breaking. "Ford and I aren't doing so hot right now."

"What happened? Is he still there with you?"

"Actually he went up to Gloucester a few days ago. He heard about a couple of boats looking for crews, so if he doesn't come back I'll know he went out. He's broke and he said he just isn't cut out to build boats. He's a fisherman and building one instead of working on one made him feel like a freaky wimp. We argued about it for days. Me telling him that macho stuff was for kids and him telling me that fishing wasn't macho, it was a way of life. His way of life. He thinks I want to change him, but I don't. I just didn't want to lose him in some Atlantic storm. Then he accused me of not thinking he could do the grueling work . . ." She sighed and Meg heard her light a cigarette. "By the time he left we were barely speaking."

"Maybe he just needs some time."

"A fishing boat is not the place to think about personal problems. And he won't. It's all about the money and his father's way of life that he grew up with. He doesn't know how to do anything else." She drew a shaky breath. "This hurts ten times worse than when Porter cheated on me."

"I'm sorry, Kate."

"Yeah, me, too. I love him and I miss him so much." Meg heard the sniffle, then a sob. Her sister crying over a fisherman was so contrary to the Kate who once said money and the right social circles were what really mattered. Falling in love with Ford had changed her.

"Sounds as if you could use some company. Remember when you said something to Bethany about shopping and clothes?"

"Uh huh."

"I told her we'd come up and shop and pig out on North End Italian. How about it? This weekend maybe?"

"I'd love it. Maybe it will get my mind off worrying."

"Probably not, but look for us Saturday morning."

Chapter Seventeen

Bethany and Brandt strolled through the mall sipping huge cups of soda. They'd messed around in the video arcade, she'd bought a new CD and stopped at all the store windows that were already showing summer clothes. While Brandt hung out with a couple of guys, she made a mental list of what she would buy when she and her mother went to Boston.

But aside from those few moments of anticipation, she was bored. Bored with Brandt, bored with school, bored with life. She wondered what was the point, and she couldn't help but think Caleb might have killed himself because life sucked and he just plain ran out of reasons to put up with all the shit. Dad hassling him about college, Mom fawning over him like he was a baby, then he was getting ranted on all the time because he and Donnie were friends.

As they wound through the mall walkers, she glanced up at Brandt, desperately wanting that rush she'd always get when she was near him. But the rush didn't come. Ever since she'd bj'd Brandt, she felt like a dirty virgin. He was still cool and cute and dangerous. That was the trio girls wanted and a lot of them wanted Brandt. She had him and it didn't matter anymore. If Caleb was here, he'd tell her:

"Hey, twerp, you're gettin' smart. He's a loser. 'Bout time you figured it out." And Erica had about the same opinion.

Brandt dragged her closer, whispering. "Hey look, there's the fag. Your brother's favorite secret pal." Donnie was across the mall sitting with a skinny kid in a *Star Trek* tee-shirt.

She sucked up the last of her soda and set the cup down beside a leafy tree in the mall rock garden. "Don't be such a snot, Brandt. They were friends."

"Ain't what I hear."

"Well, you heard wrong."

Donnie and the other boy walked toward one of the movie theaters.

"Whoa. They're going in to jack each other off. Let's go watch."

"No!"

"You know what? You're no fuckin' fun," he snarled. "What's the big deal? You can do me if you don't wanna watch."

"You're disgusting." Then Bethany saw three of the guys who had been at the party. One of them, wearing a tee that read, MEAN GIRLS SUCK, NICE GIRLS SWALLOW, signaled Brandt, who grinned and nodded.

"Let's go."

"I don't want to go to the movies."

"Who said anything about a flick?" He gave an indifferent shrug. "Do what you want. You'll miss the fun."

She grabbed his jacket, twisting the suede into her fist. "Don't, Brandt. Please. Donnie never did anything to you."

"Hey, you're messin' up my suede," he snapped, squeezing her wrist until she let go. He straightened the material. "Go sit on the bench with the old ladies. If I think of it, I'll pick you up on my way out." He turned from her and sauntered toward the other three.

"In your dreams! I won't be here!" she yelled, but he didn't turn around, didn't pay any attention. He'd acted like a jerk ever since the party, ever since she'd "proved" she loved him. She pressed her arm against her stomach, holding down the rise of sickness. She clenched her shaking hands, raising her head when she heard Brandt and the others laugh. Swaggering, they disappeared into the corridor that led to the theater.

She turned her back, holding her breath to stop her tears. She hated herself; she hated what she'd done and she hated Brandt.

"Okay, twerp, you gonna let that loser dump on you?"

She whirled around, expecting Caleb to be perched on the back of the bench. She'd heard his voice, she knew she had. Nearby was only a harried woman with a stroller and her crying toddler who didn't want to ride.

Bethany sorta believed in ghosts from the time she and Erica had explored the haunted barn in a field behind Erica's house. Hot and empty but for some old hay, a broken pitchfork and those wavy voices, Bethany cajoled the shaky Erica to explore. Deep in the barn, they'd heard the farmer calling his cows and they'd heard a woman and a man making love in the loft. Erica had run, but Bethany had lingered, not wanting to miss the chance of seeing a real ghost. Though she didn't, she told Erica she had and then embellished the fantasy. A few weeks later the barn burned down. The girls were convinced the lovers had done it when the farmer found them and threatened to expose them. When they related their romantic version to Erica's father, he'd laughed and said the fire department had burned it because it was a hazard. But Bethany never believed that; she was convinced the lovers sent the fireman to let their spirits escape to a new place where they'd be forever happy.

Ghosts in haunted barns were one thing; a talking spirit in a public mall, well she wasn't so sure, but she hadn't imagined her brother's voice. And no one else called her twerp but Caleb.

Figuring she had nothing to lose, she decided it was

more cool to think it was Caleb than to doubt. Her mother had always told her that faith was harder than doubt, and she desperately wanted to believe. She huddled down on the bench and whispered, "I don't know what to do." Since her brother's spirit was lounging around, she might as well get some advice. "Tell me."

She wasn't at all sure how to get a spirit to speak, but from videos she'd seen, she adopted the most common posture. She sat very still, eyes prayerfully lowered, hands clasped in her lap like she did in church, waiting for his answer to drape over her like a white angel. After a creepy silence that made her feel weird, she straightened, blinked her eyes and glanced around to see if anyone was staring at her. She ran her hands through her hair and rose. Silly. She hadn't *really* heard Caleb; she'd just imagined his spirit.

Spirits couldn't be seen and she knew Caleb was a good spirit. He wouldn't embarrass her or make her look dorky. He'd help her like he'd helped Donnie that time. But since he was dead, he'd have to talk to her in her mind. Yes. That's what he'd done, he'd floated into her heart and mind. All she had to do was believe and listen.

The boredom she'd felt earlier sank beneath an advent of energy. She jumped to her feet, ashamed she'd been sitting and shaking and scared like some wimp. Caleb would be doing something, but he was dead and he couldn't. Well, she could. And she would.

She zigzagged through the walkers toward the movie line that was already forming, ducking behind a couple with two kids. She kept herself on the other side of the line, out of Brandt's sight and eased her way down the corridor that led to tickets. The concession area was open to anyone, so she slipped in. The smell of hot buttered popcorn filled her, returning memories of when her dad had bought huge buckets for her and Caleb.

She spotted Donnie, and just as she started toward him, Brandt's pals slid into sight. They had circled around and like a rumble of gang members stalking down their prey, they surrounded him.

She searched for a way past them when an arm snaked around her neck. "Changed your mind, huh?"

"Brandt . . ." she whispered, more out of irritation than pleasure.

His hand cupped her breast. "Come on, baby, let's go watch."

She wanted to throw off his hand and tell him he was a jerk, but she allowed herself to be led to a "Keep Out" door, which he opened. Inside it was dark and narrow, smelling like sweaty feet. Brandt drew her along, obviously well-acquainted with the narrow steps that led up to the theater's balcony.

"We don't have tickets," she said, knowing someone always swept the balcony for sneaks.

"When you're with Brandt Foley, you don't need a ticket."

She stumbled toward the third row of seats, spotting Donnie and his friend in the middle of the fifth row.

"Donnie, hi!" she shouted, wincing when Brandt jerked her arm.

"You bitch."

"Let me go."

"Hey, Foley, can't you keep her collared?" Two of Brandt's pals stood with their legs spread and their arms crossed. "We're gonna take care of him. You better keep her quiet."

"No—"

Brandt's hand clamped across her mouth.

His pals started moving across the seats, stepping on the backs in a leap frog motion, bearing down on Donnie and his friend who had stood up, soon realizing there was no escape. "Scream, and your meat ain't gonna be worth beatin'," one boy warned, getting around behind Donnie. A knife flashed.

Bethany struggled and wiggled and stiffened and when

Brandt wouldn't release her, she bit, sinking her teeth deep into the flesh of his hand.

Then he did let go and she screamed. She screamed as loud as she had when Caleb pitched that no-hitter. And this scream felt just as good until Brandt hit her. Then she didn't feel anything.

Jack arrived at the principal's office for the late afternoon meeting five minutes early. The three school board members were already there, plus Arthur Squires.

"Gentlemen, I appreciate you all coming," Jack said. "Mrs. Foley, I apologize for not contacting you directly. I didn't know that you were filling out the rest of Mrs. Snyder's term."

Roberta Foley had a lavish face with makeup that tried earnestly to hide what years in the sun had produced— leathery skin and a swarm of wrinkles. Lots of rings and bracelets took attention from a conservative gray suit, and the cameo at her throat looked as if it belonged on someone else. This was not a woman who chose classy jewelry over the garish except when it suited her purpose.

"It would seem to me that a man with children in the school system would know who is on the board."

"One daughter," he said succinctly, "and my attention these past weeks hasn't been on the political appointments in Cooper Falls."

"Gee, I wonder why," muttered one of the men, glaring at Roberta.

"Calling a meeting like this is out of form," she continued, "and it probably violates the open meeting law."

Squires stepped forward. "We're only discussing an unwritten policy not a rule change, Mrs. Foley. Why don't we get started. Jack requested this meeting when I told him my concerns about a college baseball scholarship he wants to set up in his son's name. I want to stress that I understand his desire and applaud him for wanting to honor his son's memory. I sent you all a letter so that you would be aware of why I think this could be problematic."

"I've read your concerns, Arthur, and I have to say copycat suicide is a strong argument against anything that could be construed as a way to glamorize death," said Clyde Wamp, posturing as if he'd taken a course in Political Correctness 101. He had just returned from a cruise and his nose was peeling beneath his raccoon eyes from sunglasses worn too long in the sun; a gelatinous paunch clearly indicated he'd made intimate friends with the ship's lavish meals.

Jack didn't know him personally, but when Meg learned that he'd sent his kids to private school, she'd ranted to Jack of the hypocrisy of representing the public system while keeping his own in private education. Jack agreed, and he and Meg hadn't voted for him in the last election.

Dennis Kennedy, a onetime football star at Cooper Falls High was in his mid-thirties and the father of third-grade triplets. He was the manager of Team Central, a local sporting goods store. The DeWildes' credit history included years of purchases at Team Central.

Kennedy flexed a rubber ball in one hand. "No one wants to make death a winner, Clyde. Frankly, I don't see the problem here. Kids do implausible things—some explainable, most not. To make policy based on what might trigger a few needing attention strikes me as denying those kids who would benefit from scholarship assistance. Besides, followed to its logical conclusion, if one kid ever killed another kid with a baseball bat, would we ban baseball from the sports program? I don't think so. And Jack isn't even asking for matching funds—in fact, he isn't asking for anything. Caleb's unexpected death was a tragedy, but I don't see his suicide as having any connection to the standard of excellence he set for Cooper Falls baseball."

Jack nodded to Kennedy, grateful for his well-thought out support.

Roberta argued, "I take exception to you saying Mr. DeWilde isn't asking the school for anything. He wants the school's blessing and their backing. The boy had problems and I understand why, but this will set a precedence—"

"Wait a minute," Jack said. "You understand what?"

"Your son had problems. Normal children do not hang themselves."

Jack mentally counted to five. "Mrs. Foley, I asked you what you understood."

"I don't think you want me to go into that here."

"Indulge my ignorance."

She glanced at Squires who looked uncomfortable and annoyed. "I know you told me not to say this, but he asked."

Ah, Jack thought, there had been discussions beyond Squires's written concerns. Wamp leaned forward and Kennedy looked mystified. A discussion between Squires and Roberta that the principal had preferred remained that way. Interesting.

Jack kept his face neutral. Too much depended on this meeting having the outcome he wanted to indulge either his temper or disgust. No wonder he didn't like Brent or Bran or whatever her kid's name was.

Squires sighed, looking defeated. "Say your peace, Roberta."

She sat up straight and lowered her voice as if the world had their ears to the door. "Your son liked boys. That's the kindest way I can put it. Obviously he was troubled and pressured by this secret life. I heard about it from a very reliable source. While I understand how difficult this might be for you, that kind of activity does not set a good example for students."

"What kind of activity?" Jack pressed.

"Really, I don't think the details are relevant."

"Mrs. Foley, if this 'activity' is worrisome enough to

you to prevent the scholarship money from helping other kids go to college, it should be specified for those of us less enlightened," Kennedy said.

She glanced at Arthur obviously looking for support, but Squires was studying a hairline crack in the opposite wall.

Kennedy said, "Be specific, Roberta. We're all adults here."

"Very well, Caleb was the instigator of the recent homosexual activity at the high school."

"My God," Wamp said, looking as if he would rather embrace a hive of bees than discuss gay activity. "I don't see what that has to do with . . . with a college scholarship."

"Pardon me for being blunt, Mrs. Foley, but that's a goddamned lie," Jack said. "And even if it wasn't, Clyde's exactly right. What in hell does it have to do with money for baseball scholarships?" He rose to his feet. "As to my son being an instigator, if Caleb did anything, he tried to stop the homophobic harassment of Donnie Paquin by your son and his pals."

"My son was beaten up by your son, Mr. DeWilde. I didn't make an issue about it because Brandt insisted I stay out of it." She pursed her mouth and glared at him.

"You didn't make an issue because the cops arrested your kid for being drunk and threatening, and now I'm quoting what *I* was told, 'to kill all the fags.' Or did that escape your notice?"

The bluster collapsed and she looked stricken and naked and Jack felt a small pang of pity. No parent likes their kid's worst moment made public.

"That was an unfortunate remark by Brandt, but our family believes homosexuality is wrong."

"So do I," Jack said, gaining a dumbfounded look from her. "However, my personal belief doesn't give me the right to shove it in anyone else's face."

"Now that I think we can all agree with," Squires said quickly, waving his hands in a calming motion as if he could personally short-circuit the charged tension in the room. "If we could get back to the reason we're here. Jack?"

Kennedy winked at Jack and went back to flexing his ball. Wamp nodded, peering at Roberta as if he'd just seen her for the first time and wished he'd extended his cruise. Squires lost interest in the hairline crack on the opposite wall. And Roberta Foley simply stared at Jack as if unable to comprehend that they could agree and yet be on opposite sides.

Jack began. "This scholarship is as much for the students who will benefit as it is to honor Caleb. He wanted to play Major League baseball far more than he wanted to go to college. We argued about it the day he died—a regret I'll have the rest of my life." He paused, collecting himself. "I didn't encourage what I thought was a pipe dream—real life has made too much of an impact on me and my family for me to give much credence to dreams and fantasies. Now it's too late for me to make that up to Caleb, but I think he would like knowing that other boys have the chance to pursue their dreams with some scholarship money.

"I'm interested in creating an opportunity for boys who want to play ball. It's not complicated and there are no strings. Losing our only son in such a horrendous way has had a profound effect on our family. For the rest of our lives, my wife and I will be wondering what we could have done to prevent it. We can't bring him back and we can't change whatever pain drove him. This scholarship is not a substitute for Caleb, but it helps spread the ripples of positive influence his life made while he lived."

Jack sat back down, resting one ankle on the other knee. The three men remained silent as if contemplating his words. Roberta showed no response.

Finally Kennedy said, "You could do this without benefit of the school's backing."

"I've considered that, but I'm not interested in making my son a victim or the school the bad guy. This isn't about anything but money for kids for college in Caleb's name."

Squires slowly nodded. "He's right. If the school isn't part of this—and believe me the reasons why we refused would become quickly known—we will not only appear insensitive, but look as if we're denying Caleb's achievements as well as keeping deserving students from a generous scholarship. It would be a public relations nightmare."

"Then it's settled," Kennedy said and Wamp nodded. "The scholarship will be initiated this year."

"Roberta?" Squires asked.

"It was a very moving presentation, Mr. DeWilde. And I can see you've convinced Arthur to change his mind. Mine, however, hasn't changed. You've denied what I was told about your son, but you haven't told us why he killed himself. Or is it that you don't want to know?"

Jack stood, neither looking at her or acknowledging her question. He'd had enough of baited questions and irrelevant opinions. "If there's nothing else, I have to get home. I'll drop a check off tomorrow."

In the hall, Kennedy caught up with him. "Jack, there should be an assembly to announce this."

"Whatever."

"You're pissed at Foley."

"Gee, does it show?"

Kennedy grinned. "You handled her just fine. She has to have the last word. She knows her kid couldn't hold a candle to Caleb so she has to drag your son down to make hers look good."

Jack let out a deep breath. "You know, you're right. Thanks for your support in there."

Kennedy shrugged, glancing away then looking back at Jack. "I miss your son. He was a helluva good kid—an example of a teenager at his best. Whatever trouble overwhelmed him can't change that."

Jack offered his hand. "Thanks." And that was all he could manage around the knot in his throat.

Chapter Eighteen

Walking through the kitchen and into the dining room, Jack stared in disbelief. The house looked almost as bad as the cottage after Caleb and his pals trashed it. The only item in its right place was the wall-to-wall. Fear for Meg sent his gut winding tight and hot. Then he saw her coming down the stairs. Her hair spiked out like excess barbwire, her clothes looked as if she'd slept in the cellar, her expression tired and bleak.

"What happened here?" Jack pushed the dining room chairs back in place.

"I couldn't find it," she said wearily. She eased down on the steps, leaning against the balusters. Her hands lay dead on her knees, her skin pallid, her lips compressed taut enough to hold the rest of her body together. "I've looked everywhere it could be and places where it couldn't. Nothing. Not even a wadded piece of paper with his writing." She stared up at him as if he were part of some conspiracy. "Now you can say I told you so. Happy?"

"I was happy before I came in here," he said, disturbed that she could think he would delight in her frustration. "I presume what you couldn't find is the phantom journal."

"See? You never believed there could be one. I hope you're satisfied."

He ignored the bait. "Actually I would have been ecstatic if you found it. Once read, dissected and analyzed we could then get on with our lives. The difference here is that you believe Jessup's pronouncements are like some marked path to find a way out of the woods. I think he's a jerk."

"He must have thrown it away," she murmured.

"Jessup?"

"Caleb." She sighed in exasperation. "He probably put stuff in there that he was afraid someone would read."

"Like what? That he trashed the cottage, or went out and drank too much or had sex with some girlfriend. None of that is shocking."

"Maybe not to you because you did all those things when you were younger than Bethany." He had but being reminded in this context had nothing to do with comparative rebelliousness. She wanted to make sure he understood the difference between his teenage antics and their son. She'd always viewed Caleb as incapable of bad behavior. That was why she couldn't allow the tragedy to find its unfinished rest. This ongoing search, he now understood, was as much about reinforcing her belief in Caleb as it was in finding the reason why. She continued. "Caleb wouldn't have wanted us to know. You told me how upset he was about the cottage."

Upset that they got caught, but Jack kept that to himself. "Point taken. But if there was a journal—and I emphasize if—and he tossed it out, he apparently wasn't interested in doing it anymore. That doesn't mean it was filled with salacious tidbits. It could have been his fury at me for not encouraging a career in baseball."

"Don't make light of this."

Jack folded his arms, anchoring his irritation. "You get pissed if I say I don't believe there is one, and you still get pissed when I acknowledge it could have existed." If he could've performed magic and created the journal, he would have. He had reached the point where any answer that would satisfy her was the right answer. "What do you want me to do?"

"I want . . . I want you to . . ." She blinked, glancing up at the ceiling as if some answer existed in the afternoon shadows that spilled through the windows. "Oh God, I don't know." She scrubbed her hands down her face, then threw herself onto her feet and stormed down the last three steps. "Never mind. Just forget all about it. There's nothing you can do and it appears that everything I do is just one more dead end."

Jack caught her arm as she sailed past.

"Don't. I'm all dirty and smelly."

He drew her into his arms despite her protests. "I love you."

"Don't tell me that. I'm trying to be mad at you."

"Sweetheart, this has been a long month with few answers. You have to face the possibility that you will never know." He touched her mouth when she tried to protest. "Or that you might not find out for a long time. You know what sometimes happens when a couple wants a baby, and she doesn't get pregnant. They become discouraged and decide to adopt."

"Yeah, yeah, and then she gets pregnant. They quit trying and worrying and relax and things work."

"Exactly."

"But they kept making love. I have to keep looking. I mean if I just quit . . ."

"I didn't say quit, but give it a rest. If there are answers, they might become clearer when you're not so obsessed with them."

She rested against him. "I think life is already trying to convince me. I was offered and accepted a job at Bushes. Danny wants me to teach a gardening class twice a week."

While they walked to the kitchen and Jack fixed himself a glass of ice water, she explained about Hannah and other customers who had asked for advice.

"I think it's a great idea." *And please let this be the beginning of the path out of this quagmire.* "Someone probably saw all those pansies you bought and figured you must know what you're doing." He stood at the sliding doors, drinking and admiring the riot of color that genuflected beneath the Caleb trees.

"They do look like spring, don't they," she said in a brighter voice.

"It's spring and in a few weeks the Caleb trees will be loaded with cherry blossoms."

"There are some scraggly branches should be trimmed."

He put his glass in the dishwasher. "I'll put it on my list." And in the serenade of stillness, Jack rallied his courage. "Meg, I have to talk to you."

"I haven't been a very attentive wife lately, have I?"

"You've been the best wife, and more precious to me now than I can ever tell you."

She glanced up at him, eyes suddenly glistening. "Oh, Jack, what a lovely thing to say. I'll tell you what. Let me go take a quick shower and you fix us some wine. I'll meet you in the den and we can have a nice talk." She started to walk away, then turned. "Uh, the den is a bit of a mess."

"It doesn't matter."

She scowled. "You seem so melancholy. Kind of like the way you looked when we had lunch."

At the sound of car doors closing Jack glanced out the back door thinking that he couldn't have timed a better reprieve, except he no longer wanted salvation from this.

He opened the back door, and immediately he knew something was terribly wrong. "Uh oh."

"Who is it?" Meg asked, washing and drying her hands.

"Seth. And he has Bethany with him."

• • •

"The son of a bitch hit her? Seth, what the hell was going on?"

Bethany was tucked in her mother's arms, sobbing and shaking. Her cheek flared red where she'd been slapped. Looking at the two of them, if he hadn't known better he would have assumed they'd come through some horrific war. One wounded by what she couldn't find out, and the other suffering the pain of disappointed love.

"Actually she's a heroine," Seth said beaming in pride at Bethany as if she were his own daughter. "She went into the theater to stop Foley and his pals and did just that. Donnie and his friend got lucky when she showed up."

Just like when Caleb came to Donnie's rescue, Jack thought, amazed that history had repeated itself in such an obvious way.

"Daddy, they were going to cut him and his friend." She shuddered describing the unexpected appearance of a knife that Jack figured was a switchblade. "I was wicked scared and there was no one to help. Brandt wouldn't let me go so I bit him and screamed. Then he hit me."

"The prick," Jack muttered, recalling his own wariness of the kid.

"He's at the police station and his parents have to come and get him," Bethany said with frank gleefulness. "Oh, Daddy, you should have been there. The police came running in like it was a drug bust or something. They yelled and Brandt—" She giggled. "He was so scared. The cops were so cool, and Donnie—he looked like he'd had a come-to-Jesus moment."

Meg said, "Of course he did, you probably saved his life or at least prevented him from being hurt. We're proud of you, honey."

Suddenly her face glowed. "Caleb is, too."

Jack and Meg exchanged looks.

"He gave me the guts to go in there. I asked him for help and he gave it to me." With her parents staring, she chattered, waving her hands in dramatic gestures that were wonderful reminders of her bubbliness that Jack hadn't seen since before Caleb died. "Oh, he wasn't there like in person. That would be too weird. But he wasn't a ghost. They don't appear in malls," she said authoritatively. "It was more of a presence, like a guardian angel or a spirit. I know it was him 'cuz he called me twerp."

Meg covered her mouth, her eyes blinking rapidly. Jack winced, visualizing some screwball psychic in their future. Jessup was enough of a problem.

"Come here, cupcake." When she did, he put his arm around her. "I understand what you mean."

"You do?"

"Caleb loved you and worried about you and you know that didn't change when he died. When you believe someone is watching out for you, then that gives you courage to do the right thing. You knew how Caleb helped Donnie and since Caleb couldn't, you went in his place."

Bethany beamed. "You do understand! Oh, Daddy, yes!" Her arms circled around him like a clamp, and he treasured the moment.

Then she drew back, peering at him with grown-up practicality. "But the police needed to come, too, and they did."

Jack grinned. "I'd say you've got it all figured out, sweetheart. No argument from us."

"Brandt was a jerk and a loser just like Caleb said." She looked down. "After he died, I got messed up 'cuz I was mad at him for dying. Going with Brandt made me feel like I could handle things without my brother. I should have stayed away from him."

Jack hugged her. "It's called the experiences of growing up. The bad ones usually teach us the most. I'd say you've learned well."

They stood, her arms circling him and Jack welcomed the trusting weight of his daughter. It had been a long time.

Meg touched her back. "Let's get you cleaned up, okay?"

Bethany looked closely at her mother. "What happened to you? And to the house?" she asked as they walked into the dining room.

"I was looking for something and I sort of tore things apart."

"What was it?"

"It's not important right now. You're what's important."

Once they were out of earshot, Jack, basking in the revival of his closeness with Bethany and the family's unity, leaned back against the counter and gave Seth a studied look. His friend lifted both eyebrows as if he'd done nothing more noteworthy than give Bethany a ride home.

Jack said, "Notwithstanding Caleb's angelic intervention, and Bethany's quick thinking, it seems mighty handy that the cops showed at just the right moment."

"Cooper Falls officers are some of the finest in the state. Always there when you need them."

"Hmmm. And when did Detective Eidson appear?"

"Oh, I called the police. Mind if I take a piece of this candy?" Jack shook his head. "Cell phones are handy in that way."

"And I suppose you just happened to be going to that dreadful flick about oozing creatures from space. I know how your taste runs in that direction."

He shuddered. "I'm a forties movie fan myself. Loved Rita Hayworth and Barbara Stanwyck." He unwrapped a lime sour ball, popped it into his mouth and tucked it into his cheek, continuing. "Actually, Mazie and I were checking out the Victoria's Secret window. New lacy racy duds for spring. They had this thin pink thing with cups that wouldn't have held up whiffle balls, but there was my Mazie who looks dazzling climbing out of sweatpants weaving some gossamer fantasy to enrich my imagination."

"Fascinating."

His cheeks reddened. "Well, yes, it was." He cleared his throat. "Anyway, I glanced across the mall and there was Bethany and Brandt. From where I stood it looked as if they were arguing. Brandt stomped off after his friends, and Bethany didn't look happy. I thought she'd turn around and head in the other direction, but she sat down—"

"No doubt when the vision appeared."

"Don't know. Never been a vision guy myself. But after a few minutes she followed him."

"And you sensed trouble?"

"Nope, I wanted some popcorn. Love that movie popcorn."

"You're full of it, Eidson," Jack said, amused.

"Only early in the week. By now I'm usually up to speed. The Foley kid is a smug moron, thanks to his indulgent parents. And he has continued the tradition of ornery nastiness without a pause for a redemptive moment. He's earned my rapt attention every time I see him. Seeing him piss on your daughter, and then seeing her follow him . . ." He shifted the candy to the other cheek. "So I sent Mazie into the store to buy that pink fantasy, and I decided to buy some popcorn. When the Foley kid took her through the back way to the balcony, I made a call."

"You're something else, you know that?"

"Nah, I was worried about the kid if he tangled with your daughter. I think she has an aggressive personality like her old man."

Jack considered all that might have happened if Seth hadn't followed. Donnie and his friend cut, Bethany . . . my God, he didn't want to think what might have happened to her.

"I'm grateful, Seth. One of these days I hope I can return the favor."

Eidson crunched the last of the candy. "You could do something for me by doing something for yourself. Get rid of that cancer that's eating you up."

Jack's ears rang with the ferocity of a fire alarm. He was going to protest, feign confusion, blow off the comment with a curt denial. But he wasn't fast enough and he knew exactly how Eidson read the silence.

Eidson opened the back door. "Meeting with the school board go okay?"

"Yeah. They okayed the scholarship. Listen, Seth—"

He glanced at his watch. "Better run. Mazie is probably trying on that pink thing and I want to enjoy the show."

And he was gone leaving Jack feeling as wrung out as a shammy. Eidson had reeled out a pole on some fishing expedition, and he'd bitten like a flounder. No damn wonder he was a good cop. He never missed an opportunity to make his mark. Well, it didn't matter—Jack was more than ready to exorcise the cancer.

He poured two glasses of wine, walked into the den, pushed aside the pile of books on the couch so she had someplace to sit.

He sprawled in the desk chair, stared out the window and waited.

". . . she's going to be fine in more ways than the physical. It seems odd to credit a bad experience, but mistakes teach more profoundly than the good experiences." She paused, smiling at Jack.

He could smell that rose soap she used. Her hair was shiny and tamed. He noticed she wore one of his old shirts over light gray leggings and when she leaned across him to pick up her glass, the soft press of her breast meant she wore no bra. Their eyes met and he saw love and desire escorting her happiness.

What irony. Meg's sending signals that a few days ago would have had his total attention and cooperation and now, he's about to dynamite her joy.

"I so appreciate you calling, Mrs. Paquin," she said, winking at Jack. "Well, that's a very nice thing to say. Yes, we're very proud of her. I'll tell her. Good-bye."

She tossed the portable phone onto the window seat, planted a very wet kiss on his mouth before scooping up her glass of wine, then grinning widely before she collapsed on the couch. Not a drop of wine lost. He hadn't seen her this happy in weeks, which made what he had to say barbaric.

"She was sweet to call, wasn't she?" When he didn't respond, she sat up, sipping from her glass. "Jack?"

"Meg, I have to tell you something and there is no way to lead up to it that will in the end make it less hurtful."

She went still, wariness in her eyes. "Is this about Caleb?"

"Not directly. It's about the day he died."

"All right," she said, her eyes confused. He guessed she was trying to recall his demeanor, but for both of them so many details of those early hours were a blur. She took a swallow of wine then held the glass balanced on her knees that were pressed close together. Jack sat back in his chair, sure that every thumping organ in his body was about to gasp its last.

She stared at him, waiting. The stillness in the sparse space clanged louder than a four alarm fire.

Too late to run. No excuses. No defense. Just get on with it.

"I had sex with Vicki Slocum the day Caleb died," he said flatly, amazed that the words didn't cause an implosion. Instead they sucked up all the oxygen and Jack quit breathing.

Meg didn't respond, she didn't move, she didn't even blink. He found his voice and started to explain about hearing the siren and later realizing that it was for Caleb and feeling the awful weight of horror. But when her glass tipped forward, splashing wine on the carpet, and he reached for her, she shrank back from him as if she'd been hit.

He put her glass aside, stood up and closed the den door.

He didn't move toward her, but jammed his hands into his pockets to keep from trying once more to touch her. He couldn't bear it if she fought him, and she would. She would scream and fight, he was sure of it and he almost grabbed her to reassure himself that she still cared enough to react.

"Meg?"

She turned away, slapping her hands in the air as if not even wanting him to utter her name. Her silence went on and on. Rage, hysteria, sobbing, bring them all on— please—any of those he expected. That's what his mother had always done when she caught the old man cheating; then she'd gotten past her anger and taken him back.

That's what Jack wanted. Anger and tears and fury, but then it all would subside and their lives and their marriage would continue. Of course, he'd be remorseful, of course it wouldn't happen again. But this silence . . . he didn't know what to do with it.

"Say something, for Christ's sake."

She turned around, her eyes shuddered, her fingers picking at the shirt buttons. "My marriage 101 manual didn't list proper responses to a cheating husband." The whispering sarcasm was as thick as a summer fog on Narragansett Bay.

"It's not and never was an affair. It only happened once."

"And you've been harboring this, sparing me for all these weeks? How chivalrous of you." She slowly got to her feet and started toward the door.

"Wait a minute. We need to talk about this."

"Why? Is talking going to change it, make it go away? You've eased your conscience and made your confession.

I think I have at least the right to refuse to hear the details." She opened the door, pulling away when he tried to stop her.

"Meg, you have to listen to me."

"Excuse me? I *have* to listen? I wish I hadn't heard what I did. Allow me to sort that out before you bombard me with the excuses, reasons and I'm sure a well-thought out defense."

"You're wrong. If I had a defense I would have presented it before I admitted what happened."

For a blessed moment she seemed taken off guard, and Jack thought he might get her back in the room and the door closed . . .

"Bethany and I are going to Boston," she said abruptly, moving farther away from him as if touching him might change her mind. "I'd planned to leave Saturday morning, but tonight suddenly has much more appeal. By the way, Kate told me that Ford is working on a fishing boat. Seems that their relationship has hit a bad patch, but then you never did think they belonged together, did you? It would appear you know all the answers. Maybe while I'm gone you can try and figure out why I should forgive you. That is what this is all about, isn't it? Meg forgiving Jack for his transgression. Jack cheats on Meg, but Meg, the dutiful, loving, forgiving wife rises above the deception and betrayal . . . and she . . ." Then she burst into tears and fled the room.

He watched her hurry up the stairs, and in the distance he heard the bedroom door close. Not slam. Just close. Slamming doors would have brought Bethany running. And from that small gesture, Jack drew hope.

He slumped against the jamb, his head hanging low, his eyes smarting. He'd believed that telling her was the hardest part. Now he knew the hardest part was going to be saving his marriage.

Chapter Nineteen

Meg leaned back against the closed bedroom door, her eyes teary, cheeks pale, her body shaky and cold. Jack and Vicki having sex while Caleb was dying. My God, these past weeks she'd functioned in a surreal world where the people she loved and had fiercely believed in were strangers. First an unexplained suicide and now a confession of adultery. She shuddered anew.

In the bathroom, she soaked a washcloth in cold water and pressed it to her face. Just a little while ago, she'd stood here with flushed cheeks and sparkling eyes eagerly anticipating private moments with Jack. She'd actually thought that whatever was bothering him could be easily cured by her understanding and their mutual intimacy.

She drew a deep breath, stunned by her own naiveté. But unawareness wasn't the same as self-induced blindness. She'd never seen any overt signs of interest in Vicki by Jack, but then would she have recognized an overt sign? Probably not. She trusted him therefore she wasn't reading ulterior motives into his every move or mention of Vicki. Now, of course in hindsight, it was easy to judge every past move or casual mention as suspicious. Just a few days ago, Kate had floated the idea of *something* after uncovering some of Vicki's background and motives, and admittedly Meg had taken the anticipated leap that there could be *something* intimate between Jack and Vicki. But she'd swiftly dismissed the possibility as disloyalty to Jack. Not Jack. Not her Jack.

Well, it was Jack. Her Jack. And she no longer had to be concerned about ignoring facts, thanks to her husband's need to tell her.

Meg had a couple of acquaintances whose husbands had had affairs. Long affairs—one for three years, one for five years—in neither case was a confession a factor until those husbands were caught. Hide and lie had been their instinct. The wives had been devastated, their trust mutilated, their deep hurt finding no solace in explanations or excuses. Both marriages collapsed.

Meg knew her own marriage could follow that same path. The breach of trust that now swamped her raised troubling new questions. Was his disinterest in learning why Caleb chose suicide part of keeping his secret? Was his not going to the assembly because he was going to see Vicki? Were those hang-ups that seemed more than usual really Vicki calling, hoping to get Jack? This last one seemed a bit extreme, since Vicki could get him anytime she wanted on his cell phone.

But one element of what he'd confessed nagged at her. If he and Vicki only had sex once and there was no possibility it would happen again, why did he tell her? She could have happily lived out the rest of their marriage without knowing. Ignorance, of course, was much safer than reality. The bubble of protection that Jack had always enclosed her in should have applied to this, shouldn't it? A husband taking the step of admitting adultery when he hasn't been caught seemed bizarre. She knew her friends found out via gossip and stumbling upon a tryst. Yet Jack had come to her, told her straight out and thankfully avoided being defensive or blaming her by formulating some "I felt neglected" excuse.

Then a new possibility occurred to her—it didn't diffuse

her anger and hurt, but it shed some light on Jack's confession. Perhaps Jack had no choice. His guilt, betrayal, his love for her and for Bethany, his deep need to hold his family together no matter what the cost—these would certainly drive her husband. Perhaps the confession was more about holding tight to his marriage, more about extricating Vicki out of his personal life and more about how one mistake can have catastrophic consequences.

Meg rubbed her eyes, glanced over at the travel bag she'd laid out to pack. She had no interest in shopping in Boston, but she also wanted to get out of the house. She needed to get some distance from Jack; she didn't want to be talked to, to be asked to forgive, or allow Jack to be conciliating and charming. She didn't know what she was going to do, but the very least he deserved was a long weekend to worry about it.

"Mom, please, just a couple more pairs of shorts and a few shirts. Please? I mean it's not like I won't wear them forever." At Meg's raised eyebrows, Bethany grinned. *Uh huh,* Meg thought, *she'll wear them until she decides she doesn't like them, or they no longer match the current "in" label.* Bethany draped another tee-shirt over her arm. "I can't wait to get home and show Erica. None of the kids have cool stuff like this." She threw her mother a dazzling smile before heading once again for the dressing rooms.

It was late Saturday afternoon and Meg, Bethany and Kate had been shopping since midmorning. They'd lunched on Newbury Street, browsed the shops and ended up in Filene's.

Meg was beginning to wonder if the department store could simply ship the entire junior department to Cooper Falls and save everyone time. Bethany had picked out enough clothes to last the next five years, yet if this array was still "cool" by August, Meg would be amazed.

"After a while they all look alike to me," she said to Kate who was holding up lime linen slacks and the matching jacket. "I like the color, but it looks a little bland for you."

"You're right." She started to hang it back on the rack, then held it up so that it was parallel to Meg's face. "Stunning. This color would look great on you. Why don't you try it on?"

"I don't think so."

"Why not? You haven't bought a thing for yourself."

"I don't need anything."

"Need, need, need. How about buying it because you want it?"

"I don't want it either."

Kate rolled her eyes. "I give up," she said, putting the outfit aside. Then she glanced over her shoulder, catching Meg with an unguarded agonized expression. "Meg, what's going on? You've been preoccupied since you and Bethany got here last night. To be honest, you look pale and a bit demented."

"Demented? Thanks a lot."

"Never mind trying to change the subject. You know I'm going to dig until you tell me."

Meg pressed her lips together and turned away.

Kate touched her back. "Honey, tell me. Are you sick? Is Jack all right? I mean he didn't run off with that terminally sweet Vicki, did he?" Then when Meg's face took on a sickish gray, Kate froze. "Oh my God. Meg, my God, I'm sorry. I swear it was just a stupid crack. I didn't mean—"

"Shhh." Meg looked to see if Bethany was coming out of the dressing area. "I don't want Bethany to know."

"Oh God."

"It's not what you think. He didn't run off with her." Before Kate looked too relieved, she added, "But it's close. He had sex with Vicki the day Caleb died." Until the words were out of her mouth she didn't realize she had parroted his confession. Raw and straight with no embellishments. How like Jack even when so much was at risk.

Oddly, she realized in that moment that she appreciated his straightforwardness even though she wasn't happy about the information.

"Oh, God."

"Can't you say anything else?"

"Oh, God."

Meg sighed, not at all surprised by her sister's astonishment. For all Kate's sophistication, she was a real prude when it came to infidelity. Meg saw the spring of tears and found herself suddenly wanting to comfort her sister. Despite all her blather about cheating men, Kate really had believed Jack was different.

"Funny, I expected you to either erupt or remind me that you warned me she was in love with Jack."

"I have to sit down. God, I can't believe you're so calm and reasoned and not totally freaked into hysteria. Did that little bitch tattle to you?"

Meg chuckled. "From terminally sweet to little bitch, but no, she didn't tattle. Jack told me." She recounted to Kate those minutes in the den; of her shock and horror, of her anger and her defensive outrage. "I was tough and nasty to him," she said, now realizing that the barbed sarcasm and verbal payback had been but a momentary defense against the numbness that had set in since.

"Why did he tell you?"

"What?"

"Why Friday? I mean if it only happened once and it was weeks ago, what prompted the confession now?"

Meg shrugged. "Time has passed since Caleb and his guilty conscience wasn't going away. He seemed so overwhelmed by it, in retrospect I think he couldn't live with the betrayal any longer."

"For someone who's the victim in all this, I have to say you're being very broadminded. He cheats and you're feeling sorry for him. What's wrong with that picture?"

"It wasn't an affair—just the one time."

"And you believe him?"

Meg hesitated, the affirmative answer bubbling up and then sliding back down. She wanted to, she desperately hoped he wasn't lying. This was the question she needed to answer not only in her mind, but deep in her soul. Strangely enough, the degree of involvement and the depth of the relationship mattered more to her than she would have thought.

"I haven't answered that yet. Right now, I'm still trying to get a handle on some of my own reactions. I feel so inadequate and ashamed."

"You're ashamed? Ashamed of what?"

"You'll think it's stupid."

"No doubt. Tell me anyway."

"I don't want to throw him out." She looked at her sister, her eyes naked and fearful. "I know I should hate him, be feverish with outrage and demanding he walk on hot coals or chew broken glass—you know, the scorned woman gets revenge. But I'm just sad. Sad for him because I know these past weeks haven't been easy because of Caleb, and Jack, especially, has always been the solid rock for his mother and Ford—then for Bethany and me—shh, here comes Bethany."

"Okay, I'm done," her daughter announced, her arms overflowing. "I can't find anything else I want."

"Probably because there's nothing left in your size." Meg got out her credit card and they made their way to the saleswoman who had rung up some earlier purchases.

It wasn't until much later that night after an Italian dinner that had both women swearing they would never eat again and Bethany sound asleep in Kate's extra room, that the conversation came back to Jack.

Kate poured glasses of wine and they sat at opposite ends of a yellow and peach silk Victorian sofa that Kate had purchased in a Boston antique shop. There were signs of Ford still in the apartment—a leather jacket on the coat-rack, a pack of Marlboros on the coffee table and a photo of Kate and Ford in a gilt-edged frame. Kate, Meg noted, accessing the details, wasn't ready to let their fragile relationship slip into oblivion. A major shift from when she finalized her feelings for Porter by dumping everything he owned in green plastic bags and leaving them on the curb for trash day. Kate was as dug in with Ford as Meg knew in her heart she was with Jack.

Meg began, "I'm sure Jack thinks I'm going to leave him. And that's okay. He'll worry and be testy and Fredi will want to swat him. I say, good enough. He shouldn't just skate through this. But I have to look at this beyond today and next week. If we separated, it would be horrible for Bethany. She's lost her brother, just realized what an asshole her boyfriend was, and then to have her parents' marriage in trouble? She's had enough upheavals.

"And then there's the gossip—Claire, from across the street, hasn't forgiven Jack for his remarks to her the day Caleb died. She'd have him burned in effigy if she found out about this. And she would—everyone would and what they couldn't learn, they'd invent. And in the end our family, that had the promise of survival after Caleb, would collapse. There are no winners, Kate. Ahead, I see sadness and unhappiness and more pain in the long lonely lives of all of us. I don't want to go through it. I'll lose more than I'll gain."

"You've really thought about this haven't you?"

"Since Friday when he told me." She stood and walked over to the bank of windows that looked out over the city. Boston winked a million eyes at her. "Let's see, these are the scenarios that I've played out in my mind. I've thrown him out, asked for a divorce, confronted Vicki and after I blackened both her eyes, told her she was welcome to the bastard . . ."

"So what happens when you go home?"

She turned and looked at her sister. "I'm going to deal with Jack."

• • •

Jack finished checking the new web site listings for DeWilde's that Fredi had put on the Internet. He made a few changes to the descriptive text, and reread. The site had been up for a week and already the hits had been impressive.

Too bad he didn't give a shit. Two months ago he would have been enthusiastic; today he barely cared whether the computer booted up or crashed.

Now he incorporated the changes, double-checked it online and then exited the site. For the next few minutes, he read through the contingencies in a sales agreement, refusing to allow himself any time to think about what was going to happen with Meg.

"Jack, there's someone here to see you," Fredi said at the door, then lowered her voice. "She should get you out of your grumpy mood. And she looks gorgeous."

Vicki. All tanned and smoking with noxious energy. She'd called earlier promising to be in by noon. He'd been royally annoyed when she'd said she'd try not to be any later. It was now 12:30. He flipped to a new page. "She's late for work. Tell her she should take a tour of her desk and the backed-up work before she prances from office to office with vacation highlights."

"What are you talking about?"

"Christ, doesn't anyone around here understand English?" He tossed the pen on top of the sheaf of papers and cradled his throbbing head. He rubbed the temples, seeking surcease from the headache that since Friday night had become his new nagging enemy. "I don't want to see her." He glanced up at Fredi. "Clear now?"

"You don't want to see your wife?"

Jack's eyes sprang open so fast he got dizzy. "Meg? She's here?" His heart lurched around his chest as if it had been goosed with a hot poker.

Fredi grinned. "Hmmm, I just love catching you off-guard. It happens so infrequently." She opened the door wider as Jack stood.

She *was* gorgeous. Wearing a fitted red suit with some kind of blue and white scarf whirled around her neck and tossed flamboyantly over her left shoulder. She thanked Fredi and came fully into his office.

"Can I bring you two some coffee?"

Jack couldn't take his eyes off of her. She sure didn't look like a woman in turmoil; in fact she looked about as satisfied with herself as he'd ever seen her. Confident and assured slid into his mind right along with the answer he was dreading. She was going to leave him, and she'd come to let him know in person. Rub it in and then announce she was going off to see Rivers. You're screwed, pal, and you're history.

"None for me, Fredi," she said sitting down and crossing her legs.

Jack shook his head and Fredi backed out and closed the door.

"You look terrible," she said.

"I didn't get much sleep this weekend. You look as if you didn't have that problem." Probably in cahoots with Kate on how to drill and torture him.

Instead of offering any comment, she said, "The house looks wonderful. Thank you for putting everything back in order. I got back about eight-thirty and dropped Bethany at school."

Because you wanted to avoid seeing me at home; all the better to wait and blow me off when I least expect it.

"As I was leaving the parking lot, Sloane stopped me and asked me if I was coming to the spring concert tonight. Erica has a solo on her flute."

"Yeah, I heard about it over the weekend." He wasn't sure what he was supposed to say. His plan had been not to attend and then answer Meg's questions after the scholarship announcement had been made. No matter when *he* told Meg, he figured she would conclude that the scholarship was a gesture he'd made out of guilt over Vicki. Caleb didn't deserve that and if there was one thought he'd had in these past weeks that was absolutely virginal, it had been his determination to make sure this gift honored his son.

"You are planning to go, aren't you? I understand there's going to be a tribute to Caleb."

So she knew that much. "Sure," he said because "no" would be a disaster.

"Sloane said they expect a big crowd."

He started to make a crack that nothing Rivers said impressed or interested him. However, he was hardly in a position to throw around barbs about Rivers, and Meg's raised eyebrows indicated she was waiting to point that out. So he said nothing. He sat on the edge of his desk, arms folded, waiting for the next bullet.

Meg fiddled with the band of her watch. "Well, we seem to have exhausted that subject. I was hoping you might take me to lunch. I noticed Jingles had their wonderful club sandwiches advertised for today."

"Lunch at Jingles?"

"That's what I said."

Jack felt like a rat in a maze. He'd complained recently that she never unexpectedly dropped into the office; her preoccupation with Caleb's death had all but erased the impromptu visits. Now, when he least expected it, here she was wanting to go out to lunch.

Her gaze remained steady with no trace of an ulterior motive, her voice calm and absent of malice, body language open and relaxed. He closed his eyes, then opened them slowly, half believing she would have disappeared.

"You're puzzled," she said.

"Amazed. I either missed some cue or my confession last Friday was some imaginary nightmare."

"Oh, you made the confession. Now, I've made a decision."

Finally. "Yeah, that's what I'm afraid of."

She stood, walking to the mahogany and brass coatrack she'd surprised him with the day DeWilde's was officially opened for business. She lifted his jacket and handed it to him. "Come on, I'm starved."

Jack put it on and followed her, feeling like an old dog promised a cookie before the needle that knocked him into forever.

At Jingles, they got a table by the window—the same table where Jack's attorney had breakfast the morning Jack had unloaded on Ford about Kate. He'd told his brother to dump her; now he was about to suffer that fate from Meg.

Jack's mother waited on them, chattered to Meg about the photo albums she'd assembled from a box of snaps Meg had given her while Meg described the memory scrapbook she and Bethany had been working on. Jack listened, nodded and smiled at appropriate moments while his insides screeched like the tires on the loser's car in a chicken race.

They ordered club sandwiches with coleslaw and glasses of iced tea. Their food arrived and after Meg and his mother made plans to get together to show off their respective projects, Hazel left them alone.

Jack stared at his food, then decided his appetite was as phony a pretense as this entire scenario. If she was gonna leave him, then dammit, he wanted to know.

He poked his fork into the slaw without lifting it to his mouth. If he tried to eat, he'd gag. An advantage of getting this said in public was the damage would stay within the crevices of cordiality. The disadvantage was that he wanted to pound the table, swear and bellow.

Like your old man, pal. Just like your old man.

He set the fork down. "Okay, Meg, you've successfully confused and raised my anxiety level. How about clueing me in? You want a separation? I don't like it, but I can deal with it while we work things out. If divorce is what you're thinking, then I'm warning you right now, I'll fight it. I'm not making any excuses for what I did, but it only happened once and . . ."

He fumbled for something spectacular and original to add to an already desperate plea. She watched him, silent, continuing to eat. Finally, she laid her sandwich aside, swallowed and took a sip of tea; she blotted her mouth with the napkin.

"And what?" she prompted as if he only needed a bit of prodding to scrape out his guts.

"I don't know," he snapped, flinging his napkin down. "What the hell is going on? What do you want?"

"You."

"Good God, Meg. I've never seen you like this. I don't know what to say or what you want me to do."

"Did you hear what I said?"

"Yeah, you want revenge, but instead of just shooting me, you want to filet me and watch me bleed."

"I said I wanted you and you think I meant revenge?" She sat back, assessing him. "You really believe I'm like that?"

"I don't know what I believe anymore. I had—" He looked around and lowered his voice to just above a whisper. "I had sex with another woman. Most wives would be lying in wait with a long, sharp knife. Maybe that's what I expect or deserve, but this twisting me like a hooked fish on a line—it's just not like you."

"It's not like me because I've never had to deal with a husband who cheated on me."

"Ahh, God." He sat back in defeat.

"I'm not most wives, Jack," she said, her voice catching. "And I'm not the same wife as I was before March twenty-first. You do remember the sweet, obedient woman with the perfect family, the ideal husband and a marriage she never doubted?"

"I remember," he said grimly, realizing he'd rarely dwelled on the day-by-day wonder of the life they'd had. He'd just expected it to be that way. Always.

"I could throw you out," she said calmly as if she were talking to a dying houseplant. "I could pay you back by going to bed with Sloane—he told me the night we had drinks that he loved and wanted me."

"Jesus."

"I thought about both seriously." She paused and he held his breath. "I've made a decision."

He pushed his chair back. "I don't want to hear it."

"Why? Because it might force you to realize that this is all my decision? Because you can't charm, cajole or talk me out of it as you've done in the past when I suggested something you didn't like? And I didn't decide with cold calculation. I made it the way you hate decisions being made. I listened to my heart—some advice, by the way, that Vicki gave me. I've made my decision without asking your opinion and I have no intention of changing my mind."

Jack sank back, his eyes gritty from the sting of salty moisture. A chilly desolation circled his bones and smothered him as if the lid on a coffin had closed for the final time. It was over. His life, his marriage, his sanity. Nothing left but naked remains and a vast hopelessness. Dying looked good; it looked easier and less painful. And with that grim knowledge came an understanding of what Caleb must have experienced. Something horrible and untenable had propelled his son to the tree in Sawyer's Woods.

"Let me have your hand," she said.

Jack extended it, going through the motions of a man who has seen the future and was acting out his own demise. He stared at the lines embedded in his palm; they were not the craggy, unrepentant leathery scars of his old man. His palm was as silver-tongued as his charm, the flesh smooth, the fingers adept at useless talents such as fancy knots in silk ties. He expected to feel her rings drop into his hand, but she confused him again when she turned his wrist so that their palms faced. Then she carefully laced their fingers together.

When he looked up, she said, "I'm a wife who loves her husband enough to be saddened and disappointed. I thought about leaving you. Then I made myself consider what I was feeling beneath all that anger and hurt, and what would be lost. I don't want one very bad mistake to destroy our marriage and our family."

Jack felt his entire body resurrect.

"But I want to know one thing." She paused, her tone very serious. "Why did you do it?"

He let out a long breath, leaning forward a bit, keeping their fingers locked as though this might be the last time he'd be allowed to touch her. "I figured I could handle any move she made. I went over there because she'd just had her first big sale and she was pumped with excitement. I knew that euphoria from tough sales I've pulled off, plus I felt a bit like her mentor in that I'd guided her through some of the potholes of small-town real estate. Anyway, I went. It was stupid and insane and a bad case of an inflated ego. I had handled women coming on to me in the past so I figured if she made any moves, I could handle her. Well, I couldn't and didn't." He gripped her hand tighter as if he could physically compel her to believe him. "It would be easier to say it was a midlife crisis moment, or I had too much celebratory champagne, or I was testing my finesse with a younger woman, but they would be lies. The truth is I had a puffed-up ego about my ability to handle any situation. I ran into one I couldn't and instead of getting the hell out of there . . ."

Jack didn't know what else to say so he sat and waited, hoping she believed him for he had no other explanation.

Meg said, "Giving into temptation is as old as Samson and Delilah."

"You don't believe me," he said wearily.

"Yes, I do. What you told me would have been much harder to make up than falling back on any of the excuses men usually make." Obviously amused, she said, "I really should have a camera. I've never seen you so . . . so . . . I don't know—silently befuddled? Staggered?"

Am I hearing things? he wanted to ask. Instead he said

what most terrified him. "I thought you didn't believe me. I thought you would say you were definitely leaving me."

"And toss you to that woman? I might be furious, but I don't despise you. Besides, Vicki would never make you happy because she's not me."

In any other context, Jack would have chuckled at her wonderful arrogance. Now he was simply grateful for her confidence. "You have to know that not *once*, not for a second did I ever consider leaving you for her."

"But the issue is me leaving you, and I'm staying for a quite selfish reason. I've worked too hard on this marriage to throw it away because you were an idiot."

"This is unbelievable."

She gave his hand a final squeeze before unlacing their fingers. She then settled back like a victorious street fighter who'd just reclaimed the neighborhood from the enemy. She was impressive, sure of herself and sassy.

"What exactly don't you believe? That I'm not screeching in hysteria? Or that I'm telling you I have no intention of kicking you out?"

"Both."

"Surprise." She picked up her glass of iced tea. "Eat your sandwich. You look as if you haven't had a good meal since I left."

"And you strung this out to make me twist and squeal."

"I wouldn't have missed it. You were quite frightened."

"Terrified," he admitted, not trying to hide his deep relief. He picked up one of the fat toasted club triangles, his appetite reinvigorated.

"Jack DeWilde terrified of anything is a miracle. Admitting that terror is a gift." Then she looked at him. "But do this to me ever again . . . ever . . . and I won't be giving you a second chance."

"Yes, ma'am."

She leaned back and watched him eat, while nursing her glass of tea. And Jack fell in love all over again.

• • •

They went to the high school concert in Jack's Lexus. Bethany was at Erica's house because she wanted to ride over with her and Sloane.

"How did Bethany seem to you?" Meg asked Jack. The three of them had eaten pizza together at Pizza Hut before dropping her at Erica's.

"Happy with her new clothes. Bubbly like she used to be. Excited about the tribute to Caleb."

"Hmmm, I think the entire episode with Brandt just sort of slid away."

"She's a tough kid. He blew it when he treated her like low rent. Our daughter is classy, smart and almost as pretty as her mother."

"Not a bit prejudiced, are we?"

"Damn right."

Meg chuckled. "What did you think about her belief that Caleb talked to her?"

"It's more of her own instincts, plus knowing how her brother had no use for Foley because of what he tried to do to the Paquin kid."

"I envy her that fierce belief in her brother's spirit," Meg said.

He nodded. "I do, too."

Jack parked, and they walked into the packed auditorium. The Spring concert had always been a huge draw and seats were filling quickly. They nodded to friends, spoke to those close by with Jack going out of his way to speak to Claire. She'd dressed in yellow, closely resembling a drooping daffodil, but her smile was wide and warm, and hovering with forgiveness. Jack figured her gossip antenna had honed in and learned of the scholarship—nothing else he'd done would have garnered a second look.

Hazel called out from her seat with Jingles's wife, Belle, and Jack and Meg waved.

"I want to think that a lot of this big crowd is because of the tribute to Caleb," Meg said.

Jack shrugged. "Hard to tell." For Meg's sake, Jack was glad the two events were combined. He doubted there would have been a huge turnout otherwise. It had been over a month and for most, life had moved on. Even for the DeWildes—despite all the hoopla over a phantom journal—the shocking disbelief had eased, not every conversation reverting back to Caleb. The most significant irony: Meg's forgiveness of him would not have happened if he'd confessed a few weeks ago. That didn't cause him relief, only a humble gratitude. Miracles do happen.

Meg's hand was firmly clutched in his as they wound their way to two seats Jack spotted midway in a row on the left side.

They settled in, their shoulders brushing, their closeness that of reunited lovers, rather than a long marriage nearly toppled. He leaned closer to say something and she nodded, then they both smiled.

From their vantage point far to the right and one row behind them, the Eidsons grinned like two doting matchmakers observing their successful work.

"Oh, Seth, isn't it wonderful," Mazie said, hugging her husband's arm. "What a difference in Jack from this past weekend."

Mazie had glimpsed for only a few minutes the Jack that Eidson opened the door to at two A.M. on Saturday morning. Drunk would have been understandable, but DeWilde was cold sober and edging very close to an empty despair that had Eidson hauling him inside and sending Mazie off to bed. Eidson was just old-fashioned enough that he didn't want his wife to see the dissolving of a fine man. And when they were alone, Seth never prodded or poked. He didn't need to. Jack unloaded like a man who had been wrestling a dozen cobras.

Later over a waffle breakfast, and with Mazie knowing the essence, she assured Jack that Meg would make the right decision. To wit, Jack had muttered, *"Yeah, she'll dump me."*

"They're a fine family," Eidson said now, never in doubt that the DeWilde marriage would survive. He'd not been so sure about Jack.

"He was convinced Meg would leave him."

"Yep."

"And you didn't try to assure him she wouldn't."

"Don't know Meg as well as I know Jack. A false hope is worse than no hope."

"Think he'll tell you what happened?"

"We don't need the words, my love, we're looking at the result."

The concert lasted nearly forty-five minutes, with Erica getting enthusiastic applause for her flute solo when the chorus and band took their final bow.

"Ladies and gentlemen, faculty and students. As the finale tonight, Cooper Falls High School wants to take this opportunity to pay tribute to one of its finest athletes— Caleb DeWilde. Caleb's death stunned and shocked us, and from the number of students who got counseling and expressed to me how much they missed him, there's no question he will be remembered as a huge asset to the school and the community."

Principal Squires paused, then cleared his throat. "It is with great pleasure that I announce The Caleb DeWilde Memorial Sports Scholarship. This is a gift from the DeWilde family and will be awarded to a graduating senior who has participated in one of the school's sports programs. Caleb was a superior athlete and had aspirations of playing Major League Baseball. This scholarship is to help others aspire to their own hopes and dreams."

Meg clutched Jack's hand. "What is this? I didn't know anything about it."

"I know." This was one secret he reveled in her now knowing.

"I'm flabbergasted. Speechless. Thrilled. A sports

scholarship because he loved baseball." Tears glistened and she choked up. "Oh Jack, it's a wonderful gift and an honor to his name."

Jack couldn't speak. Her happiness, her approval, her generous spirit warmed him beyond his ability to express it.

The principal finished up with the details, the applause drowning him out as the entire auditorium came to their feet.

They wanted this, too, Jack realized with a newfound awe. They wanted to clap and praise and whistle for Caleb because he was a great kid and had made his mark in the school and in the community. The ripples of a life never end. His son would not be forgotten.

Chapter Twenty

Three days after the scholarship announcement, Meg threw away the box of stale Pop-Tarts. The gesture was a passage of sorts. Not a finale of the connections she'd kept of her son, but a lesser need for some reminders she'd clutched with such frenzy in those early days. His clothes that she'd folded into the drawers in his room remained tucked safely away like selected keepsakes of his history.

If only she could locate the elusive journal. Her failure to find any trace frustrated her and forced her to consider that Jack could be correct and the journal did not exist.

An excited Kate called Thursday night. Ford had returned to Gloucester, but instead of bar sloshing with the other fishermen, he had pocketed his take of cash and driven down to Boston. They were happily together and that's all that mattered, Kate had gushed with hyper giddiness. Meg let her sister's enthusiasm carry her, too, for to argue, lecture or offer a cautionary opinion wouldn't have been heeded anyway.

When Meg related all of this to Jack, he merely shrugged.

"No comment or prediction or advice?" she asked, removing the needlepoint pillows from their bed and turning back the covers.

"It's their life. I'm keeping my two cents in my pocket." He stood at the bathroom sink, brushing his teeth.

"But you do have an opinion." She opened the bedroom windows a few inches, welcoming the cool night air.

"Nope." He rinsed his mouth and wiped it with a towel. "You finished in here?"

She nodded, stepping out of her clothes and pulling on a clean nightshirt from the drawer. "This is quite a switch."

"Just following the advice of my lovely wife." He flipped off the bathroom light and tossed his shirt onto the top of the hamper. "Ford's a big boy and doesn't need his nose wiped or his life assessed to meet my approval. If it works for them, I'll help celebrate. If it doesn't and Ford wants some support, he knows where I work and where we live."

She considered stating her approval of his hands-off approach, but stayed silent. His mother, too, had taken a sober direction since Caleb's death. How ironic that tragedy provided unanticipated benefits. Jack had been anchored to his obligations after his father's death. Now after his son's, he'd embraced this wiser course.

Meg crawled into bed, curling under the puffy quilt and doing one of the things she loved best—watching him undress. "You're very handsome, Mr. DeWilde."

Jack glanced up. "I'm getting a gut," he said pinching a soft roll at his waist. "I need to start running again."

"I'll wake you extra early."

"Yeah, might as well get back in the habit." He slid naked into bed and turned out the light. "So what are you doing tomorrow?"

"I'm going down to Bushes. I understand about twenty-five signed up. Isn't that great?"

"I'm not surprised. Danny has been telling everyone. A family that came in the office today asked me if I was related to you."

"Seriously?"

"Hmm, I could call myself Mr. Meg and bask in your

limelight." He stacked his hands behind his head, eyes squinting despite the darkness of the room. "I can see it all now. Today a workshop at Bushes, tomorrow seminars at the Boston Flower Show."

She laughed. "You're really happy I'm doing this?"

"Yes, ma'am." He shifted, then as if not wanting the conversation to end, he said, "So you start when?"

"Officially on Monday with the first workshop at ten-thirty. These will be novices so I want to focus on winter cleanup and what they can plant to have some early color."

"Pansies."

"An excellent choice, sir."

"I owe it all to the brilliant gardener who I have the pleasure of sleeping with."

"She thanks you, sir, for the compliment."

"Maybe a compliment. For sure a fact."

Neither moved. From outside came the yowl of a tom and Meg winced. Her pansies carpeting the ground around the Caleb trees better not be torn up from some cat fight. She punched her pillow and settled her cheek so that she faced him. He didn't look at her. Their mutual silence slipped from ordinary to strained.

Meg waited, wanting him to turn toward her, take her hand, touch her hip, anything . . .

They hadn't made love since before his confession. Meg had been skittish and unsure of her own motives in wanting him after the scholarship announcement. When they got home, it seemed bizarre that her desire would have been so thick and she wasn't sure she trusted it; making love might be the glossy icing after such an inspiring evening. And while she'd faced his infidelity and made her decision, she wasn't as decisive about sex. Would he compare her to Vicki? Had he ever? These were her worries, but asking him, well, she simply couldn't. At the same time, she could find no reason to refuse him that wouldn't immediately support the idea that she wanted him to continue to pay for cheating on her. If she'd truly forgiven . . .

Maybe he was unsure and scared, too. Maybe he was waiting for a signal from her, for her to want him.

She stretched out against him, her fingers flat against his belly. She felt his muscles tighten beneath her touch. Her fingers wandered, brushing the soft hair, sliding lower before his hand gripped hers and brought it to his mouth where he kissed her palm and then placed it back.

"It's been a long time," she whispered.

"Ten days."

"You haven't said a word." The fact that he hadn't attempted seduction, when he was so good at it, made him more dear to her.

"I didn't want to hear no. And if we did, I didn't want it to be just sex."

"You wanted me to come to you, didn't you?"

"I wanted you to want me because you still loved me in that way."

"Oh, Jack." She slid over on top of him and framed his face with her hands. "I love you in every way," she whispered, kissing him and rejoicing when his arms circled her. Their kisses deepened, leaving them both gasping. She lay against him, panting. He eased her up and astride him, while she pulled off her shirt.

He cupped her breasts, and she leaned down so that he could kiss them. "I remember watching Caleb take milk from you," he murmured pressing his mouth into her softness.

She threaded her fingers through his hair, aware and amazed that the mention of Caleb didn't swamp her with sadness. "I liked having you watch me." She kissed him. "I still like it."

"You are a gift, my love. One I don't deserve, but one I'm grateful to have." He then tumbled her onto her back and slid into her. The feel of him filled her with more than flesh and desire, he completed her.

A new beauty lay in the simplicity of their coupling without foreplay or sexy talk. Their joining sealed them, blending their orgasms, and spread a fresh layer on their repaired marriage. This wasn't a healing as much as a new turn into their future.

A weekend rainstorm brought down tree branches and limbs in addition to overflowing the storm drains, causing flooding of the streets and water in more than a few basements. Jack spent Sunday checking the sump pumps at his house as well as at his mother's and his mother-in-law's. Meg, too, had been back and forth to her mother's over the weekend. Lorraine would be returning from Florida and bringing her friend Ben. Meg had promised to have the house as inviting as if her mother had just been out for the day.

She bought groceries, fresh tulips and daffodils as well as hiring Merry Maids to come in and freshen the rooms.

On Monday, she started work at Bushes while Jack had driven to Newport to interview two potential agents. Bethany and Erica had stayed after school to work on a statewide school literacy project that would get books into the hands of students in inner-city schools.

After finishing at Bushes, Meg did errands including a trip to her mother's to make sure everything was done for her arrival later that evening. She planned to pick her and Ben up in Providence.

She turned into her driveway, a grin still tugging at her mouth. Her first workshop had been challenging and satisfying, and despite some cancellations, it still turned out bigger than she'd anticipated thanks to Hannah who signed up six people just in her own neighborhood. Meg came home dizzy with the flush of being employed to teach about a subject she loved, plus getting paid for it, too.

She got out of her Expedition, picked up the mail and unlocked the door into the kitchen. She quickly separated the junk and dumped it before pressing the answering machine for messages. There was a message from her mother that they'd changed their flight and wouldn't be coming in until noon on Wednesday. "Terrific," Meg muttered, thinking that she'd have to leave her class early to get to the airport. Well, it couldn't be done. She'd just call her mother and tell her she'd be late. She and Ben could wait for her or take the shuttle.

Another message was from Bethany saying she and Erica were eating at Taco Bell after they finished at school. Finally Jack: "Hi babe. I'm running late so don't start supper. I'll pick up Chinese on the way home."

In the backyard, a barking dog sprinted across the lawn drawing her attention until she saw a broken limb dangling from the largest of the Caleb trees. She and Jack had picked up the small branches that had come down during the weekend storm. This one must have snapped in one of those wind gusts that whirled earlier that morning.

She went outside to inspect, looking up to see where the limb hung, swinging enough that if it fell the weight would crush her pansies. She took a few steps to get a better view of the break and assess if it was caught enough to stay put until Jack and she could ease it down.

Then she saw the jagged stump where the limb had snapped and caught on a forked limb.

"Oh my God."

She whirled around, heading for the garage and returned moments later with her stepladder. She leaned it against the tree, heedless of mashing flowers and climbed.

Her heart slammed and her breathing was so ragged, she nearly hyperventilated.

She reached behind the snapped branch for the wet Ziploc bag and clutched it, leaning her forehead against a weighty limb, feeling her body shudder.

She didn't remember coming down the ladder or racing into the house to rip open the bag.

Only when she held it did she sob.

She'd found Caleb's journal.

This writing junk down was Jessup's idea, and I feel kinda dumb doing it, but he told me to do it anyway. I don't know what to write—Jessup says to put down anything—what I like and what I hate, what I want and what pisses me off.

Okay my dad pisses me off cuz he doesn't believe I'll be a pitcher for the Red Sox. I will!!!! The coach says I'm the best and I'm gonna get better. How come he thinks I can be some brainy nerd at some university, but he won't believe I can pitch a ball good enough? How come he has no faith in the me who is the real me? It's not fair and I hate it. And Mom, she's okay, but she fusses over me like she did when I was five. All she thinks about is making Dad happy like if she didn't we might turn into one of those weirdo dysfunctional families.

School started last week and I got all these tough subjects that are gonna kill me. It's heavy stuff and I'm gonna be a ballplayer not some dumb college geek. New kid in school who's sorta quiet and shy. Donnie asked if he could hang with me cuz he doesn't know anyone. Told me he heard I was a jock and a chick magnet. I think he's trying to ring my bells, but hey, works for me.

Donnie's got trouble. He's a fag and a lot of guys are razzing him. Kinda shitty, but goes with being gay, I guess. One guy wants to ice him out. That pisses me off since Foley is a piece of crap. Like who made him a moral warden. Not cool.

Today was the best day of my life. I got a job working for this gorgeous chick. Doing stuff like raking leaves and helping her shovel the crap out of her dead aunt's house. Dad got me the job. He told her I was a good kid, I worked hard and then said I could be trusted to do whatever she needed done. I like that last part. Yeah, I like that. Dad is okay sometimes.

Vicki is so cool and she smiles whenever I come to work like she's really glad to see me. I wonder why she doesn't have a boyfriend. I'm gonna ask her.

Shit, she does have one in Boston. Jesus, if she was my girl I wouldn't let her out of my sight. Ha! I wouldn't let her get dressed.

I wanted to scream at them, Twerp too, last night at supper when they smirked and teased me about having a crush on Vicki. Crushes are for kids. I don't feel like no kid when I'm with her. She treats me like a real guy, like a grown-up. And she likes me! Wow!

Meg closed her eyes and pressed her hands on the scribbled pages. The fragments of teenage angst, swagger and a raw truth from her son saddened and comforted her—his thoughts were so normal, so wonderfully Caleb when he didn't think any adult was looking—or reading. Nothing she'd read sounded like depression or thoughts of suicide.

She gave me some extra money today and then she squeezed my hand and told me I was the best. Guess I kinda blew her away by doing more than she wanted, but I couldn't let her lug all those boxes out of the attic. And cleanin' and washin' her car was no big deal. I'd do anything for Vicki even if she didn't pay me. I love her.

Bummer. She's gone back to Boston. I feel crummy and depressed. I don't like going over there and not seeing her. School sucks. That piss-ass Foley and his trashy pals tried to beat up Donnie. I kicked him and punched him and got suspended for it. Who cares. Donnie and me are friends and friends don't duck when the shit flies. The black eye I got was worth it.

Oh my God, it's a miracle. She's back. I saw her wearing a red dress and talking to the mailman. Maybe she came back cuz she couldn't stay away from me. Uh huh I like that idea. I wanted to leap over the hedge and throw my arms around her, but I'll be cool and just sorta wander over and act surprised on Saturday.

She was crying. She looked so sad in her robe and with her hair all tangled like the Twerp looks when she's bawling about something. I didn't know what to do. Then she looked up and tried to smile and held out her hand to me. I took it and put my arm around her. I was shakin' so bad cuz I didn't want to do anything that would make her think I was a dork about a woman crying. Her boyfriend croaked and she was sad and lonely and she didn't have anyone. She had me! She smiled and said thank you and that I was HER BEST FRIEND. I told her I loved her and I wouldn't ever let her be sad and lonely.

And wow, she put her arms around me and held me like I was some solid rock or something. I kissed her and she kissed back. A real kiss! She was shy, but then—oh God oh God oh my God, she really kissed me and I thought I was gonna come right there. Oh man, then it just happened. I was scared and shaky and sure she was gonna call me a little kid and laugh, but she didn't. We did sex. I thought if this was heaven I never wanted to come back to earth. It was sooooooooo good and hot and she told me I was the best. THE BEST. Oh wow . . .

The words blurred, her body anesthetized while her mind rocked from disbelief to shock to fury.

Vicki Slocum had sex with her son. *Sex with Caleb.* Her sixteen-year-old son, who loved Pop-Tarts and baseball and defended his friends with a ferocity that made her proud; her teenage son with a harmless crush that an adult had twisted into an abuse that made Meg sick all the way to her soul.

She left the journal on the kitchen table, retrieved her handbag, extracted the keys and walked out of the house. Her ears were ringing in sync with her hammering heart. She got into the Expedition and drove to Vicki's.

Her car wasn't there. She called the office and lowering her voice so Fredi wouldn't recognize her, she asked if Ms. Slocum had left for the day.

"I'm sorry, but she has."

Meg turned off the cell and pulled away from the curb, driving around for fifteen minutes before returning and seeing Vicki's car and a light on in the kitchen.

She got out of her truck and went around to the back door. She opened it and entered without knocking. Vicki was on the phone, twirling the cord around her finger, leaning against the wall, laughing. Meg walked over and yanked the cord out of the wall jack.

Vicki whirled around, her pretty eyes wide and confused. "Meg."

Then Meg slapped her so hard across the face that Vicki staggered back and lost her balance. Grabbing for the counter edge, she pressed her hand against her red cheek.

"Listen I can explain. It's not what you think," she said in a rushed voice, running out of breath. "There was this chemistry and Jack wanted me."

"Did he now? And I suppose you're going to give me the same excuse for my son."

"Y-your s-son?"

Meg got right in her face. "His name was Caleb and he was sixteen years old. Sixteen years old!"

Vicki turned away, and Meg grabbed her arm swinging her back. "Don't you dare feign embarrassment or shame now. The time for that was when you were violating my son."

"Let go of me. You don't know what you're talking about."

"God, how I wish I didn't, but you know exactly what I'm saying. I read his journal. I read of his crush and his desire to please you and how upset he was when you went back to Boston. Then you had to come back after your married lover died and bring all your dramatic sadness. My son comforted you and instead of accepting that as a warm and caring gesture and leaving it there, you had sex with a young boy who idolized you. You took that trust and boyish crush and abused it."

Tears rolled down Vicki's cheeks. She slid down the wall, pulling her legs up and hugging them to her chest. "Oh Christ, I never meant it to happen. It just did. And God knows I prayed you and Jack would never find out." Her eyes got huge, the color draining from her cheeks. "Does Jack know?"

And suddenly Meg wondered if he did. Was this the real reason he was so disassociated from helping her find the truth? Why he'd scoffed at the idea of a journal? She tried to swallow down the sour bile rising from her stomach. No, this was about Vicki and her son, not about Jack. Meg noted that Vicki was more shaken by the thought that Jack knew than she was about what she'd done.

"Oh no, no . . ." Vicki finally said, taking Meg's silence as confirmation. She looked up at Meg, her hands twisting and wringing. "Swear to God. I didn't plan it to happen, it just did."

"It just did? Sex doesn't just happen. You let it happen. You were the adult, you were the one to say no."

Vicki bit her lip and Meg suddenly wasn't so sure she was an adult. Just a self-absorbed twenty-eight-year-old more concerned about what made her happy at any given moment. Relieve her sadness with a vulnerable boy, exercise her sensuality with Jack. It was all the same, it was all about what was good for Vicki and it made Meg sick with disgust and revulsion.

Vicki rose to her feet, staying out of reach and began to talk fast. "I told Caleb it couldn't happen again. I know I told him that. But he kept coming over and I just knew he thought I loved him. I stayed away from him and made sure I wasn't home when he came to work. I would leave him a list and his money on Friday. He was upset with me, but I was afraid to be nice in case he took it the wrong way. I only saw him about three times after it happened. Honest."

Meg said nothing. She was too swamped with regret that she hadn't probed more thoroughly for reasons behind his lower than usual grades, his escalating arguments with his dad, the bouts of quietness that she'd thought were teenage reflection. His trashing the cottage—that had troubled her, but not Jack, and yet he'd kept it from her. To spare her the worry? To show he could discipline as well as criticize? How could she blame him when in the past she'd chided him for leaving the lecturing to her? Nevertheless, if she'd known, maybe she would have put it all together and heeded Caleb's cry for help. But even now, Meg knew she would have never guessed sex with Vicki—that was too off the charts, too horrible . . .

Now, in hindsight, she beheld the whole piece complete with sadly believable motives—Caleb was carrying an explosive secret, coupled with loving Vicki and her ongoing rejection of him. As emotionally exhausting and mentally painful as an unlanced boil, instinctively he knew he couldn't tell anyone. What a dragging burden that must have been.

Meg glanced at the flinty young woman she and Kate had joked about, the self-assured agent with the high sales record, the pretty luncheon companion who raved about Caleb and had made Meg proud all over again of her son.

Speaking with only the barest of inflections, she said, "You had sex with my son, sex with my husband and wanted to be my friend. How do you look at yourself in the mirror without getting sick?"

Vicki blinked, looking baffled by the trio of comparisons. "I really liked you. The thing with Caleb—it was an accident, he was such a sweet boy and so understanding, what happened just happened. But Jack . . . I loved Jack. I've loved him since I met him."

Meg stared, speechless by her utter cluelessness. It was as if the three incidents had nothing in common, no binding reality of betrayal. She had invaded the DeWilde family with her twisted idea that what she wanted was more important than the pain and destruction she had caused.

"I don't ever want to see you again," Meg said, so suddenly weary she could barely get her words out. "Once Jack knows what happened with our son, you'll be fired." Meg turned to leave.

"No!" Vicki reached for her arm and when Meg eluded her, she grabbed her purse strap, sending her handbag to the floor with the contents flying. "You can't tell Jack. You can't," she babbled as Meg bent down and swept up the contents.

She pushed the items inside, pausing and frowning at the photo.

Vicki, arms huddled against her shaking body, wailed, "Please, please don't tell Jack. He'll hate me and I couldn't stand that."

But her voice was an echo, her words droning chatter. The photo drew Meg's attention. She'd never seen it before. How had it gotten into her . . . ?

Oh yes, one of Caleb's friends had given it to her the day she went to the high school to ask questions. She'd put it away because she couldn't bear to look at it and completely forgotten about it.

Caleb stood with Gregg and another boy on the outside steps of the school auditorium. They were mugging for the camera, certainly not the demeanor of a young man who in a few hours would hang himself. She started to put the snap away, when a detail caught her attention. The sweater was wrong.

It was the sweater that Vicki returned, the sweater that this very minute was folded into her keepsake drawer. But if Caleb was wearing it, then how—?

She raised her eyes and looked over at the woman who was now dabbing at her eyes with a tissue.

"Where did you get Caleb's sweater?"

She sniffled, tears leaking. "What?"

"The red-and-gray sweater that you gave to me when we had lunch."

"I told you. Caleb left it here."

"When?"

"I don't know when. He always left things here. I found it outside on the ground."

Meg took a step closer. "When? What day? What time?"

Vicki backed up, raising her arms as if to protect herself. "I want you to leave or I'm calling the police."

"Answer me."

"I don't know. I don't remember."

"It was the day he killed himself, wasn't it?"

"No! I don't remember. It could have been there for days." Her voice rose and the words raced. "It was way over near the side of the garage. I hardly ever go over there. Caleb used to take the shortcut across the backyard. I thought I was doing you a favor by giving it to you."

"He was here, wasn't he? He was coming to talk to you. You were the friend he told Donnie he was going to see."

"I don't know. I didn't see him."

"You didn't see him because you were too busy having sex with my husband."

Vicki shrank back, color racing out of her cheeks at Meg's accusation. "I didn't know. Do you think I would have given you the sweater if I'd seen him?"

The question astonished Meg in that even in the muck of

Vicki's anorexic morals she was trying to justify herself. "The tragedy is that Caleb saw you! He saw you betray and reject him with his own father. The shame, embarrassment, the humiliation left him so demoralized that he couldn't imagine his life ever being normal again. It would have been wretched enough if he'd never been intimate with you, but the combination was so unspeakable that he . . ." She covered her mouth to trap the words. It was all so clear, so coldly clear and painfully true.

Vicki lit a cigarette with shaky fingers, while Meg stared at the coiled phone cord.

It would be so easy to strangle her. To wrap the wire around her neck and pull it into a tight knot. Making her dead. As dead as her son was and the justified act was so logical that Meg picked up the cord. She wrapped it around her hands, then unwrapped it.

"What are you doing?" Vicki asked, taking more steps away from Meg.

"Thinking about how good it would feel to choke you."

Chapter
Twenty-one

Jack knew something was wrong when he saw the ladder against the tree, when the Expedition was gone and the back door was unlocked. Meg never did that.

He shoved the bag of Chinese food onto the counter. "Meg!" he called on the off chance that she'd let someone borrow her truck. No answer.

He listened to the three messages: from her mother, from Bethany and shut it off when his own came on. Then he spotted the notebook on the table. Caleb's journal. She'd found it. He opened it and read standing up.

"God in heaven," he whispered.

His first stop was at Vicki's, but when he didn't see Meg's car he drove on by. Using the cell, he tried places he thought she might be, but either got no answer or she hadn't been seen.

Erica Rivers answered the phone at her house.

"She's not here, but do you want to speak to Bethany?"

Jack could hear his daughter laugh. She knew nothing. Thank God. "Yeah, let me speak to her," he said sliding through a stop sign and then turning left.

Jack drove past Jessup's, slowing down because the place wasn't well lit, but the only vehicle in the yard was Jessup's dirty pickup.

"Daddy? Hi, what's up?"

"I'm trying to find your mother."

"Oh Daddy, you really do worry too much. She was going to the airport to get Grandma, remember?"

Jack had heard the change in plans on the answering machine. At the same time he didn't want to alarm Bethany. "That's right. Okay, so what are you and Erica up to?" They were on their way to Taco Bell and Mr. Rivers would drop her off about eight o'clock. It was just after six o'clock. "I'll see you when you get home, sweetheart."

"See you. Love you."

"I love you, too."

So now what? he wondered, driving past his mother-in-law's house in hopes Meg was there. She wasn't.

Idiot. She's read about Caleb having sex with Vicki just days after he'd confessed his own stupidity. Christ, she's probably on her way to Vicki's to wring her neck . . .

Shit. He punched her number out and while it rang and rang his belly buckled with a pee-down-the-leg fear.

No answer. He drove by her house once again, but still no Expedition. Okay, get a grip here. Maybe she's just driving around, trying to sort it out. He called Eidson.

"You want me to have her picked up?" Eidson asked after Jack gave him a scrubbed version. Meg had found out some painful stuff about Caleb and he was concerned about her.

"I don't know. I'm worried, but I don't want her hauled home like she's some bubble brain."

"Your wife on her worst days wouldn't be a bubble brain. How about this. I'll call the station, and the dispatcher will ask the patrol cars to keep an eye out for her vehicle. Give me the plate number." Jack did. "I'll call you if we get anything."

"Thanks. I'll keep looking." But he didn't know where to look.

• • •

Before she went into the house, Meg took a long-handled shovel from the garage and in the middle of the pansies beneath the Caleb trees, she dug out one of the plants. Then she reached into her purse and took out the picture tearing it into small bits. She pushed the pieces into the damp earth, covered them and replaced the pansies.

Her decision to not show Jack the photo was instinctive rather than complicated. Because of all they'd been through, because this was a secret too wrenching to tell. Jack had obviously been afraid to learn what had happened to Caleb because of where he'd been when Caleb was dying. Showing him the picture would certainly be justified, for in a very real way, he had pushed Caleb into suicide. Yet, Meg knew that horrible truth would shatter him. It likely could destroy him. For sure he would live with a guilt that no amount of forgiveness would change.

Nothing would be gained by this final revelation but continuing sadness. Certainly it would slice a new depth of guilt. And yes, it would carve forever in his mind that his mistake with Vicki had caused their son's death. However, Meg saw neither as having a good outcome for their marriage or most of all for Jack himself.

Meg wanted her family back and revealing this final and tragic detail . . . Well, she just didn't know what would happen if Jack carried this unbearable burden. And given the past weeks, Meg wanted nothing to do with creating deliberate uncertainty.

She couldn't . . . and wouldn't.

Caleb had hidden the journal because it held his secrets. Meg buried the photo because it held a terrible secret—a secret that had so shattered Caleb that he killed himself. Her question of why he died had been answered, and her knowing was burden enough.

She returned the shovel to the garage and then the ladder. As she walked across the asphalt, Jack turned into the drive. The vehicle screeched to a stop, with Jack out and running toward her while the Lexus still rocked.

Immediately she knew he'd read the journal.

In those stark seconds, she saw new lines of age and worry, a sadness of soul that draped around him like a permanent anguish. She knew she'd made the right decision. He gathered her into his arms and she felt him shudder.

"Meg, sweetheart, I've been going crazy trying to find you."

"Did you read it all?" she asked, amazed at the steadiness of her own voice. "I stopped after I learned about what she did."

"I read some. It's about a young man's yearnings and not understanding why she's refusing to see him, why she doesn't see how much he loves her."

"I wanted to kill her."

"I wouldn't have blamed you if you had."

"I came close, Jack. So close it didn't even feel wrong."

He drew her close. "I'm just so sorry for Caleb and what he must have been going through. He was overwhelmed by a tangle of guilt and desire and love. A very potent combination."

"Yes," she said softly.

They stood in the drive, the sun settling into a lazy ball behind the Caleb trees. Inside the house, Meg picked up the journal while Jack poured her a glass of wine.

"What are you going to do with it?" He set the glass down and she didn't touch it.

"Put it away with the other things I've saved. I can't bear to throw it away because it's so sad and haunting. It's like knowing the ending and still being drawn into the missed moments, the squandered opportunities, the decisions and happenstance that if we'd known, we might have changed."

"But I understand why he never told. He loved Vicki

and if we'd known what had happened, I would have fired her, plus sex with a minor is against the law. She would have faced criminal charges. Caleb probably knew that and he wanted to protect her as much as he wanted to guard his secret."

"It was a terrible dilemma for him." She walked over to the French doors that framed the Caleb trees. "They will be in bloom in another week."

"Meg, I'm going to fire Vicki."

"Yes, I knew you would."

"Honey, are you sure you're okay?"

She turned. "Yes, actually I am. I know why he killed himself and I confronted Vicki. I feel as if we can finally begin putting our lives back together."

Jack took her into his arms. "I love you. I want us to be okay. Okay with each other and okay with Bethany."

"We will. Caleb would want it that way."

Bethany came home, bouncing in and kissing them both before disappearing upstairs to finish a book report. Meg tucked the journal away in the drawer in Caleb's room and shut the door, giving her a sense that she'd closed this final chapter of his too short life. Jack's wonderful idea of the scholarship would allow him to live on and Meg intended to dwell in her wonderful memories of Caleb, for they were many and fulfilling.

Later as she lay awake listening to the whispery spring breezes floating through the open window, she curled next to Jack's warmth and felt a deep contentment.

It was time to enjoy living again.

Epilogue

Meg knew about time being a healer, a flow of months that like a balm softened and blunted the painful edges. In the sooner or later, the days rewarded her with new paths and virginal possibilities so that hours actually slipped by when Caleb's death wasn't foremost in her mind. Now, in the past few weeks as spring blossomed with warmer days and the Caleb trees burst into full bloom, she'd decided to have a party at their cottage in Jamestown.

All afternoon, she'd been busy with food preparations and when Jack arrived earlier than she'd expected, she talked him into a stroll on the beach before their guests arrived.

In the past year, they'd made a habit of taking walks together in the early evening. It offered a wind-down after a workday, encouraging a new vigor to their marriage and an opportunity to hash out family issues before they became problems. Bethany, in the full bloom of teenage angst and expectation, had observed this closeness as mushy-gushy junk, but Meg and Jack hadn't missed the pleasing return of her sunny disposition.

"Bethy is coming with your mom. It seems that the new boyfriend—Dan or Don or—"

"Dana."

"Whatever. Anyway he was supposed to stop by and her hair was a mess and her legs were disgustingly white and she'd bought some tanning spray or else she'd have to wear jeans and long sleeves like some wintered-over dork instead of a summer outfit you bought her in Boston. I called her while driving down here and she said the tanning spray had worked and she couldn't wait to show it off at school on Monday."

Meg laughed. "I love it. She sounds so normal."

"Yeah, she does," he murmured, the pride and delight evident in his voice. Jack let her take the lead as they made their way down the path to the beach that welcomed Narragansett Bay.

The beach expanded before them like an endless sweep of coastline, the sandy mile pristine and smooth not yet disturbed by the onslought of summer people.

"Mazie called me," Meg said. "She heard from Claire the name of the first winner of the Caleb DeWilde Memorial Scholorship."

"My favorite gossip," he muttered.

"But this is good gossip. It's a young man whose family has very limited resources for college. The scholarship will make it happen for him." They walked side by side, Meg noting how tightly Jack held her hand. "You're pleased, aren't you?"

"It's what I envisioned to honor Caleb. Yes. I'm very pleased."

"I have some other news," Meg added. "Kate and Ford are seriously talking about marriage. They want to have a chat with us tonight after everyone leaves."

"I'm not voicing an opinion." His visible shudder harked back to when he always had an opinion of what his kid brother should and shouldn't do.

She squeezed his hand. "But tell me what you think. They seem so opposite and yet so much in love."

"I think they need to make a decision and go with it. It's not as if they're starry-eyed twenty-year-olds. Besides, who can predict or guarantee a happy future."

"But we can't stop living when the future isn't what we expected, can we?"

"No."

And they both knew they were talking about Caleb.

They stood quietly for a few moments, listening to the water roll onto the beach, watching some eager sailboaters enjoying the warm afternoon breezes.

Turning they embraced and then returned to the cottage to welcome their family and friends.

Turn the page for a preview of
The Secret Stones
Dee Holmes's powerful new novel

Coming soon from Berkley Books!

The last time she'd rushed to the hospital emergency room had been when Jessica was five. She'd been bitten by a dog and while her daughter had charmed all the nurses, Mattie had been terrified of infection and rabies.

This time wasn't like last time.

"I'm Mattie Caulfield," she said to the receptionist. "My daughter, Jessica, was brought in after being in a car accident."

"Go right through those doors and take a left. I believe your husband is already here."

Mattie barely heard the last sentence. Her chest was tight from holding her breath and her ears were ringing. Somewhere between the phone call and the frantic five-mile drive to the hospital her heartbeat had soared to rocket speed. Please God, don't let her die. Please. She rushed through the doors and straight into her ex-husband's arms.

Stephen wrapped himself around her like a waiting warm blanket. He held her secure, stilling her shaky body, whispering, "Shh, you're shivering like a wet puppy." His voice had the calming effect of a beloved friend ready to blunt any adversarial news, and Mattie leaned a bit harder into him. They hadn't been this physically close since before their divorce six months ago.

In a raspy voice she asked the questions that had cemented themselves into her mind since the phone call. "How did this happen? Is she okay? How bad was she hurt? What have you been told?"

He pulled back, his eyes searching hers with a kind of misty nostalgia Mattie had seen often when they discussed their teenage daughters. "You always did pop questions out faster than I could answer," he said, trying for a smile. "How did it happen? From what I've heard the driver lost control of the car, bounced off a guardrail and flipped into a culvert. Jessica was badly hurt and I haven't been told much beyond the good news that she is alive and they're trying to get her stabilized. They called Tom and he's coming in."

Tom Egan was their family physician and the fact that he was notified should have comforted Mattie but it simply added another layer of worry. Was there something the emergency personnel hadn't told Stephen? Like a head injury? Paralysis? Or some dreadful prognosis that required gentle preparation by an old friend?

While she appreciated the effort, the reality was that if the news was bad it wouldn't get better or easier just because the bearer wasn't a stranger. Mattie was already preparing for the worst as if the very act of accepting a potentially tragic outcome would give her an emotional buffer.

Stephen had guided her to a chair where she perched on the edge, tense and tight and chilled despite the warm May night. Doors slammed, doctors were paged, somewhere the clang of a gurney was followed by a woman screaming. Mattie shivered. A doctor and two nurses came from the right, rushed through swinging doors and disappeared. She wondered if they were working on Jessica. The big clock above the swinging doors read 10:18. The five minutes she'd been here felt like five hours.

"Where were you anyway?" Stephen asked.

He stood above her, hands deep in his pockets, jacket open, tie loosened, his hair more gray than she'd realized and mussed as if he'd dragged worried fingers through it over and over. She wanted to comfort him, but managed only a press on his arm. He was a handsome man, charming, affable, a devoted father and looking at him now, she could understand why her parents were so upset when she and Stephen divorced. He seemed so . . . so strong and supportive.

"Is where you were a secret?" he asked when she didn't answer right away.

"Of course not." Reminding herself not to be defensive, that the question wasn't out of line, that she would have asked him the same thing—well, actually she wouldn't have. So out of courtesy, she said, "I was at the store getting the month's receipts ready for the accountant."

"At ten o'clock at night?"

"It's been a busy week."

"And Hannah? Where is she?"

"She's spending the night at Mom's." And then she gritted her teeth and refrained from telling him she didn't appreciate being grilled as if she were a neglectful mother.

She had no obligation to explain perfectly normal activities, or even blissfully sinful ones for that matter. She certainly didn't have to feel guilty for not being home. And that's why his questions irked her. To Stephen her not being home was tantamount to carelessness and disregard for her family.

With her warm fuzzy feelings of before now evaporated, she folded her hands and said, "You didn't say if you knew anything about the other girl."

He glanced away, drawing a sharp breath, his sadness thickening his words. "She died. No seat belt, according to what I heard the police say. Jess wasn't wearing hers either. How could they have been so goddamn stupid?"

"Not stupid, Stephen. Just kids believing they're invincible."

He nodded toward the couple across the room. "I doubt that will be much comfort to her parents."

Mattie stared at the obviously distraught couple. Heartfelt empathy brought tears to her own eyes. When the couple turned, the woman was being literally helped to her feet by the man next to her. They moved to plastic chairs where they hunkered down in disheveled grief.

But even grief couldn't disguise the loud clothes, the overdone makeup and hardness of demeanor. Mattie didn't recognize the woman and that puzzled her. She knew, at least by sight, the mothers of both her daughters' friends. Between swim meets, choir practice and PTA, it would have been difficult not to recognize the parents. "Who was the girl with Jessica?"

"Arlis Petcher."

The name meant nothing to her, but since Stephen seemed to know it she assumed he knew her. "Was she Jessica's age?" Which was nearly eighteen, as her daughter reminded her almost daily.

Stephen shrugged. "Probably a new friend. You know how friendly Jessica is. Just like her mother." He beamed fondly at Mattie.

"How odd. She never mentioned her to me."

"Probably because you were busy at the store."

Mattie scowled. "Please, Stephen. Working is not a synonym for neglect."

He raised both hands in a peace gesture. "Honey, don't be so defensive. You're here now. That's what counts."

Truthfully she had been busy for the past few weeks—setting up the auction at the Landry house had absorbed immense chunks of time, and then there was Wyatt Landry. She'd turned down a date with him tonight because her books for the month *had* to be at her accountant in the morning. She could only imagine Stephen's reaction if she'd been out with Wyatt when she was notified.

As for her not being home every minute, Jessica and her

sister, Hannah, were seventeen and fifteen respectively—
young responsible adults, for heaven's sake. They were
never in trouble and Mattie hated that Stephen could make
hackles of guilt rise up along her spine with the most
benign comment.

A police officer came through the doors and went over
to speak with the Petchers. Mattie rose, settling her bag
strap on her shoulder. "Wouldn't you think they could wait
awhile? My God, those poor people have just lost their
daughter."

"What are you doing?"

"I'm going to offer sympathy and find out what happened tonight."

The officer glanced up when Mattie and Stephen
approached. While Stephen said who they were, Mattie
spoke to the couple.

"I'm so sorry about Arlis."

Then as if Mattie's sympathy had been a match to dynamite, the Petcher woman screamed, "You! You're sorry?
You're fucking sorry? Like that means shit?"

"Mrs. Petcher," the cop said, "take it easy."

"I don't have to. Her kid killed my baby as sure as if
she'd shot her!"

Mattie took a step back as the woman reached to grab
her. The husband restrained her, but not the spew of accusations.

"Your kid made my baby steal our car. My Arlis never
did nothin' wrong and she meets up with Miss Prom
Queen and now she's gone. Drinkin' and speedin' and
killin' my baby. That's what she did. She k-killed my b-ba-
baby." She began to sway and her husband settled her into
a nearby chair.

Mattie retreated, speechless, swamped by the implications for Jessica. Stealing? Drinking and speeding? Not her
Jessica. No. There had to be another explanation.

When the officer finished with the Petchers, he told Mattie and Stephen that he would want to speak with their daughter as soon as she was conscious. Mattie asked about the accusations.

"We did find beer cans in the car, and damage to the car plus skid marks indicate excessive speed."

"Was the car stolen?" Stephen asked.

"The Petchers claim no one asked permission to take it, so until we get your daughter's statement, we have to assume they're correct."

"Was our daughter driving?"

"We haven't ascertained who had control of the vehicle. Neither were wearing seat belts and no one was behind the wheel when the investigating officers arrived."

"Christ," Stephen muttered. "Jessica could be in a lot of trouble."

"If you could let us know when we can talk to her, we'd appreciate it." The officer left and Mattie and Stephen went to inquire if there was any news about their daughter. When the answer was no, they found a coffee station and helped themselves.

Mattie sat staring at the paper carton, trying to process the accusations and what she knew about Jessica.

"Honey, the woman was hysterical. She wanted to blame someone—"

"What if she's right?"

Stephen scowled. "Don't you think that waiting for Jess's side of the story before we find her guilty would be prudent?"

"Of course I want to hear her side. But none of what I've heard tonight sounds anything like what our daughter would do. It's so bizarre that I can't help thinking there are some missing pieces here, or we don't *really* know her. Even her being with this Arlis Petcher is odd. I know I sound elitist, but Jessica didn't hang around with kids who have coarse, sewer-mouthed mothers."

"Apparently she sometimes did, for they were together tonight."

"Yes, and for what reason? Jessica told me she and some friends were going to the mall, and then they were having a sleep-over . . ."

"Go on. Where was the sleep-over?"

Mattie drew a blank. "I assumed it was at Callie's since she has the big house. No, I know it was at Callie's because I asked Jessica if she wanted me to drop off some sandwiches and she said no because I made them last time."

"Then check with Callie's mom tomorrow. Simple."

"But what if she wasn't going to Callie's? What if she let me assume she was when all along she was planning on going somewhere with this Arlis? Somewhere she didn't want me to know about? Oh God, Stephen, you don't think she was going to buy drugs?" At the drain of color in his face, she shook her head. "No, we know our daughter. She wouldn't. She wouldn't." But a small nudge in her gut whispered, *Maybe she would.*

Then a doctor approached and introduced himself. "We have Jessica stabilized, but she still hasn't regained consciousness and her condition remains critical. If you want to see her, you can, but only for a few minutes. She's in intensive care. Fourth floor. Tell the nurse on duty who you are."

Upon stepping into the hushed air of the ICU, and then walking softly to where their daughter lay among monitors and tubes and bandages was a moment forever seared in Mattie's mind.

How could this have happened and where would it all end?

Stephen drew her close as they stood listening to the heave and blip and tick of the machines. Mattie touched her daughter's cool cheek and felt the pulse in her jaw. Tears coated her eyes as she bent down and kissed her. "You're going to be fine, sweetheart. You're going to get well. We love you very much."

The nurse indicated they had to leave and that Dr. Egan

was waiting for them down in the visitor's area on the first floor.

Seeing the physician, obviously called from some kind of gathering since he wore a boutonniere, brought Mattie's fears rushing back.

After patting her hand and shaking Stephen's he suggested they sit down.

Neither did, and Mattie felt the sweat break out across her back immediately followed by a prickly chill.

"I saw Jessica before they took her up to ICU, and I've spoken with the attending physician. While she's not out of danger, she's in better shape than she was when Rescue brought her in. She sustained some serious injuries in the abdominal area as well as internal bleeding." He paused. "There's also been some head trauma. She's slipped into a coma."

"Oh God."

"Jesus," Stephen whispered. Then holding Mattie's hand, he asked, "Is she going to die?" And although Mattie shrank from the question, she waited, breath held, for the answer.

"We don't know, but the odds are good that she'll recover."

Both let out the breaths they were holding. Mattie asked, "This coma? How long before she wakes up?"

"It's anybody's guess. Could be a few days, a few weeks or a few months."

"Can't you be more definitive than that? When we were told you were coming in we assumed you knew something more than the guys rolling the gurneys."

Tom Egan looked from one to the other, clearly not pleased at being questioned. Mattie agreed with Stephen. She expected more, too.

"Actually I do know something more than the guys rolling the gurneys. I wanted to tell you in case you didn't know."

"Didn't know what?"

"That Jessica was pregnant."

Stephen stared. "That's impossible. There must be a mistake."

Tom shook his head. "No mistake. We couldn't save the fetus." Then he frowned. "Mattie?" When she simply stared at him unblinking, he took her hand, patting it. "I'm sorry for having to tell you this tonight. And from your reactions, neither of you knew. But I didn't want to put it off for fear word would get around and you heard it from someone else. It's just so sad when kids fear confiding in their parents."

Mattie's mind reeled, desperately sifting through her chaotic thoughts for some smidgen of missed information that would make all of this at least understandable. Right now it felt as if her daughter had been living someone else's life. "How far . . . ?" she swallowed, cleared her throat, but the words wouldn't come.

"How far along? Just a few weeks. I'm sure she intended to tell you." He glanced toward a door that read No Admittance. "I have another patient to see while I'm here." Again he patted her, and she wanted to fling his hand away. *How could he be so blasé, so routinely solicitous. Oh, your daughter's in a coma, and oh, you didn't know she was pregnant? And oh, she would have told you, and by the way I have another patient so good-bye.*

Stephen put his arm around her. "Come on honey, I'll take you home."

Jessica stiffened and pulled away. "No. I'm staying here tonight."

"Stephen's right, Mattie. Go home and get some rest. Jessica is in good hands."

"Rest? You think I can just go home and sleep as if this was just another night?" She backed away from both of them, her voice breaking. "My daughter's been accused of awful things. She's in a coma for God knows how long, then you say she was pregnant. I would say, Dr. Egan, that rest is the last thing I'm going to do tonight or for a lot of nights to come."